AND FOR YOUR INFORMATION . . .

A BUTTERFLY NOVEL

Denise Deegan is the best-selling author of four novels and one book of non-fiction. She has been published in Ireland, the UK and Commonwealth, Germany, Holland and Korea. She is a regular contributor to the Irish media.

Denise lives in Dublin with her husband and two teenage children.

www.facebook.com/butterflynovels

www.twitter.com/denisedeegan

AND FOR YOUR INFORMATION . . .

DENISE DEEGAN

HACHETTE
BOOKS
IRELAND

First published in Ireland in 2011 by Hachette Books Ireland
An Hachette UK company

A CIP catalogue record for this title is available from the British Library

ISBN 978 1 4447 2120 1

Typeset in Sabon MT by Hachette Books Ireland

Printed and bound by Mackays, Chatham ME5 8TD

Hachette Books Ireland policy is to use papers that are natural, renewable
and recyclable products and made from wood grown in sustainable forests.
The logging and manufacturing processes are expected to conform to the
environmental regulations of the country of origin.

Hachette Books Ireland
8 Castlecourt Centre
Castleknock
Dublin 15

Hachette UK Ltd
338 Euston Road
London NW1 3BH

www.hachette.ie

To Laura and Little Bird,
with love and butterflies

PROLOGUE
Sushi Rainbow

We're sitting at the sushi counter in Dundrum. Bowls of different colours glide by on the conveyor belt. It's embarrassing, having just one bowl of the cheapest stuff. Alex and Rachel have a rainbow of colour. They keep telling me to help myself. I just take one prawn katsu from Rachel's stash – my favourite. FYI, it's not like I'm poor or anything. I'm just not minted, like them. My money runs out, like, all the time.

'*So*,' I say to Alex, leaning in like I want all the goss – which I do. 'What was San Diego like? I can't believe you stayed for six weeks. You're so lucky.'

She gives me a look. The one thing you never tell Alex is how lucky she is.

'It was great,' she says and, unfortunately, leaves it at that.

I googled it, San Diego. Sun, sand, surf and, crucially, surfers. They've an amazing zoo. It's, like, huge. With so much land for the animals to roam. And the best thing: you can ride around on segways. The website for the zoo has live webcams of polar bears, elephants and apes. My favourite, though, are the pandas. I still watch them.

'And David?' Rachel asks.

Alex smiles automatically and goes all dreamy. Then she's looking at Rachel, the way she never looks at me, like a best friend. It used to be the three of us, hanging out, all getting on the same, i.e. great. Then Alex's mum died. I didn't know what to say to Alex. The harder I tried, the more I messed up. Rachel's good at stuff like that. They got closer. I try not to mind.

'He was amazing, Rach,' Alex is saying. 'I can't believe I nearly didn't go. He taught me to surf. At least, he tried.' She smiles. 'We got so close.'

'Oh my God, you had sex, didn't you?' I ask, leaning in. She laughs like I'm being ridiculous. 'Oh my God, you did. Didn't you?' She can't stop smiling. Which is, like, a dead giveaway. '*And?*' I ask. Obviously.

'I am *not* discussing my sex life with you.'

'Ooh, so there *is* a sex life.'

Rachel looks stunned.

'Not that it's a big deal,' I say to make her feel better. 'Actually, I think it might just be the world's biggest disappointment. After Santa.'

Alex looks at me comfortingly. 'It's different with someone you love.'

I look at her like I'm deeply offended. 'Are you saying I don't love Simon?'

'*Do* you?' She looks shocked.

'Don't be ridiculous,' I say. And we laugh. I'm not stupid. I know the first rule of survival: don't love someone who doesn't love you.

'It *is* different, though,' she says, like she wants me to find love. She's not the only one. I don't make the same mistake twice and tell her how lucky she is to have David but she *is* lucky. I look at the necklace he gave her and wonder what it's like to be in love. Really in love. To have someone who'd *die* for you. To have someone you'd die for. Simon has his good points. Sometimes, though, I wake in the morning (obviously) and wonder if today's going to be the day my life starts, the day I fall in love. I look at Rachel, who's helping herself to the last prawn katsu, and wonder what it's like to have your life totally sorted. To be with a guy you love. To know what you want to be. To do and say everything right – automatically. Sometimes, when I'm around Rache I mess up on purpose, just to get it over with.

She catches me looking. 'Oh, sorry. I took the last one.'

'It's OK. I'm totally full,' I lie. 'Let's go shopping.'

At my favourite cosmetics counter, I pick up an eye shadow. It's bluey-green, like peacock feathers. When I move it under the light, it sparkles. I find a tester and try it out. Oh my God. It's amazing. It makes my eyes stand out. In a good way. Not like a frog's or those people you see with thyroid problems. I check the price. And put it back. I try to think of a way. If I went without smoothies for a week … But then you can't exactly sit with nothing in front of you while your friends suck away for hours.

'Sarah?'

I turn. Rachel's holding up two eye shadows.

'Which one?' she asks.

I hesitate. They're practically the same.

'Oh, what the hell, I'll get them both.' She smiles, like she's totally mad. She goes to the counter – so easily, like money's air.

Alex is at a clothes rail. But she's barely touching the clothes, just gliding the hangers along without really looking. I know she's thinking of David. Having the person you love on the other side of the world must be so *romantic*. All that anguish. All that longing. Alex and David were meant to be together. Like Dolce & Gabbana.

I look back at the eye shadow. Would they really miss one? I mean, how many just roll off the counter every day and get kicked under? Not that I'd take one. I'm not that kind of person. I run a finger over the colours. Longingly. Then I slip one into my palm. Just to see how easy it would be ...

Very easy. All I'd have to do is put my hand in my pocket and let go.

I walk over to Rachel, the eye shadow still in my hand. It's no big deal. I can put it back at any moment. Only, I'm not putting it back. I'm slipping my hands into my pockets. Just to see ...

That's when I remember security cameras. They must have them. Every shop does. Oh God. My heart starts to pound. I try to look casual while I check, glancing around as if for no particular reason. Jesus, they're everywhere. OK, don't panic, I tell myself. But my heart is really pounding now. My mouth is dry. I can't believe I'm in this situation. Now, there's only one thing to do. Keep walking. Over to Rachel. Who's at the checkout now.

I stand beside her. Fold my arms. She looks at me and smiles. I smile back. But I'm freaking. Alex is coming over. If I get caught, I *will* die.

'Find anything?' Rachel asks her.

'Nah. I'm kind of tired. Must be jet lag.'

The checkout girl hands Rachel her change and a paper bag with rope handles. Oh my God. We're going. Moving. Towards the exit. My heart feels like it's going to burst through my chest. I'm going to be stopped, called. Caught. Any minute.

'Was that *seriously* extravagant?' Rachel asks me. We're walking through the door.

'What? Eh, no. No, it was fine.'

We're three steps from the shop. Five. Ten. Fifteen. Could I have made it? Could there really be a God? I glance at Rachel and Alex, chatting away like it's another ordinary day. They wouldn't believe me if I told them. Which makes me feel wild. And dangerous. And free. I put my hand in my pocket and feel the compact. I didn't have to rely on anyone for this. I didn't need Mum's money. I didn't need to borrow from my friends. I did this myself. *I* was in control. I lived on the edge. And flew.

1
LITTLE BLACK DRESS

There's this dress that I love? It's short and black and sleeveless with big square leather patches on each side of the waist. It has this cute belt. And it would be amazing with knee-high black boots. Or actually tan-coloured boots – to match the belt. I've tried this dress on, like, three times. And I've been saving up for it for so long it's almost a joke. Every time I go into the shop, I'm afraid it'll be gone, that someone with money will have come and snatched it up without thinking.

I'm in the fitting room. Again. I'm looking at myself in the mirror. Only, in this dress, it's not me. It's someone confident and successful and gorgeous. I know how easy it would be to take it. I knew that the moment I walked into the cubicle and saw a shirt already hanging there. If I put the dress in my bag and replaced it with the shirt, I'd end up with the same number of items I came in with. Just the possibility has my heart pumping.

I think about the shop being down all that money – two hundred and sixty euro. Then I think of insurance. These places are covered for this. They expect a certain amount to be taken. There's probably even a name for it. If I listened in Business Studies, I'd probably know. I slip out of the dress. I tell myself that, actually, *they're* the real robbers, here, charging so much.

I get dressed back into the Abercrombie top that Alex didn't want anymore and the skinny jeans I got for practically nothing in Penneys. I'm me again. I look in the mirror and remember how I felt when I took control. Took what I wanted. I want to be that person again.

I check for security cameras. Then wise up. They can't have cameras in fitting rooms – because then pervs would be getting jobs in security. I look myself in the eye. And decide. I'm going to do this.

Quickly, I roll the dress up as small as I can get it and, heart pounding, I slip it into my bag. I zip it up, collect all the other dresses I brought in with me, add the shirt, take a deep breath and walk out. Jesus.

I hand the bundle to the assistant. Can she tell I'm freaking?

'Nothing was really great,' I say and can't believe how calm I sound.

I leave the fitting rooms. I force myself to look around at a few more things, then I'm walking towards the exit. It seems to take forever to get there, like everything has switched to slow motion.

I'm almost at the door when the bleeping starts. Oh my God. Is that me? It couldn't be. There wasn't a security tag. I checked. Could I've missed one? Oh God. Maybe I checked the wrong dress. I had four. My heart is pounding so fast. I know I have to keep walking. I try to look natural, like this has nothing to do with me.

A hand falls, hard, on my shoulder and I jump off the actual ground. I tell myself to chill. Be cool. I can talk my way out of this. Of course I can. I take a deep breath and turn. The security guard is huge – like an Eastern European Robocop. For one totally mad second, I think about making a break for it. Then I imagine how that would look – running down Grafton Street with a uniformed security guard after me.

I make my eyes big. 'Yes?'

'Come inside.' His voice is deep with authority. Like he's used to this.

I glance into the shop. The girl at the cash register is staring. Customers too. I feel myself blush. Thank God Rachel and Alex aren't here. They'd be so shocked. So disgusted. They'd *hate* me.

'Inside,' he says.

I have to get out of this, get away. 'Look, I'm in a huge hurry. This has nothing to do with me. Those things go off all the time.'

'Inside,' he says again, like it's his favourite word.

'Seriously. This is a mistake.' I've almost convinced myself now.

'I *said*, "Inside",' he says, through gritted teeth.

The only reason I do is so I can be out of sight, away from the eyes, the scene. And as I follow his huge bulk deeper into the shop, I'm seriously starting to freak. Will they call the police? My mum? Which is worse?

The room he takes me to is small and poorly lit. Racks of clothes line the walls. Two or three handbags are thrown in a corner. Is that a good idea, I wonder, leaving bags where they bring shoplifters? A stock of toilet paper juts out from the top of a cupboard. He closes the door and stands in front of it, folding his arms, and staring at me. Oh God. He could do anything. I take a step back, feel for my phone, wrap my hand around it. If I screamed, people would hear ...

The door opens and he moves aside. A dark-haired woman in a black trouser-suit walks in. She's in her thirties and looks like work is her life.

'Open your bag,' she says.

My heart jumps. My mouth is dry. Should I ask for a lawyer like they do in the movies – do nothing, say nothing, in case I incriminate myself? What am I talking about? I don't have a lawyer. And this isn't Hollywood.

'Open your bag,' she says again. Like I've no option.

I shift the strap on my shoulder, trying to think of a valid reason why my bag contains a little black dress with the security tag still on.

'Look, that thing just went off. It has nothing to do with me.'

She looks at me like I'm stupid. 'We have CCTV.'

'In the *fitting rooms*?'

They look at each other, knowing they have me. And I know now why lawyers tell you to say nothing.

'The bag,' she says.

I can't do it.

'Do you want me to call the police?'

Oh God. My stomach knots. If they call the police, do I go to jail? I look down at the bag. But then I picture my mum's face and hesitate. I look up and try to think of something, anything I can say. The Suit puts out her hand for the dress. I close my eyes. Take one second. Then I'm doing it, unzipping the bag, taking out the dress. Why didn't I just keep saving? Why didn't I wait? She snatches it from me.

}|{

'Shoplifting is a crime.'

Ten minutes ago, I was a normal teenager. Now I'm a criminal. She looks at me like I'm every dirty thing squished together. Which is pretty much how I feel.

'What age are you?' she asks.

Suddenly, hope. 'Sixteen.' Maybe they can't prosecute.

'We need to call your parents.' I almost throw up. 'And the police.'

I stare at her. 'I thought you said you weren't *calling* the police.'

'I never said that.'

I can't let this happen. 'Look. I'm so sorry. This was a mistake. I've never done anything like this before. I swear.' OK, I'm lying. The important thing here is, I'll never do it again. 'If you just forget about this, I'll leave the shop and never come back. I swear.'

'Forget about it!' she scoffs. 'This may come as a shock to you, but I'm trying to run a business here. I'm trying to keep staff employed in a recession. Do you know how hard that is with people like you swanning in here and just helping yourselves?'

'People like you.' She says it with such disgust, lumping me in with every single person who's ever stolen. To her we're all the same. But the real shocker is, maybe we are. Or maybe I'm worse than people who steal for a living. Because I don't need the stuff. Not really. Not desperately.

'I need your parents' number.'

I swallow. My parents haven't had the same number for three months.

2
ROBOCOP

I don't know if, in situations like this, they deliberately make you sweat? But they've left me alone in here for ages. (With the handbags.) When the door finally opens, it's my dad. Last time I saw him, he was leaving home. Everything he said then sounded like it came straight from a manual. A manual entitled, How to Tell Your Children You're Leaving in Ten Simple Steps. Seems like years ago now. He looks different, hair shorter, clothes trendier. He doesn't look like a dad. He looks like someone's 'partner'.

'You OK?' he asks. I want to run to him and feel his arms wrap around me like they used to when I was a kid.

'Where's Mum?' I ask, like I don't need him.

'Coming.'

That's what I was afraid of.

Robocop carries in a few stools. Dad thanks him, but ignores the stools. Robocop leaves again.

'How're you doing?' Dad asks, softly.

I shrug. If I speak, I'll cry.

He looks at me for a long time. 'I've missed you.'

}|{

I thought I'd got over it. Completely. Seeing him here, all concerned, makes me realise I so haven't. I wish he'd leave. Go back to his life. Back to her.

I make my voice hard. 'Your choice.'

He shifts. 'I didn't leave you, Sarah. I left your mother.'

'I don't want to talk about it.' Which is why I've been avoiding his calls. I don't want to know. I don't want to know where he's living now. I don't want to know what she's like. I don't want to know how pretty or young or sexy she is. Unless she's a complete hag. Which wouldn't be so bad. Except that it wouldn't explain why he chose her over us.

'Sarah, we need to talk.'

'Are you coming back?'

He doesn't answer. Which is an answer. Should I be happy that he looks guilty?

'Then there's nothing to talk about,' I say.

'I'm still your dad. We can still get together, do things together.'

'What about Mum?' He mightn't feel any loyalty to her. But I do.

I hear people outside.

He looks towards the door, then at me. 'This is serious, Sarah.' Referring to the stealing, not the leaving. Which, if you ask me, is pretty serious too. But it's not a crime. So it's OK, right?

The door opens. It's The Suit. With my mum. Oh God. She looks at me. Then at my dad.

'Hello, Joanne,' he says, his voice flat, cautious.

She closes her eyes and shakes her head like she's nothing to say to him. She sighs, then looks at me and, I swear to God, I can hear her thoughts: *You've surpassed yourself this time.*

}|{

The room fills. In comes Robocop with a uniformed policewoman. She's young and pretty. And I hope that means she isn't a total bully? The Suit introduces her as Sergeant Carmody. Then all eyes zoom in on me. I swallow.

Sergeant Carmody takes out a notebook and pen. She looks at me, then at my parents.

'I need to take a statement.'

Does this mean I'm being *arrested*? I look at Dad in panic.

He clears his throat. 'Excuse me, Sergeant. I wonder if I might make a point in Sarah's favour?'

She looks at him. We all do.

'This is the first time that Sarah,' he glances at me like a loving father, 'has done anything like this. She's a good kid … We've had some … family issues …'

I roll my eyes. Oh my God, he's not bringing that up.

'I understand that, Mr Healy,' she says politely. 'But if the shop wants to press charges—'

'We do,' The Suit interrupts, cow that she is.

Dad's caught off guard. Which is when Mum finally comes out with what sounds like she's been holding in since she got here. 'This is your fault, Michael.' Since he left, everything is. Broken dishwasher. Cracked vase. Dog pooing in our garden.

And suddenly, I'm tired of it. 'No. It's my fault.'

She ignores me. Looks only at Dad. 'You got us into this. You get us out.'

He looks at Sergeant Carmody. 'I wonder if I might have a moment alone with my family?'

Family. Doesn't sound right.

The sergeant looks from Dad to Mum. Then, slowly, she nods. She glances at the other two, as if to say, 'let's go'. The

}|{

Suit doesn't budge, at first, but finally wilts under Sergeant Carmody's gaze. When the door closes behind them, Dad turns to Mum. He looks tired.

'I don't know what you think I can do. They're pressing charges.'

'Convince them not to. You're the psychologist. Manipulating people is your forte, isn't it?' She says it with such bitterness. And I want to leave, just walk straight out, screw the consequences.

Head down, Dad starts to pace. He runs his fingers through his hair. Finally, he stops. And turns. He looks at her.

'I mentioned family issues. I could suggest a therapist. As an alternative to the legal route.'

'A *therapist*?' I say in shock. I'm not the one who needs a therapist here. 'Isn't there anything else?' I grew up with a therapist. They screw you up.

'Community service, maybe.'

'Yeah, OK, community service,' I say. Anything but a shrink.

Mum glares at me. 'You are in no position to be picky, young lady.' She looks at Dad. 'I don't care what you suggest. Just make this go away.' Now she's looking back at me like she wants *me* to go away. Not for the first time, I wish I was someone else, someone like Rachel who never messes up, who makes her mother proud.

In a deal hammered out between Dad, Sergeant Carmody and The Suit, I'm barred from the shop. I have to see a shrink. *And* do community service. Everything is to be monitored, forms filled and returned to the police. You'd think I murdered someone. I thank Sergeant Carmody because I know

}|{

that, without her, it would have been worse. She's saved me
from a criminal record. And though The Suit looks at me like
I'm some kind of spoiled, lucky piece of poo, I thank her too.
If I didn't, my mum would never let me forget it.

We leave the shop together, the united family. We've probably gone twenty metres when Mum turns to me.

'What the *hell* were you thinking? Don't you *get* enough?'

We're on Grafton Street. She is shouting. I want to die.

'Are you *completely* stupid?' she asks.

The answer is, yes. But if I say it, she'll think I'm being
sarcastic. And that would make her go completely psycho.

'This wasn't your first time, was it?'

I look down at my feet.

'Jesus, Sarah,' she says.

I just want to go home. Start over. Be the person she
wants me to be. Or at least try.

'This is the *last* time you *ever* take anything that doesn't
belong to you. Do you hear me?'

It'd be hard not to. I nod so that she'll stop.

'Why don't we discuss this somewhere quieter?' Dad says.
'Where did you park? I'll walk you to the car.'

She turns on him. 'We don't *need* anyone to walk us to the
car. We are perfectly *capable* of walking to the car, thank
you very much.' I feel like throwing up. She looks at him the
way The Suit looked at me – like he's nothing. 'Just let me
know when you've everything set up.'

Dad looks at me. 'Stay out of trouble,' he says but gently
and with a smile. Then winks, like he used to do.

'It's all a joke to you, isn't it?' she says to him, then.

He looks tired. 'Goodbye, Joanne.'

He turns and walks away. And leaves me with her. And
her anger.

3
FINGERPRINT

She breaks the lights and curses at totally innocent people –
a little old woman not crossing fast enough, a guy in front
of us who stops at an orange light. I look out the side window and try to pretend I'm with someone else.

'It's that school,' she says. 'Hanging out with kids who
have too much.'

I stare at her. This has nothing to do with my school. This
has nothing to do with my friends.

'I knew it would be a mistake,' she says, like she's glad to
prove Dad wrong. He chose Strandbrook. Another 'mistake'
with his name on it.

'It's a good school,' I say. 'It gets the grades.'

'I don't see any evidence of that,' she says, like she wants
an argument. 'All you've got since you went in there is an air
of entitlement.'

I look out the window again. She's wrong. I'm not like
that. My eyes well up. I can't do anything to make her
happy. Ever. She always thinks the worst of me. Then I
always end up proving her right.

}|{

My phone bleeps.
She sighs loudly. Like *I* sent the text.
Which makes me take out my phone.
It's from Simon. 'Want to hook up?'
'Sorry,' I text back. 'Not feeling well.'
It's not a lie.

We pull up outside the house. She gets out fast, slams the door and marches up the path. I let her go, taking my time, keeping as much distance between us as possible.

Inside, though, she's waiting in the hall.

'Don't you *ever* do that to me again.' It's like this is a drama, created for her to have a starring role.

'I didn't do anything to you.'

Then, wham, she slaps me across the face. I stare at her, holding my stinging cheek. She's never slapped me before. And I swear to God, I feel like slapping her back.

Louis, the brother I hardly know, appears out of the kitchen.

'Was that necessary?' he asks her, as if he's the parent not the son.

'Don't you start,' she says. She looks back at me.

'I don't know why I ever had children,' she says. 'I just don't know.' And then she's gone, running up the stairs like something out of *Gone With The Wind*.

'You OK?' Louis asks.

'Do I look OK?'

'What happened?'

'Nothing. Forget it.' I walk past him, into the downstairs loo. I check my face in the mirror. The outline of her hand is highlighted in red. Like the Ulster flag.

Louis appears in the doorway. 'She's under a lot of pressure.'

I swivel, angry. 'Doesn't give her the right—'

'I know.' Then he walks into the bathroom, takes me by the hand and pulls me out, like I'm three years old. 'Come on,' he says. 'I'll make you a … Coke.'

I look up at him. 'You'll *make* me a Coke?'

'Well, I was going to try making a smoothie but … it'd probably be a disaster.'

'A Coke will do,' I half smile.

In the kitchen, I sit at the island. He pours two Cokes. I reach for mine.

'Wait,' he says, holding up a hand. He goes to the freezer and takes out the ice tray, whacks it against the worktop and drops ice into the drinks. He slices a lemon and pops that in. Then he hands me my Coke.

'What, no straw?' I tease. It's so not like Louis to go to this trouble.

'That's more like it.'

We sit for a few minutes, just drinking our Cokes, the silence welcome after all that noise.

'So, what happened?' he asks eventually.

I shrug.

'I'll hear anyway. Might as well give me your side.'

I look at him and sigh. 'I took a dress.'

'You *took* a dress?'

'OK, stole a dress.'

His eyebrows pop up. 'Impressive.'

'It's not a joke.'

'You're right. I'm sorry. It's not.'

'And you better not tell anyone.'

'Come on, Sarah. What do you take me for?'

'Ever. OK?'

He nods, his face serious. 'Of course I won't tell anyone.' He looks at me. 'You OK? They didn't call the cops or anything?'

'Yeah. They did.'

'Shit, Sarah. They didn't press charges, did they?'

'No. Dad talked them out of it.'

'*Dad* was there?' He sounds relieved.

'You make him sound like a superhero.'

He smiles at that. 'He's good at stuff like that, though.'

'Are you saying Mum isn't?' Someone tell me why I'm defending her.

He says nothing. From the back pocket of his jeans, he pulls out his tatty leather wallet. 'How much d'you need?' he asks, like he's the dad now.

'Nothing! I'm fine.'

'Come on. I know what it's like when your friends are loaded.'

He's working part-time now at the Jitter Mug Café and part-time at a local pub. Mum won't let me work, though. Not till I'm finished school. He pulls out a twenty.

'It's OK. I'm fine. Seriously.'

He puts it down on the counter. 'Take it before I change my mind.'

I feel guilty. This is all about me. 'How're things with you?' He's my brother but we're practically strangers.

'Grand.'

'Bet you wish you could move out, though,' I say.

'The thought *had* crossed my mind.'

I look at him. 'It's kind of weird.'

'What?'

'Us … talking.'

He raises his eyebrows and nods slowly.

'How's that friend of yours, Alex?' he asks after a while. 'That thing with the stalker, wow. What actually happened there?'

I sit up, loving these kinds of conversations. 'Oh, yeah! This, like, total nutter thought she *loved* Alex's dad or something? She was, like, some obsessed, fan he'd called up on stage once. Anyway, when Alex's mum died, she got it into her head that he'd ask her to marry him. Weird, right? He didn't even *know* her. So he got this barring order but that didn't stop her. She followed them over to San Diego.'

'What were they doing in San Diego anyway?'

'This is so sweet. Alex's Dad wanted to give her a chance to get back with her ex, David, because she's like totally in love with him. And, actually, after the whole stalker thing, that's exactly what happened. They're together again. So it turned out really good for her in the end. Those guys were seriously meant to be together.

Louis slides the twenty over, pats it and gets up. 'Right. I'm off.'

Surprised and actually kind of disappointed, I wonder if I was going on a bit. 'OK,' I say.

'Listen,' he says, 'don't worry about today. It'll blow over. Everything does in the end.' His face becomes serious. 'I wouldn't do it again, though. You don't want a criminal record. You might want to get into the States sometime, right?'

I look at him. Would it really have been that serious? Could one stupid mistake really stand against you for the rest of your life?

*

In my room, I take out the very first thing ago, the Mac eye shadow. I roll it between thumb, watching it sparkle, remembering how I fel when Mum freaked at me about something and I slipped my hand into my pocket and felt the eye shadow like a ray of sunshine. Now, I dip my finger in. The grooves of my fingertip are highlighted in blue. A tiny circle at the centre is surrounded by increasingly bigger circles, like spreading ripples. There are lines cutting through the grooves, damaging them. And it makes sense to me that I wouldn't have a perfect fingerprint.

I close the compact and fling it, hard, into the bin. I will be a new person. A better person. I will try so hard.

I spend the rest of the day in my room. She doesn't call me for dinner. And when I'm practically starving to death, I raid my chocolate stash rather than go down.

At nine, my ancient Nokia rings. Rachel's name appears on the scratched screen. I know she's calling about tomorrow – the three of us are meant to be going to Dundrum. Now, though, the thought of going near a shop makes me feel sick, the thought of facing my friends even sicker. What if they've, somehow, found out?

The phone stops ringing. Oh God. I never not answer my phone. She'll know something's up. She'll wonder what. I have to call her back. And I have to go. Of course I do. Alex is just back from San Diego. There is no excuse good enough not to.

Sunday. I get up ear.   .n the house. This is the new me,
the person who makes m. mum happy – or at least tries to.
It is also the me who has to tell that same mum she's going
out in the afternoon.

I start in the kitchen, cleaning up Louis' usual trail of
destruction. Then I hoover and mop, feeling like Cinderella.
I wonder if that's how Mum feels. No. She's way too angry
to ever feel like a Disney character.

I work for literally *hours*. And the scary thing is, I'm actually proud of the shine I've brought to the place. When
Mum finally comes down and sees the result of my hard
labour, she looks surprised. Then, instantly suspicious. She
throws me a look that says: I know what you're up to.
Instead of screaming, I unload the dishwasher. She makes
coffee and lights up. I go back upstairs.

An hour before Alex is due to call, I start to get ready. I
need to be at the door before the bell rings, so she doesn't
get to meet my mum. This is a standard routine – given
Mum's moods. Today, though, I especially can't risk what

)|(

she might say, what remarks she might make. They can't know what I did.

I straighten my hair, take it easy on the makeup and just wear Uggs, denims and a hoodie – so there's one less thing for her to give out about.

Mum's still in the kitchen when I come down. At the end of a cigarette and looking out the window.

'I'm going out for a while,' I say. I try to sound casual. Like it's no big deal.

She turns, whisking the cigarette from her mouth. 'No you're not.'

'But it's arranged.'

'Well, unarrange it.'

'I can't. Alex has been away for ages. If I don't go, she'll be, like, insulted.'

She squints at me then. 'I can't *believe* you'd want to go out after yesterday. I mean, don't you feel *any* remorse?'

Don't you? I want to ask. She still hasn't apologised for hitting me and I know she won't. But I say nothing. I just want to get out. 'Of course I feel remorse.'

'So you won't mind being grounded then.'

'Oh my God. I'm going to see a shrink. I'm doing community service.' Whatever that's going to involve. I don't even want to *think* about that.

The door bell goes. I look at her. One last try, 'That's them.'

'Well, then you better tell them you can't go.' Oh my God, what does she want, blood?

When I open the front door, Alex is standing there. Alone. She smiles.

'It's just the two of us,' she says. 'Rachel has to help her mum with some catering thing.'

Now I really feel terrible that I can't go. Alex never goes out with just me. And now, this one time she wants to, I let her down.

I grimace.

'I can't go either.' I look towards the kitchen, then back. I want to tell her the truth – that I'm grounded. But she might ask why. 'Mum wants me here,' I say. It's not enough. 'We're having guests. She just told me. I was about to call you. I'm really sorry.'

She just looks at me for a minute like she can't believe it. 'It's OK,' she says then. 'Don't worry about it.'

I feel so bad. 'We could go tomorrow after school – if you like.' Then I remember. I'm grounded.

Her face brightens. 'Yeah. Mike could pick us up. And we finish early tomorrow anyway.'

'Cool,' I say, only because I can't back out again. And as I walk Alex to the car, I try to work out how to do this – keep everyone happy. Mum doesn't get home till seven. If I get back by six, she'll never know. I feel bad. But then remind myself that she thinks the worst of me anyway, no matter what I do. At least, this way, I keep Alex happy.

We get to the car. I give Mike a little wave. I *love* Alex's driver. He's just so cool. He hardly talks and when I look at him from behind (the usual view), I imagine he's a cowboy from an old black-and-white movie, chewing on a toothpick or blade of grass. I flirted with him once, just to see if an actual *man* would ever be interested in me. He wasn't. And that, I realised after, was a major relief. He's Alex's driver. And, like, at least thirty.

I stand back as Alex gets in.

'Sorry,' I say again.

'It's OK.'

'What'll you do?'

'Probably just have a jacuzzi and take it easy.'

My idea of total heaven. 'Cool. See you tomorrow.'

An estate agent would describe our house as a three-bed semi with attic conversion. They're always optimistic. If it was flattened out, our house would fit, completely, into about a quarter of Alex's ground floor. (Another reason not to have her around.) The attic conversion is my room. My dad turned my original bedroom into an office for himself and converted the attic for me. Then, he left. Still, I'm glad he did it. I love my room, tucked away up here at the top of the house, away from everyone. I feel like Rapunzel but with internet access and a mobile phone.

I hide out up here for the rest of the day, keeping out of Mum's way and using all my energy to hate her. Not just for being a stone-cold bitch about what happened, but for being the reason Dad left. If she hadn't been so angry all the time ... if she'd kept herself good-looking ... if she hadn't made him choose ... But I'm not thinking about that right now. Or ever.

About The Other Thing, though – would it have killed her to give me a break? I took two things. Two things. I said I was sorry. And I am. I'm seeing a goddamn shrink. And doing community service – which no one has even bothered to explain. I mean, what'll I be doing? And how long for? Britney Spears got community service, I'm pretty sure. But I can't remember what she had to do. Someone famous had to pick up litter. I know that. Oh God. Is that what I'll be doing – picking up litter? What if someone sees me? I try to stop thinking about that. I lie on my bed and zone in on my wall of Caliente Men, a huge collage of the hottest international actors, models, rock stars, footballers and generally beautiful people I've collected from magazines since first year. It's not growing all the time. Sometimes I go off a face and get rid of it.

I look at Robbie Williams and try to think only of Robbie Williams – not usually a problem. Today, though, it's not working. I can't forget what happened. I can't forget that my mother hates me even more than usual now. Or that, tomorrow, I have to go back to school and face people who might have seen, heard, found out. Oh God. Maybe I could develop a sudden debilitating sickness.

Next day, on the basis that I can't hide out forever, I go to school. At first, I don't trust the calm. I expect to be outed, any minute. When first break passes without incident, I start to hope. The big test is lunch. No one holds in a scandal beyond lunch.

I'm queuing in the canteen with Alex and Rachel, afraid to look around. Simon strolls up to me. 'Hey, babe.'

'Hey.' I've been so worried about The Other Thing I've pretty much forgotten Simon. Then I remember: on Saturday, I told him I wasn't feeling well. I haven't heard from him since. 'I'm fine, by the way.'

He looks confused.

'It was just a tummy bug.'

'Oh. Right. Yeah. Cool.'

Cool? I know we're not serious. I know we only hook up once a week and when that doesn't come off, we just kind of leave it, but 'cool'? Seriously? I look at him and wonder. If

}{{

we didn't actually see each other, would we have a better 'relationship'? We get on so well on Facebook. It's like we're different people. Funny, flirty, fun. Then we hook up and he's just Simon. And maybe he thinks the same about me because he's telling me he'll see me later and is walking off. I watch him sit with another group – Amy and Orla and a few of the guys. Simon still moves around, like he always did. His life hasn't changed because of me. I don't mind. Thing is, I probably should.

It's quarter past one. No one has called me a criminal. Or a liar. No one has given me a funny look with a smart comment. Can I hope that this means that they won't? At lunch, the three of us sit together. Then Mark joins us. Since David moved to the US, Mark's the only guy sitting with us – and the only person who thinks that is working is Rachel, who is in love with him. Ever since we got back to school, he's been edgy. Today, like every other, he's silent while we eat. And as soon as we're finished, he's looking around like he wants to be somewhere else. I get that, though. I mean, who wants to be the only guy sitting with a bunch of girls, even if he does love one of them? He finishes his drink and puts it down like he's made a decision. He turns to Rachel like he's going to say something. But when he looks at her, his face softens and he doesn't say anything. A nearby table bursts out laughing. I remember the shoplifting and turn slowly, expecting the worst. It's the jocks. But whatever they're laughing at, it's not me. I breathe a sigh of relief. Then notice Mark, looking over at them, like that's where he wants to be. Then he turns to Rache.

'I might head off for a bit.'

She looks surprised. 'Oh. OK.'

He puts a hand on her shoulder like he's sorry. Then he's gone.

'It's hard for him without David,' Alex says.

'I could ask Simon to sit with us,' I say, not exactly sure he'd want to.

Rachel looks at me. 'It's OK, thanks. No offence or anything but Mark doesn't really get on that well with Simon.' What she really means is: he doesn't like Simon. 'He'll probably just hang out with his rugby mates for a while. I don't mind.'

He lands at their table, sits down and in seconds he has them laughing. I feel kind of sorry for Rache.

'Guess who's coming back to Dublin?' Alex asks.

I look at her. Not David!

'Marsha!'

'Oh my God. I *love* Marsha,' I say. She's the only stylist I've ever met. And she's amazing. I couldn't believe it when she left. I turn to Alex. 'So your dad's hired her back?'

'They're going out.'

'What? *Oh my God*,' I say, totally excited.

But Rachel's looking at Alex like this is bad news, like she knows something I don't. Which wouldn't be a first. I look at them and think of two electrons on the same shell. I think of a third electron on the next shell out – me. And I can't believe I'm comparing us to science. I hate science.

'I'm OK with it,' Alex is saying to Rachel. 'Honestly. In the States, I really thought I'd lost Dad. When the stalker attacked, there was all this blood. And the scariest sound, like he couldn't breathe.' Alex looks so pale, so worried, like she's living through it again. Then she seems to wake up.

She looks at Rachel and says, 'After that, nothing seems like such a big deal, you know? And Marsha's not the total worst, I guess. We all make mistakes, right?'

What mistakes? I'm wondering.

'How did they get back together?' Rachel asks.

'*Back* together?' I ask, totally confused. Marsha and her Dad weren't going out.

Alex looks at me, kind of apologetically. 'They had a, kind of, one-night stand thing before she left. Actually, that's why she left – I walked in on them.'

'What, like, kissing?'

'Worse.'

'Ee-ew.' God.

'I was upset.'

'I bet you were.'

'So how *did* they get back together?' Rachel asks again.

'When Marsha heard about the attack, she dropped everything and flew straight to San Diego. She spent so much time with him, in the hospital and afterwards while he was getting better. I was with David pretty much all the time. In the end, Dad asked if I'd be OK with them seeing each other.'

'He asked your *permission?*' I ask. '*Seriously?*'

She shrugs. 'He just wanted to make sure I was OK with him seeing other people, you know, after Mum.'

'Wow. That was so *thoughtful.*' I try to imagine my dad asking my permission to do anything. And almost laugh. I wish, when you were born, you could pick your parents, the way you pick good fruit. Squeeze them, tap them, shake them. The only thing is, you'd be a baby so you wouldn't know what you were looking for and even if you did, you wouldn't be able to talk, so you couldn't ask important questions like, 'will you like me?' or 'will you stay together?'

'So where's she going to live?' Rachel asks.

'In an apartment in Dalkey.'

'What about her design business?' Rachel asks.

This time, I don't even ask.

'Oh, she's going to try it from here.'

I think about her flying across America to be with Alex's dad. I think about her moving back to Ireland to be with him. 'Love,' I say, dreamily, as someone else finds it.

'Oh, it's not *love*,' Alex says, making a face. 'They're just seeing how it goes.'

That's when I realise Alex might be OK with them being together. But not in actual love. And I get that. It kills me that my dad is with someone else. When I let myself think about it.

We go back to class. The rest of the day goes by in the usual way. Nothing happens. No one says anything. By the time we're walking through the school gates, I'm so relieved I want to cry. So, it hasn't followed me here, after all. I feel so lucky, like I've been given a second chance. I can go on being me, just me, not some loser who got caught shoplifting, not someone you can't trust. I close my eyes in relief. And make myself a promise – I will never steal again.

5
HELLO

After school, Mike drops us to Dundrum. We head for the shops. Normally, I'd be leading the way. Today, I'm lagging behind. I force myself to follow Alex into the first shop. It is part of the same chain that I was caught in on Saturday. What if they talk to each other? What if they warn each other about shoplifters? My stomach twists into a knot. My heart starts to pound. My mouth is dry. God, I'm even breathing funny.

'Are you OK?' Rachel asks.

'What? Yeah. Fine.' I aim for cheery but sound kind of scary.

She's squinting at me. 'You don't look too well, Sarah.'

'I'm grand.'

Alex, who shot off to have a look around the minute we hit the shop, comes back.

'God, their stuff is really crap. Want to try Tommy Hilfiger?'

Phew, I think.

We leave the shop. Only problem is, it's not the only shop.

We're almost at Tommy Hilfiger when I decide I can't do it.

'I think I'll wait outside,' I say.

Rachel looks instantly worried.

Alex just looks puzzled. 'You love Tommy Hilfiger.'

I make a face. 'I just want to people-watch for a while. See if there are any cute guys.'

'Ah,' Alex says, as if that makes total sense.

'Want me to come with you?' Rachel asks.

'Do I look like I want competition here?'

Her face relaxes into a smile. 'You sure?'

'I'll be over by the escalators.' I start walking to the busiest part of the centre. When I get there, I hold on to the chrome railing and look down at the level below. People are milling around like ants. Slowly, I start to calm down. I don't know how long I'm there but I'm miles away when a hand falls on my shoulder. It feels like I'm having an actual heart attack. I turn.

But it's just the guys.

'Jesus, Alex, you frightened the crap out of me.

'See anyone interesting?' she asks.

I'm still holding my heart.

'Are you *OK*?' Rachel asks. 'You look terrible.'

'I didn't expect you back so quick.'

She checks her watch. 'We were, like, twenty minutes.'

'Were you?'

They look at each other. Then back at me.

'You sure you're OK?' Rachel asks.

'I wasn't great over the weekend,' I say to cover up.

'Why didn't you say so?' Alex says. 'I'll call Mike.'

'No, no, it's OK, I'll be fine.'

‘Sarah you look like death,’ Rachel says.

‘I’ll sit down, I’ll have a frappuccino.’ With Louis’ twenty.

‘We’re going,’ Alex says.

‘You sure?’

It’s the first time in my life I’m happy to leave Dundrum.

We pull up outside my house and I’m stressing again. Mum’s car is outside. I’m dead. I hurry up the path. I open the front door really quietly and start to sneak upstairs, hoping she hasn’t noticed I’m not home.

‘Sarah?’

Crud. I stop. No point going on. Especially as she’ll only come after me. I sigh, then turn around and trudge back down. I open the door to the kitchen, preparing to be decapitated.

She’s standing, leaning with her back against the sink, smoking. It hits me, suddenly, how much weight she’s lost, especially on her face. And she wasn’t exactly fat in the first place.

‘Where were you?’

‘At Alex’s. Doing a project.’ She makes me lie. I swear to God, she makes me lie.

‘You’re grounded. Remember?’

‘For school work?’

‘For everything. Unless you check with me first. What’s the project on?’

‘Fashion,’ I say, starting to blush.

‘What about fashion?’

Jesus. ‘Is it, like, a form of expression?’

‘Let’s have a look.’

‘What?’

'At what you've done.'

'It's in Alex's.'

'Why were you going upstairs when you came in?'

'To change.'

'You saw my car, didn't you?'

I don't answer. But I look down. And I know she knows.

'Set the table,' she says, sounding as tired as she looks.

In silence, I set three places, knowing that Louis won't be home. Louis always has an excuse. If it's not 'college' it's 'part-time job'. We never see him. But she insists on setting a place for him anyway. Because we're 'still a family'. I pour water into three glasses and carry them to the table. She strains the potatoes into the sink, steam rising all round her face. I imagine her in a sauna throwing water over hot coals. She could do with a sauna more than anyone I know.

Sometimes – when she's not angry – I want to tell her it'll be OK. But what do I know? And it's not like she listens to me, anyway. It used to be different. We were close, once. OK, maybe not as close as Rachel is with her mum or Alex was with hers. But close enough. I could tell her things and she wouldn't freak. Now she's more likely to say, 'do your homework' than 'let's go to Ikea'. We never go anywhere together any more. I don't know when it changed. It wasn't a sudden thing. I just know that, over time, I began to spend less time at home and more time at other people's. I've never told anyone, but I loved Alex's mum. I seriously miss her. Which is probably wrong, right? She was Alex's mum. I know that half the problem with my mum is that I don't achieve. She totally blew when I did so badly in my Junior Cert exams. Then again, Louis doesn't achieve either. But there's something about Louis. He can melt her somehow. I've never learned how.

When I've set the table, I hang around, knowing that if I try to go upstairs, she'll just call me back. Finally, she lands the plates down. Soggy broccoli, gloopy mash and dried out chops. I thank her. Because I value my life. I pick up my knife and fork, trying to decide which looks the least yuck. I cut into the dry meat and slide some wet potato onto it, hoping that one will cancel out the other. I've tried convincing her to let me have money for school lunch so she won't have to cook. That would cost her a fiver, as opposed to whatever she spends on dinner for three, that's eaten by one. She never touches food herself, just lights up and smokes her way through. So it's a total joke when she says that she wants us all to sit down for a meal. Like eating (or pretending to) is going to bring us magically together.

The only sound is the grating of my knife on the plate. She looks out the window and puffs away. She turns back and taps the ash onto her side plate. Then she looks at me like she's remembering I'm here.

'So how are your friends?' She says it like she doesn't like them. Which is unfair given that she doesn't really know them (I try to avoid exposing them to her). The irony is that her ideal daughter would be a Rachel. Someone organised, focused, in control. Someone who knows what she wants in life and goes after it. Someone who never messes up. Maybe, instead of giving out about my friends, she should call up a few of her own. If she has any left.

'How's Ellen?' I ask, inspired.

She looks surprised. 'Ellen? I don't know. I haven't seen her in ages.'

'I wonder how she is.'

'Happily married with kids that don't give trouble.'

I stare at her. She only sees what she wants to see. I took

her side. Cut Dad off. Because of her. She's never once seen that. I get up from the table.

'You're not finished.'

'Neither are you.'

'Eat your meal,' she says. Like I'm two.

Is that what it is? I think but don't say. I'm not suicidal – yet. I go over to the bin and slide in the last few bits of dried meat. She gives me this look, like I'm the spawn of the devil or something. And I feel like becoming the spawn of the devil just to spite her. She's my mother but she doesn't know anything about me. She doesn't know that, despite her, I can be happy. She doesn't know that I love my friends. She doesn't know that I've a boyfriend. That I've had sex (just as well or I'd be dead). She doesn't know that, if I could, I'd be miles away from here, from her.

6
SHARK

On Tuesday, some sort of diplomat is giving us a talk on what she does. It's either the most boring job in the world or she's just making it sound that way, talking to us like we're three, like we haven't a clue what goes on in the world, like we're actually slow. She's doing my head in.

'So,' she says, finally. 'Does anyone have any questions?'

'Why are you still here?' Alex whispers, looking innocently ahead.

'Are you always so boring?' I whisper.

'Could you use more hand actions?' Her hands haven't stopped moving since she got here.

'Can you repeat everything you just said? Only more slowly.'

'If I'm in Brussels and you're in Brussels when's the next train out of Brussels?'

'Is that your hair or did something die on your head?'

Alex giggles.

It's so great that she's back to normal, back to the way she used to be before her mum died, over a year ago. I missed her.

After school, surprise, surprise, none of us is in a hurry to go home. When Rachel suggests the Jitter Mug, I can't say no. These are my friends, for God's sake. Just for half an hour, I tell myself. I can cover for half an hour if my mum finishes early.

The place is mobbed as usual. The only difference is that Louis is at the till.

'What are you doing here?' I ask.

'I work here.'

'At weekends.'

'They upped my hours. What can I say? Customers like me.'

Yeah, I think. *Women customers.*

Louis sees Alex and breaks into this huge smile. 'Hey, Alex. Glad you survived that frenzied attack in California.'

'You make it sound like a shark,' she says. He laughs. 'When really it was just a mad psycho who almost killed my dad.'

His face goes serious. 'Glad you're OK though.'

She nods. 'Yeah. Thanks.'

It's weird. It's like they know each other. I mean, outside of her just being my friend. Louis catches me looking. And snaps out of tunnel vision mode.

'So, what can I get you, ladies?' he asks, like he's at the bar not the coffee shop.

'Three tropical smoothies,' I say.

'Paying separately?'

'I'll get them today,' Alex says. 'To celebrate my *survival*.' She directs this at Louis. He smiles like they're sharing some kind of private joke. I so don't get it.

We wait for our smoothies at the end of the counter. I

watch Louis dealing with the next customer. He acts like we're not there. But he's gone all perky, like he knows someone's watching. Finally, we collect our smoothies from another guy and go sit down.

I look at Alex. 'So. What's the story with you and Louis?'

'What?' She looks appalled.

'I don't know. You just seemed so pally.'

'Yeah!' Rachel says, like she's as surprised as me.

'There *is* no story. He slagged me. I slagged him back, Jeez.'

I shrug. Then I remember. 'He asked for your number. Weeks ago.'

She shrugs. 'Don't know why.' She takes a sip of her smoothie.

'He didn't ring?'

'I'm not Louis' type,' she says, without looking up from her drink.

'Does Louis *have* a type?' Rachel asks.

I clear my throat loudly. 'Louis *is* my brother.'

Rachel looks at me. 'No offence, Sarah. But he is a bit of a player.'

I'm about to argue, but then I look over and catch him flirting with the next customer – a young mum who is actually carrying a baby.

'You're right,' I say. 'He has no shame.'

When I get home, Mum's there again. Waiting for me in the kitchen. What is up with the health services in this country, letting their social workers sneak off early like that? Please God, let this not be a pattern.

'Sit down,' she says. 'We need to talk.'

This is Mum at her scariest – when she doesn't shout. When she says we need to talk. I sit at the kitchen table, knowing that something's coming. Something awful. She sits opposite and places her cigarettes on the table like a weapon. She puts her cheap blue lighter on top. Then takes her hand away.

'I've been on to Our Lady's Abbey. They'll take you.'

'What?'

'You're moving school, Sarah.'

'What? No way.' She can't be serious. 'I'm not leaving Strandbrook.'

'You don't have a choice.'

Oh my God. 'You can't do this.'

'I *am* doing this. It's happening.'

'Without any *discussion*?'

She blows. 'I'm so *tired* of discussion. I'm so *tired* of doing things your father's way. Softly, softly. Talky, talky. You're spoiled. And I'm putting my foot down. Like I should have done long ago.'

In that case, I'll put mine down too. 'I'm not going.'

'Who'll pay your fees?'

'Oh my God. That's so low.'

'Not if it's the best thing for you.'

But I'm not listening. If she won't pay the fees, Dad will. But then, I'm not talking to Dad. I don't want to talk to him. I especially don't want to ask him for anything, to owe him. So I try harder.

'All my friends are at Strandbrook. You can't do this—'

'You'll make new friends. Who won't have celebrity parents and everything money can buy.' Oh my God, that's what this is about. 'Normal people. Whose future isn't secure. Who know the meaning of the word "work".'

'I work.'

She laughs bitterly. 'Really?'

'All right then, I will work. Really hard.'

'Actions have consequences, Sarah. The sooner you learn that, the better.'

'I'm going to a psychologist. I'm doing community service—'

'They're your father's department. Moving school is something *I* want.'

'Mum, I took two things. I said I was sorry. I'll never do it again. I swear. You can't move me.' Strandbrook is the one thing that's right in my life. But I don't say that. She'd think I was getting at her.

'What was the other thing you took?' she asks, like it was something the size of the American lottery.

'Makeup. Just this tiny thing of eye shadow.'

She reaches for the Marlboro pack and taps a cigarette out. She puts it to her mouth, then snaps her lighter. She inhales deeply. Then points the cigarette at me.

'You know, I was never in favour of that school in the first place.'

Oh my God. I'm in the middle of someone else's war. 'This is my *life*.'

'Exactly. And you get one shot at it. I'm not going to let you blow it.'

Not for the first time, I wish she wasn't a social worker. I wish she wasn't so obsessed with how hard 'people out there' have it. Because they have it tough, we should too. Or something.

'Our Lady's Abbey was good enough for me. It'll be good enough for you. You're moving school. And that's it.'

I feel like clicking my heels together, saluting and saying,

'Heil Hitler.' Instead, I pound upstairs. I pace my room, trying to figure out what to do. Because I'm not going to let her do this. I'm just not. This is *my* life.

There's only one thing to do. It's drastic. But necessary. I pick up my phone, take a deep breath and call Dad.

'Can we meet for coffee?'

There's a pause. 'Are you OK?'

'She's kicking me out of the school.'

Another pause. This one longer. 'Let's get that coffee, OK?'

'You have to *do* something.'

'How about the Royal Marine Hotel at half five?'

'You wanted me to go to Strandbrook. It was your idea. Remember?'

'I'll see you at half five, OK?'

'I mean, that's half her problem. It was your idea.'

'Sarah? Half five, OK?'

'OK. But you can't let her take me out. OK? You just can't.' He owes me this much.

I'm early. Biting my sleeve, I'm going over the arguments in my head. It was his idea. And he was right. It's a great school. I'm happy. I've great friends. And I'd die if I had to move. People make mistakes. OK, mine was stupid. But it's not like I'm a bad person. I'm prepared to take the punishment. But that punishment is already strong – without this as well.

As soon as he has a coffee in front of him, I spill it all out.

He says nothing. Being a psychologist, that's not unusual.

But being a psychologist's daughter, I know what to do. I stop talking. Just look at him.

)|(

Silence.

Finally, I break. '*You* could pay the fees, couldn't you?'

He looks at me. Expressionless. 'Sarah, your mother seems to have her mind made up on this one.'

'Yeah but what you want matters too, right? You're still my dad.' So he keeps telling me.

'Well, of course, but I don't want to step on her toes.'

Suddenly I get it. 'Because that would mean talking with her, asking her for something. Is that it?'

He sniffles, clears his throat. Shifts in his seat. 'Things are tighter now, Sarah, financially. I'm not sure we can afford Strandbrook any more.'

Oh my God. Things are tighter for one reason. Her. I'm going to be wrenched from everything I know. And his priority is to Her. I stand up.

'I should have known I was wasting my time.' I start to walk, blinking back tears.

'Sarah?' He stands up. 'We need to talk about the community service.'

I turn. 'You can ram the community service up your bum.'

The whole coffee shop is staring. But I don't care. I march out, thinking I don't know which of my stupid parents is the worst.

I get the DART to Blackrock. The Jitter Mug is mobbed. There's a huge queue. Louis looks as chilled as usual. I go straight up to him.

'Louis, I need to talk to you.'

'I'm working,' he says, then turns to this girl who's so obviously into him. 'That'll be five-fifty.' And there it is, that Louis smile.

'It's urgent,' I say.

He gives the girl her change, holding her eyes for crucial seconds longer than is necessary.

Her 'thank you' is suggestive, then she is gone, leaving a waft of perfume behind. It's Tommy Girl.

Louis looks at me. 'Can't this wait till we get home?'

'No. Because you're never home. I need your help, Louis. Seriously, it's urgent.'

He looks at the line of people growing ever bigger. He checks his watch. Then he fishes in his jeans and throws money in the till. He orders a tropical smoothie.

'Go sit. I'm due a break in twenty.'

'Thanks.'

I walk past the table with Flirty Girl. She glares at me – probably for interrupting. I give her a smug smile. Like he's my boyfriend or something.

It's a half an hour before he gets free.

He sits down. 'What's up?'

'She wants me to move school. She thinks I'm hanging out with the wrong people.'

'Alex and Rachel?' he says, like they're pussycats.

'They've too much money. She wants me to hang out with people like us. Who've none.'

'*Why?*'

'She thinks it's their fault I took stuff.'

Suddenly, I see it. This isn't just unfair. It's flawed. She's blaming my friends, my school, for what I did. The person who's always going on about taking responsibility.

'Actually, Louis, forget it.' I stand suddenly. I wanted him to talk to her. Now I just want to get home. He stands too, looking bemused. On a whim, I hug him.

'Jesus, get off me. I've a reputation to keep up.'

I smile. 'See you later.'

'Good luck.'

'I'll need it.'

She's in the kitchen, scraping carrots at ninety miles an hour. She doesn't even notice I've walked in. I stand watching, waiting till she's done. Finally, she sees me and puts down the carrot peeler.

'Where were you?' she snaps. 'You're supposed to be grounded, Sarah. Don't you get the concept?'

'Mum, we need to talk.'

She reaches for her cigarettes (never far away). She opens the pack and sticks one in her mouth. She has to flick the lighter twice before it flames. She inhales deeply, closing her eyes. Then, without saying a word, she walks over and sits at the kitchen table.

I take a deep breath. And follow.

'OK, shoot,' she says.

And it's so hard, when she says it like that. Like she's got some sort of stopwatch and I have to go when she says go. I try to get my thoughts together. But then, I guess, there is just one.

'Mum, you and dad have always taught us to take responsibility for our actions.' I pause. 'Well, I need you to let me do that. I took that stuff. No one else. Not my friends. Not my school. And if you blame them then it stops being my fault. You need to blame *me* here. OK? Just me. I'll do the community service.' (That I just told Dad to ram up his bum.) 'I'll go to the psychologist. I'll work harder in school. Just please, give me a chance to prove myself, OK? I can do it, Mum. I can be a good person.' The person you want me to be.

She takes a drag of the cigarette. And takes ages to reply.

'Sarah, I've spoken to the principal. I've made plans.'

And then I say it. 'Don't use me in your war against Dad.'

She squints. 'What did you say?'

All I can do now is keep going. 'Don't take me out of Strandbrook just because it was Dad's idea for me to go.'

'That's not what this is about.' She stubs out her cigarette like her problem is with it. 'This is about you.'

'Is it, though?' I can't believe I said that. Then again, I'm desperate. I'll do anything to stop this. Strandbrook is my life.

She stares at me like she can't believe I said that. I expect her to blow. But she gets up and walks to the window, her back to me. She runs a hand through her hair, takes a long drag on her cigarette. Then she turns around. For the first time, she looks unsure.

'I don't know,' she says. 'Let me think about this.' She puts a hand to her forehead, making her cigarette point skyward. 'I need to think.' She sounds so hassled. And I know she makes my life hell but she just looks so stressed, standing there, I almost cry.

'Do you want a hand with dinner?' I ask.

She looks surprised and I don't know whether it's because she'd forgotten about dinner or because I offered to help.

'Yeah. OK. That'd be good. Thanks.'

I nod. 'OK.'

I hope she didn't think I offered just to get on her good side. Because I didn't.

7
OESOPHAGUS

After dinner, I go on Facebook. Simon has posted on David's wall.

'What are Californian girls like?'

Oh for God's sake.

'Californians,' David has posted back. Go David.

'What percentage have had boob jobs?'

Oh my God. This is on David's *wall*.

David doesn't reply.

Next thing, the words, 'Hey, babe,' come up in my chat box.

'Why did you post that on David's wall?' I ask.

'What?'

'The thing about boobs.'

'I was joking. That guy's no sense of humour.'

'Simon. It's sexist. And California-ist.' I don't tell him that it's also an insult to me.

'It was a joke, Jeez.'

'Yeah, well, it just makes you look like a loser.'

'Why do you care?'

}|{

I'm wondering exactly that when there's a creak on the stairs outside. I click out of Facebook and into a study website. A knock, then the door opens. I look up. Innocently.

It's only Louis, dressed in his bar gear and smelling of aftershave.

'Well?' he asks. 'Did you talk to her?'

'She says she'll think about it.'

He looks surprised. 'Excellent.'

'It doesn't mean yes.'

'It could have been an outright no.'

'I guess.'

'OK. Well, don't give up. Tickle her. Make her laugh.'

I give him a look. I could *never* make her laugh. Only he can do that. 'I'll try.'

'Atta girl.' He winks then is gone, his aftershave hanging on the air.

Wednesday morning and, as usual, Mum's left for work when I get down. Before he moved out, Dad would always be still here at this time, knocking back a last-minute coffee before rushing out the door with his hair sticking up and a tie slung over his shoulder. I turn on the radio to block out the silence. I have to change the station from news to Spin FM, the players of happy music. I have breakfast while packing my lunch. Then, with no reason to hang around, I go, leaving the radio on so there's noise when I get in.

On the DART, I hook up with the guys as usual. I try not to think that soon it might not be 'as usual', that soon I might be going in the other direction, to a school of strangers.

'You look shagged,' Rachel says to Alex.

'I was talking to David till one.'

I imagine what it must be like, not being able to hang up on someone because you love them so much. 'That's so romantic.'

'There's nothing romantic about time difference.'

'What?'

'By the time he gets out of school and everything, it's already midnight here.'

'Oh God, I never thought of that.'

'Roll on weekend.'

'How's he doing?' Rachel asks.

Her smile is dreamy. 'He says being over there makes him feel Irish. He misses you all.'

'Aw, bless,' I say. I really like David.

We get off the DART and walk up to school. Today, it's like seeing everything for the first time. And the last time. The hockey pitches I don't even play on. The school building. The statue in front. I love this school; I love the look of it, the smell of it, the sound of it. I love the atmosphere, the people. This school is part of who I am. Was my mum *ever* a teenager? Was she *ever* younger than forty? Seriously.

'Are you OK?' Rachel asks.

'What? Yeah,' I say quickly.

'Sarah. You're crying,' Alex says.

'What? No I'm not.'

'What's wrong?' Rachel asks gently.

'Nothing.' I whip a tear away. But then, they look so concerned, I can't help it, I tell them.

They look like they can't believe it.

'She wouldn't do that,' Rachel says. 'I mean, why would she?'

'She went to Our Lady's.'

'*So?*' Alex says. 'You've been going here since First Year. Why change now?'

I shrug. What else can I do? Tell them I was caught shoplifting and lose them forever?

'You're happy here,' Alex adds. 'It's your school, for God's sake.'

I can't believe she's getting angry – for me. I'm so touched. And guilty for not telling her everything.

'What does your dad say?' Rachel asks.

Suddenly I feel sick. I look away. 'He doesn't care,' I say quietly and well up again.

Then Rachel's arm is around me.

'Don't worry,' Alex says. 'We'll think of something.'

I force a smile. 'It mightn't happen.'

'Exactly,' Rachel says.

'Don't say anything. To anyone, OK? Not even Simon.'

'OK. Sure. Of course,' Rachel says, straight away.

'Don't worry,' Alex says. 'This isn't going to happen. You're going nowhere.' And though I know there's nothing she can do, I feel better just knowing they both care.

I promised to work at school. And I'm trying. But I don't have the brain for school. It wanders. All the time. I'll look at a teacher and, instead of taking in what she's saying, I'll wonder where she got her top. Or if she's had Botox. Or if she'd ever consider a nose job. I'll wonder what her husband's like – if she's married. Or why she's not – if she's not. Same problem with study. I have to keep pulling my mind back from all the interesting places it's wandering off to and see only the words in front of me. Words like 'doth' and 'oesophagus' and 'pi-r-squared', if that's a word. Even if I could concentrate, there's another problem. Just the *mention* of the word exams sends me into a frenzy so that instead of actually studying, I have to do something to calm down. Like watch *The OC* or *Desperate Housewives*. Or *Wife Swap* (the American version).

At least, today, we've French first. I can listen in French. Everyone gives out about Madame Reilly. They don't think we learn anything in her class. And I guess we don't learn a whole lot of *French*. But I like her. I like her attitude. She's not beautiful but she does the best with what she's got. Her hair is dark, her cheeks rosy. Not naturally dark. Not naturally rosy. But so what? She looks like Snow White. Just older. She wears bright colours: reds, greens, blues and always a scarf draped over one shoulder that never falls off. She has 'panache'. (I searched for a long time for that word. It's perfect for her.) Madame Reilly is not French but acts like she is.

And, OK, she might spend more time talking about France than actually teaching the language. That's because she loves the place. I think it's *interesting* that Napoleon was afraid of cats. And that the French deliberately broke the lifts on the Eiffel Tower so Hitler couldn't make it to the top when he took over Paris. I listen to her and I'm there. In Paris. Strolling the boulevards. Smelling the croissants. Having coffee in a small, corner café. And looking up from my pain au chocolate to see a total stranger who is so beyond caliente, smiling at me like he's just fallen in love. Yup, I can see the point in learning French.

So when Mark asks Madame Reilly for the French word for 'tangent', I don't laugh like everyone else. I frown at him like he's *très* immature. But then I think, *maybe he's right*. How am I ever going to learn the language if she doesn't teach it? Oh my God. I have become my mother.

After French, we have Debating, one of the classes I dream most in. The great thing about debating is that it's not an exam subject, so I can go on dreaming. While Rachel argues the case for the importance of keeping the Irish language alive (how could she?), I scan the class. Is Orla Tempany looking a little too often at Harry Marsh? I'm going to keep my eye on that. After debating, we have Film Studies. And it's amazing how boring a person can make something entertaining like movies. The day goes on. And on.

Finally, it's over and I go straight home – which almost kills me.

At seven, I make sure I'm studying when Mum comes in. I make sure I'm doing it somewhere obvious (kitchen table). I make sure I look like I'm concentrating (frown). She raises an eyebrow. But says nothing. I learn French verbs while she prepares dinner. Nobody talks. Which is good. Because no one's giving out.

At dinner, I wait for her to tell me what she's decided. My stomach feels like there's a fist around it. I'm so tempted to bring it up myself, just get it out there. To at least know. But I say nothing. In case her answer is the wrong one.

'I took your advice,' she says.

I look at her. I don't remember giving any.

'I called Ellen.'

'Oh.' I'm so surprised, I only just remember to ask how she is.

'Separated.'

'Seriously?'

'Two years ago.'

'God. Poor Ellen. What happened?'

'Her husband left her.'

'For someone else?'

'Sarah, a man never leaves a woman unless there is some-one else.' She doesn't sound bitter. She sounds like this is just a fact. 'Anyway, we talked. It helped.' Speaking of talks, this is the longest conversation I've had with Mum since … I don't know when. 'I think we'll stay in touch,' she says.

'Cool.' I'm happy for her. She could seriously do with a friend.

'By the way,' she says, and something about her changes, her voice turning hard. 'Your father has set up your community service.'

I think of litter. 'What is it?'

'Visiting a home for the disabled,' she says casually.

If she knew anything about me, she'd know not to be casual. These places freak me out. That Alzheimer's home, last year … Oh my God … All those people totally out of it, thinking I was trying to poison them. I start to feel sick. And I'm not even there.

'What'll I have to do?' I ask cautiously.

'I don't know. Whatever they need. I'll drop you off, Friday, after school.'

'This Friday?' It hasn't even been a week since I got caught.

'This Friday,' she confirms.

'Won't you be working?'

'I'll finish early.'

'It's OK. I'll get the DART.'

'No. I'll bring you.'

Suddenly, I get it. She wants to make sure I go. I want to tell her she can trust me. But then I guess I've shown her that she can't.

'Then you've the psychologist on Saturday morning.'

Oh my God, this is seriously depressing. Did she have to bring one up right after the other? And Saturday? Jesus. 'Do they even work on Saturdays?'

'Don't moan. She's fitting you in. Be grateful.'

And just like that, it's back to the way it always is between us.

Thursday, at break, Alex asks if I want to go for a walk.

I look around. 'Where's Rache?'

'Gone somewhere with Mark,' she says.

'Probably the cafeteria.' Like normal people. Why the walk? It might be spring. It's cold outside. And walking? Not, like, my favourite pastime.

'Let's get our coats,' she says, cheerily.

I look at her and think, *Something's up*.

Outside, I turn my collar up and shove my hands in my pockets. I look at her, waiting for whatever it is she's going to say. But she doesn't say anything. For ages. Just walks. I'm beginning to think that maybe this is really just about walking when she says, 'So, any news from your mum on the school thing?'

I feel suddenly down. 'No.'

She looks off into the distance, then back at me. 'I was wondering ... you know ... if it's a money thing ...'

I feel myself blush.

'I just want you to know that you don't have to worry. My dad went to Strandbrook and he's been meaning to do something for the school for ages. So, he's, like, setting up this fund for people who are kind of stuck for their fees and stuff, you know, with the recession, and that? Anyway, after next week, anyone in, like, trouble can apply for a grant ...' She looks at me, questioningly, like she wants to know if this will make everything OK.

And I'm so touched. That she would go to her dad. And get the whole thing moving. For me. When I haven't always been the best friend in the world.

'Thank you so much, Alex.' My hand is on my heart because I just can't believe it. 'It's so sweet of you. Of your Dad.' I pause. 'But it's not money.' I wish I could tell her. And still stay friends.

'Oh.' She looks so surprised.

'But thanks, Alex. Really, thank you.' And I wonder if you really only find out who your true friends are when you're in trouble.

8
BINGO

Last night, I googled the home I have to go to. There were photos of the people in there. I got the hell out of the site. And have been dreading it ever since. Now Mum picks me up from school with a, friendly-for-her, 'How was your day?'

'Fine,' I say, thinking, *It's not over yet.*

We drive the, unfortunately short, distance to the home. It's near the sea, halfway between school and home. Outside the single-storey, modern building, she cuts the engine and looks at me. I know there's no point arguing, so I just open the door.

'You can leave your bag in the car,' she says. Like I give a shit about my bag.

I walk towards the home. I stop and look back, waiting for her to leave. She doesn't. She just sits there, looking at me until I go through the front door. And it's not like I can hide in some corridor and sneak back out when she's gone because I've walked straight into a huge, bright, open room, full of people – people in those modern wheelchairs with engines and headrests and gadgets. They're organised into a giant semi-circle, all of them facing me, well, actually, facing some kind of podium that's in front of me. It's like some talk is about to begin. All these strangers are looking at me like they're trying to figure out who I am and what I'm doing here. There are helpers too, sitting with the residents, people like me dressed in ordinary clothes. I wonder if they just volunteered or if they're on community service too. Mostly, they're middle-aged and kind of mumsy looking. So, volunteers, I guess. Someone in scrubs with a pretty face is coming my way, wearing the biggest smile. She's the first non-scary thing about the place. So I focus on her.

'You must be Sarah,' she says, holding out her hand.

I'm embarrassed because mine is clammy. I wipe it on my coat before we shake.

'Eh, yeah. Hi.'

'I'm Christina. You're just in time for Bingo.'

'Oh.'

She looks around the room. 'Everyone loves Bingo.' Then she looks back at me. 'So, what would be great is, if you could help someone with their counters, just put them on the board for them.' I look at her blankly, no clue what she's talking about. She lowers her voice. 'Some of our residents can't see that well; others can't move their hands. So, it'd be great if you could sit with someone, like John over there, and give him a hand.'

I look at John and remember the photos on the website.

'Come on, I'll introduce you,' she says.

I follow her when all I want to do is run. As we approach John, I start to feel sick, then guilty that I feel sick. Oh God. This is so not me. This is not what I'm good at. John's head is tilted to one side, like he can't support it. His face is twisted into a tight, uncomfortable expression. I force a smile. And when he doesn't smile back, I know it's because he can't. I take a deep breath and pretend I'm Rachel. I'm good with people. All people. I'm cool in all situations. Oh God, I'm not fooling myself. This is not working.

'John, this is Sarah. Sarah's going to give you a hand today.'

'Hey, John,' I say.

Only his eyes say hello.

Christina puts a chair beside his wheelchair.

'There you go,' she says to me.

'Thanks,' I say and sit. Be cool, I tell myself. Just look at the board. Look at the big, blue buttons that must be counters. And try to work out how to play Bingo.

It feels wrong, though, sitting beside him, like he's not here.

'So,' I say making my voice cheery, 'someone just calls out random numbers and, if we have any, we cover them with counters, right?'

He looks at me and groans really loudly like he's trying to answer. Oh, sweet Jesus. He can't talk. I look over at Christina in panic. She should have told me. I think of John, the man inside the body, trying to communicate and not being able to. My heart kind of breaks for him. He needs a Rachel here – not a Sarah. I've never felt so useless in my entire life.

This one guy who's been turned away from everyone else, just staring out the window, turns his whole wheelchair around and glares at me like I'm a total idiot. I die again. Blush and look away. Oh God, if only this thing would start.

If only someone would just come and call out some bloody numbers. Please. Somebody. Anybody. Hell, I'll call them out.

The guy at the window goes back to staring out. It's like he doesn't want to be here. Which makes two of us. I look at him. Everything about him is different. The way he's facing. The way he looks – his hair a mess, his beard unkempt. Even from over here, I can feel his anger. And I can feel that people are avoiding him as much as he is avoiding them. I can feel that he is trouble.

At last, a voice at the microphone. I turn. A middle-aged, tubby, soft-looking woman has taken to the podium.

'Everyone ready?' she asks cheerily. 'Great prizes today. Our best yet, I think.'

I glance over, knowing, automatically, that the guy at the window won't be impressed. I'm right. His head falls back against his headrest, like things just couldn't get any worse.

For me, things get better. It's easier with something to do. And Bingo really is just matching numbers. It takes a while, though, to cover the whole board. And it's not our lucky day. We're beaten to it every time. Someone called Mary wins bubble bath. Someone called James wins a candle. A guy called Brian wins a box of chocolates. They all get genuinely excited. It's so lovely. The prizes are tiny. It's only Bingo. They're in wheelchairs. But none of that seems to matter. These people are happy. They live in a home with so many restrictions, but they are happy. Well, all except the guy at the window.

After about an hour, I'm holding a big, blue button in my hand and sneaking a look around the room to see where everyone else is at. We have only one number left uncovered on our board. I look at John. He raises his eyebrows. I LOVE that he can do that. Then, she calls it – our number. Four.

I shout, 'Bingo!'

John groans with excitement. I realise that I've jumped up. We look at each other and I swear to God, I can make out a smile. I slap him gently on the arm. He makes a sound like laughter. He is definitely laughing. Oh my God, I wish he could high five.

'Wow,' I say. 'That was brilliant.'

I sit down. And another game starts. I look around, feeling part of this now. Feeling at home. Me, the person who wanted to run. And I wonder if there's something magical about Bingo. Or this place.

When it's time to go, I'm not running to the door. Actually, I wouldn't mind another game. It's so warm here, so friendly. Everyone is just so up. I think about home, the radio trying to fill the empty kitchen with sound. I wonder if there's anything else they want me to do. Christina's coming up to me. Smiling.

'Thank you so much,' she says. 'You were great. Fitted right in. Didn't she, John?'

John groans. And instead of freaking, I simply understand. I smile and put my hand on his shoulder. 'Bye, Partner, see you next week.'

He groans again and I actually hug him.

Christina walks me to the door.

'Wow,' I say. 'Everyone's so happy here.' Then I remember the guy by the window. I look over.

She follows my eyes.

'Is he OK?' I ask, when what I really want to know is

what's wrong with him. The top half of his body is perfect. His legs, though, seem wasted.

Her eyes fill with compassion. All she says is, 'Shane's new to this.' *She's a nurse*, I think. She's probably taken vows of secrecy or something. 'Anyway,' she says. 'Thank you *so much* for coming. I think everyone enjoyed your company. So we'll see you next week?' she asks.

'Yeah, sure. No problem.'

Then I push open the door. Cool March air chills my face. Suddenly, I feel lucky to be walking out, lucky to be walking at all.

I get the DART home. Mum's car is outside. Beside it is one that I don't recognise. I walk into the kitchen expecting someone new. What I'm not expecting is to see my mother crying in their arms.

Ellen, Mum's friend, sees me first. She lets Mum go. Then Mum turns and sees me.

'Is everything OK?' I ask nervously.

'Everything's fine,' Mum says quickly. She clears a tear with the back of her hand.

'Did something happen?' I ask. Mum never cries. Anger is her thing.

'No. Nothing happened.'

'Nothing new, anyway,' Ellen says, so I know she means Dad leaving.

'OK,' I say. I back out of the kitchen.

Upstairs, I raid my chocolate stash. I don't want to see Mum sad. But she's sad Dad left. Which is good. Because it means she did love him. She did care that he was going. And maybe it wasn't easy, after all, for her to make him choose.

Or maybe I'm reading too much into a few tears. I don't want to give her a break unless she deserves one. And I don't know that she does. I suck on a Curly Wurly (they last longer that way) and try to think of something else.

Today it's easy. Because of the home. I wonder what it must be like being in a wheelchair. Maybe it's not that bad when you get used to it. I go over to my swivel chair, sit on it and pretend it's one. I wheel around my room. I can reach the light switch. I can open my drawers. I can't get anything that's hanging up, though. After a while, I need to go to the loo. I scoot over to the bedroom door and open it. Then I'm stuck. I can't go downstairs. Unless I pretend that the house has been adapted and that we've a lift. I pick up the chair and carry it down to the bathroom. Inside, I wheel over to the loo. Then I'm stuck again. I can't get on without standing up. How do they do it? Oh my God. Don't tell me they need help to go to the loo. I'd die. I look over at the shower. How do they do it? I sit there trying to figure it out. Then I have to get up and go to the loo before I burst. Afterwards, I carry the chair back upstairs. I lie on the bed. And wiggle my toes. I look at them wiggling. Appreciate them wiggling. It's something I have never appreciated before.

At eight, Mum calls me for dinner. I go down, hoping that everything's back to normal – or as normal as they are in our house. I walk into the kitchen. Mum's at the table, opening two pizza boxes. We never get takeout. I stare at her.

'Cooking doesn't make me a better mother,' she says, misunderstanding.

'I know.' I've been trying to tell her that.

She sits at the table. I join her. She slides a box my way.

'Thanks.'

She pours two Cokes.

I look at her. 'I thought you hated Coke.'

'I love Coke.'

She takes up a slice of her pizza – without actually putting anything on a plate, without insisting on knives and forks.

'How did the community service go?' she asks.

'Good.'

'What was good about it?'

I shrug. 'The people were so positive, I guess.'

'In what way?'

She wants to talk? She wants to have an actual conversation? Not just go through her usual agenda – Have you done your homework? Have you tidied your room?

'I don't know. They were all in wheelchairs and they seemed really happy.'

'What did you do?'

'Helped them play Bingo, moved the counters for them and stuff.'

'Bingo?'

'Yeah, they love it,' I say, kind of animated.

She puts down her pizza and looks at me for a long time. 'I'm sorry for hitting you, Sarah.'

I almost choke.

'The shoplifting thing. I panicked. I've seen too many people go down that road.'

I don't know what to say. So I don't say anything. Neither of us does, for a while.

She takes a deep breath. 'I'm going to start seeing someone, a therapist.'

'*Really?*' I thought she felt the same about them as I do.

'I don't want to be like this, angry all the time, taking it out on you and Louis. I need to talk to someone. Ellen gave me a name.'

'OK.'

'Maybe it's a good thing you're going to someone too. Maybe the shoplifting ...' Her voice trails off. 'I don't know.'

Maybe the shoplifting what? I want to say but don't.

She looks at me, her eyes sad. 'I've forgotten you in all of this.' She starts to cry.

And before I know what's happening, I do too.

'I'm so sorry,' she says.

I swallow back tears. 'It's OK.'

'No. I've been too hard on you, Sarah.' I want her to stop crying. 'But the shoplifting ... You have to promise me you'll never do anything like that again.' She looks kind of desperate.

'I won't, Mum. I swear.'

'You have to be responsible. Work hard. Stay out of trouble. It's up to you. Your whole life is up to you. You have to make your own way. Depend on no one.'

I know where this is coming from. I've heard it before. Don't depend on men.

'I want your grades to improve, and I mean *drastically* improve, at the summer exams.'

I sigh. Back to this again.

'I'm giving you a chance, Sarah. You can stay at Strandbrook. As long as you stay out of trouble and your grades improve.'

Oh my God. Seriously? 'They will. They will improve. I swear.' I don't know how but they will.

'Life is serious, Sarah, OK?'

'I know.'

}I{

'Good. OK. That's it then.' She nods, once, firmly, like she's decided. 'Let's try and get on with our lives.' Then she does something I haven't seen her do in a long time. She smiles.

Normally, the first person I'd ring is Rachel. After her offer of help, though, it's Alex I call.

She answers the phone with, 'This is the command centre.'

I smile. 'No, *this* is the command centre.'

'This is the *global* command centre.'

'Well, this is the *universal* command centre.'

'Shut up,' she says, laughing.

'No, you shut up,' I laugh back. And suddenly I want to tell her in person. 'We're still on for tonight, right?'

'Yup. Want Mike to pick you up?'

'Nah, it's OK. I'll get Louis to drop me over.' I want to tell him. And Mum gives him the car when he's working at the pub so he can get home OK at two in the morning. 'So, eight, right?'

'Yup. Don't forget your togs.'

'God, I love your house.'

I change out of my uniform and into my togs. I throw on my Juicy bottoms, an Abercrombie T and a zip-up hoodie. I leave the door open so I can hear Louis come in from the Jitter Mug.

At the sound of a familiar pounding on the stairs, I go out onto my tiny landing, lean over the banister and call down to him.

'Can I bum a lift to Alex's?'

He looks up. 'I gotta shower.'

'It's OK. I'll wait.'

Fifteen minutes later, I'm not even ready when he calls up for me. I throw everything into a bag and run down – because he *will* go without me.

In the car, he turns to me. 'So, go you. Staying at Strandbrook.'

'How do *you* know?' I was looking forward to telling him.

'Just tried to put in a good word for you with Mum.'

'Aw, thanks, Louis.'

'For what? You did it yourself.'

He drives with the window down, elbow out and a cigarette hanging from his mouth.

'It's freezing!'

'Fresh air's good for you,' says the smoker. He's just too relaxed to be normal.

'Don't you *ever* worry?' I ask.

'Eh. No.'

'Not even about exams?'

He laughs.

'Did she tell you? If I don't do well in the summer exams, she'll move me.'

'So do well.'

'It's not that easy.'

'Why not?' asks the guy who thinks everything is.

'Doesn't matter.'

Eminem's 'I'm Not Afraid' comes on the radio. I turn it up. The two of us shout the lyrics. Which is weird. Louis starts swerving the car from left to right, messing. Which is when I decide I'm not going to worry. I'm not going to think about it. At least, not for tonight.

Louis is getting very paternal. He waits in the car at the bottom of the steps until Alex opens the door.

'I can stay at Strandbrook,' I say, as soon as she does.

She screams and throws her arms around me. Then she grabs me and starts bouncing me up and down. I laugh. She's tiny compared to me.

Louis pulls away, shaking his head.

We go up to Alex's room. Rachel hugs me too. She seems really pleased but doesn't go as mental as Alex.

'What made her change her mind?' she asks.

'I don't know. She's been talking to this friend of hers who's also separated. And I think that's kind of helping.' Then, after telling myself I wasn't going to worry, I tell them about having to do well in the summer exams.

'Are there even exams in Transition Year?' Alex asks.

'They'll probably have something,' Rachel says.

'You'll be grand,' Alex says confidently. But she doesn't know what it's like to be me.

'We'll help,' Rachel says. 'If you like.'

'Can you do brain transplants already?' I ask. It's sweet of her to offer. But I imagine Rachel trying to explain stuff to me. I'd feel even stupider than I am.

She smiles. Then says, 'You'll be great, Sarah. And there's loads of time. She opens out a white cloth she's been holding in her hand. It becomes a triangle. 'Come on. Back to work.'

'What are you doing?' I ask.

'Putting on a sling.' She looks at Alex. 'OK, give me your arm. Let me try again.'

I sit on the floor, leaning against the bed, watching them, so happy to be here, not getting ready to move schools. Homer comes over and rests his head on my lap, making it the perfect moment.

Rachel turns the piece of cloth this way and that, trying to work out how to do it. She has a safety pin in her mouth.

Alex groans.

'What's wrong?' Rachel asks.

'You're hurting me.'

'How could I be hurting you?'

'My arm's *broken*, remember? You're yanking it around all over the place.'

'Oh. Sorry.'

I check out the diagrams in Rachel's first aid book which is open on the bed beside me. I stand up. 'Here, let me try.'

'It's really hard,' Rachel says.

I don't see why, but say nothing. Just put it on.

'Hey, how did you *do* that?' she asks.

I shrug. 'Just followed the instructions.'

'In, like, seconds.'

'Maybe I'm like Forrest Gump. A fucking genius.'

We laugh.

Rachel squints at the diagrams again. 'Let's take a break.'

We go downstairs and Barbara makes us smoothies. God I'd love a Barbara.

Rachel raises her glass. 'To Strandbrook.'

'To Strandbrook.' We all clink together.

'Oh my God, Barbara – these are *amazing*,' I tell her. 'Like, the best thing I've ever tasted.'

She bursts into a wide smile. 'You would like another one?' Her French accent is so exotic. I love this house.

'Would you *mind*?' I ask. Seriously, they don't use her half enough. If she was in my kitchen, I'd live in it.

'So where were you rushing off to today?' Rachel asks.

I wasn't going to say anything, but because things seem to be working out now, I say, 'I've started helping out at a home.'

'A *home*?'

'For disabled people.'

)|(

They stare. 'But you hate places like that.'

'It was actually fine.'

'Why are you helping out at a home?'

I shrug. I feel sick, having to lie. And try to make it as short as possible. 'Mum's idea.'

'She's been getting a lot of ideas lately,' Alex says.

I'm shrugging again. 'She wants me to be a better person or something.'

Rachel gets cross at that. 'What's wrong with you? You're perfectly fine the way you are.'

Her concern makes me want to cry.

'What's wrong with the people in the home?' Alex asks.

'I don't really know.'

'Have they Down's syndrome or something?' Alex asks.

Rachel looks appalled. 'People with Down's syndrome aren't disabled.'

'What else can you call them? You can't call them retard-ed, can you?' Alex says. 'That's just politically incorrect.'

'So you just say they've Down's syndrome. Or some-thing,' Rachel says.

'They're in wheelchairs,' I say. 'I don't know why.'

'And what do *you* do?' Rachel asks.

'Help them play Bingo.'

'Bingo?'

I nod. 'They love Bingo.' I tell them about it. And how happy everyone is. Apart from the guy at the window.

'What's wrong with him?' Rachel asks.

'I don't know. I think he's paralysed or something.'

'No wonder he doesn't want to play Bingo.'

9
WHOLE NUT

Saturday morning, Mum pulls up outside an old Georgian house close to the city. I look up the steps to a purple door with a shiny brass knocker. Then I look back at Mum.

'How many times do I've to go?'

'As many as it takes.'

I sigh and slowly open the door. 'I'll find my own way home.'

'OK. Good.' She pulls away.

I watch the car disappear down the street. At the end, there's a Starbucks. I'm so tempted to spend the next hour there. But I know she'd find out. So, I climb the steps. Like Everest. The plaque on the wall reads: 'Mary Gleeson, Clinical Psychologist'. I don't know why she has to tell the world. I stand blocking the sign, my back to the street, while I push the bell. I stay there till the door buzzes open. Then I don't hang around.

Inside is just a hallway. I stop, confused. I look around. The first door on the right has her name on it. Hesitantly, I open it. Inside is a waiting room, posher than a GP's surgery, but not by much. It's empty. Directly opposite is a door

}|{

to another room. It also has her name on it. Her office, I assume. I imagine her inside, on a comfortable chair with a notebook and pen. I imagine a patient, lying back on a couch. Maybe it's just her, though. Maybe there's no one in front of me. And she's just waiting inside for me. I don't know whether to knock or wait. So I wait. Because the less time I'm in there, the less talking I'll have to do. I look around. Sigh. Sit down. On the coffee table are the usual magazines. Out of date. But not totally dog-eared. I pick up a copy of *Hello* and try to be positive. The community service turned out OK.

I can't concentrate. Weird, since it's *Hello*. I stand up, restless. I walk to the window, look out. Then I start to freak that someone might see me, so I come away again. I walk around the room, wondering how many times I'll have to come here. I took two things. I don't have mental problems. It can't be many. Maybe just enough to keep the cops happy. Hopefully.

The door to her office opens. A boy of about seven comes out. He's blond and kind of angelic looking. I can't believe that a kid that young would need to see a shrink. He doesn't look at me, head and eyes lowered, walking silently as if he wants to disappear. 'It's OK,' I want to say to him. 'I know. It makes you feel a like a loser but that doesn't mean you are one.' But, of course, I say nothing – because that would just make it worse. His parents (mum pretty and worried-looking, dad rugby-ish and kind of caliente) follow immediately behind him. She doesn't see me at first because she's miles away, but when she does cop that I'm there, she looks at me like she's wondering what's wrong with me. And I have to remind myself, I wondered the same about her son.

After a few minutes, Mary Gleeson appears at the door to her office. She wears a long leather skirt, high boots, a fitted black shirt and a smile. She's younger than I expected. And prettier. Not how I imagined her at all.

'Sarah?'

'Eh, yeah.' I stand up and start to walk over.

She holds out her hand.

I make sure my grip's not too limp, but not too firm either. Normal.

'Thanks for coming,' she says.

I meet her eye – because honest people do. 'Thanks for fitting me in.'

'Come on in.' She smiles.

I follow her in, not believing that, at a time like this, I'm wondering where she got her boots. She gestures to an armchair, then lowers herself into one opposite. I'm relieved I won't have to lie back and close my eyes. I take a seat and wait. She crosses her legs. I wonder if any of her patients fancy her. I know Simon would.

'So,' she says. 'Welcome.' Her voice is suspiciously calm, like she's been practising. She takes a notepad and pen (ha!) from the arm of her chair and she puts them on her lap. 'Before we start, I want you to know that anything we discuss here is completely confidential. It stays between us. I also want to reassure you that I was recommended to your father by a colleague but I don't know him personally.'

I nod, wondering how much Dad's told her.

She smiles. 'So, why don't you tell me why you're here?'

She knows why. You don't just land into a psychologist's office with no explanation, no background. She just wants me to say it, admit it. And I resent her for that, sitting there in her smug leather skirt, judging me. Still, the last thing I want is to have to come back so I do my best to give her what she wants – and still hold on to a bit of dignity.

'I took a dress. From a shop. A dress that didn't belong to me.' Funny all the words you have to use to avoid saying 'stole'. 'It was a mistake. I'm really sorry about it. It's not going to happen again.' Can I go?

She looks at me calmly. 'And why do you think you "took" the dress?'

She's using my word back at me. Trying to put me at ease. But I'm not at ease with "why?" I hate why. I've grown up on why.

'I took it because I wanted it and I didn't have the money.' Simple.

'It wasn't your first time, was it, Sarah?' She says it like she knows, and I think that Dad must have told her.

So I tell the truth. 'No, but I only took one other thing. Eye shadow, that's it.'

She nods. 'And when did your parents split up?' Like they're linked.

And that's it, the reason I didn't want to come here. 'What's that got to do with anything?'

'Your father moved out, didn't he?'

'So? Loads of people separate. It's not the end of the world.'

'Do you miss him?'

'No.'

'You're very sure of that.'

'Yes, I'm very sure of that.' I feel my jaw clenching.

She writes something in the jotter. 'You have a brother?'

'Louis. And before you ask, nothing bothers Louis. Not my parents splitting up. Nothing. Ever.'

She tilts her head, like she's considering that. 'I don't know, Sarah. Don't you think we're all affected, in some way, by what happens around us?'

'No,' I say. Then to sound reasonable I add, 'Not always.'

'How often do you see your father now?'

Hel-lo. 'Look, I told you. This has nothing to do with my dad. I'm fine about my parents splitting up. I took two things – because I needed them – not for any other reason.'

'You needed them?'

'OK, *wanted* them, then. The thing is, I'm not here because I've psychological problems. I'm here so I don't get a criminal record. So could we just talk about the stealing?'

'Good,' she says.

'What's good?'

'That's the first time you've actually come out and said you've stolen something. The first part of solving a problem is admitting you have one. You've just done that.'

Oh my God. 'No I haven't. Because I don't have a problem. I stole – twice. I've explained why. I'm sorry. I won't do it again.'

'How do you know?'

How retarded is this person? 'Because I don't want to.'

'Sometimes that's not enough.'

'So what, I'm like *addicted*?' I ask sarcastically.

'Shoplifting can be addictive,' she says matter-of-factly. 'More importantly, it can be a cry for help.' Oh my God! 'I'd like to explore the motivations behind your actions, to make sure you don't offend again.'

Offend. 'There are people out there doing a whole lot worse than I have.'

'Sarah,' she smiles calmly, the way she does everything. 'I've been given a job to do. And it's my responsibility to the person who hired me, to the police, and to you, to do it well.'

She looks like the bloody Mona Lisa with that wishy-washy smile. But I know she's won. If I don't co-operate I'll be coming back forever.

'So, has your father tried to contact you?'

I take a deep breath. 'Yes, but I've nothing to say to him.'

She writes something. I feel like knocking the notepad off her lap.

'Does Louis see him?'

So, she's good with names, big deal. 'Yes.'

'And do they get on well?'

'I don't know. Probably.' They do.

She uncrosses her legs. Then crosses them in the other direction. She settles further back in the chair.

'When did your parents separate, Sarah?'

'Months ago.'

'How many months?'

And suddenly, I flip. 'Oh my God. You people are all the same, reading stuff into stuff. I told you. This has nothing to do with my family.'

'Your father's a psychologist.'

'*So?*'

'I'm feeling a lot of anger. I'm just wondering if it's towards him.'

'It's not,' I say through gritted teeth.

'Not for walking out on the family?'

'What are you trying to do, *make* me angry?'

'No, but if you *were* angry, it would be perfectly understandable. Anger is a very honest emotion.'

I feel like telling her to fuck off – and my language is usually pretty good.

'How's your Mum doing?' she asks.

'Fine.'

'She's not angry?'

'Yes, she's angry. She's furious. With everyone. All the time. My mum has enough anger for everyone. OK?' Happy now?

'And you don't want to be like her?'

'Of course I don't want to be like her. Who would?' I stop suddenly. I shouldn't have said that about Mum. Who is trying now. She's going to see a shrink. She apologised. I feel so disloyal.

'Well, Sarah, I think we've made great progress here today.'

Is she kidding? I was fine before I came here. Now I'm so angry I could shove her off her chair. And I don't do anger. As she so wisely pointed out, I don't do my mum.

'So I'll see you the same time next week?'

Great, I think. *Something to look forward to.*

I hurry down the steps, across the road, straight into a newsagent's. I reach for two bars of chocolate. Don't care if they're Dairy Milk, Whole Nut or Fruit & Nut – they're chocolate. I rip the wrapping off the first bar and bite into it before I've even paid. I close my eyes. Concentrate just on the chocolate, the taste, the smoothness.

'I need the wrapper to scan,' the checkout guy says.

'Oh, right, sorry,' I say. I hand it over, feeling like a lunatic. How many does he get in here on an average day?

'No problem, love,' he says kindly. Giving me the answer. *Lots.*

I pay. And leave.

Her office faces me on the way out. And it all comes back.
I bite down hard on a chunk of chocolate. Some psychologist. I was fine when I went in there. Now I'm this angry person. Angry with everyone. My father for leaving. My mother for being angry. But mostly I'm angry with Mary Gleeson for making me angry. I feel like screaming. I feel like running (and I don't even like running). I feel like punching something (Mary Gleeson ideally). I march down the street towards town. I bump into people.

'Watch it!' I say like it's their fault. Like everything is.

I pound around town, walking the streets, avoiding the shops, until finally, all walked out, I get the DART home.

I'm half way up the stairs when she calls me.

'Jesus,' I say. I turn around and start back down.

She comes out of the kitchen and looks up.

'How did it go?' she asks. Her voice is gentle. Caring, even. Then my anger vanishes and I just feel bad – for ratting her out.

'OK,' I say.

'Come have some hot chocolate or something,' she says – the one time I want her to be a bitch.

We go into the kitchen. She puts on the kettle.

'I'll just have water,' I say, going to the sink. All that chocolate has made me thirsty. I drink a whole glass, then lean against the sink.

'You OK?' she asks.

'Yeah.'

'I was thinking. It's been a week. You've probably been grounded for long enough.'

'Thanks.' I might have had to break out tonight otherwise.

'Ellen wants me to go to a movie,' she says.

'Tonight?'

'Is that OK?'

I'm amazed she asked. 'Yeah. No. Sure. Of course. You should.'

'I don't know.'

'It's just a movie.'

'And maybe a drink after?' she says, like she's talking about five hundred of them.

'Live dangerously, Mum.'

She actually smiles. 'Ellen's good for me,' she says, like she's excusing going out. 'She makes me feel like I'm not the only one.' She looks at me like she's hoping I'll understand.

And I think, *maybe I should make friends with a shoplifter.*

Oh my God. I seriously need to go out tonight. To just listen to the music and dance. Pity Alex isn't coming. She's staying in to talk to David on Skype. Probably for hours. So, it'll just be Rachel and Mark, Simon and me, and a few others Simon asked along – Amy, Orla and I'm not sure who else.

Sometimes I think the best part of going out is the dressing up. The shower, the makeup, the clothes, the shoes, the music. It's better though with your friends. Louis drops me off at Simon's place in Dun Laoghaire. We're going, together, from there.

Simon's parents have split up. He lives with his dad in this really cool penthouse that overlooks the sea. Everything's modern and sleek like a five-star hotel. His dad has a new girlfriend and they're never home. Which makes me wonder

}|{

if *my* dad is out all the time now. If his new 'partner' wants him to go all sorts of places with her. If she's demanding. Exhausting. If he'll come home. OK, scrap the last one. I'm not completely stupid. I know he's not coming home. But why think about all that? Simon's buzzing me up.

His hair is gelled and kind of tousled. The top two buttons on his shirt are open. He smells of Polo Ralph Lauren.

'Shmexy,' he says when he sees me.

'You ready?' I ask, wanting to get going.

'What's the rush? Thought we could have a drink here first.'

'OK. Cool.'

He helps himself to vodka and Cokes from his dad's stash. I look out at the lights of Dun Laoghaire and pretend we own the place, that we're, like, twenty-five, and we've got these amazing jobs, are seriously minted and totally in control of our lives. Then he's coming towards me and I know from his eyes what he wants.

'Simon, no. I've spent ages getting ready.'

He just smiles and takes the drink from my hand. And, I think, *there are some things you have to do to keep a guy*. But as he runs his hands over me, I can't help thinking that what I'd love right now is a boyfriend I could sit on the couch with and tell everything to, a boyfriend who would just cuddle me and rub my hair and tell me it's going to be OK even if he didn't know for sure. If I told Simon I was seeing a shrink or I'd been caught shoplifting, he'd dump me. On the spot.

'Simon, turn off the lights. The blinds are open.'

He ignores me.

'Simon!'

He laughs, then backs me into his bedroom which, at

least, has the blinds down. And as he starts to take off his shirt, I wonder why I always attract guys who don't want anything from me except this. Still, at least I'm not some sad loner sitting at home alone, biting her nails or pigging out on chocolate.

I thought sex was supposed to be *good*, though. Maybe guys get more from it than girls. Simon certainly does. Afterwards, he even talks.

'So do you think Alex should get a boob job?'

'What?'

'Have you *seen* the hotties on David's wall? Alex has some serious competition.'

'No she doesn't.' He doesn't get that people could be made for each other.

Just my luck. I've been dying to get out and dance, like, all day. And I finally get here and no one else wants to. Simon's too busy chatting to Amy and Orla, like they're his own personal harem or something. And I don't want to butt into Rachel and Mark's cosy conversation but I'm desperate.

'Come on, Rache, let's dance.'

She looks at Mark.

'Go on,' Mark says. 'My shoes are killing me anyway,' he jokes.

Thank *Christ*.

On the dance floor, I close my eyes and let go, forgetting everything, losing myself in the music. Then Rachel's tapping me on the shoulder. She's looking back at the others.

'Do you really think you should put up with that?'

'What?'

'Simon. Don't you think he's a bit too friendly with Amy?'

}{{

I so don't want to ruin this moment. 'They're friends.'

She gives me a look.

I shrug. 'He's just flirting a bit. Sometimes you got to put up with stuff, right?'

'No, Sarah. You don't.'

I close my eyes and go back to the music. It's different for her. She's with someone who loves her. I just want a boyfriend. He doesn't have to be perfect. Just there.

10
OH. MY. GOD.

After school, Monday, Rachel suggests the Jitter Mug.

'Is there anywhere else?' Alex asks. 'I'm tired of the Jitter Mug.'

'Where else is there?' Rachel asks. 'There's nothing decent till Dalkey. And that's too far for Sarah and me.'

'OK,' Alex says.

When we get to the Jitter Mug, Alex heads for a table.

'I'll hold this while you get the smoothies.'

Rachel and I look at each other. We never hold tables. Even if we did, it would *not* be this one. In the middle of a draught and miles from the action.

I look around. 'There isn't exactly a rush on, Alex.'

But she's ignoring me, rooting in her wallet for money. Which she hands to Rachel.

'The usual,' she says.

'What's up with her?' I ask Rachel as we go up to the counter.

'No clue,' she says, looking back.

The queue is short and soon we get to Louis.

'Where's the third musketeer?' he asks, straining his neck and looking around.

Oh. My. God. I get it. Or at least I think I do. 'Alex is over there if you want to talk to her,' I say, nodding in the direction of our table (all you can see of Alex is her school bag). I watch him carefully.

'Why would I want to talk to her?' he asks. But he sounds defensive.

We collect our smoothies and make our way back to the table.

'Why are you hiding from Louis?' I ask.

She looks shocked. 'I'm *not*.'

'And why's he asking about you?'

'Is he?' She looks worried.

'What's going on?'

'Nothing! God.'

'Oh my God, he asked you out, didn't he?'

'Sarah, seriously. You're being ridiculous.'

'Prove it.'

'Fine. I will.' She stands up but then runs out of energy. 'How?'

I think for a moment.

'Go up there and ask for ... a croissant.'

She marches straight up to Louis. I wish I knew what she was saying but it's taking longer than simply asking for a croissant. He looks at us, then back at her. His face is so focused on her. That's when I see it. Oh my God. He loves her. My commitment-phobic, playboy brother loves my friend. Who is in love with someone else. How the hell did he let that happen? He hands over a croissant, forgetting to ask her to pay. She forgets to pay.

Oh. My. God.

Eyebrows up, she holds the croissant in the air all the way back.

'Not sure what *that* was supposed to prove,' she says lightly, sitting down. She hands me the croissant. Like it's some kind of medal.

I look back at my brother. Poor Louis; he *finally* falls in love and it's with someone who can't love him back. And how the hell did he fall for her in the first place? They hardly know each other.

Next day in school, 'Upper' (Ms Morrison) is seriously excited. But that's nothing new. What *is* new is her latest idea. She wants us to set up our own businesses. She wants us to become 'Young Entrepreneurs'.

'You can sell a product or a service,' she says, 'working in groups or individually. Now, I don't want you to just buy something cheap and sell it more expensively because where's the challenge in that? I want you to be creative. Now, split into groups and brainstorm on the type of businesses you could set up. The sky's the limit. We can discuss the feasibility of the projects later. Off you go now.'

Automatically, Rachel, Alex and me find each other. Then Mark appears. Then, surprisingly, Simon. Followed by Amy and Orla.

We drag seven chairs together. It seems too much.

'How about the oldest profession in the world?' Simon says, enthusiastically. 'We could be your pimps.' He looks at Mark.

'Speak for yourself,' Mark says.

'Very funny, Simon,' I say, embarrassed.

Rachel and Alex just look at each other.

'I was joking,' he says. 'Jeez.'

'How about something to do with mobile phones?' Orla says. 'We could make cool covers and sell them.' I feel like thanking her.

'But mobiles are all different sizes,' Alex says.

'Oh, yeah,' Orla says.

'We could do iPod covers,' Amy says, then frowns, 'but they already have iPod covers.'

There's a long silence. But then Orla looks like she's had a breakthrough. 'Cakes,' she says. 'Let's just make cakes. They're easy and everyone buys them.'

'Right, I'll just get my apron,' Simon says. 'I am *so* not making cakes.'

'Well, I am,' Orla says. She takes our her jotter and starts to doodle. Like she's sorted.

'I'll go with cakes too,' Amy says. I can almost hear her switch off.

'Any other ideas?' Simon asks. He looks at me like he's remembering I'm here. 'Sarah? What kind of things do you like?'

I look at him and think, *you're supposed to be my boyfriend. Shouldn't you know?*

'What about you, Rache?' Mark asks.

'What about first-aid classes? Like, giving them, you know?'

I think of her efforts with the sling. 'Don't you have to be, like, qualified?'

Her face falls. 'Probably.'

Then I feel guilty. 'But you could do, like, a blood pressure service or something, you know, where people pay to have their blood pressure taken.'

'That's a great idea,' she says. She looks at Mark.

'We could do it together, in supermarkets and stuff. We could get white coats and everything.'

He makes a face. 'Maybe. What about you, Alex?' he asks. And I know he hates the idea.

'How about an invention that could beam you to the other side of the world whenever you wanted?'

'You wouldn't be thinking California, would you?' Mark asks, smiling.

She smiles back. 'I might.'

'I'll work with you on that one.'

Rachel's giving him daggers. 'Come on guys, this is serious.'

Mark gives her an irritated look. 'I thought the sky was the limit.'

'She just meant be creative.'

'And what are we doing?' he asks.

I want to stop them arguing. 'I've an idea,' I say, though I haven't.

Everyone looks at me. And I don't know where it comes from, the idea. But straight away I love it.

'A pet-minding business.'

'That's brilliant!' Alex says.

Then I remember. 'Mum hates dogs.'

'Oh.'

'Cats?' Alex suggests. I see Rachel still glaring at Mark. Luckily, he doesn't see it.

'Maybe cats would be OK,' I say, but I'm thinking, *she probably hates cats too*. The more I think about the idea, the more convinced I am that it wouldn't work. For starters, who'd trust me with their pets? Would I even trust myself?

*

My dad has an ambition – to write a newspaper column on psychology. He used to talk about it all the time. One of his strategies was to start a blog, build up a following, then approach a newspaper. As soon as he converted my room to his office, he started the blog. Sometimes I read it – don't know why. I hate psychology.

Tonight I go into his blog. His photo is one he took before he left, when he looked like a dad, not a partner. I'm glad he hasn't changed it. Not that anything he does matters anymore. I look at the title of his latest blog. And go cold. Oh my God. He's written a column on shoplifting. The warning signs. The reasons. The solutions. How could he? How could he write something so personal to me – as if I'm some sort of lab rat whose life gives him ideas? What if people I know read it and guess where he got his inspiration?

I'm so angry, I don't think. I just pick up the phone. She answers. She answers his private mobile phone. Doesn't she realise he has a family, a daughter who mightn't want to be reminded of Her?

'I want to speak to my father,' I say through gritted teeth.

'Is that Sarah?'

Fuck off, I think. 'Just get me my dad.' I wish I hadn't heard her sugary, sweet, pathetic voice. I know I won't be able to forget it.

'Sarah?' He comes on the phone, sounding worried.

'What the hell did you write about shoplifting for?'

There's a pause. 'You read my blog.'

'Glad I could be of service,' I say sarcastically.

'Sarah—'.

'You know I am a *person*. Not an experiment. My life is not a stepping stone for your career.'

'I know that,' he says.

But I'm not listening. 'Oh and I love that whole "cry for help" thing. You think everything is about you, don't you? You think I'm messed up because you left. You know what that makes you? A full-on arrogant bastard.'

I hang up. And fling the phone onto the bed. I'm breathing funny. My heart is pumping hard and fast. I can't believe I called him a bastard. But I hate him. I actually hate the guy. He is the most selfish person I know. My phone starts to ring and I ignore it. It keeps ringing and ringing till I turn it off. Minutes later my mum is calling me. And only because I don't want her to come up, I open the door and shout, '*What*?'

'Your father is on the phone.'

'Tell him to eat shit and die.' Then I slam the door.

On Friday, I have a crappy day at school. Tip Toes, my favourite teacher (not), gives out to me for not paying attention. I snap at Rachel when she asks if I'm OK. And instead of being able to go home to the peace of my room, I have to do my bloody community service. Great. Just great.

I get off the DART two stops before my usual and trudge up towards the home. I drop into a newsagents to buy a new pen. Because today being the wonderful day it was, mine ran out. The shop's busy and I have to wait in line. The girl at the checkout is taking forever with a woman who looks like she's buying the whole shop. I stand facing a massive sweet display. Suddenly, I need to take something. Badly. No one would miss a simple pack of Maltesers. They probably cost the shop two cents or something. Two cents is *nothing*. They'd let you off two cents if you didn't have enough.

I pick up a pack like I'm going to buy it. I hold it in my

hand. The wait goes on. The cashier pushes two bags of shopping to the woman who clearly doesn't know what a supermarket is for. She hands over the change. The woman leaves and the cashier turns to the next customer, a man who wants cigarettes. When she turns to get them, I slip the Maltesers into my pocket. And just like that, my heart is thumping again in that crazily satisfying way. The girl at the checkout moves on to the next customer. Me. I hand her the pen. She takes it and scans it without even looking at me. She hands it back and asks for the money. *Bored people are the easiest*, I think. *They just don't care.* I pay for the pen, then I'm walking out.

Outside, like a cold, fresh wind, it hits me. What I've done. I've just risked everything for a packet of Maltesers. I've risked being caught again. I've risked Mum going ballistic again, losing her trust again, being taken out of Strandbrook. All for a packet of Maltesers. What is *wrong* with me? I take them from my pocket and let them fall to the ground. I can't look at them. Can't touch them. I want to forget I ever saw them.

'Hey!'

Oh God. Oh no. I turn.

'You dropped your Maltesers.' It's a boy of about twelve. He's picking them up and handing them to me. I look at him with such incredible relief.

'It's OK. You have them.'

'Really? Cool.'

I start walking. And seriously worrying. Was Mary Gleeson right? Is this an addiction, an addiction that could ruin everything?

*

I'm late arriving at the home. Bingo hasn't started but someone is already sitting with John. Christina comes over to me.

'Sorry I'm late.'

'No problem,' she says. She glances over at the guy by the
window. It's like he hasn't moved all week. 'Why don't you
go over to Shane today?'

It seems like a bad idea. 'He doesn't look like he wants
company.'

'I know. But I have to try something. And nothing else is
working.'

'What's wrong with him?'

She hesitates. Then she says, 'He's had some bad news
lately.'

I don't tell her that's not what I meant. Because I guess
she knows that. I'm embarrassed now for asking, like I'm
this nosey person who wants all the scandal. Suddenly, I
want to do something good. For a change. Make up. If I can.
So I go get a board and some counters. Before I even get to
him, though, I know it's a mistake.

I arrive by his side. If he notices, he doesn't let on.

'Hello,' I say.

He turns his head and looks at me. Expressionless.

'Would you like to play?' I lift the board.

'Bingo? You want me to play Bingo?' And it's not just
words coming at me but anger.

'OK. Sorry. My mistake.' I turn to go.

'Wait!'

I stop and turn.

'What's your name?' he asks.

Why does he care if he doesn't want me there? I think,
suspiciously. But he's looking at me for an answer and I better give him something.

'Sarah,' I say, cautiously, turning to go.

'Sarah, right. Well, Sarah, answer me this …' He pauses. And I know what's coming isn't good. 'Do you feel sorry for me?'

'Sorry?' I ask, not believing.

'Do, *you*, feel, sorry, for, *me*?'

Oh my God. It's like a trap. I say yes, then there's something to feel sorry for. I say no, then I've no sympathy. So I just stare at him. Stuck.

'Come on. What are you waiting for? It's either yes or no.'

I'm blushing. And panicking. I look over at Christina. But she doesn't see me.

'You do, don't you?' he says.

'No,' I rush, defensively.

'You *don't* feel sorry for me?' he says, like I'm a stone-cold bitch.

Oh my God.

'I'm stuck here in a freaking wheelchair and you don't even feel *sorry* for me?'

My eyes smart and I think, *I am not going to cry. I am not going to give him the satisfaction.*

'What have I ever done to you?' I ask quietly.

'Oh, that's easy,' he says. 'You come here and use people like me to feel better about yourself.'

'What?'

He smiles. 'A word of advice, Sarah. Next time you feel like doing an act of charity, don't come near me.' He plugs in his phone and turns away.

And I want to die.

'Sarah?' Christina calls. 'Could you come give John a hand, please? I've something I have to do.'

Oh, *now* she calls me. I go over.

'You OK?' she asks quietly.

I nod. But really I'm trying hard not to cry.

'I'm sorry,' she says. 'I should never have sent you over.'

I shrug, afraid that if I say anything I'll cry.

'Sit here with John,' she says.

'Hey, John.' I smile at him. All he can do is turn his eyes to me. But those eyes say, 'It's OK.'

I turn my chair so my back is to the window. To him.

Then, after a 'testing one-two, one-two', that would normally make me laugh, Bingo starts.

'One and five, fifteen.' I check the board.

'Two fat ladies, eighty-eight.' My eyes fill. I can't stop them. The numbers blur.

'Three and five, thirty-five.' A tear falls.

'Two little ducks, twenty-two.' I drop my head so no one sees. And all I can think is, *I steal. I lie to cover up. I use people to feel better about myself. Worst of all, I hate someone who's in a wheelchair.*

11
Subconsciously

Next morning, I'm freaking that Mary Gleeson will ask me if I've stolen anything and I won't be able to hide it and I'll never get out of this cycle of shoplifting and going to her.

She looks even more pretty today, even more perfect. If she'd any sense, she'd ruffle herself up a bit for people like me.

'So, how've you been?' she asks.

'Good.' I sound upbeat. Maybe too upbeat.

'How are things at home?'

'You know, my mum isn't as bad as I made her out to be last week. She's things on her mind, you know? And she's trying. She's going to see a counsellor now. So that's good.'

She smiles in agreement. 'And how's your father?'

Oh *great*. Here we go again.

'You're still not talking to him?'

'No.'

'So there's nothing you want to say to him?'

There's plenty I want to say, I think. 'No.'

'Last week we spoke about anger.'

)|(

I close my eyes. *Not again.*

'You said you weren't angry with your father. But you *were* angry.'

'You made me angry.'

'I *hope* that what I did helped you see that you had anger. Sarah, do you think there's anything to be gained by not expressing it?'

'What?'

'Sorry. Do you think that if you don't get angry with your father, he might come back? And *that's* why you're not talking to him, so you don't get angry with him?'

'No offence, but that's rubbish. I got angry with him this week.'

She looks surprised. 'So you *did* speak?'

I shrug.

'How did this come about? Did something happen?'

Did something *happen*? 'He wrote a blog about shoplifting. He used his own daughter to educate the masses.' I fight hard not to get upset.

'Did he mention you in person?' She looks stunned.

'No, but people could easily work it out.'

She looks relieved. 'What did he say?'

I look out the window. 'The usual "cry for help" crap.'

After a pause, she asks, 'And you don't go along with that?'

I turn back. 'Yeah, sure I do,' I say sarcastically. 'I wanted my father back in my life so I took a dress.' I roll my eyes. 'Like I couldn't have picked up the *phone*?'

'But you *haven't* picked up the phone,' she says gently. 'Apart from this isolated incident, you haven't picked up the phone just to talk to him.'

}I{

'I don't *want* to pick up the phone.'

After another pause, she asks, 'Would your mother like you to?'

'What? Are you kidding?'

'Is that why you haven't?'

'Look. There's such a thing as loyalty.'

She puts on this kindly face. 'Sarah, your mum wouldn't be human if she didn't hurt. But don't you think you're a bit young to take on her problems?'

'I'm not taking on her problems. I'm just taking her side. *Someone* has to.'

'Not so.' She takes a deep breath and leans forward in her chair. 'Sarah, I know you don't want to talk to your dad but there are things you need to say to him, feelings you need to let go of. Bottled up emotions find other ways of coming out.'

'What? Like shoplifting?' I ask, cynically.

'Like illness, depression, stress. You're lucky, Sarah. Your subconscious took over before that could happen. It made you do what you, consciously, wouldn't do – get back in touch with your father. You need to talk to him, Sarah. You need to tell him how you feel about ... well, about everything.'

'I stole again,' I say, because, suddenly, I need to tell someone.

She doesn't look surprised. 'All the more reason to talk to your dad.'

'You think I should just let him have it – like in general?'

She nods. 'I think you should say whatever you need to say. Don't hold back.'

'And *if* I talked to him, would that be the end of the shoplifting?' I really need a 'yes' here.

'Let's take this one step at a time, Sarah. Talk to him, then see.'

She's just so confident about everything. And I need someone to be confident. Because I'm so afraid I'll do it again.

When I get home, Mum looks different. It's her hair. It's shorter. And a different colour. Lighter. With some warm highlights.

'You look nice.' Like, five years younger.

She touches it. 'You don't think it's too much?'

'No. I think it's great.' And I would love to know that this means she's finally started to look after herself. 'I could give you a manicure some time, if you like.'

'You can do manicures?'

'You are looking at the manicure expert.'

When she smiles, it makes me feel warm.

'I could give you one now – if you're not busy.' She's always busy.

'Have you time?' she asks.

'I'll go get my stuff.'

I run upstairs and start to grab my things. I make sure to remember everything. If I have to interrupt the session, she might remember she has something else to do.

On the kitchen table, I spread out a warm towel from the airing cupboard, the softest I could find. I fold it in two. I get a bowl of boiled water and put in a few drops of lavender oil. Then I set up all my tools. I work fast – just in case.

'Ready,' I say, as soon as I am. I pull out a chair.

She comes over, sits down. She starts picking up my stuff and looking at it.

'Very professional,' she says, like she's impressed.

)|(

'So just put your fingers in the bowl and let them soak.'

I put on some sounds, a CD I got once for a euro that I've never listened to. Sounds of the sea. It seemed like good value at the time.

Finally, I sit at the table with her and start to get my creams ready.

'So, how did you get on today?'

Oh God. Just when I'd forgotten. I feel guilty all over again. 'She wants me to talk to Dad.' I watch her carefully. 'I don't have to.'

'You do. A good mother would have encouraged you to – long ago.' She looks guilty.

'You *are* a good mother.' Kind of.

'I haven't been.' She looks at me. 'But I'm trying to be better, to think of you. And Louis. I'm not the only person who's been hurt by this.'

I still feel I should explain. 'She thinks the shoplifting was a cry for help. She thinks I need to say stuff to Dad.'

She looks at me intensely. Then nods. 'Do you miss him?'

'No.'

'*I* miss him,' she says. 'All the time.'

Then we're looking at each other and both of us are welling up.

'You can take your hands out now,' I say quickly.

She looks down at them. 'Oh, right. OK.'

'I'm just going to push back your cuticles.'

She nods. I pick up my gadget and take one of her hands. We both look down as I get to work.

'It's OK to miss him, Sarah,' she says, without looking up. 'You're not being disloyal to me. He's your dad and he loves you.' Now she looks up. 'If you decide you want to keep in touch with him, that would be a good thing.'

I bite my lips together and say nothing because meeting up to let him have it is one thing. Keeping in touch is something completely different. A giant step I can't even think about right now.

I want to get on with my life. Be normal again. So, after dinner, I call him.

'The shrink says I should talk to you,' I say, flatly.

There's a pause. 'OK. Good, I'm glad. When are you free?'

Oh God. Do I really want to do this? 'I don't know.'

'How about tomorrow morning?'

I need to stop shoplifting. I need to stop seeing the shrink. 'OK,' I say, before I change my mind.

'Will I pick you up?'

I think about him calling to the door. How hard that would be for Mum. 'No. I'll meet you somewhere.'

'Where?'

Not in some public place. I might want to shout. Not in his new home. Where she might be. 'At the bus stop at the end of the road. At eleven.'

'OK.'

In the morning, when I'm about to leave, I can't decide whether to tell Mum or not. I don't want to bring him up, depress her. But then I don't want to sneak around behind her back. I go into the kitchen. She's taking a piece of gum from a wrapper and putting it in her mouth.

'Chewing gum?' I ask. She hates the stuff.

She holds up the pack. It's Nicorette.

'Oh my God, are you giving up smoking?'

'I'm going to try.'

I so don't want to tell her now. She looks at me, with my coat on.

'You going to see Dad?' she asks.

'Yeah.'

She smiles. 'Good luck … God, this stuff tastes disgusting.'

I don't want her to give up. 'There's an inhaler thing that you suck.'

She smiles. 'Don't suppose there's any chance of a hug?'

I almost cry. If I was her, I wouldn't want my daughter seeing him; I wouldn't want any connection with him, at all, ever, after what he did. I go to her. And when she hugs me tight, I have this feeling that she doesn't want to lose me either.

'See you later,' I say, to remind her that she will.

'Hey,' he says brightly, when I get into the car.

'Hey.' I can't look at him. Because I'm still thinking about the blog. And Mum.

He pulls away from the kerb. For a while he says nothing, then the predictable. 'How are you?'

I shrug, look out the side window.

'How's it going with the psychologist?'

'No clue.'

Another pause. 'So, where to?'

'Sandymount Strand.'

'Good idea.'

We drive in silence, then, after twenty minutes, he pulls up at the beach. The tide is out and there's nothing but sand for miles. You could scream and no one would hear. I zip up my coat, take a deep breath and get out of the car. For a long time, we just walk. Then he turns to me.

'I'm sorry about the blog, Sarah. It wasn't a conscious decision to write about shoplifting. I honestly didn't think.'

'So, you're telling me that I didn't cross your mind once when you were writing it?'

He looks guilty. 'I guess once I'd started—'

'You just don't care, do you?'

'Of course I care. I'm sorry. It was stupid—'

'It was selfish, that's what it was.'

'I know. I know. I should have stopped … I'll be more thoughtful in future. I promise.'

'It's just my life, you know?'

He puts a hand on my shoulder and looks me in the eye. It feels so deliberate. Like he knows this is the right thing to do in this situation.

'Sarah, I'm sorry. I love you,' he says it so gently, I want to cry. I want to believe him. But he has taught me often enough to judge people by what they do, not what they say.

'You left us.' I say it simply. Because everything boils down to those three words.

'Sarah, I didn't leave you, I left your mother.'

And boom. Just like that, I could rip him apart. Because he *did* leave me. And he just called her '*your mother*'. Instead of 'Mum'.

'I hate you,' I say.

He's silent. He looks at me, scratches his head. 'I'd hate me too.'

'Oh my God. Do you have to be so condescending? You walked out on us. All of us. You chose a total stranger over us. We were your family. Didn't that count for anything?'

He opens his mouth to speak.

'And you left me with Mum's anger. Months and months

of rage. Do you think that's fair?' All of a sudden I'm crying. When I so don't want to be weak.

He reaches for me.

'Don't touch me.'

'Sarah, I'm sorry.'

'And stop saying sorry. Sorry's a word. Anyone can say it.
It takes two seconds and no effort at all. It's a word. Like
"fuck" is a word. And "hate" is a word. And "piss off" is a
word. OK maybe two words.' Then I stop talking because
I'm making no sense. Anyway, there's no point. And I'm in
serious floods now.

He hands me a handkerchief, a real cotton handkerchief.
He's always carried one around. And it's a relief to know
that he still does, like maybe there's one thing about him
that hasn't changed. But that just makes me cry harder.

'I love you, Sarah.'

'Yeah, you already said that. But a person who loves you
doesn't leave. You're my dad. You've responsibilities. You
can't just walk out.' And I realise then that I'm not just
angry that he left but that I miss him. I smell his aftershave
on the air and I remember – he was the one who flung us
high. He threw us up, knowing he'd catch us. It was only
later that everything he did became so deliberate, as if he'd
read somewhere it was good parenting practice. Oh God.
This was a mistake. I shouldn't have come. I don't want to
remember.

'Sarah, I didn't plan this, any of this. I didn't plan on
falling out of love with your mother. I didn't plan on
meeting someone else—'

'Stop,' I say. 'I don't want to know.' That he fell out of
love. That he met someone else. 'I'm here because of the

shrink. I'm here to tell you how I feel so I don't shoplift any more. That's it. OK? So let's just leave it at that.'

'Sarah. I still want to be a father to you. I want to hook up with you, hang out.' He sounds like a hippy.

'It's all about what *you* want, isn't it?'

'I still love you.'

'Not enough to stay.'

'I love Anthea.'

'Good for you,' I say and think, *what a crappy name.*

'Look. Maybe we could do something. Maybe your mother and I could go to counselling—'

'Get real, Dad. You're not coming back, so what's the point? Anyway, she doesn't need you to go to counselling. She's doing that without you. Actually, she's doing fine – in general – without you.' *Oh God*, I think. What if Mum doesn't want him to know that she's seeing someone? I shouldn't have said anything. I should never have come.

'I'm glad she's seeing someone,' he says, like he's some sort of kindly saint.

'I want to go now.'

We drive back in silence. Was this supposed to make me feel better or just stop me shoplifting? Because I sure as hell don't feel better. And if it hasn't stopped me shoplifting, Mary Gleeson is a dead woman.

'I think that session went well,' Dad says when he pulls up outside the house.

I stare at him. 'I'm your daughter, not your patient. That was not a session.'

He looks embarrassed. 'You're right. I'm sorry. It wasn't.' He pauses. 'So can we do this again soon?'

'I gotta go,' I say and hurry out of the car.

12
HUMAN RESOURCES

Saturday night and I'm getting ready to go out with Simon, Rachel, Mark and a few others. Music blaring, I'm right up to the mirror, putting on mascara.

'Careful you don't fall in there.'

I get such a fright I poke myself in the eye. I turn around. 'Shit, Louis. Ever hear of knocking?'

'I *did* knock.'

I turn down the music. He comes in, sits on the bed. I look at him suspiciously. Louis never comes in and sits on my bed.

'Heard you saw Dad,' he says.

I ignore that. Go back to my eyelashes.

'How did it go?'

'Brilliant,' I say sarcastically, without turning around.

'You going to see him again?'

'Nope.'

'Why not?'

I stop what I'm doing and turn. 'Louis, you better not be turning into some kind of corny father-figure type person or something.'

He has a good laugh at that.

'I don't want to talk about Dad, OK?' I put away my mascara and reach for my lip gloss.

'OK. But you only get one, right? And he's not the worst.'

'Thanks for that, Louis.'

'When we get together, we have a good laugh.'

'I'm thrilled for you. Was there anything else?'

I expect him to go. But he doesn't. He just sits there on my bed.

'So, any news?' he asks, finally, like he's the man of the house now and we should have a chat.

'No.'

'Going out?'

'Ye-ah.' What is wrong with him? He's never this dumb.

'With the usual suspects?'

I see his face. It's so obvious. I have to stop this right now.

'Look, Louis, forget it. You haven't got a chance, OK? She's in love with David.'

He pales. 'What're you talking about?'

'Alex. I saw the way you look at her.'

'*What?*'

'You love her.'

He gets up from the bed. 'You are completely stupid if you think I love *anyone*.'

'OK, well, I'm just saying. Don't waste your time. That's all.' I sound harsh. But life is harsh. And he better get used to it.

'Alex is a kid, OK? I don't waste my time with kids.'

I'd be insulted for her if I knew he meant it. 'Good. Don't.'

'Don't worry I won't.' And he's gone, as quickly as he arrived.

I'm not asking him for a lift, after that. So I walk to Simon's. He answers the door with a quick 'hey,' then disappears back to the couch. There's a rugby match on their huge flat screen.

'Ready to go?' I ask.

'This'll be over in a minute,' he says, without taking his eyes from the action.

'What is it?'

'Toulouse versus Wasps.'

'What?'

He doesn't answer. I sit beside him. Look at the screen. I try to see what the attraction is. Some of the players are pretty cute, I guess.

'Who's that guy? Number ten?'

He doesn't answer. It's like I'm not here. I get up and start to wander around, looking at their paintings and stuff. Their coffee machine is the one George Clooney advertises. If I liked coffee, I'd make myself one. I look over. No offer of sustenance from the couch. I help myself to a Coke from the fridge. Finally, I wander back over. Sit down again.

'I met my dad,' I try. Normally, we don't do personal.

He stares at the screen, leans forward and starts shouting. He stands suddenly and punches the air. Maybe I should have told him he was going bald.

The final whistle blows.

'Great,' I say, standing, 'let's go.'

'Hang on. I just want to get some of the commentary.'

And I swear to God, I feel like leaving without him. Instead I go to his father's drinks cabinet and add some vodka to the Coke.

*

)I(

Sunday. I'm in Dundrum with Alex and Rachel. And I have to leave. I have to get out. Before I take something. I can't believe it. I should never have trusted Mary Gleeson.

They're walking towards BT2 now.

'I can't do this any more,' I say, stopping.

They turn. 'You can't do what?' Rachel asks.

'This. Shop.'

Alex smiles. 'Why not?'

'I don't know. There's nothing in the shops. It's all crap.'

They look at each other.

Alex shrugs. 'Actually, you know what? You're right. Let's go see a movie … On me.'

Oh God. She thinks I'm stressing because I'm broke. Which makes me feel like a total shit.

'What's on?' Rachel asks.

'Only one way to find out,' Alex says and starts to walk. I tell myself that she genuinely does love movies.

I'm relieved to leave the shops behind. I still worry, though, that this hasn't gone away. In the cinema, we decide on a romantic comedy. Alex promises to kill me if it's bad.

It's seriously good. Watching the screen, I forget everything. I laugh and cry for someone else. Walking out of the cinema, I turn to Alex.

'So, are you going to kill me?'

'I'm thinking about it.'

'What? That was a great movie.'

'It was a bit unreal though.'

'Yeah,' Rachel says. 'That guy was way too good to be true.'

'No, he wasn't,' I insist.

'No guy's that nice,' Rachel says.

'Oh my God, I'm so telling Mark,' I joke.

'Go ahead,' she says. 'He could do with a kick in the ass.'

I stare at her.

She shrugs. 'He's driving me mad.'

'With *passion*?' I tease.

'No, Sarah. Mad in general. He won't get down to study.'

'Hel-lo. We're in Transition Year. There *is* no study,' I say, then remember that, for me, there should be. I feel kind of sick.

'We both want to do medicine,' Rachel says then. 'Have you noticed the points you need?'

'Rache. You're, like, a total genius,' Alex says.

'We should, at least, be keeping up our languages.'

'If my mum heard you,' I say, 'she'd adopt you on the spot.'

But Rachel doesn't hear. 'He comes back to my place to study, right? But he doesn't want to study at all.'

'Oh, *really*?' Alex says. 'And what *does* he want to do exactly?'

She smiles.

'Couldn't you do both?' I ask. 'You know, alternate?'

She rolls her eyes, but she's smiling. You can tell she loves him. And that he's totally mad about her.

'I'd just like to know when he's going to start taking things seriously, that's all.'

'He takes *you* seriously,' I say. 'That's, like, pretty amazing. Simon doesn't notice me half the time.'

'Simon doesn't deserve you,' she says.

'He's OK. I was just saying—'

'Sarah, he doesn't appreciate you. That is a fact.'

'He does in his own way.' I just wish it was more than physical.

Monday morning. I come down to the kitchen, still climbing into the last bits of my uniform. With one hand still
searching for a sleeve, I stop. There's a stranger in my
kitchen. A woman. In a fitted trouser suit. Her dark hair is
twisted into a bun. She's putting bread in the toaster like
she's at home. She doesn't look like a burglar. I find where
my arm goes and shove it in.

'Hello?' I say. As in: explanation please.

She turns. 'Oh! You must be Louis' sister.' She smiles
widely then walks towards me, hand outstretched.

'Eh, yeah.' My brain slowly computes. A friend? A lectur-
er? She has to be at least thirty. She couldn't be anything
else. Could she?

She pumps my hand. 'Miriam,' she says, cheerfully.

'So you *know* Louis?'

She smiles the way you'd smile at a kid who's just said
something cute and innocent. 'You could say that.' She's got
one of those husky voices, the kind that jazz singers have.
'We met last night. At the pub.'

I swallow. 'Where's he now?'

She laughs like a smoker. 'Oh, still recovering.'

I'm actually blushing. Sometimes I wish I didn't have such
a good imagination.

'Would you like some toast?' she asks me, like I'm the
guest. Classic Louis, letting an assertive sex beast wander the
house. Mum's house. Oh my God. What if she comes back?

'Eh, no thanks.' I check my watch. 'So do you, like,
work?' Hint, hint.

'Yes. I'm in Human Resources.'

I look at her blankly. Then decide to get on with my life. I go to
the drawer below the oven and grab the Coco Pops.

'Oh, so *that's* where you keep the cereals,' she says.

I sit at the table and start into breakfast. She's not the only one with somewhere to go. She joins me, making this the weirdest breakfast in the history of my life.

'So, what class are you in?' she asks, brushing crumbs from the side of her mouth with her pinkie. Like everything else she does, it oozes sex.

'Transition Year.'

'Yeah? What's that all about?' she asks.

I feel like telling her to go have some kids and find out, instead of sleeping with nineteen-year-olds.

'Back in a sec.' I run upstairs. Knock on his door and burst in. The room's a mess. But that's nothing new.

'Louis, wake up.'

He's unconscious. His hair sticking up all over the place. I poke him.

'Louis. Get *up*.'

He groans.

'Come on. Your *girl*friend's downstairs.'

'Who?' he asks groggily, rubbing an eye. Louis was never a morning person.

'*Miriam.*'

'Miriam … Miriam … Oh, yeah.' He smiles this really stupid lazy smile. '*Miriam.*'

'Louis, seriously, you can't let a total stranger walk all over the house. What about Mum?' There'd be war. Total war.

He sits up, scratching an eyebrow. 'What time's it?'

'Quarter past eight.'

He flops back on the pillows. Mum leaves at seven-thirty. 'What's she doing down there?'

'Having breakfast then going to work. She's in Human Resources.'

He looks at me blankly. Then turns over.

}|{

'Aren't you going *down* there?'

'She's going to work, right?'

'I have to go to school. I can't leave her down there on her own.' A lot of normal-looking people are kleptos. I should know.

'Course you can. I'll get up in a minute.'

I know he won't.

'OK. I'm going to school. If she takes anything, you're responsible.'

'Fine.' He pulls the duvet over his head.

I run back down. She's reaching for her bag.

'How do you get to school?' she asks.

And without thinking, I say, 'DART.'

'Great. You can show me where to get it.'

Oh my God. I have to walk my brother's cougar to the DART.

She talks all the way. Like some sort of wind-up toy. At last, we get to the station.

'OK, see you later,' I say. I rush ahead with my weekly DART ticket, knowing she'll have to queue to buy a single.

Five minutes later, I'm waiting on the platform, when she comes up to me like a stray dog.

'Hello again!'

I stare at her. Doesn't she get the message?

She looks up at the sign for the next DART. 'Two minutes,' she says. 'Good timing.'

Or bad, I think.

Two minutes later, the DART pulls in. I scan the carriages for Rachel and Alex. The DART comes to a stop, and there they are in the carriage that opens in front of us. Naturally, Miriam gets on with me. I walk up to the guys. I turn to Miriam.

'Bye, I guess.'

'Sure, nice to meet you.' She pauses. 'I didn't get your name.'

'Eh, Sarah,' I say.

'Cool, see you, Sarah.'

Unlikely, I think, knowing Louis.

She walks on ahead.

'Who was that?' Rachel asks.

'Miriam.'

'Who?'

'She's in Human Resources.'

'What's that?'

'Exactly.'

'Jesus, Sarah, who *is* she?'

I smile. 'Someone Louis picked up at the pub.'

'OMG. She's ancient,' Rachel says.

I can see Alex checking her out.

'Bit of a sex bomb, though,' Rachel continues.

'I *know*,' I say.

Alex just smiles. 'Good old Louis.' Then she catches me staring at her. 'What?' she asks.

'Nothing.'

13
GOLDFISH

Friday. I walk up the avenue to the home, telling myself it'll be OK. I'll just avoid him. Won't even look his way. Like, what's he going to do anyway, wheelchair after me? I walk in and can't believe it. The first pair of eyes I meet are his. He's with everyone else, turned facing the podium. I feel myself blush but keep walking – over to John.

'Sarah?'

Oh my God. He's calling me. Like we're friends or something. I keep going. Pretend I don't hear. I smile at John.

'Hey, John. How's it going?'

I grab a chair and sit beside him.

'Sarah?' he calls again. And I so don't trust him.

John looks over at him like he's worried. I can feel everyone's eyes on me. I'm dying. John groans. I have to do something. I look over and try to stay cool.

'Yes?' I ask, coldly.

'I'm ready for Bingo,' he says, kind of cheeky.

'Great,' I say and turn to go back to John.

'Aren't you going to get me a board?' he calls, like he didn't practically throw one at me last week. He smiles innocently.

And I know that if I don't get him a board, I'll just come off as cruel. So, giving him a look that says 'you don't fool *me*, buster', I get up. I grab a board and counters and bring them to him. I put them down on the tray he's pulled out from his wheelchair.

'So, you came back,' he says. 'Didn't think you would.'

'Why wouldn't I?'

'I thought I'd scared you away.'

'Well, obviously you haven't.' I start to go.

'Aren't you going to sit with me?'

'I'm with John.'

'No, you aren't.'

I follow his eyes. Oh my God. Another helper is taking my seat. She's chatting away to him. Oh my God. Didn't she see that I was there? I look around. Everyone else has someone. I don't freaking believe it.

He smiles. 'Go on, pull up a chair. I won't bite.'

'Can I have that in writing?'

He actually smiles.

But I don't trust it. 'Look, you don't need me. So—'

'I do. I do need you.' He's mocking me.

Which makes me brave.

'How? There's nothing wrong with your hands.'

His eyes narrow. And I know it's coming, whatever he's been planning to ambush me with since I got here.

'So what are you, some kind of Florence Nightingale or something? Or do you just not have a life?'

Oh my God. Am I supposed to let him away with that just because he's in a wheelchair? I glare at him and lower my voice.

'For your information, I want to be here just as much as you do.'

'So why are you?' He eyeballs me.

'You really want to know?' I eyeball him back.

'Yes I really want to know.'

'I got caught shoplifting. You're my community service.'
I can't believe I told him.

He bursts out laughing. Turning into a different person.
Someone with happy eyes. And white teeth. Someone alive.
And I wonder what age he really is underneath all that fuzz.
People are looking now, like they've never heard him laugh
before. 'Wish you'd told me earlier,' he says quietly. 'I might
have been nicer.'

'Oh, you mean you do nice?'

'I'll have to now, won't I? Seeing as I'm dealing with a
criminal. Are you violent too?'

'When I have to be.'

He laughs again. And I think that the only way to get on
with this guy is to give him a hard time. Which totally suits
me.

'Come on, sit down and keep me company,' he says, all
friendly and persuasive.

'Are you going to behave?'

He puts his hands up like I'm going to shoot. 'Definitely.'

No longer afraid of him, I sit down. Almost immediately,
Bingo starts.

'Three and five, thirty-five.'

I look at the board.

'So, how long've you been shoplifting?' he whispers. Like
it's a hobby or something.

I ignore him. Just look at the board.

'What's the most interesting thing you've stolen?'

I look at him. 'I'm concentrating.'

'Go on, tell me. What's the most interesting thing you've
nicked?'

}I{

'Don't think I won't hurt you just because you're in a wheelchair.'

He bursts out laughing. 'I didn't expect you to be this interesting.'

'Yeah, well, I expected you to be this condescending.'

'Ooh, burn.' But he's smiling. 'So, am I safe?'

'What?'

'You're not going to steal me, are you?' I smile. 'On second thoughts, do. Steal me. I'm up for being stolen.'

I laugh. People look over. I blush and shut up. I concentrate on the numbers.

'Five and one, fifty-one.'

I cover it with a counter.

He looks at me like I'm mad. 'You're not actually *playing*, are you?'

'That's why I'm here.'

'I thought you were on community service.'

'I am. Now, let me do it.'

He shakes his head.

I stay with him for the afternoon. We don't win anything. And I'm kind of glad. He'd probably just slag off the prize. But it's weird. It's like being with my friends. We slag each other the same way. Talk about stuff the same way. If someone had told me, walking up the avenue, how seriously funny he was, I wouldn't have believed them. And I wonder if all he wanted was to be treated like a normal person.

Mary Gleeson doesn't look any different from usual. She doesn't look like she's expecting any great breakthrough – the kind of breakthrough I was expecting when I agreed to speak to my dad.

'So, how've you been?' she asks, like she's happy to let this run and run. Which makes me so angry. This is my *life*.

'I thought you said if I talked to my dad, it would stop. It hasn't stopped.'

'You've taken something?'

'No. But I wanted to. This hasn't gone away.'

'OK,' she says, like she's considering that. 'You spoke with your dad. How did that go?'

'Crap.'

She raises her eyebrows, as in: how crap?

'I did everything you said. And I felt worse, not better.'

'In what way?'

'I don't want to talk about it.'

'OK.'

'I told him I hated him.'

'Do you?'

'I don't know. I felt like I did when I said it.'

'Then you needed to say it. How did he react?'

'He was OK.'

'Did he apologise?'

'For what, leaving?'

She nods.

'Yeah, but so what? He's still living with her.'

'It's good, though, isn't it, that he accepts the blame for how you feel?'

'Yeah, well he should.'

She smiles. 'Let's leave that for now,' she says patiently. 'I want you to remember back to the very first time you took something from a shop. I want you to tell me how you felt immediately afterwards. I'm talking about good feelings here.'

The fact that she expects them makes me feel a little less guilty. 'I felt kind of buzzed.'

'Go on.'

'I felt like, I don't know, kind of like, a winner? Like I could beat the system, get what I wanted without depending on anyone. Not my mum. Not my friends.' She nods me on. 'It made me feel powerful.'

'Because it gave you the one thing you really needed – control over your life. Think about it, Sarah. Your dad left. Your mum was angry. You'd no control over any of that. This was the one thing you could control.' Suddenly, it's like she's on my side. 'You talked about depending on your friends for money. Have they more than you?'

'Are you kidding? They're minted. Seriously minted. I can't keep up.'

She nods, then, after a while, asks, 'Have you ever tried making your own money?'

'Mum won't let me take a part-time job. She wants me to study.'

She thinks for a while. 'I see that,' she says at last. 'I also see that if you were to earn your own money, you'd feel a lot more in control. I think it's important, Sarah. How would your mum feel about you babysitting?'

'I don't know anyone with small kids.'

'You could advertise.'

'I guess.' I'm not sure I even like small kids. My cousins are psychos. I'm more comfortable with animals. 'In school, they want us to start our own businesses. It's like a Young Entrepreneur Scheme? I was thinking of a pet-minding business but Mum hates dogs. So that's the end of that.'

'You like animals?'

'I love animals.'

'Have you asked her about the business?'

'No point. Even if she was OK with it, which she so wouldn't be, who'd take me seriously? I'm a teenager.'

'I'd leave my dogs with you. In fact, if you start a pet-minding business, I will.'

'Seriously? You'd leave your dogs with me?'

'I know a lot of people who would. Have you ever seen a kennels?'

'No.'

'Then you should go visit one. No one wants to leave their dog in kennels.'

'What kind of dogs do you have?'

'King Charles.'

'Aw, they're so cute.'

'Sarah. No one sails through the break-up of a family. It's very common to feel out of control. You've a chance to regain it. Ask your mum about the business. If she's against it, think of another idea. Something you'll like. The important thing is to get cracking.'

Suddenly, that's exactly what I want to do.

'How *is* your mum?'

Two weeks ago, that question would have stopped me. Now I'm smiling. 'Better. She's going out a bit. She got her hair cut and let me give her a manicure. Which is, like, amazing for her. But the best thing is, she's doesn't want to be angry any more. She's trying. It's good.'

'Sarah, I'm very encouraged by this session. I know you think things didn't go well with your dad, but it was important to let him know how you feel, to let that out. You wanted to shoplift. But you *didn't do it*. You want to put this

behind you. And you will. I want you to put all your energy
this week into starting a business. If you need me to write to
your mum to emphasise the importance—'

'No. It's OK. I'll ask her.'

For the first time, I leave Mary Gleeson's offices feeling
better.

You don't just spring a request on my mum. You prepare
what you're going to say. You gauge her mood. You choose
your moment. I prepare all the way home. My moment pres-
ents itself over lunch when she is actually eating, instead of
smoking, and she's just made a comment on the weather.
There will never be a better time.

'Mum?'

She looks up from her plate.

I almost back out. But I think of Mary Gleeson and force
myself on. 'You know the way you want me to be independent and look out for myself and stuff?'

She looks at me like she knows something's coming.
'Yes?' she says cautiously.

'Well, in school, they want us to run our own businesses.'

'Really? That's great. What kind of businesses?'

Here we go. 'Pet minding.'

'They want you to run a pet-minding business?'

I could lie. And God I'm tempted. 'No. Any kind of business. I just want to mind pets.'

For a moment she says nothing, then, 'How would that
work?'

I can't believe the conversation isn't over. 'Well, when
people go away, I'd mind their goldfish and stuff.'

'*Goldfish*?'

'Well, and dogs and stuff.'

'Dogs?'

'I wouldn't have to mind them here. I could ask people if they'd be OK with me minding them in *their* homes.'

'What, you mean like you'd stay there when they're away?'

She'd never allow that.

'No. I'd just go there a few times a day and feed the dog and bring it for walks and play with it for a bit.' I'm working this out as I go along.

'Wouldn't they be lonely on their own all day?'

She's actually concerned about the dogs? 'They might be.'

'Mind them here,' she says matter-of-factly, like it makes total sense. She's forgotten something.

And I know I shouldn't remind her but ... 'You hate dogs.'

'No I don't.'

'Then why don't I have one?' I nagged her for years.

She takes a deep breath. 'Sarah, in marriage, parents should show a united front.'

'What are you saying, that Dad didn't like dogs and you just went along with him?'

'When you're older you'll understand.'

'But what about what *you* wanted?'

'Your dad was the parenting expert.'

'Because he was a *psychologist*?' She doesn't believe that, does she?

'Sarah, we're getting off the point here. You want to run a pet-minding service. I'm saying that's fine with me.'

I break into a smile. 'Really? You're serious, right?'

'Am I ever otherwise?'

OMG, is that a joke?

'But you have to be responsible,' she says. 'This is a business. You have to go about it in a professional manner, think of all the eventualities, anything that could go wrong, and prepare for it. If a dog gets sick, what next?'

My face falls. And I think, *maybe I can't do this*.

'It's OK. I'm not trying to put you off. I'm just saying. You'll be responsible for other people's pets. You have to live up to that. If a dog gets sick, you take it to the vet and get the owner to pay the bill when they come home.'

'What if they refuse?'

'That's why you have to think ahead. Everyone leaving a pet with you must sign a legal agreement.'

Oh my God. 'A *legal* agreement?'

'Of course. If they were leaving their pet in a kennels they'd have to do the same. It's just an agreement between two people outlining where everyone stands. Don't worry, I'll help you with it and I'll get our solicitor to look over it. I just want you to think it all through, know what you're getting into. Be professional. That's all. This will be an amazing experience, Sarah. A great opportunity. I'm so proud of you for picking such a responsible business idea. Some people will probably just bake cakes.'

I smile. That's what most people are doing. I can't believe I almost didn't ask. I can't believe she said she was proud. I especially can't believe that she likes dogs. I think about what she said about Dad being the expert. And, for the first time in my life, I wonder if being married to him had a downside.

14
DON'T LIKE HER

Rachel says she wants a break from Mark tonight. David's not here. And there's no way I'm bringing Simon. So it's just the three of us, in a tiny pizzeria in Dalkey. The Italian waiters fuss over us a bit. Which is nice.

I'm doing the pet-minding business,' I tell them while we wait for our pizzas.

'Really? Great,' Rachel says.

'What about your mum?' Alex asks.

'You're not going to believe it. She likes dogs after all.' I explain about how mum wanted to keep a united front and I feel kind of sad. 'It makes me wonder what else she went along with. Everything?'

Rachel shakes her head. 'No. You couldn't do that for an entire marriage. It would do your head in. You'd end up killing someone.'

Or being seriously angry all the time. Suddenly, I don't want to think about that.

'I thought I'd do posters and put up little notices, you know in supermarkets and stuff.'

'I'll give you a hand if you like,' Rachel says.

'Hey,' Alex says, 'if you're going to be walking dogs, I could come with Homer.'

'Oh my God, that'd be so cool.'

I still can't believe this is really going to happen.

Our pizzas come and look delicious. We don't wait.

'So,' Rachel asks Alex after a while. 'How's Lover Boy?'

She smiles. 'Good. I didn't think this would work, just staying in touch on Skype. But it's OK, you know? And we'll see each other over the summer. Which is, like, only weeks away.' She closes her eyes. 'I can't wait.'

'Who's that girl who keeps posting on his wall?' Rachel asks.

'What girl?'

'I don't know. Jenny someone?'

'Oh. She's in the group he hangs out with. I've met her. She's OK.'

'I don't like her,' Rachel says.

'Yeah, I know. She fancies him. It's OK. We joke about it.'

'Still don't like her.'

'Thanks for caring, Rachey,' Alex says, reaching over and pinching her cheek and wiggling it around.

'Get off, Jesus.' Rachel slaps at her.

We laugh.

'What's up with you and Mark?' Alex asks Rachel.

'I don't know. He's just bugging me, the way he keeps going on about going to California when he's finished school.'

'Rachel, everyone goes on about California,' I say.

'And we're not leaving school for two years,' Alex says. 'A lot can happen in two years. Like he could change his mind.'

'It's just that when he goes on like that it's like he wants to get away. From me. You know?'

'You're being too sensitive,' Alex says.

'Yeah,' I say.

'You think?'

'Definitely.'

'Phew,' she says, sighing. 'I really needed to hear that.'

No one asks about Simon. And, by now, I don't expect them to.

All week, I work on setting up my business, designing posters on the computer and printing them off, putting them up anywhere I can, making smaller notices for places that won't take actual posters, designing flyers with little cut-off bits with my phone number on. Mum takes flyers to work. Louis takes them to college, the Jitter Mug and the pub. Friday, I recruit an unexpected helper.

Miriam's in the kitchen when I come down – which makes this, what, a second one-night stand? She's already at the table. Eating my Coco Pops.

'Hey,' she says like we're friends.

'Hey.' I get a bowl and reach for my Coco Pops.

'These are great,' she says, picking up the flyers. 'Is this your business?' I nod, kind of embarrassed. 'Go you. How many pets do you get a week?'

I wish. 'I've just started.'

'Oh my God, I know so many people who'd use this service. Can I bring some to work?'

'Sure,' I say, surprised. 'Thanks.'

'No problem. It's a great idea. So, you DARTing today?'

'Eh, yeah.'

'Great! Company!'

For someone her age, she doesn't act so ancient. There's probably someone upstairs who'd agree.

On the DART, she waves a cheery goodbye and carries on up the carriage. Rachel raises an eyebrow.

'Is Louis actually *going out* with her?'

'I'm thinking, second one-night stand,' I say.

'What's she like?' Rachel asks.

I shrug. 'Nice. For her age.'

'Yeah, but she's ancient,' Rachel says, looking at her.

Alex says nothing.

After school, I have to go to the home. I'm walking up the avenue, trying to think of good places to leave flyers. I don't see Christina till I'm almost at the door.

'Hey,' I say, surprised she's outside.

'I was waiting for you.'

'Is everything OK?'

'Yes, I just wanted a word. It's about Shane.'

Something's wrong.

'I don't know what you did last week, but I'd like you to keep doing it.'

I squint at her. 'I don't know what you mean.'

'When you left, he went over to John and apologised for taking you away. It was the first time he'd spoken to anyone since he arrived. He's started to come out of himself a bit. I was hoping that, maybe, you could sit with him again.'

I hesitate. 'I'm not sure he'd want me to. He doesn't actually *need* help. And he's got this thing about charity.'

She thinks about that. Then nods. 'You're right. I just got a little over-excited by the progress.' She smiles. 'Look, don't worry about it.'

I shrug. 'Sorry.'

'No, no. You're right.'

I follow her in. And there he is, sitting next to John, chatting away like John can chat back. He sees me and waves. Everything about him looks cheeky. I hike my school bag up and go over.

My 'hey' is a general one to both of them.

Christina sits beside John and starts talking to him. Shane moves away to give them space.

'You coming?' he asks.

'Eh, yeah, sure.'

I walk with him. He stops at the edge of the group.

'You're sitting with me, right?'

'Depends. Are you playing Bingo?'

'If I have to.'

'You have to.' I go get the board and counters. There's a lovely hum in the room from everyone chatting. I put the things on his tray and go get a chair. Finally, I sit.

'So,' he says, in a low voice. 'Pull any heists this week?'

It's like he thinks I'm cool because I got caught shoplifting. 'I'm not exactly a criminal mastermind, you know.'

'You're as close to one as I'll get.'

'Except I don't do it any more.'

He seems to sense that it's a sensitive subject and backs off with a 'I was only messing.' Then he looks at me with this exaggerated, deep-meaningful expression. 'So, how've you been?'

I feel like laughing. 'You sound like my shrink.'

'You've a *shrink*? God, you get better and better.'

'I try.' I can't believe I've told a practical stranger stuff I can't tell my friends.

'So why're you seeing him?'

'Her.'

'OK, why're you seeing her?' he asks, like I'm fascinating.

'I'm nuts. Clearly.'

'How nuts? Out of ten.'

I smile. 'Dangerously nuts. You never know what I'm going to do.'

He interlaces his fingers and places his hands in an arch, like a professional shrink. 'I think we should start with your childhood.'

I smile. 'Shut up.'

'All right then, let's keep it simple. What's your surname?'

'Healy. Yours?'

'Owens. Age?'

'Seventeen. You?'

'Nineteen.'

'*Seriously?*' I ask. I stare at him. 'You're kidding, right?'

'It's the beard.'

'That's not a beard. That's a bush.'

He laughs. 'Maybe I should get rid of it.'

'Maybe,' I say, sarcastically. 'Nineteen, Jesus.'

He's smiling. 'Where d'you live?'

'Glenageary. You?'

'Killiney. But *I'm* asking the questions here. School?'

'Yes,' I say, just to annoy him.

He smiles. 'Which one?'

'How are any of these questions going to help my mental health?'

'Bear with me,' he says and sounds so like Mary Gleeson that I laugh. 'So, school?'

'Strandbrook.'

'Ooh, poshy.'

'I'm not posh.'

'OK, liberal.'

I've no clue what he means but it doesn't sound good. 'Shut up.'

'So how d'you get into the whole stealing thing?' Like it's a career option or something.

'Shocker, but I'm not actually proud of it.'

'So you're a good girl, then?' he asks, sounding disappointed.

'Not totally rotten, I guess.' It's so weird. He's the first person who has made me see that.

'Shame.'

'Want me to go?' I pretend to be offended.

'Nah, stay. No one else to talk to.'

'Gee, thanks.'

We're quiet for a while. He glances out the window. Takes a deep breath. 'So what's happening out there?'

'Depends what you want to know. I'm pretty crap on current affairs. But if you're interested in celebrity news …'

'Celebrity news sounds good to me.' He smiles.

I tell him the latest stuff. He looks at me like he's amused. 'Where d'you get all this stuff?'

'Perez.'

'Where?'

'Who. Jesus. Perez Hilton?'

He looks blank.

'Oh my God, where have you been? You've never been on perezhilton.com?'

'Eh, no.'

I shake my head in disbelief.

'Testing one-two, one-two.'

We both look up. Then look at each other and try not to laugh.

Bingo starts with 'Two little ducks, quack, quack. Twenty-two.'

I check the board, then glance up. To find him looking at me.

'Hi,' he says, cheekily.

I ignore him. Look back at the board.

'Legs eleven,' Mary calls.

A number we have. I look at Shane.

'What?' he asks.

'Eleven.'

'Ooh.' He shakes his fists like he's excited. But he does cover the number on the board. 'So. Hobbies?' he whispers.

'Bingo,' I whisper back.

'Favourite band?'

'Frank Sinatra.'

He squints at me. 'Do you take *anything* seriously?'

'Do you?'

He smiles. And despite his total lack of concentration, we actually win.

'Wahoo,' he says, punching the air. I think he's being sarcastic. But I'm not *actually* sure? People stare at him. He is presented with a soap collection. He hands it to me.

'Here. You did all the work.'

His smile is beautiful. Even behind the fuzz.

OK, so I actually like him. Officially. Weird.

I've just left when Christina, standing at the entrance, calls me back.

'Sorry, Sarah, I just wanted to ask you something.'

I go back. 'Sure.'

'I was wondering, and no worries if it doesn't suit, but do you think there's *any chance* at all you could come on

Mondays and Fridays? Just for a few weeks? You're having such a good effect on Shane.'

I think it's kind of cheeky, actually. But then, I guess, it's just because she cares about him. Which is cool, you know, for someone who just works there.

'I don't know. I'd have to ask my mum.'

'*Would* you? I'd really appreciate it. Just for a week or two. Just to keep the momentum up. He's doing so well.'

I think about how Shane would hate this if he knew. 'I'll check,' I say.

Louis is on the DART, on his way back from the Jitter Mug.

'Why are you so late?' he asks.

'Community service.'

'Oh right, yeah. How's that going?'

'OK.' I look at him. 'There's this guy who's only your age.'

'What's wrong with him?'

'I don't know. He's in a wheelchair.'

'Car accident probably. Or rugby.'

'It's so sad. He's such a cool guy.'

'I don't know how you do it. Go in there.'

'You know what? I love it. The people are amazing.'

He looks at me like he doesn't get me.

I change the subject. 'So what's with Miriam?'

'What d'you mean?'

'She was in the kitchen again this morning.'

'I wouldn't read anything into that.'

'That's what I thought.'

'She's nice and everything but married.'

'Oh my God, Louis.'

'She came on to me. What could I do?'

'Say no.' Jesus.

He smiles. 'I'm only messing. She's not married. At least I don't think she is.'

I hit him. 'You are turning into a slut, my man.'

He raises his eyebrows. 'Can't help it if I'm a popular guy.'

'There is this concept called a relationship, Louis.'

'Yeah and from what I've heard, it's overrated.'

Wish that hadn't made me think of Simon.

When Mum gets home, I tell her about Christina asking me to do Mondays at the home.

She looks surprised. 'And you'd be OK with that?'

'I don't know.' I explain the situation.

'So you're helping this boy, Shane?'

'I don't know. Christina thinks I cheer him up. But it's just that we get on, really.'

She looks at me. 'Trust me, Sarah. Cheering someone up can be a very valuable thing.'

I think of Ellen. But this is different. 'I don't, like, set out to cheer him up? And he'd hate me to, anyway.'

'But you do cheer him up?'

I shrug. 'I don't know. Maybe. We make each other laugh. A bit.'

'Well, I'd love you to do it. But only if you want to. Your community service is once a week. So it's up to you.' But she's looking at me the same way she looked at me when she said she was proud. And it's so good to get a break from being the person who keeps messing up.

'I'll go,' I say.

15
CHRISTMAS CRACKER

On Monday, when I walk into the home, everything's different. The chairs are grouped around tables and everyone's busy. Making things. Like tapestry. And embroidery. Is that a *Christmas cracker*? There's a new guy. He's waving. At me? Oh. My. God. It's Shane. His beard is gone. His hair is tidy. He looks nineteen. And *seriously caliente*. I know I'm staring. I walk towards him.

'Oh my God. Look at you,' I say, smiling. His skin looks so smooth, I feel like touching it.

He's not smiling back. 'What are you doing here?'

I freeze, thinking, Oh God, he knows. And he thinks it's charity.

'Christina asked me to come,' I say and wait for the anger.

But his face relaxes. 'So you weren't caught shoplifting?'

'No! God, no. Is that what you thought?'

He shrugs.

I don't get it. 'But you think shoplifting's cool. Or something.'

He raises his eyebrows. 'Maybe I did. Until I thought you were in trouble again.'

'Aw you care,' I say, messing, slapping his arm.

At last, he smiles. Then he lifts a Christmas cracker. 'I feel like an elf.'

I laugh. 'Want a hand?'

'Listen to this.' He picks up a joke. 'What do you get if you cross Santa with a duck?'

I think for a sec then shake my head.

'A Christmas quacker.'

'Oh God.'

'That's one of the good ones.'

We start to read them out. They're so lame that we laugh. He puts on a Christmas hat.

'You know, without the beard you are *seriously* caliente.'

He bursts out laughing. 'I do know Spanish. I *do* understand.'

I shrug. 'Well, you *are*.'

'No I'm not. Not any more.'

'Trust me. I'm a bit of an expert on this. You are caliente.'

He smiles like I've given him something. 'So,' he says, arching his hands in shrink mode. 'How've you been?'

'Don't start.'

He smiles. 'All right then, any news?'

'*Actually*. I'm starting my own business.'

'Really? What?'

'Pet minding.' I try not to sound too excited.

'Cool.' He's quiet for a moment. Then he asks, 'You take snakes?'

'Snakes? I hadn't thought of snakes.'

'I'm sure my folks could do with a break from feeding Quagmire, if you're in the market for a snake.'

'Quagmire? Like from *Family Guy*?'

He nods.

}|{

'I love *Family Guy*. Who's your favourite character?'

He smiles. 'Stewie.'

'Oh my God, Stewie's evil.'

'All part of his charm.' He says, picking up bits of a cracker and working on them. 'Who do you like?'

'Brian. You know, the way he's a *dog* but he's the most sensible one, then he goes and does something doggy.'

'Brian's great.'

'I can't believe you're making Christmas crackers.'

'It's for a good cause.'

'What?'

'Here.'

I pick up a cracker and start to fill it.

'So, Quagmire? Want to mind him?'

I think of Mum. 'What *do* you feed it?'

'Frozen mice.'

'Jesus.' When I recover, I ask, 'Where do you store them?'

'In the freezer.'

'There's no way my mum would go for that.'

'What about your dad?' he asks, and I know he's just being nosey.

'He doesn't live with us.' And that's all I want to say about that. 'Want a gossip update?'

He looks at me like he gets it. 'From Perez?'

'Who else?'

'Too late. Thanks to you, I'm addicted. Which makes me practically gay, by the way.'

I laugh. 'He's good, though, isn't he?' I say enthusiastically.

He smiles like he finds me cutely amusing. I don't mind cutely amusing. I'll take any kind of amusing. 'Any other good sites?' he asks.

'I'll send you some links. You're on Facebook, right?'

He hesitates. 'Yeah. I just haven't been on it ... in a while.'

I want to die. Of course he hasn't been on Facebook. He's been kind of busy. And what do you do anyway when you end up in a wheelchair, post pictures? God.

'But I can go on it if you want to send me some links,' he says.

'Or I could email.'

He takes out his iPhone and starts thumbing. Then he hands it to me. 'This the right Sarah Healy?'

'Yep.'

'Like your profile pic.'

It's Betty Boop, because sometimes I just feel like being dark.

He takes back his phone. 'I'll send a friend request.'

I look over his shoulder. He goes into his profile. Then he goes quiet, reading all the posts asking how he's doing. I move away to give him space. Finally, he looks up, clears his throat.

'I haven't got back to anyone,' he says. 'I kind of switched off for a while.'

Not for the first time, I wonder what happened, what kind of accident he had. It could have been anything – rugby, skiing, car accident. 'I'm sure they understand.'

'At least that gives me something to do with myself tomorrow. Let's have a look at your Facebook.' He passes me the phone.

I log in as me, then hand it back to him.

He goes into my photo albums. Scrolls through them in silence. Finally he looks up.

'So where's the boyfriend?'

I laugh. 'Who says I have one?'

'You have one.'

I smile, kind of flattered.

'Now, which one is he?'

'He's in that shot. You guess.'

'That guy?' He points to David.

'Nope.'

'That guy?' He points to Mark.

'He's the guy in the rugby shirt who looks like he doesn't play rugby.'

For some reason he thinks that's hilarious.

'Got any of him on his own? Or one of the two of you? I can't get a good look at him on this. He's tiny.'

I take the iPhone from him and scroll through the images. Then I look up, surprised. 'I don't have any.'

'Come on.'

I shrug. 'I don't.'

'What's he like?'

'How did we get on to this subject?'

'Just answer the question.'

'He's OK.'

'He's *OK*? You're going out with the guy. He's got to be more than OK. Tell me about him.'

'His name's Simon.'

'And?'

'He's in my class.'

'Oh my God. The detail – it's too much.'

I smile. 'What d'you want to know?'

'How long are you going out? Is it serious? The usual stuff.'

'Four months. And no.'

'Good,' he says.

}|{

'Why good?'

He looks straight at me. 'He's not the guy for you.'

I catch my breath. 'I'll take that as a compliment.'

'It was meant as one.' And he looks at me like no one else does. Like he rates me. He knows about the shoplifting. He knows about the shrink. And he still rates me.

When I get home, the house is empty. I turn on the heat, get some juice and go up to my room. I go straight on Facebook. I smile when I see Shane's friend request and accept it immediately. I check out his photo albums. It's like a record of everything he's lost. In all the shots, he looks so alive. Dive-bombing from the Forty Foot. Skiing. Playing rugby. Giving a girl a piggyback. Laughing. There's that girl again. And again. Here's one of them dressed up for some night out. They're smiling at the camera, like they're from *The OC*. Total A-listers. His arm is around her shoulder. He looks proud of her ... They're together.

I remember what he said about Simon. And decide he's wrong. Simon could be the guy for me – if I worked at it. I reach for my phone.

'This is the command centre,' I say.

'What?'

'Nothing.' A pause. I take a deep breath. 'I thought we could, maybe, do something after school.'

There's a long silence. I start to freak. I shouldn't have asked. We never see each other during the week. He'll think I want to get serious. And he'll run a mile.

'Tomorrow?' he asks finally.

'Or any day.'

Another pause, like he's thinking it through. 'OK, cool.'

}|{

Major relief. Then worry again – if I don't arrange an actual time, it won't happen. 'We could go to a movie tomorrow … if you like.'

'A movie?'

'Or something like that,' I say, casually.

'OK, cool,' he says.

And I'm probably a bit too happy.

'By the way, who's your new friend?'

'What?'

'Shane someone.'

Oh God. I don't want to tell him. I don't want him snooping around, making smart remarks, making a joke of it, of Shane. 'Just a friend of Rachel's. Don't really know him.'

'He's got some pretty hot friends.'

'Are you trying to tell me you're gay, Simon.'

'I wasn't talking about guys.'

Like I didn't work that out. Does he even know how insulting he is?

'So who's Shane Owens?' Alex asks on the DART the next morning.

'Oh, the guy in the home I was telling you about.'

She looks at me blankly.

'The guy at the window? Remember?'

'I thought you said he'd a beard.'

'He did. He shaved it off.'

'You never said he was caliente,' Alex says.

'I didn't know. Till he shaved it off.'

'He's like a white Lenny Kravitz,' Alex says.

'Who's Ellie Kravitz?' I ask.

She laughs. '*Lenny* Kravitz.'

'OK, well who's Lenny Kravitz?'

'A black singer. He had a part in that movie, *Precious*.'

'That movie you told me was feel-good and was so the opposite?' I say, accusingly.

'They sold it as feel-good. How was I supposed to know?'

'Which one was Lenny Kravitz?' Rachel asks.

'The orderly or nurse, when Precious was in the hospital.'

'Oh my God, yeah. He *was* caliente,' Rachel says. 'Is Shane black?'

'No.'

'So how come you're friends on Facebook?' Alex asks. 'I thought you hated the guy.'

'I did. He was an asshole. But only because he thought I was, like, this Florence Nightengaley person? He's OK now. We get on. Actually, Rache, could you send him a friend request?'

'Why?'

'Because I told Simon he was your friend.' I see her face. 'You know Simon. He'd just make a joke of the whole thing. And Shane isn't a joke.'

'OK, sure. No problem.'

'Can you do it now, like, on Alex's iPhone?'

'You'll have to wait till we get to school,' Alex says, 'for the WiFi.'

'Oh yeah, OK. Thanks.'

After school, Simon wants to go back to the apartment before going to the cinema. He says he wants to change. But I know what he means by change and I want this to be about something more than that. I tell him we'll miss the start. I tell him we'll go afterwards.

We sit together on the DART. I try to think of something

to say. He's my boyfriend. I should have something to say. Outside of the fact that I got caught shoplifting. Or that I see a shrink. Or that I don't love him, but I'm trying.

'Geoff Wiseman is such a loser,' he says, putting his feet up on the seat opposite.

I look at him. And wonder. If it was just us left in the world, would we have anything to talk about?

'Geoff's OK,' I say.

He looks at me like I've lost it. 'He plays chess.'

'Alex plays chess,' I say because suddenly it sounds like Simon's slagging Geoff to make himself sound better, cooler.

He looks at me. 'Do you fancy Geoff or something?'

'No! I just don't think he's a loser.'

Could this be going any worse?

But then, when we get off the DART, Simon takes my hand, something he's never actually done before. And I think that, maybe, it'll be OK. Maybe that's all we needed, someone to make an effort.

We get to the cinema.

'Want some popcorn or something?' Simon asks.

'Nah. You go ahead. I'm not hungry.' Fact is, I'm broke and don't want sponge.

'You've a great bod, Sarah. You don't need to diet.'

I just look at him. Who said anything about dieting?

He gets a huge tub of buttered popcorn and a large Coke. He looks like a little kid. Kind of cute, actually. I take out my phone.

'Say cheese.'

He makes a James Bond kind of face, raising an eyebrow and looking sideways. I laugh and click. It feels like we're a real couple. Maybe we can be.

Inside, we sit up at the back. And, again, I'm stuck for something to say. He doesn't seem to mind that we're not talking, though, munching away on his popcorn and happily looking around him. He turns to me.

'So, this is new.'

I shrug. 'Just thought we'd do something different. For a change.'

'I wanted to see this anyway,' he says, like it's not a total waste of his time.

I need chocolate.

The lights go down. It's another end-of-the-world movie. Simon's choice. I pretended not to mind but, actually, I do. Nature is taking over. Buildings are collapsing all round. I keep thinking, *this could actually happen*. I glance at Simon and try to imagine him in my hour of need. Leaping over flames. Jumping from moving vehicles. Springing over giant cracks in the ground. But the only image that comes to me is him pushing his way onto the last helicopter out. I look at him, beside me, fist submerged in his popcorn, chewing in time to the action. And I wonder. Can I really make myself love this person?

On our way out, he leaves his empty tub on the seat and gives the movie the thumbs up. He tells me he's glad we came but looks surprised to be. And when he slips a hand into the back pocket of my jeans, I know he's imagining himself as the hero. All muscle-y, hot and brave.

We go back to his place. Which is empty, as usual. If I owned it, I'd never leave. It's just so gorgeous. Already, Simon is dragging me to his room.

'Let's have a Coke first,' I say when really I mean, let's snuggle on the couch and chat. About something. Anything.

He goes to the fridge. I sit on the cool leather couch, waiting for him. He hands me my drink. But stays standing.

'Aren't you going to sit down, hang out for a while?'

'We've been hanging out since school.' He makes it sound like a lifetime.

And I think, *if we could just love each other*. It would be so handy.

'You're acting kinda weird today,' he says.

'So, have you thought of a business idea yet?'

'What? *No*. Jesus. We're not going to talk about that *now*, are we?'

'No. Just wondering.'

'OK because you had me worried there.' He knocks back the rest of his drink. 'You finished?'

He can see that I'm not. But he reaches for my glass anyway, takes it from me, puts it down, then he's dragging me up.

'Come on.'

In his room, he makes straight for my shirt without even looking me in the eye or kissing me. I could be a total stranger and he'd never notice. I pull back.

He looks up. 'What?' he asks.

'I'm not feeling that well,' I say.

'You were OK a second ago.'

'I wasn't. I just didn't say anything. Actually, I think I might go.'

He looks like a kid who's just dropped his ice-cream cone. I start to tie my shirt. He looks like he's trying to work out how to still get what he wants.

'See you tomorrow, yeah?' I say.

'Yeah, sure. Whatever.'

I let myself out.

)|(

Next day, as soon as we get in to school, Simon comes up to us.

'So, Rache,' he says, and I know she hates him shortening her name. 'Who's Shane Owens?'

Automatically, she looks at me.

Then he looks at me.

'A friend,' she says quickly. 'Why?'

'Hot guy.'

'So?' Rachel says.

'So, nothing. We'll all have to get together some time.'

'Why?' Rachel asks.

He shrugs. 'No reason. He just seems to know some cool people.'

Hot people, I think, miserably. Then I remember what Shane said. 'He's not the guy for you.' Somehow, that makes me feel better.

16
ALLERGIES

On Thursday, at my locker, I turn on my phone. There's a
voice message. I don't recognise the number. I put my finger
to my ear to block the noise of the locker room. I close my
eyes and try to hear the message. It's someone enquiring
about the pet-minding business. I rush over to Alex and
Rachel.

'A woman just called about minding her dog.'

'Brilliant. Call her back.'

'When I get home.' I want to prepare what to say and call
her on a landline. 'Ready to go?'

'Yup.'

On the DART, I start to make notes.

'What are you doing?' Rachel asks. I'm so not a note person.

'Trying to think of all the things I need to ask her.'

'The dog's name. What type of dog it is. How long she wants
him minded for. And when.' You'd know Alex had a dog.

'Hang on, slow down.'

'Has he any allergies?' Rachel asks.

We look at her and burst out laughing.

'He's a dog,' I remind her.

'OK, medical conditions, then.'

'OK.' I write it down.

'Remind her to bring his food, his bed, his lead,' Alex says.

'This is just an enquiry,' I say, not wanting everyone to get their hopes up. Especially mine.

'Ask if she wants to bring the dog to meet you,' Alex says.

'That's good,' I say looking at them. 'God, your businesses will be great.'

They look at each other.

'When we decide what they are.'

'I thought you were doing the blood pressure thing,' I say to Rachel.

'I don't know. I don't want to do it on my own.'

'I'll do it with you,' Alex says. 'It's easy, right?'

'Yeah, you just got to invest in the equipment,' Rachel says, sounding excited.

'No problem. We'll get it this weekend.'

'Cool.'

I call 'Betty'. When I ask if she wants to bring her dog over to meet me, she thinks I mean immediately. I don't want to put her off so have to go on a mad tidying spree and print out the questionnaire and legal document. When the doorbell rings, twenty minutes later, I take a deep breath to calm myself. I open the door. Oh my God, Betty's so cute. Tiny, like a little bird. Her anorak is the kind detectives wear. And I love that though she's old, she wears her purple beret at a tilt. She's carrying Paco in her arms. He's a chocolate-brown cross between I don't know what. One ear stands up more than the other. His eyes are full of personality and even more chocolate than the rest of him. His bum is white. I love him.

'Oh my God, he's gorgeous. Hello, Paco.' Then I remember my manners. 'Sorry. Come in.'

She does. 'Ooh you go to Strandbrook,' she says, looking at my uniform. 'I used to teach there.'

'Really?'

'Music.'

'Wow.' She puts Paco down and he hurries around checking the place out.

'Do you speak Spanish?' she asks. I squint at her. She smiles. 'Paco only understands Spanish. He grew up in Spain.'

'Cool,' I say, thinking my first pet will be international – if he *is* my first pet. 'I speak Spanish.' Just not very well. I learned it for a year when I was thirteen.

'Oh, goodie,' she says and I want to hug her.

I show her where I'd put his bed, his bowl and stuff. I show her the garden and how Paco would have plenty of room to run around but not get lost because it's walled. We let Paco out and he sniffs around. His tail is wagging.

'Look at him. He's at home already.' It's all going so well until she asks, 'So how long have you been running the business?'

I blush. 'Actually, Paco will be my first customer. I've just set up.' *She's going to back out*, I think.

'Wonderful,' she says, and claps her hands.

She asks about the money. I tell her the fee, then worry that it's too much. 'I could give you a reduction – for being my first customer.'

She looks at me. 'Not at all. Would you like money up front?'

}|{

'No, no. It's fine. Thank you. Whenever. After's fine.'

'Sure I'll give you half now and half later,' she says, like she's ordering a hit.

I smile.

As soon as she's gone, I call Alex and Rachel. Both their lines are engaged – which probably means they're talking to each other. I have to tell someone. Simon won't care. I run upstairs and go on Facebook. Shane is chatting, so I type: 'Got my first customer today :)'

'Let me guess, not a snake?'

'A dog. Speaks Spanish.'

'A talking dog?'

'*Understands* Spanish. Smart ass.'

'Congratulations :)'

'BTW, my friend thinks you look like Lenny Kravitz.'

'Really? Which friend?'

'Alex.'

'She thinks I look that good?'

'U do.' I'd never tell a guy he's good looking. That's what's great about Shane. The whole boy-girl thing never comes into it.

'Who'r u talking 2?' It's Simon.

'No one.'

'What?' Shane types.

Oh God, I've sent Simon's message to Shane. 'Sorry. Someone else is talking.'

'Who?'

'Boyfriend.'

'I'll go.'

'S'OK.'

He's gone. Oh my God. I called him 'no one'. Someone
kill me.

'Hello?' Simon types.

I'm in such shock, I get out of Facebook.

Later, though, I go back. To see if Shane is on.

He is.

'Hey,' I say. 'Soz about earlier. U didn't hav 2 go.'

'Yes I did. Lover boy wanted to talk.'

There's a pause.

'Has Lindsay Lohan had a nose job?' he asks.

'They say she had one in 2009 but no definite evidence –
well, apart from her nose. Go into Google Images and see
what you think.'

After a minute he's back. 'Definitely. See. You *are* making
me gay.'

I love the way he types out all the words. Like an adult.
'What u do tday?'

'Facebook. Back in touch with mates. Only so many
crackers a guy can make.'

'Anything worse than Christmas crackers in April?'

'Christmas crackers in January?'

'U sound like a cracker joke.'

'Is there a worse insult?'

'Eh, no.'

'Thought so.'

And I'm so relieved that I haven't hurt him.

17
JELLY TOTS

Friday morning and Miriam is at the breakfast table. She smiles and lifts her spoon in greeting.

'We'll have to stop meeting like this,' she says.

I don't know why but I'm suddenly convinced that she is actually married. I sneak a peek at her left hand. Hmm. No rings. No marks left by rings. Nothing.

'Nope,' she says, brightly. 'He hasn't popped the question.'

Oh my God.

'It's OK, I'm joking,' she says.

To hide my embarrassment, I reach for the Coco Pops then sit at the table.

'You know, you really should vary your diet. Growing girl like you.'

I look at her, surprised. 'Are you serious?' I laugh.

'This time, actually, yes.' She smiles again.

I pour my cereal and milk and for a while the only sound is my Coco Pops popping. I look at her, sitting there on her own.

'No offence, Miriam, but it's not, like, very gentlemanly of Louis to stay in bed while you get up.'

She smiles. 'There's nothing gentlemanly about Louis,' she says, like it's a compliment.

'I'll take your word for it.'

After school, I go to the home. Shane's outside. Wearing a woollen hat with flaps down the sides. There's a pom-pom at the end of each flap. It makes him look cheeky, like he doesn't give a shit. He sees me, breaks into a smile and waves. It's like he's been waiting for me.

'Hey,' I say when I get to him.

'Wanna go for a walk?' he says.

I look towards the building.

'It'll be OK,' he says.

'I'll just go tell Christina.'

'OK. I'll start off.'

Jesus. I run inside. Christina smiles when I tell her. She looks out the window at him disappearing up the avenue.

'This is great. He's never wanted to go out till now.'

I run back out and after him. He's half way up the avenue.

'Hey, thanks for waiting.'

'You're welcome,' he says, speeding up.

We leave the quiet, leafy avenue. The street outside is busy, traffic racing past. Normally I'd jaywalk. That's not going to work here. I look up and down the street. About a hundred metres up, there's a pedestrian crossing. The path dips on either side.

'Over there, I guess,' I say casually.

'Oh right, yeah,' he says. 'Then we can go down to the sea. Seems like ages since I've seen the sea.'

We cross no problem, then make our way along the path. It narrows at a bus stop and I let him go ahead. We turn

}|{

down left, to the sea. There's a shop on the corner, across the road. I'd love some Jelly Tots. But someone has thrown their car across the dip in the path. There's no way Shane could get across. So I leave it. We carry on. People have parked cars up on our path all the way along. He goes first, I follow. We make it to the end of the road and have to cross another. It's exhausting. I'm so not used to thinking where I walk.

'There's a pedestrian crossing,' I say.

'That's miles away. Here, you take the handles at the back, tilt the chair, I'll wheel across then you tilt again when we get to the other side.'

'Will you be fast enough?'

'Course I will.' He takes off across the road. 'If I'm not, they'll just have to wait.'

'Jesus,' I mutter.

He laughs. 'You should see your face.'

We cross and it's fine.

'Wow,' he says. 'This is amazing. Just to get *out*. Feel that *air*.'

Normally, I don't walk. I don't 'feel that air'. I don't look at the view. For the first time *ever*, I think I might be missing out on something. I breathe in the salty air. And do feel better. Finally, we get down to the sea. Shane stays on the path while I jump down onto the stones. I collect a handful and climb back up. I hand him most. Then from my own supply I start firing them, one by one, into the sea. Smiling, he does the same. Without anyone saying anything, it becomes a competition. I'm seriously losing. Some of my shots don't even hit the water. One goes backwards and nearly hits him.

'Oh, Jesus. Sorry.'

He laughs. 'Clearly you don't play tennis.'

}|{

'Clearly.'

'What do you play?'

'I don't.'

'You play no sport?' he says, like that's impossible.

'If you must know, I'm totally unco-ordinated.'

He laughs.

'What's so funny?' I ask, offended.

'Some pair we make.' He looks down at his legs.

I smile then, relieved. We give up on the stones and just stay watching a ship leave Dublin Bay.

'What would you do if you'd only a year to live?' he asks, kind of dreamy.

I look at him. 'Oh my God, I love these conversations.' They're the kind I'd have with Simon if he wasn't Simon.

'OK, first off, I'd fall in love.'

'I thought you *were* in love.'

'I mean properly.'

'So you're not properly in love?'

'Can we get back to the question?'

'We can.' He smiles.

'I'd get married, have a kid—'

'Hang on. Woah, slow down. You'd get married, have a kid, then drop dead? Wouldn't that be kind of tough on them?'

'You think too much.'

'Probably.' He smiles.

'OK, I'd quit school, travel the world. Skydive. Scuba dive. Seduce Robbie Williams.'

He laughs. 'You're definitely not in love.'

'I'd try every single bar of chocolate I haven't tried yet.' I look at him, suddenly curious. 'What about you? What would you do?'

'I'm still trying to figure that out.'

}{{

Speaking of love. 'Who's that girl all over your Facebook page?'

He loses his smile.

Oh, shit. 'I'm sorry. It's none of my business.' Why did I open my big mouth?

'It's Emma,' he says. 'My ex.'

I'm not going to ask what happened.

'She couldn't handle my diagnosis,' he says, looking at me with meaning.

'What diagnosis?'

'So they didn't tell you?'

'What?'

'I've motor neurone disease.'

'I don't know what that is.'

'Neither did I.' He smiles. He says nothing then. And just when I think he isn't going to, he explains. 'My muscles are wasting away. I'll be dead in one to five years.'

'What?' I ask, so quietly.

'You thought I was paralysed, didn't you?'

I can't speak.

'I'm not. My leg muscles are too weak to move.'

'But the rest of you is OK,' I say desperately. 'The rest of you is fine.'

'For now. It creeps up. Takes over. When it gets to your chest muscles, you can't breathe.'

I put my hand over my mouth.

He gives this big smile.

'Oh my God,' I say in relief. 'I thought you were serious. That is so not funny.'

'I *am* serious.'

I squint at him. 'Then how can you smile? How can you sit there and smile?'

'Are you angry with me?'

'No. I'm not angry with you. Of course I'm not angry with you.' I just feel like punching something. 'I just don't know how you're not screaming your head off.'

'I've been screaming my head off for the past three months – just silently. Now? I prefer talking to you. And, by the way, you're the one making me smile.'

I'm totally winded. He's going to *die*? 'I don't believe it,' I whisper.

'It takes time to sink in,' he says. 'But you get used to the idea. Eventually.'

I'll never get used to it. 'There must be a *cure*, something they can do.'

'Nope,' he says cheerfully.

'Research. There must be research going on …?'

'Oh there's research all right. Stem cell research. Early days. And controversial. I'll be in a jar on my folks' mantelpiece long before they find a cure.'

'Stop,' I say crossly. 'Don't joke.'

'You kind of have to.'

Oh God. I'm going to cry. I open my eyes wide and look left, then right to spread the tears.

'Hey. Don't go all Florency on me now.'

I force a smile. A single tear lands on his hand. 'Sorry,' I say, not just about the tear.

He winks. 'S'OK.'

No it's not, I want to say. It's terrible.

'Come on, let's get out of here,' he says.

We don't speak. All the way up to the shop. I'm thinking back. Rearranging everything in my mind. Now that I know the truth. No wonder he was at the window. No wonder he hated me, swanning in there with my two legs, with my *life*.

}|{

I thought he had it bad, in the wheelchair. I had no clue. And that girlfriend just cutting and running. What a bitch!

This time, we're on the right side of the road when I seriously need chocolate.

'Back in a minute,' I say. I rush in, get two slabs of Dairy Milk and two packs of Jelly Tots.

'I hope you paid for those,' he jokes.

'Very funny,' I say. Weird thing is, it's the first time I've been in a shop when I haven't thought about taking something. Yeah, well I'd things on my mind. I hand him a bar of chocolate and a pack of Jelly Tots.

'Jelly Tots? Wow. I haven't had Jelly Tots since I was a kid.'

'Trick is, don't chew, just let them melt on your tongue,' I say, like everything's normal.

'Thanks, Nigella.'

As we go back, I remember his question – what would I do if I'd a year to live. I remember his answer – 'still trying to figure that out'. I can actually feel my heart ache.

We get back to the home.

'You OK?' he asks me.

'Am *I* OK?'

'I should have told you sooner. But we were having such a laugh. I didn't want to ruin it.'

I nod.

'I'm sorry,' he says.

'I know.' I feel tears coming again. 'I'm gonna go, OK?'

'OK. See you Monday, I guess.' He looks like he's checking. Wondering. Unsure.

'Course you will.' But all I can think about is getting away.

18
HUNKY

Mum calls me for dinner. I don't come down. After a lot of calling, she comes up.

'Oh, sweetheart,' she says when she sees me. She hasn't called me sweetheart since I was, like, two. 'Is it Dad?'

I shake my head.

'Did something happen at school?'

After a few more questions, I just tell her. She sits on the bed beside me and brushes my hair back, over and over.

'He's such a nice guy, Mum. It's just so unfair.'

She says nothing, just strokes my head.

I look at her. 'We just don't have any problems, do we?'

She looks at me for a very long time. 'No, I guess we don't.'

We fall quiet. For ages, nothing. Just her hand moving over my head.

'Would you like to do something tonight?' she asks finally. 'We could catch a movie. Get a bite to eat.'

I've cancelled on Rachel and Alex, not up to going out. But this is something else, this is an offer from my mum, something that never happens. 'Really?'

And For Your Information . . .

}|{

'Really. Here, give me your hand.'

She pulls me up so fast, with such force, that I laugh.

'Come on,' she says. 'We've a lot of catching up to do.'

I look at her, and even though I'm so happy about that, I start to cry again.

We go to the romantic comedy I saw with Alex and Rachel. Mum wants to see it. And I liked it so much I don't mind watching it again. Why wouldn't I? The girl gets the guy.

It seems even better a second time, which is kind of weird for a romantic comedy.

'Whoa, that guy was seriously hunky,' Mum says, as we're walking out after.

I laugh. 'Hunky.'

'He was, though.'

He's like half her age.

'They're kind of predictable, though, romantic comedies,' I say, just to see what she says.

'Come on. You don't believe that!'

I smile, relieved. 'No. I guess not.'

We go to the Asian restaurant across the way. It's one I love. Casual and modern. We get a table on the balcony under the heaters. We look out at the giant fountain.

'How're you feeling?' she asks, reaching for a prawn cracker.

I remember why we're here. 'I just can't believe it.'

She sighs. 'Life can deal some pretty pissy cards sometimes.'

I look at her. Mum *never* curses. It makes me want to laugh. She takes a sip of wine. She who never drinks.

'How are you?' I ask.

'I'm good, Sarah.' She nods a few times. 'I'm really very

good.' She says it like someone recovering. Which, I guess, she is. 'It's good to be out like this, just the two of us. We've missed out on this.'

I shrug. 'Doesn't matter.'

'Actually, it does.' She takes a deep breath. 'I'd like to explain.'

'You don't have to.'

She lifts her napkin and fiddles with it. Then puts it down again. Looks up at me. 'I loved your dad, you know that. But we weren't good for each other, Sarah. I know that now. A person can lose themselves in a marriage, forget who they are. I didn't even realise it had happened to me. I had all this anger and didn't know why.' She looks at me. 'But now I'm beginning to remember who I was.'

'Someone who likes pizza and Coke and dogs and wine and cursing.'

She laughs. She reaches across the table and takes my hand.

'I love you, Sarah. Always have, even when I was at my worst.' She pauses and looks so suddenly sad. 'I'll never forgive myself for that slap. Never.'

'Well, I forgive you.' And I do. You just don't know what's going on in people's lives, even people right under your nose.

Before I go to bed, I go on Facebook, just to say goodnight.

'Night, night,' I type on his wall. Just so he knows I haven't headed for the hills, like his girlfriend.

Suddenly, he chats, 'Hey.'

'Hey.'

'You OK?' he asks.

'Yup.'

'What's your phone number?'

I tell him.

Then he calls.

'Hey,' he says again.

'Hey.'

'Bit of a shocker.'

'A bit.' I smile at the understatement.

'I should have told you sooner. I'm sorry.'

'Forget it.'

'The time never seemed right for a dramatic announce-ment.'

'I'm so sorry, Shane.'

There's a long pause. 'Sarah?'

'Yeah?'

'Don't pity me, OK? You're the one person who never has. If I lost that ...' He stops.

'You won't,' I say. But he already has. How can I not pity him? He's going to bloody die.

'So what are you up to?' he asks.

'My mum brought me out for a movie and a meal.'

'Cool.'

I take a deep breath, and decide to be honest with him. The way he's been honest with me. 'It hasn't always been. Cool, I mean. We've been kind of a mess, me and my mum.' I tell him everything – about Mum, about Dad leaving, about the mess that is our lives. It feels good to let it all out, let it all go.

When I finally stop talking, there's silence.

Then Shane says something very simple. 'I guess some people just weren't meant to be together.'

And at that exact moment, I think of Simon.

Next morning, Mary Gleeson asks how I am. And I can't answer honestly without telling her about Shane.

She listens very carefully and seems concerned. 'Is he speaking to someone, a therapist?'

'I don't know.'

'Because something like that is a lot to take on for anyone, especially someone so young.'

'I know.' I can't imagine what I'd do.

'What is his support like?'

'What d'you mean?'

'His parents. How are they with him?'

'I don't know.'

'Do you know why he's in the home?'

I'm confused. 'Isn't he supposed to be?'

'Well, he could live at home, if it was adapted for wheel-chair access.'

'I don't know,' I say again. And I'm beginning to think there's a lot about Shane I still don't know.

She looks at me for a long time. 'Do you think you can handle this, Sarah?'

'What d'you mean?'

'If you're finding it tough, I could recommend an alternative community service.'

'No.' God, no. I can't imagine not seeing him again. 'I just don't know what to say to him. How I should act. He doesn't want me to pity him, but how can I not? So, now I'm stuck. If I go see him, he'll know how I feel. If I don't, he'll think I've walked out on him, like his girlfriend did.'

She frowns while she thinks. 'OK, well,' she says at last, 'it seems to me like you've only one option if you want to keep seeing him. Treat him like you always have. With absolute honesty. Or it won't work.'

'You're right,' I say, then it hits me again, the fact that Shane is going to die. I hear my voice go high. 'You know, I thought I had it tough. Shoplifting? Big deal. Parents splitting up? So what? You know? You get one life. One life. And look what I'm doing with mine. Not talking to my dad – I know I'm angry with him but he's still my dad, he still loves me. And I know he drives me completely mad – but I do miss him. We could all die tomorrow, you know? Then there's Simon.'

'Simon?'

'My so-called boyfriend. Who I don't love. I mean, what's *that* all about?' She opens her mouth to speak but I keep going. 'I know what it's about. It's about not wanting to be on my own. Well, what's so wrong with being on my own? It's better than being with *him*. I mean, do I even *like* him?'

'Don't be so hard on yourself, Sarah. There was a reason you didn't want to be on your own. You saw what it was doing to your mum.'

I look at her, surprised. Could that be right? It sounds right. It also sounds subconscious-y. I look at her. And I get it finally. The whole psychology thing.

'I'm going to talk to my dad. I'm going to try again. At least listen to him. Yeah?'

She nods. 'Good.'

I stand up. 'Can we be finished for today? There's something I gotta do.'

She nods. 'Sure. I'll see you next week.'

When I leave Mary Gleeson's office, I get the DART to Dun Laoghaire. I make my way to Simon's apartment, knowing what I have to do. But as I near it, I start to feel guilty. He doesn't know what's coming.

He buzzes me up. And when he opens the door, I see that, for a change, his father is home.

'Let's go for a walk,' I say.

He stares at me. 'But you hate walking.'

So, maybe he picked up something about me after all. 'I feel like a walk today.'

'What's up?'

'I want to talk.'

'Sounds ominous,' he says, joking. 'I'll just go get my shoes.'

Suddenly, I wish he was being more difficult. I stand at the door, taking in, for the last time, the fabulousness of the penthouse.

He reappears. Then claps his hands. 'OK. Let's go.'

Going down in the lift, I feel so bad.

'So! What d'you want to talk about?' he asks.

Maybe I should wait. No. I have to do it now. If I don't, I never will.

'I can't do this anymore, Simon. This. Us.'

He stares. 'What are you talking about?'

How do you tell a person you're breaking up with them without implying they're not good enough? It's not you, it's me? No one believes that. So I go for the truth.

'Life's too short, Simon. If I can't have love, I don't want this.'

'What's that supposed to mean? You want me to love you?'

'No. I want to be in love.' I shrug.

The lift opens and he walks out. I follow. He turns suddenly, his eyes wide. 'It's *him*, isn't it?'

'Who?'

'Shane Owens.'

Oh my God. It would be funny if it wasn't so sad. 'It's nobody.'

'Then *why*?'

'I don't love you. You don't love me.'

'I like you,' he tries.

'*Do* you, though? *Do* you even like me?'

'Of course I do. What's *wrong* with you? This was never about love.'

'Maybe it should have been.'

'So you're just going to dump me?'

'Simon. You could have this with anybody.'

'Newsflash, Sarah. No one likes being dumped.' He goes quiet. He shoves his hands in his pockets, looks out the glass door of the empty lobby, then, finally, back at me. 'OK, for the record, can we say I ended it?'

I stare at him. Then think, *What the hell*? Because life really is too short. 'Say what you like.'

I walk home. Fast. Weirdly, I want to. With every step I take, I feel more relieved. Next time he flirts with someone, it won't be an insult to me. Next time he makes some stupid sexist comment on Facebook, it won't be my problem. I don't have to do anything, put up with anything, anymore, to hold on to him. Yaay. I feel so free.

When I get home, I go up to my room, change into my pyjamas and put on my Uggs. I want to stay in. Be myself. Not have to say wise and funny things for anyone, especially him. I lie on the bed. And am still. I don't look at my caliente wall. I don't go on Facebook. I don't text Rachel or Alex. Just look up through the Velux window at the blue,

blue sky and send a silent thank you to Shane.

Later, Mum calls me for lunch.

'Aren't you going out?' she asks, looking at my PJs.

'Nope.'

She looks surprised. 'Good to have a rest every now and again,' she says.

I sit with her at the table. I'm about to tell her how happy I am that I ended it with Simon, when I remember. She doesn't know about Simon.

'How did it go with Mary Gleeson?' she asks.

'Good. Yeah. Really good.'

'It's five weeks now since you started going. Maybe soon you'll be able to stop?'

'No, no. I like going.'

She looks surprised. Then says, 'It's good to talk, isn't it?'

I feel a bit sorry that I can't talk to her. Tell her everything.

'Would you mind if I went out tonight?' she asks.

'Mum, I would love you to go out.'

Later, I call my dad.

'Sarah?' He sounds surprised. 'Is everything OK?'

'Yeah. I was just wondering if you wanted to do something, like, together, sometime.'

A second. 'Sure. Absolutely. When?'

'I don't know. Maybe next weekend or something? I'm minding a dog for a few days, starting today.'

'You're minding a dog?'

'I'm running a pet-minding business.'

'Really?' He laughs. 'That's wonderful.'

'You don't like dogs, Dad.'

'No. But you do.' He clears his throat. 'So, would you like to go for a bite to eat?'

I think about that. Mum wouldn't have to cook. She could go out. 'OK, yeah. Thanks.'

'Great. It's a date. I'll call you during the week. How's everything going?'

'Fine, yeah, good.'

'Good, good. Excellent. So I'll give you a ring in the next day or two.'

'OK, thanks.'

19
CURLY WURLY

Paco arrives. And I start trying to remember my Spanish. I text Rachel and Alex to say he's here. They want to come over. Mum's been in such good form lately, I decide to risk it. I really do want them to see him.

It's hilarious. With all the attention he's getting, Paco has started acting like a celebrity, holding his head up and trotting around like he owns the place. He deserves celebrity status, though. He knows all the tricks. Fetching. Giving the paw. Rolling over. Like, hours of entertainment in one dog.

Mum, busy taking photos, is not acting like she thinks my friends are a bad influence. And I begin to relax about them being here.

Finally, we let Paco into the back garden to calm down. We've kind of made him hyper. We pour some juice and sit around for a while. Mum wanders off.

I tell them about Simon.

'You OK?' Rachel asks.

'Kind of relieved actually.'

'Was he OK about it?' Alex asks.

'Pretty much. No one likes being dumped, right?'

'That's true.'

'He wants to tell everyone he broke it off.'

'What? You're kidding!' Rachel says.

'I don't mind.'

'You're going along with it? Why?' She sounds like I've lost it.

I shrug. 'Life's too short.'

They look at each other like the world's flipped. I know why. My reputation used to be my big thing.

'Shane is going to die,' I say. I tell them everything. 'The thing that really pisses me off is the girlfriend. I mean what kind of person drops you when you get sick?'

'Maybe she didn't love him,' Alex says.

'Or maybe she's just a selfish cow,' I say. I look at Rachel. 'Would you stay with Mark?'

She nods. 'Yeah, I'd stay.'

I look at Alex. 'Would you?'

'Well, yeah, I would now. But early on, I don't know. Watching someone die kind of kills you, Sarah. I don't think you can judge a person until you're in that position.'

'I'd stay,' I say, 'if it was someone I loved.' I'm absolutely sure about that.

'No offence, Sarah, but you have a kind of romantic view of love. Sometimes it's hard, you know?'

I say nothing. What can I say? I've never been in love.

Monday morning, I'm at my locker. Simon walks past and ignores me.

Fine, I think. *Be like that.*

I wait for Rachel and Alex. Together we go to the Home

Economics room where we're due to start a week-long cookery course. We're late and everyone's pretty much there, huddled into the usual groups. Simon's talking to Amy and Orla. They look at me. It's like the subject of the conversation has just turned up. I feel like asking Simon a) when he turned into a girl and b) what age he is. But I just smile like I don't care.

The instructor turns up, someone from outside school. Incredibly good looking. Like Taylor Swift.

'Ten out of ten,' Simon says, loud enough for everyone to hear. It's like he's trying to be a lad, or something.

The instructor ignores him, introducing herself to the class with a voice like honey.

'What about your number?' Greg Black says.

'Grow up, Greg,' Mark says, like he's the mature one.

If we were in the wild, they'd be fighting over her.

She acts like she doesn't notice. She tells us she's going to teach us to make French toast. If she'd said we were going to climb Everest, she'd have every guy in the class queuing up. Including Mark. She wants us to cook in pairs and chooses those pairs alphabetically. I'm with Amy.

Great, I think as she walks over. Her smile is mean and there's something behind it. So I ignore her, just watch Taylor Swift show us how to make French toast.

'Lick your fingers,' Greg whispers. 'Go on, lick your fingers.'

I'm about to turn round and tell him to shut up when Amy whispers one word. 'Slag.'

'Excuse me?'

'I can't believe you two-timed Simon.'

'What?' Oh my God. 'Is that what he said?'

'The guy's on your Facebook page, Sarah.'

I stare over at Simon. Does he really think I'm going out with Shane? Or is he just making this up to get at me? One thing: I feel no loyalty to protect his story now.

'Look, Amy, believe what you want. But, for the record, I ended it with Simon. Because Simon is Simon. Not because there was anyone else involved.'

'He said *he* ended it,' she says, like she doesn't believe me.

'Simon says a lot of things. Doesn't mean they're true.'

In the canteen, the rumour spreads. It comes back to us via Mark, who joins our table to warn me.

'It's OK. I know. He thinks I'm going out with this friend of mine.'

'Who?' Rachel and Alex ask together.

I shrug. 'Shane.'

They stare at me.

'We talk on Facebook so we're, like, going out or something.' I roll my eyes.

'Who's Shane?' Mark asks.

'Oh just this friend from outside school.' I don't mention the wheelchair or the home because they do not sum up my friendship with Shane.

'But that's crazy,' Alex says.

I don't know if it's crazy because she knows I wouldn't two-time someone or crazy because Shane's in a wheelchair. Or both.

'You better do something,' Rachel says.

I look over at Simon, the idiot. 'He'll get tired of it.'

'He mightn't,' Rachel says.

'Then people will get tired of listening. 'I mean, what

more is there to say? He ended it because I two-timed him.
End of story.'

'Yeah but it *is* a story. It is a lie.'

'And it's your reputation,' Alex says.

'No one's dying, though, are they?'

Alex looks at me for a long time. 'You've changed,' she
says, like it's a good thing.

I was worried how I'd be with Shane, but when I see him
waiting for me outside the home with his cap on like it's just
a good day for a walk, I know it's going to be OK. I smile
and wave.

'Yo,' he says.

'Yo, yourself.' And I just want to hug him.

'Ready to go?' he asks.

'Sure. You checked with Christina?'

'Yep.'

'Cool.'

We're off.

'Can't stay too long today,' I say. 'I've got to get back to
Paco.'

'You see, with a snake you wouldn't have that problem.'

'No. I'd have the frozen mouse problem.'

'They're frozen. What can they do?'

I smile and am so glad to be here, chatting like normal.

'So any news?' he asks.

'Actually, yeah. I ended it with Simon.'

He looks at me and smiles. 'Excellent move.'

'Feels like it.'

'Was he devastated?'

'No.' I think about school. 'But no one likes being
dumped, right?'

He stares ahead like he's remembering something.

Suddenly, I'm angry. 'I can't believe your girlfriend left just because you got sick.'

He stops wheeling and looks at me. 'I ended it with Emma.'

He did? 'Why?'

'What kind of life would it have been for her, watching me shrivel away?'

'Yeah but you didn't have to end it. You could have let her decide to stay or go.'

'She'd have stayed – out of guilt. I didn't want that. So don't blame her. It was my idea.'

'She didn't have to listen to you. She could have kept showing up, kept coming, climbed up on that chair of yours and snogged you to death until you changed your mind.'

He laughs. 'Is that what you'd do?'

'If I loved the person. Absolutely.'

He looks at me. 'You're a good person.'

'You know I'm not.'

'I know you are.'

I smile. He has this incredible knack of making me feel good about myself.

We stop at the shop for treats. I take a photo of him eating a Curly Wurly. He looks so cheeky with the hat and everything.

'Can I put it up on Facebook?' I ask. He makes a face. I show him the picture. 'Come on, it's a great shot.'

'All right, go on then.'

Back at the home, Christina asks Shane if he's got her pen.

'Oh God, sorry, I left it in my room. I'll go get it.'

'Can I come?' I'd love to see his room.

It's beige and modern and spacious with big windows and an en suite. It's kind of calm or something? But it could be anyone's. No posters. No gadgets. Nothing to show it's his.

'It's nice,' I say.

He shrugs. 'It's home.'

I remember what Mary Gleeson said, but I don't ask about his family and why he's not with them.

'Hey. I'm glad I told you.'

I smile. 'Me too.' I put my hand on his so he knows it makes no difference.

'Wow, you just made history.'

'How?' I smile.

'You're the first non-medical person to touch me since I got sick.'

I lose the smile.

'People are afraid I'll break. Or something.'

I look him in the eye and squeeze his hand. Hard. 'I'm not afraid.'

20
CONSUELA

It's lovely to come home to a welcome. Paco's jumping up on me and barking, his tail lashing around. We go out to the garden and play. For ages. I brush him, give him fresh water and food, then decide I better get rid of the doggy smell and all his hairs or it might be the end of my business. I open all the windows and take out the hoover. Paco trots around beside me. Little pal.

I finish up. Now that the floor's clean, though, the rest of the place looks manky. I get out the Pledge. It reminds me of Consuela in *Family Guy*.

I look at Paco. 'We have no more Lemon Pledge,' I say in a Mexican accent.

He goes mental, barking and jumping, like he knows I'm messing. Genius dog.

He follows me up to my room. (It'll be our little secret.) I upload all my recent photos onto Facebook. I put him on my lap and show him himself. Then I click on the photo of Shane.

'This is the person I talk to when I get in from school,' I say. It's been so great coming home to Shane every day, instead of an empty house. He's the one person I can talk to, be myself with – totally. He knows everything about me and it's, like, so what? He wants me to be blunt, not careful, around him, say whatever pops into my mind. And I do. Funny thing is, when I'm not being cautious, I make less mistakes. I've never had this kind of friendship with a guy before. I never thought it possible. I can't believe what I've been missing.

I check to see if he's on chat – and am disappointed when he isn't. He's probably having dinner, I decide. And anyway, we've seen each other already today.

I get up and fuss over Paco. I try to teach him to play dead but it's a bit tricky. In the end, I give up and lie on the floor beside him. I look around my room. And think of Shane's. And how bare it is. Then I'm running downstairs to get one of the high stools. I lug it upstairs. Then I climb up on it and start to take down some of the luminous stars from my ceiling. I also remove the crystal that hangs in my Velux window and breaks the light into tiny rainbows. I wrap them up and put them in my school bag.

Later I'm at the kitchen table, trying (genuinely) to study, when Mum comes in late. Paco runs to her. She bends down and smiles at him.

'Look at you. Look, at, you,' she says in the kind of voice you use with babies, 'giving me a big welcome home.' She looks up at me, still smiling. 'Have we any treats for him? What are you smiling at?'

'Nothing.' She's turning into such a softie. I give her the bag of treats. She throws him one. He jumps, four legs in the air, and catches it. Mum looks at me as if to say, 'did you see that?' Then she notices the kitchen.

'Have you been cleaning?'

'A bit.'

Her face softens. 'Aw, thanks, Sarah. That was really thoughtful.'

I know why I cleaned up and feel a bit guilty. 'Why don't you go up and have a shower or something and I'll make some French toast for dinner?'

'Can you *make* French toast?'

'We learned in school today. It's pimps.'

She looks at me like I've changed. Which is funny because she's the one who's changed. 'What a treat. Thank you.'

She heads off.

I put on some sounds and get out the eggs. And it's so lovely, just pottering around with the dog at my feet. I make a salad to go with the French toast. By the time Mum comes back, I've everything set out on the table.

'This looks amazing.' She kisses the top of my head (wow!) then sits beside me and looks down at Paco.

'So. How's our baby?'

I smile at the 'our'. 'He's gorgeous. I want to keep him.'

'Me too.'

Next morning, at my locker, Simon walks up to me. He reaches up to the top of my door and holds it. He's towering over me. I take a step back.

'What?'

'See you've got a new photo on Facebook.'

'I've loads of new photos on Facebook.'

'You know the one I mean.'

'Actually, I don't.' But I do. I collect my books in my arms. 'Could you take your hand off please? I need to close my locker.'

He takes his hand away. I lock up.

He's still there. 'You could have waited,' he says.

'For what?'

'You didn't have to sneak around behind my back. You could have ended it first.'

'What are you talking about?'

'That guy, Shane.'

'Oh my God, Simon. Shane is a friend. When are you going to get that?' I could tell him that Shane's in a wheelchair and that would be the end of it. But I'm not doing that to Shane.

'I'm not stupid,' he says. 'It's not Rachel he talks to on Facebook. It's you.'

I shrug. 'If you don't want to believe me, then don't believe me. There's nothing I can do about it.'

'You'll be sorry.'

'I'm already sorry – that I went out with you.'

'Ooh burn,' says Rachel, coming up to stand by me.

He walks off.

'Oh my God,' I say. 'How did I ever go out with him? Seriously?'

'He's got worse, Sarah. He really wasn't that bad.' I know she's just being kind. 'Come on,' she says. 'We better go.'

We look over at Alex. She's at her locker, staring into space. We go over.

'Don't tell me you missed that?' Rachel says.

'What?' she asks like we've woken her up.

We look at each other. She missed the whole thing.

'Come on,' I say, wanting to forget about it.

We're walking from the locker room when one of the nerds comes up to us.

'You're so right, Sarah.'

I squint. 'What?'

'That guy. On Facebook. So much more caliente than Simon.'

I think two things. Oh my God. They're starting to use 'caliente'. And when is this going to end?

On the way home on the DART, we're coming to my stop. I stand up.

'So, I'll see you later,' I say to Alex.

She looks like she's coming out of a coma. 'Sorry?'

'Aren't we going to walk Paco and Homer?'

'Oh God. I'm sorry. I'd totally forgotten.' She looks like she's thinking. 'Can we do it another time? I'm kinda tired.'

I shrug. 'Sure.'

I see Rachel looking at her. But neither of us says anything.

I go home. First thing I do is let Paco out. Second thing is remove Simon as a friend on Facebook. Normally, I'd talk to Shane but, after being in all day, Paco really needs a walk. I put on his lead and we're off. He trots along and though he doesn't say anything (obviously) he's great company. Peaceful, or something. We walk for ages. When we get back, we do our tidy-up routine. I hoover. Paco provides the backing vocals.

I go up to my room to chat with Shane. I plan to make it quick, though, because the exams are now only weeks away.

We start to chat and end up on the phone. He tells me that some of his mates called round to say hi.

'That's great,' I say, so happy that he's hooking up with them again, hooking up with his old life.

'It *was* good to see them. But they didn't know what to say.

It was awkward. None of the usual stuff we talk about came up – rugby, girls – and I'm pretty sure it's because I can't do any of that anymore. I should have just invited Peter.'

'Peter?'

'My closest mate, I guess. We go back. He's pretty cool with illness and stuff. His little sister has cerebral palsy.'

I don't ask what that is because I've enough with motor neurone disease.

'So how are you?' he asks.

'Yeah, OK. Simon's being a bit of a prick. He thinks I was two-timing him.' I decide to just admit it. 'With you.'

He bursts out laughing. 'Does he know I'm in a wheel-chair?' he asks, like he's still amused.

'He doesn't know anything about you except that you're my friend on Facebook.'

'Hilarious,' he says.

'It's not that hilarious.' I tell him about the way Simon's been going on.

'Just tell him I'm in a wheelchair.'

'No. It's none of his business. And anyway, a wheelchair wouldn't stop me going out with a person.' I hear Mum coming in downstairs and can't believe we've been talking so long. 'Listen, I gotta go and do some study. I'll talk to you tomorrow, OK?'

'OK, sure. But don't take any shit from that guy.'

'I won't,' I say. And mean it. I feel so much more deter-mined after talking to Shane.

I go to my desk and take out my books. I try French. For ages. But nothing's going in. The words dance on the page in front of me like they're playing with my mind. I switch to Maths. Disaster. I try English – for at least an hour. Finally,

I take a break and go down to play with Paco.

Only I can't find him.

In the TV room, he's snuggled up on Mum's lap. I laugh. 'I was wondering where he was.'

She looks down and strokes him. 'He's a cute little fellow, isn't he?'

'Gorgeous. What're you watching?' She never watches telly.

'*Desperate Housewives*. Thought I'd see what all the fuss is about.' She looks at me, like she's surprised. 'It's good.'

'I know.' I sit on the couch beside her.

We watch in silence. I don't remind her about dinner. I can make a sandwich later. Every so often I peek at her. She looks so chilled, her hand constantly petting Paco. She's changed so much. But then I think, *maybe she hasn't changed at all. Maybe she's finally herself again.*

Next day, Alex is really pale. I notice the minute I get on the DART.

'Are you OK?' I ask.

She nods. There are black rings under her eyes. 'Just didn't sleep.'

Rachel looks at me like something's up. She says nothing.

For the whole day Alex is quiet. Miles away. At lunch, she doesn't eat. She says she's fine.

'How's David?' Rachel asks.

'Fine,' she says but looks like she's going to cry. Suddenly, she gets up and hurries out.

We exchange a worried glance.

'I hope they're OK,' Rachel says.

'D'you think they'd a fight?'

'I don't know.'

'Maybe she's just missing him.'

'Then why doesn't she say so?'

'Point.'

We know Alex too well to go after her. So we wait. She doesn't come back till the bell goes and it's time to return to class. Her eyes and nose are red. She smiles but I'm not fooled. No one says anything. Because there's no point. Alex is the most private person I know.

Today, Taylor Swift has us making shepherd's pie. I'm just thinking how disgusting the mince looks when Alex passes out. Just drops to the floor. Rachel and me are the first to her. We drop to our knees beside her.

'Turn her on her side,' Rachel says. She moves fast, turning Alex over and bending her leg up so she doesn't roll back over.

I take off my jumper and put it under Alex's head.

'OK, stand back everyone,' Taylor Swift says. 'She needs air.' She loosens Alex's tie and opens the top two buttons of her shirt. 'Someone wet a clean dishcloth and bring it to me. Quickly.'

One of the nerds actually moves. It's weird to see her go.

Taylor puts the damp cloth on Alex's forehead.

'I'm fainting tomorrow,' I hear Simon say. I turn around and glare at him.

He makes his eyes big.

I roll mine.

'Hey,' Rachel says, gently.

I turn around. Alex's eyes are open. Rachel's smiling.

'You had a little faint,' Taylor says. 'How're you feeling now?'

Alex tries to get up.

Taylor puts a hand on her arm. 'Stay there a moment.'

}|{

'Your blood pressure's probably low,' Rachel adds.

I look at her and think, *cardio-thoracic surgeon here we come.*

Even though she argues (fiercely), Alex has to go home. We wait with her in the office until her dad comes. Then it's back to shepherd's pie. I don't think I'll ever eat the stuff again. When school's finally over, I hurry to get my stuff from my locker. I'm so worried about Alex, I forget about Simon. Until he puts his hand on the door of my locker. Again. Seriously, I'm going to have to stop using it.

'Why did you remove me as a friend on Facebook?'

Oh my God, what is he, a stalker? 'Simon, go away.'

'When you answer my question.'

'Why do you *think* I removed you? You haven't exactly been *acting* like a friend.'

'You dumped me. Amn't I allowed be a little bit pissed?'

'You've been dissing me to anyone who'll listen.'

'You were playing around.'

'You know I wasn't.'

'No. I don't.'

I don't even ask him to take his hand off – I just jerk the door and it falls off. Then I slam it shut and lock it. 'I'm not going there, OK?' I push past him. Rachel's waiting. We walk off together.

'Want me to get Mark to talk to him?' Rachel says.

'No. It's fine. He'll get bored eventually.'

But all the way home, my stomach's in a knot. I wish I'd never gone out with him. I wish he'd leave me alone. I get home and Paco rushes to me like a best buddy. He's going mental, jumping up, whining in excitement, wagging his tail. I burst into a smile and bend down. He launches himself into my arms. I laugh and carry him into the kitchen, talking to him all the way.

'Did you miss me? Did you miss me?'

He licks my nose. I put him down and open the back door. He rushes out but straight back in again when he realises I haven't gone with him. God, he's so cute. I put the cleaning on hold and go get his ball. I can't believe it's our last day together.

After I've fed and walked Paco, I text Alex to see if she's OK. She calls me back.

'I'm fine. I don't know what all the fuss was about,' she says crossly. 'I didn't need to go home.'

'You sure you're OK? You've been kind of pale lately and stuff.'

'What stuff?'

'I don't know, kind of miles away.'

She says nothing.

'Maybe you should take tomorrow off. Just in case.'

'Sarah. I'm fine. I'll be in school tomorrow.'

'OK. Cool.'

'How's Paco doing?'

'Going home tonight.'

'Already?' She sounds sorry.

'I know I'm really going to miss him.'

'We'll just have to get some more posters up.'

'You sure you're OK?'

'I'm sure. Say bye to Paco for me.'

I close the door behind Paco and Betty. I walk into the hall, then throw the three twenties up in the air. I scream and do a little dance. I know I charged it, I still can't believe I earned it. When Mum comes home, I hand her a note. She looks at it.

'I'm not taking that.'

'It's your house. You looked after him too.'

'It's *your* business.'

'Yeah but—'

'But nothing. I'm not taking your hard-earned cash. You did a great job, you Young Entrepreneur, you. I'm so proud of you, Sarah.'

And maybe it's sad how much that means. I look down at the money, then up again, smiling. Par-tay.

Next day, after school, I get off the DART in Dun Laoghaire and go on a shopping spree. In Boots, I get mascara for Alex and Rachel and, because there's a promotion, a free one for myself. It's a new brand we've been waiting for. I can't believe I'm the first to get it – and for everyone. I get lilies for Mum (she loves lilies). I buy a pair of novelty shades for Louis in Penney's (to thank him for that twenty). Shane is a toughy. I try to think of what I'd want if I was in a home. A break from routine. McDonald's! I get him a Big Mac, large fries and a large Coke. Then, so it doesn't go cold, I have to get a taxi to the home.

He's not in the day room, so I go to his room. I'm about to knock, when the door opens. I'm standing with my fist in the air when a woman appears in front of me. A crying woman. Oh God. I stand back. She walks out, a man behind her. In the corridor, he puts an arm around her and they walk out together. The man is a well-known TV presenter. His surname is Owens. I can't believe Shane never said.

I'm still standing there, watching them leave, when Shane

}|{

comes to close the door. He looks so serious, so sad. Then he sees me and says, 'Oh.'

'I'll go.'

'No … Come in. It's OK.'

'It's not a good time.'

'Is that McDonald's?'

I hold up the bag. 'Got paid for my first job.'

'Well, then, what are you waiting for? Let's celebrate.'

We go in. I hand him the bag.

'What about you?' he asks.

'Not hungry.' Actually, I've run out of cash.

He takes out the burger and offers it to me anyway.

'No thanks, seriously. I got it for you.'

He bites into it. And closes his eyes. When he opens them again, he says, 'I can't believe I forgot how good McDonald's is.'

'Sorry for barging in.'

'You didn't barge.'

'Your parents, right?'

He watches the door like he can still see them leave. 'Yup.'

I just nod. Don't ask.

'They want me to come home,' he volunteers.

So I feel I can ask, 'Why don't you?'

He shrugs. 'They don't need this.'

'But if they asked …'

He shakes his head. 'I used to make them proud, Sarah. Now look at me.'

'They still love you.'

'They'd have to change the place for me.'

'So?'

'I'll be dead in a year.'

'You don't know that. Some people live for five. And then there's Stephen Hawking who's lived forty years with motor neurone disease.'

'So who's been on Google?' he asks smiling. Then he's serious again. 'I'm working off fourteen months, Sarah, the average lifespan for someone with this.'

I ignore that. 'I bet your parents would give anything to have you home.'

'I used to have a future, Sarah. I was going to be an architect. I was going to pay my way, pay them back for everything. They've done enough. They don't need this.'

I remember his mum's face. 'Can't you let *them* decide that?'

He looks away. 'Can we drop it?'

'Why do you keep telling people what to do – your girlfriend, your parents ... me.'

'Thanks for the McDonald's,' he says.

'You're welcome.'

We fall silent.

I want to say something. Anything. 'Architecture ... You must be pretty brainy.'

He shrugs. 'I used to be.'

'Motor neurone disease doesn't affect the brain. You're still smart. Do you have a portfolio?'

He shrugs. 'At home.'

'I'd love to see it.'

He says nothing.

'So what buildings do you like?'

'You're not going to give up, are you?'

'Nope. What buildings?'

He sighs. 'The Sydney Opera House. The Guggenheim in

New York. And, I guess, the art deco library in Ringsend.'

I nod, trying to memorise them. I decide not to give him the stars or the crystal. Not yet.

Mum loves the flowers.

'They're only Tesco,' I say.

'They're beautiful.' Immediately, she takes out a vase and starts to arrange them.

'The house is so quiet,' she says, looking up. 'You really miss him, don't you?'

I should tell her. 'I called him, Mum. We're meeting at the weekend.'

'I presume you're talking about Dad,' she says with a smile. 'Aren't *you*?'

'No. I was talking about *Paco*.' We laugh, but then she gets this sad, dreamy look like she's remembering that her marriage has broken up.

'You did the right thing, Mum, making him choose.' I've been blaming her for so long – when actually what she did was really brave – making herself the bad guy.

'I don't know, Sarah. If I hadn't made him choose, he'd still be here for you.'

'Maybe not. He could have left anyway. Even if he hadn't, it would have been a lie. And you'd have still been angry. And lost. It's better now. Really it is. Because it's not fake. And you can be you.'

She smiles. 'Thank you. For understanding.'

'You're welcome!' I smile brightly. Because I know, suddenly, she's going to be OK.

21
STARS

'You left in a pretty big hurry last week,' Mary Gleeson says. Her smile doesn't seem fake any more. And her curiosity doesn't make me feel like running.

'I ended it with Simon.'

'And how are things?'

'Better.' I tell her, for the first time, all the stuff I put up with to stay going out with him. I take a deep breath. 'I can't believe I was so needy.'

'But you've changed, Sarah. And well done you.'

For a while we're silent and it's nice because her last words kind of hang there.

'So, outside that, how've you been?'

I tell her about Paco. 'Thank you so much. If it wasn't for you, I'd never have asked my mum.'

'Did she mind having a dog in the house?'

'That's the amazing thing. She loved it. She adored Paco.' I smile. 'She didn't want him to go.'

'How's your mum doing in general?'

'So good.' I look at her because I'm about to admit

something I've never before admitted. 'I was so upset when they split up. I mean devastated. I know that people split up all the time, but it felt like the end of the world. I didn't want to talk about it. I especially didn't want to think about it. But seeing Mum become herself again, I don't know, it makes me think that maybe it's not the end of the world after all. Maybe it's better for her. She's not angry. She's doing things she likes to do. She's so much nicer and easier to live with.' I shrug. 'It's weird. But good weird.'

'That's wonderful, Sarah. And you're talking more?'

'Yeah. Definitely. I mean not total heart-to-heart conversations or anything. But it used to be just her asking about homework and stuff. Now we actually talk.'

She nods and smiles. And says, 'wonderful,' again, almost to herself. Then she looks at me. 'And your dad? You were going to contact him?'

'He's bringing me for lunch later.'

'Don't expect too much. Bit by bit. Slowly, slowly.'

'OK.' It's weird how confident I am in her advice now.

'And the shoplifting?'

I'm almost offended she's brought it up. Which makes me want to laugh. When we started, that's the only thing I wanted to talk about, the shoplifting. I look at her, so amazed at how everything's changed.

'I don't even think about it any more.'

She smiles. 'I knew that. But you understand I had to ask?'

I nod. And think how amazing she is.

'So, a pet-minding business,' Dad says, like he's impressed.

He's brought me to this really nice seafood restaurant in Monkstown, though I told him McDonald's would be fine. I tell him about Paco. And, for a while, it's easy between us.

}|{

But then I run out of things to say.

'So, how's the community service going?' he asks.

'Good.'

He takes a bite of the bread and chews. Finally, he says, 'I wonder if you've done enough?'

I think of Shane. 'No! I like it. I want to keep doing it.'

'OK. Cool.'

Cool? My dad? I squint at him. 'What is she like?' I ask before I can help it. 'No. Forget it. I don't want to know.'

He says nothing.

I look at him. 'You and Mum weren't good for each other, were you?'

He gawps at me like he doesn't know what to say.

'She's happier now,' I add.

'She said that?'

'No. But she is. She's taking in dogs. Eating pizza. Going to romantic comedies. Watching *Desperate Housewives*. She's doing what she wants to do. Not what *you* want her to do.'

He looks shocked. 'Is *that* what she said?'

'No.'

He looks confused.

'She lost herself when she was with you.'

He looks even more confused.

'She doesn't blame you, by the way.'

'OK.'

'And it's better at home now.' I butter a piece of bread. 'Actually, it's pretty good.'

Monday morning, on our way to class, without warning, Alex dashes into the loo. Rachel looks at me.

I shrug.

'Better wait,' she says.

A few minutes later, Alex comes out smelling of sick. She smiles like nothing's wrong.

'Have you just been sick?' I ask.

'A tiny bit. I rushed my breakfast.'

Rachel eyeballs her. 'Alex. You're sick. Go home.'

'I'm fine.'

'You don't look fine,' Rachel says firmly.

All of a sudden Alex's eyes well up.

'Oh God, Alex, what is it? What's wrong?' I ask.

'Nothing.' She takes her books back from Rachel. 'Come on.'

With no other option, we follow.

Class starts. Twenty minutes later, Alex rushes out. We look at each other. Then Rachel gets up and walks out after her. The teacher looks at the door that's just closed behind her.

'Where are they off to?' she asks, looking at me.

'Alex is sick,' I say. And I can't believe how much you can get away with when you actually go for it. You think teachers are going to explode – and then they don't. I'd get up myself but I know Alex. Me being there would only make it worse.

Fifteen minutes later (I'm checking), Rachel comes back on her own. She tells the teacher that Alex has gone home sick.

'Is she OK?' I ask as she passes me.

'Yeah, she's OK.'

And straight away I know. There's something she's not telling me.

*

}{{

Later, when I get to the home, Shane's busy with more Christmas crackers. I sit with him. It's automatic now.

'What's up?' he asks, after a while.

'Hmm? Nothing.'

'Come on. You can't keep things from Uncle Shane. Uncle Shane knows when something's up. Uncle Shane notices *everything*.'

I sigh. 'It's nothing, really. Just that sometimes I feel a bit left out.' I tell him about Alex and Rachel.

'Hang on. How do you know Alex told Rachel what was wrong?'

'I just knew by her when she came back from the loo.'

'But you weren't actually there. So, Alex couldn't have told you if she'd wanted to.'

'Yeah but Rachel could have. And she didn't. She'd plenty of time before school ended. Like, maybe Alex asked her not to.' And that hurts so much.

'Or *maybe* because Alex wants to tell you herself?'

I feel a bit better. 'Do you think so?'

'I don't know, but she'll probably be in tomorrow.'

And just like that, I feel like hugging him. 'Thanks.' I get up. 'I'll be back in a sec,' I say, like I'm going to the loo. I grab my bag.

I go to his room, take out the crystal and hang it next to the window. Like magic, the sun comes out from behind a cloud and rainbows appear all over the room. I smile. Then I get the stars. I stand on his bed and stick them to the ceiling. And now for the grand finale. I take out pictures of his favourite buildings that I found on Google Images, blew up, printed off and put into glass frames that I got cheaply once (on a trip to Ikea with Alex and Rachel). I turn around and there he is, watching me.

'I can't believe you did that,' he says, his voice all soft.

I shrug. 'No biggie.'

'It is to me.' He comes in. 'Thank you.'

I wave it away. 'So, have you got your portfolio?'

He smiles, then wheels to the cupboard and pulls out a huge, black, leather portfolio. He passes it to me.

'Cool.' I sit on the bed and zip it open, dying to see what's inside.

'Oh my God, this is amazing.'

'No it's not.'

'Shut up. You know it is.' There are loads of brilliant designs. A kids' crèche and playground. A pool area for a posh hotel. A school canteen.

'You're so talented.'

'No I'm not.'

This time I just give him a look. I go back to the portfolio. I could look at it all day. There's so much detail in each drawing.

'What do *you* want to do?' he asks.

I look up.

'When you're *big*,' he jokes.

I feel bad. I have a life and don't know what to do with it. 'I'm not sure I'll have much choice.'

'Why not?'

'You're looking at the classic dumb blonde here.'

'There's nothing classic about you.'

'It was the dumb I was worried about.'

He smiles. 'You are so not dumb.'

I tell him about my problem with studying and exams – and what will happen if I don't improve.

}|{

'So you're just going to have to improve.'

'Yeah, just like that,' I say sarcastically.

'What's your best subject?'

'I'm not totally hopeless at French.'

'Ooh, the confidence.' I make a face at him. 'What's your worst?'

'Business.'

'Do you fail?'

'Regularly. I just don't get Business.'

'You're running one.'

Oh, yeah, I think. I *am* running a business. 'That's different, though. It's practical. I learn nothing useful in Business. Nothing you'd use in a real business. So I can't remember anything.'

'Then give it up. Take another language if that's what you're good at. Spanish is easy. I could give you grinds.'

Ooh, I like the sound of that. 'I did Spanish in First Year.'

'Well then.'

'Mum wants me to do Business.'

'Why?' he looks baffled.

I sigh. 'She has this thing about independence. Especially since Dad left. She probably wants me to run my own business some day or something.' I feel suddenly tired.

'Still. You didn't think she'd let you run a pet-minding business. And she did. So ask her, she might surprise you.'

'So you think I should do Spanish instead?' And I don't know whether it's because I'm upset with Rachel and Alex, or that I just like being with Shane, or both, but suddenly I love the thought of spending more time with him. Even if it would be to study.

'It's easy. And you're good with languages. You've nothing to lose. Except having to do Business.'

I imagine what a relief that would be. 'Thanks, Shane.'
'For what?'
I shrug. 'Helping, I guess.'
He looks at me. 'I haven't done anything yet. But do you know how good it would be to help?' He looks down at his legs. 'Since this happened, all the help has been one way.'
And I want so much to hug him.

That night, getting ready for bed, I get a text.
'Have you seen the stars tonight?'
I smile, turn off the light, lie back on my bed and look up at the ceiling, at the missing spaces left by stars that I know he's looking at now. It feels like we're connected.
'Night, night :)'

When I get on the DART next morning, Alex and Rachel are deep in conversation. It stops the minute they see me. Rachel smiles.
'Hey,' she says.
I think of electrons and outer shells. I want to sit somewhere else, tell them they can have their secret. But they're my best friends. And I love them. So I pretend that I don't notice that I'm on the outside again.
No one says much for the rest of the way. When we get to class we go straight to our desks. I'm fiddling with my pen when I feel the atmosphere change. I look up. Amy has just walked in. On Simon's arm. She looks up at him like he's some kind of superhero. He stands tall. Chest out. On display. I think two things: They deserve each other and maybe now he'll get off my case. Then I think of a third thing: She looks like a puppet, with her long, rectangular face, square chin and

}|{

slash of a mouth. He's going out with a puppet. They get the usual slagging, which just makes them smile wider. Amy looks at me like she's won. I think, *Just wait*.

After school, I'm feeling pretty low. All I want to do is go see what now feels like my one true friend.

'Hey,' he looks pleasantly surprised. 'What are you doing here?'

'Sorry, didn't you say you'd help me study? You're not backing out, are you?'

He smiles. 'Never.'

'I convinced Mum. I'm doing Spanish.'

'*Bueno*! There's your first word.'

'Come on, Shane. Even *I* know that one!'

Every day, after school, I call to see Shane. On Thursday, Rachel asks, 'You going to the home *again*?'

'Yeah. So?'

'Nothing.'

But it's like they've got the world sussed. And I haven't.

Shane, as usual, makes me feel better. With him, I don't even mind studying. Actually, it doesn't even feel like study. YouTube has Spanish lessons. French lessons. Stuff on history. And I don't know why but it seems to go into my head when it's not coming out of a teacher's mouth or a book. It's not all study, though. We play games on Miniclip. We watch music videos. Movies. *Family Guy*. It's such a relief to escape that left-out feeling, to be away from Simon and Amy and their stupid looks. And to be able to tell someone about all of that. Someone who actually cares.

22
CELERY

'Sarah, I know you've waited a long time to hear this, but I think our work here is done.' Mary Gleeson shocks me with this on Saturday morning.

I look at her, suddenly nervous. 'Are you sure?' I need her.

'We go on any longer and you'll come to depend on me. You don't want that.'

'I know, but ...'

She smiles. 'You're not shoplifting. You've come to terms with your parents' separation. And you are very much in control of your life.'

'I sound pretty together,' I joke.

'You are,' she says, with so much conviction I want to hug her.

'Thank you. You're good.' Something I never thought I'd say.

She smiles. 'As are you. It's been a pleasure, hon.'

She called me hon.

And before I leave, she gives me a hug.

I get home just in time for my next customer. Roxy is a tiny

Bichon Frise with a woolly coat like a lamb. She's so quiet
and feminine compared to Paco. She doesn't make a sound.
Her owner, John, is a neighbour. He's younger but much
more formal than Betty. He fills out the form and hands over
Roxy's things. All he says about her is that she gets a bit
'excited' when she knows she's going for a walk. *What dog
doesn't?* I think.

'Just give her a treat and she'll be grand.'

When he goes, I let Roxy get used to the place and me,
just let her sniff around and chill. When my phone rings, I
don't expect it to be Alex.

'Did Roxy arrive?' she asks.

'Yeah, she's here.'

'Want me to walk her with you?'

'Eh. Yeah, sure. OK.' *What's up?* I think. *Is she going to
tell me? Is that what this is?*

About an hour later, she is here, stooping down, talking
to Roxy while I get the lead. When Roxy hears it, she goes
mental, jumping up, barking and wagging her tail. Normal
dog behaviour. But then, as I'm trying to attach the lead to
the collar, she starts to go weird. Her whole body goes into
spasm and she starts to wheeze. It's like she's having a fit.
Her legs look like they're going to go from under her.

'Oh my God. I'm choking her.'

'You couldn't be, you haven't tightened her collar, have
you?'

'No.'

'Just leave her for a sec.'

'OK.'

We watch her. Slowly she starts to return to normal.

'She seems OK now. Want me to try?' Alex asks.

‧{‧

'Yeah, thanks.'

Roxy goes weird again. Alex lets her go. 'Did her owner say anything?'

'Only that she gets a bit excited when she's going for a walk.'

'Maybe this is just her getting excited.'

'You think?' I ask uncertainly.

She shrugs. 'Here, you hold her still while I get the lead on, then we'll just start walking and see what happens.'

We clip the lead on quickly, put her down and start to walk, like nothing's wrong. Roxy runs ahead, happy.

'Dog whisperer,' I say to Alex.

She looks down at Roxy and smiles. 'She's so light compared to Homer. I can hardly feel her at the end of the lead.'

It's like everything's normal between us. Which it isn't.

We walk for a good bit, not saying much, then she turns to me.

'How's it going with Shane?'

Suddenly, I'm defensive. 'Fine.'

'You're going to see him every day now. Wow.'

'So?'

'Nothing. That's just a lot, though, right?'

I feel a lecture coming on. 'He's helping me study.'

'Oh right, cool.'

We're quiet for a while.

'You know, Sarah,' and it's like she's determined to say whatever it is she wants to say, 'the closer you get, the more it's going to hurt.'

Oh my God. 'So, what, I should abandon him? Leave him there to rot like his girlfriend did?'

'No! I'm not saying that. I just think you should be careful not to get too attached.'

}I{

'What does that even mean?'

'The more time you spend together, the more you're going to miss him when he's ... gone.'

It's like a punch in the stomach, the thought of him not being there. Of not seeing him after school, of not chatting on Facebook last thing at night, of not looking up at my stars knowing he's looking up at his too. I feel my eyes smart. And I think, *Oh my God, if it hurts like this now, what's it going to hurt like when he really is gone?* But then I think of Shane, the guy I tell everything to, who makes me laugh, who helps me out, who rates me no matter what, and there is *no way* I'm going to walk out on him. I'm not dropping him. Yes, it's going to hurt. It's probably going to kill me. But I'll take that when it comes. I couldn't throw what we have away if I tried, however much I'm going to miss him.

I look at Alex coldly. 'And this is, like, your business, why?'

'Sarah. You're my friend. I don't want to see you get hurt.'

'I'm your friend? Really? That's interesting. So why do you leave me out all the time? Why do you tell stuff to Rachel and not to me? You say you don't want me to get hurt. But the way you treat me hurts.'

She swallows. Her eyes go watery. In seconds, she's full-on crying. Oh my God. What did I say?

'Alex, what's wrong? I'm sorry. I didn't mean to upset you.'

She takes a huge, deep breath. She closes her eyes. 'I'm pregnant.'

Everything stops. 'What?'

'You can't tell anyone.'

Oh my God. 'Alex, I so wouldn't. But are you *sure*?'

'I mean no one.'

I can't believe it. 'I won't, I swear.' Roxy jumps up on me, trying to get us to walk again. I ignore her, just put a hand on Alex's arm. 'Are you OK?' Then I think, what a retarded thing to say. How the hell could she be OK?

'No.' But she smiles.

'I need to sit down.'

'Me too.'

We sit on the wall beside the path. I look at her. 'I can't believe you were worried about me seeing Shane when you're *pregnant*.'

She shrugs. And I think what a great friend she is. A friend who's in so much trouble now. God. I can't believe it. I really can't believe it.

'Have you been to the doctor?' I ask.

'I'm going to a clinic this afternoon.'

'So it hasn't actually been confirmed? That's great. Maybe it's OK.'

'Pregnancy tests are almost one hundred per cent accurate, Sarah. I've done four.'

'Still.'

'Yeah, well I'm not getting my hopes up.'

'What does Rachel think?'

She looks at me. 'Sarah, I didn't tell Rachel. She guessed. I was just so sick in school.' It makes so much sense. And it changes everything. 'I wasn't leaving you out. If it hadn't been for Rache, I'd still be pretending it wasn't happening. She made the appointment with the clinic.'

'I'm sorry for biting your head off.'

'It's OK. I haven't told anyone else. Just you and Rachel.'

'Not your dad?'

She bites her lip. 'I can't.'

I think of my parents. They'd kill me. Especially Mum.

Actually, I don't know who'd be worse, Mum or Dad. They'd both lose it. Poor Alex.

'I need to move,' she says, getting up suddenly. And I know it's because she's freaking.

It begins to feel a bit better, walking. Like we're moving forward.

But then she's stopping again, suddenly, looking at me, eyes wide. 'Sarah, I don't know what to do.'

Oh Jesus, I think. *I don't either.*

'I'm so scared. Everything was going so well with David.' Her eyes well up. 'What'll he say? Oh God. I can't believe it.' She drops her face into her hands.

I put an arm round her. I think of Rachel, and wish she was here. 'Let's just see what happens today, OK? I'll come with you, if you like.'

She nods. 'OK. Thanks. Rachel's coming too. The more the merrier,' she jokes, but she looks so sad. Then she closes her eyes. 'Please, God. Please. Let it be a mistake.'

When we get back with Roxy, Mum is unloading the shopping.

'Hello, girls. Alex how are you?'

Alex smiles. 'Fine, thanks.'

I think of everything she's going through. The worry. The stress. Hiding it from everyone. 'Want to go upstairs?' I ask her.

'Yeah, OK, sure. I'll just call Mike, though, 'cause I gotta have lunch and stuff.' I know what she means – she's got to get ready for the clinic. I can't believe it.

We hang out upstairs for a while, watching some *MADtv* sketches on YouTube. Neither of us brings it up. Because there's nothing we can do now except wait.

}|{

Alex's phone rings. Mike's downstairs. I hug her.
'I'll see you later, OK?'
She nods. 'I'll call for you around half two.'
'OK, I'll be ready.' And I'll have chocolate.

When Alex has gone, I do something I never usually do. I stand still. I try to let the news sink in. Try to believe it. I want to ring Rachel and say, 'Oh my God.' But actually, I don't. Because that would be gossip. And this is too serious to gossip about. Poor Alex. I don't know what I'd do. All I know is that my life would be over.

Mum comes out into the hall. 'Are you OK?'
'Eh, yeah, fine. Thanks.'
'Everything all right with Alex?'
I imagine what she'd say if she knew. 'Fine, fine,' I say quickly.
'That's good,' she says cheerfully. 'You don't mind if I go out tonight?'
I look at her, glad. 'Course not. Who with?'
'Ellen and some friends.'
'You going to the movies?'
'Ellen's cooking dinner.'
'Cool.'
'Want lunch?'
'Maybe later. I think I'll just go upstairs for a while.'

In my room, I sit on the bed in shock. Sixteen and pregnant. I think of the show. Of how hard life becomes. How impossible. You have to grow up. Just like that. Never have fun again. Be responsible for this tiny person. Change nappies twenty-four-seven, never go out. It's like so, much, pressure.

}|{

Everything gets serious. You fight with your boyfriend, like, all the time. *If* he hangs around. I can't believe they weren't more careful. Alex and David, for God's sake. Like is there anyone more sensible? Outside of Rachel. I swear to God. I'm never having sex again. It is so not worth the risk.

I think about the whole pregnancy thing. Of her stomach getting all bloated and swollen. Stretch marks. I think of people noticing, staring, bitching. People like Simon. Oh my God, you can get piles.

We go together. And even though it feels like the three of us again, I can't help wishing it was the three of us going for coffee, not this. Poor Alex. She's so white. So quiet. We wait together in silence, Alex ripping an information leaflet into tiny shreds. She doesn't even know she's doing it. At last, they call her in. She stands up. Rachel and I look at each other, not knowing whether to stay or go with.

Alex looks down at us. 'Aren't you coming?' She looks so afraid, we stand immediately.

We go in slowly, like we're about to face a firing squad.

The doctor is female, which is a relief. She introduces herself and asks us to sit. There's this chair situation – we have to find one more. Rachel does, at the back of the room. We sit in a line, facing the doctor, one of us on each side of Alex.

There are a lot of questions, many of them about dates, all of them embarrassing. Alex is probably wishing she didn't ask us in. Finally, the questions stop and the doctor asks Alex to lie up on an examination bench.

'Do you want us to go?' Rachel asks.

'Only if you want to,' the doctor says. 'This is just a quick external examination. And I'll be pulling a screen.'

Even that's embarrassing.

When they reappear from behind the screen, the doctor takes Alex's blood pressure, weighs her and gives her a jar to pee in. Alex takes the jar away to the loo.

We sit facing the doctor.

'Not an easy time,' she says.

'No,' Rachel says.

'She'll need her friends around her now.' It's like she already knows that Alex is pregnant.

We look at each other, then at the door – which is opening. Alex, looking about as humiliated as a person can look, hands over the jar. Our eyes follow it like it contains the inner secrets of the entire world. The doctor takes it to the sink. Her back is turned to us so we can't see what she's doing. Alex's future is in her hands right now. Does she know that?

She turns around.

And, from her face, we know.

Then she confirms it.

'Oh God,' Alex says. She practically folds in two.

The doctor talks about counselling. And options. But Alex looks so shocked, I know that she's not taking it in. I know I wouldn't be. I try to listen for her, so we can tell her later. Finally, the doctor puts a business card in Alex's hand and tells her to call when she wants to talk.

We all stumble out.

We end up out on the street, standing around, not knowing what to do next. I hand out the chocolate. No one speaks till we've eaten a few squares.

'I don't want to go home,' Alex says.

'Will we go for coffee?' Rachel asks.

'On condition we don't talk about it,' Alex says.

We find a Starbucks and order frappuccinos. They don't taste as good as usual.

'Remember that game we used to play,' Alex says. 'Where we'd make up stories for everyone in the coffee shop.' I know what she's doing. Trying not to think of her own.

'OK,' I say to Alex. 'That guy over there.' I nod to a man in his thirties, wearing a suit on a Saturday.

'Job interview,' she says. 'For like, McDonald's or something. He hasn't done it yet. He's psyching himself up with caffeine. He's a thing for Scarlett Johansson. He cuts his own hair. Obviously. He has a pet snake.' I think of Shane and automatically feel calmer. 'He is a Pisces, but hates water. He's a vegetarian, but hates vegetables. His favourite TV programme is *The News*. He sleeps in his socks ...'

She goes on for way, way longer than usual. I've never heard her as creative. I feel like hugging her.

Going back on the DART, I hate that we are going to have to leave her. To go home alone. To tell her dad. Or not. To think of her options. Or not. To tell David. Or not.

My stop is first.

'Want me to come home with you?' I ask Alex.

'No thanks, I'll be fine.'

I hug her goodbye. Squeeze her extra tight. 'Call me any time, OK?'

'OK.'

'Middle of the night. I don't care.'

She smiles. 'See you Monday.'

It doesn't seem right that life will just go on as normal. School on Monday.

Much, much later, I'm crashed in front of the TV with Roxy on my lap watching *Legally Blonde*, and trying not to think about Alex. Mum comes in after her night out. I hear her in the kitchen. Talking. I sit up, wondering who's with her at one in the morning. She comes into the sitting room.

'Thought I saw the light on,' she says, cheerfully.

I nearly drop Roxy. There's a man with her. Middle aged and kind of boring looking. She sees me looking at him and turns to introduce him.

'Sarah. This is Éamonn.'

He looks like an Éamonn. 'Hey,' I say.

He looks at the TV. '*Legally Blonde*. Excellent.'

Is he gay or just into Reese Witherspoon? And what's he doing with my mum?

'We'll leave you to it,' Mum says to me.

'Actually, I was just going to bed. So I'll see you in the morning, I guess.'

Mum smiles. 'Night, night, Sweetie.'

It's one in the morning but there's no way I'm going to sleep. Not with a man down there, with her. What's he doing here, anyway? She'd better not like him. Oh my God, she better not be dating *already*.

In the morning, at breakfast, she's humming. Oh my God.

'Who was that guy?' I ask.

'Oh Éamonn? Just a friend of Ellen's. He wasn't drinking so he offered me a lift home.'

'So you're not seeing him again?'

'No.'

'Did he ask?' I have to know.

'Sarah, I'm not ready for anything like that. Right now, I feel I'll never be ready again.'

Good, I think, *because I'm not sure if I could take any*

Éamonns hanging around.

'So what are you doing today?' she asks.

'Walking Roxy. Studying with Shane.'

'Have you time to go to Ikea?'

'Seriously?'

'Thought we could have some girly time.'

'That'd be great ... What time does it close on Sunday? I really need to study.' Translation: I really need to see Shane, since I missed him yesterday.

'Seven, I think.'

'OK, I'll go see Shane early. Cool.'

'I can pick you up from the home if you like.'

'That'd be great, thanks, Mum.'

I can't believe it.

Shane's rented a DVD.

'You went out and got this yourself?'

'Are you trying to insult me?' he says, popping the disc into the player in his room.

'Course I am,' I say, joking. But it's so great. If he's going out by himself now, doing normal stuff, maybe some day he'll want to move home.

The movie's seriously corny. Until this one scene involving celery that is so outrageous we can't stop laughing. I'm crying I'm laughing so much. Then we're looking at each other and suddenly it's like everything stops. Our smiles fade and we're just looking at each other – in a way that says, 'I'm into you.' I want time to stop. I want this moment to last forever. But he looks away. Embarrassed, I go back to the movie. But my heart is hammering. I look at the screen and only the screen but I'm only aware of one thing, the person next to me. And how badly I want to be with him. How the hell did that happen?

When the movie's over, he zaps it off. 'So, crap, right?' he says.

'Crap.'

And I don't care how cool he's acting, something has started. Something that I don't want to stop.

'I'm starving,' he says. He checks his watch. 'Great, almost dinner.'

It's a hint. And, hurt, I take it. 'I better go.'

He nods. He sees me out in silence. And as I walk through the door all I can think is, *I wish he'd kissed me.*

I've wished for this. I've wished for a mum who'd suggest trips like this, a mum who'd want to hang out with me, no agenda. And it *is* great. I haven't seen her so happy in so long. She's looking at everything and commenting. She's lifting stuff up and examining it. She's even making jokes. But all the way round Ikea – and it's a long way – I'm thinking of Shane. And how badly I want us to be together.

When we get back, we bring Roxy for a walk. Then I'm saying goodnight. I'm going upstairs. I'm closing the door. I'm lying on my bed, eyes closed, imagining his face, imagining his lips on mine. Is it possible for your whole body to ache for a person? Because mine is aching for him. I open my eyes to my wall of caliente men.

'Well, gentlemen. It's been fun.'

I get up and, one by one, I take them down. Even Robbie Williams.

23
POSITIVE OPTIONS

In school, Simon and Amy go everywhere together. He even sits with her at the canteen. Like, all the time. They look so happy, as if all he needed was to find the right person. Which makes me feel rubbish. He catches me looking and gives me a look-what-you're-missing smile. Which makes me feel better. Because it reminds me what a creep he is. I think about Shane and how he makes me feel. Good about myself. I think about Shane all day. I think about Shane in a way I've never thought about him, till yesterday.

After school, I tell the others to go ahead. I go to the bathroom and change into my skinny jeans and my best hoodie. I put on some mascara and lippy. I have to slip into an empty classroom to curl my hair.

Sitting on the DART, I start to stress. Is it too much? Too obvious? Maybe I should change back. But where? I tell myself to stop freaking. It's Shane. It'll be OK.

But when I get to the home, it's not OK.

I go over to him, sit down, grab a chair and say, 'Hey.'

'What are you doing?' he whispers.

'What d'you mean?'

'Your clothes. Your hair.'

I feel myself blush.

There's a really long silence. He's just staring at me.

Then he says, 'I can't give you anything.'

'What?'

'I'm going to die.'

It's like missing the bottom step. And for a second I don't know what to say. But I recover. 'We're all going to die.'

'You should be out with your friends.'

'You *are* my friend.' I feel I'm fighting for him now.

'You're spending too much time here.' He says it like he's determined.

And then, I know what I have to do. The exact opposite of what I want to.

'Oh my God! You think I *fancy* you, don't you? You think … what do you think … that I want to go out with you?' I make it sound ridiculous. 'What is it with guys? A girl likes you and *automatically* you think they fancy you. I like your company, Shane. We have a laugh. And for the first time in my life I can study. Why do you have to complicate it?'

He grimaces. 'I'm way off the mark here, amn't I?'

I give him a look. 'Way off.'

He grimaces again. 'Sorry.'

'You should be.'

'No. I really *am* sorry.' He runs a hand through his hair. 'I had to make sure. I mean, the last thing you want to do is get involved with someone like me.'

'Yeah well you needn't worry,' I say, like I wouldn't go out with him if he was the last guy on earth. But all I want to do is kiss him. And hug him. And cry.

Next day, even though I want to more than anything, I don't go to the home. I can't. Instead, I go with Alex and Rachel to the Jitter Mug.

'How're you doing?' Rachel asks Alex. I expect her to say, 'fine'. And leave it.

But she looks at Rachel. 'I just want it to go away.'

Oh my God, I think, *she doesn't mean—*

'I'm just so tired of hearing about "positive options". Everywhere I go, everything I read, it's positive bloody options. I'm sorry but what's positive about becoming a parent before you've even grown up yourself? What's positive about carrying a baby around for nine months then giving it away like you've no responsibility to it at all? What's positive about killing it? There are no "positive options". When people start using the word "positive" you know you're in trouble. I'll never use "positive" again. As long as I live.' And then from talking so fast, so angrily, her eyes fill. 'I wish my mum was here.' She sounds so young. So lost.

'We're here,' Rachel says, and holds her hand.

'I should tell my dad, shouldn't I? I should at least tell Dad. I mean I can't tell David till I decide what to do.'

There's a pause.

'Maybe you could decide together,' Rachel says. 'I mean you're in it together.'

Alex's eyes widen. 'What if we're not? What if it's just me?'

'Come on. David, of all people, he's a good guy.'

Alex closes her eyes. 'I don't know if I can do it, find the words …'

'You don't have to tell him. All I'm saying is it's an option.'

'I haven't been able to talk to him properly since the tests.'

}|{

'But that's good,' Rachel says. 'He'll know something's up. It won't come as a total shock.'

Alex looks at her hopefully. 'You think?'

Rachel nods. 'I'd tell Mark, if it was me.'

Alex nods. 'Yeah. Maybe.' Two seconds later, she's saying, 'I don't know.'

For the rest of the week, I stay away from the home. I try to concentrate only on Alex. On helping her. But she has gone back to not wanting to talk about it.

On Thursday night, Shane calls.

'Are you OK?' he asks.

My heart stops. 'Yeah, fine.'

'You haven't been in.'

'I've been hanging out with my friends.' Like he said I should. I don't mean to sound hurt, it just comes out that way.

There's a long silence. 'I'm sorry, Sarah. I just want you to have a life.'

'I *have* a life.'

There's a pause. 'Can we start again?'

'What d'you mean?'

'Just forget what happened. Go back to the way it was.'

I don't want to go back. If it weren't for that wheelchair, that freaking disease, we'd be together now. I know we would.

'What's up?' he asks.

'Nothing.'

'So you coming for Bingo?'

I sigh. If I don't go, I may as well never go again. And I don't want that. If it's friends or nothing, I'll take friends.

'Yeah. I'm coming for Bingo.'
'Cool.'

If I didn't know it was Friday, I'd know now. Miriam is in the kitchen when I come down. And it's weird. She's as familiar to me as Coco Pops. I still hardly know anything about her. Some day, I'll google Human Resources. Today, though, I watch as she helps herself to Mum's muesli. Which is a good thing because the Coco Pops are running low. I pour myself a bowl and join her at the table.

'So you from around here?' I ask.

'Other side of the city.'

'So you just, like, travel to Louis' pub, once a week?' Seems a bit stalkerish.

She smiles. 'I do night classes in Blackrock on Thursdays.'

'Ah.' I get curious. 'What kind of classes?'

'Pole dancing.'

'Seriously?'

'No.' She laughs. 'Why all the sudden questions?'

I shrug. 'We see each other every week now and I don't know anything about you.'

'What do you want to know?'

'I don't know.'

We laugh. She's nice. And suddenly I don't want her to get hurt.

'Miriam. Louis isn't the kind of guy you end up in a serious relationship with. You know that, right?'

She points a spoon at me. 'That's all part of his charm.'

'OK.'

'So,' she says, pushing the empty bowl of muesli away and starting into toast. 'Does he talk about me at all?'

I thought she just said . . . 'Eh, no.' I blush.

'Good,' she says and laughs.

Never thought I'd say it, but I need to get to school.

School's different for me now. In French, instead of dreaming of boulevards and pain au chocolat, I have my verb book open and I'm trying to figure out something that's always confused me – the difference between the two past tenses. I glance up. Simon's looking at me. He rolls his eyes like I'm an idiot. So I just smile like he's the idiot. Then I think of Shane. But that doesn't cheer me up like it normally does.

After school, I'm totally nervous. I mess my hair, make my uniform extra sloppy so it looks like I don't give a shit. All the way to the home I'm wondering if I'm mad going back. This could be my get-out-of-jail-free card. Just never go back. Never get hurt more than I'm already hurt. But I can't do it. I can't not turn up.

He sees me and smiles so widely, so automatically, that I know he's glad I'm here. And I can't help it, I smile back. I go over.

'I missed you,' he says. 'No one to slag.'

'In that case, I missed you too.'

'Hope you haven't been slacking off on the old study.'

'Actually, I've been doing pretty well without you.' I hold his eyes so he gets the hint. I don't know why I'm being like this. I don't want to be. Not really.

'So, you going to sit with me?'

'If I do, will you think I fancy you?'

His face falls. 'Look, Sarah. I'm sorry about that. I—'

'It's OK. I was joking.' And I wonder if we'll ever get back to where we were.

We play Bingo. Say little. It's the first time I haven't been able to talk to him.

When the last game's over, I stand up and smile. 'So, I guess I'll see you Monday.' For some stupid reason I feel like crying.

'What? No study?'

I make a face. 'Do you want to?'

'Course I do. There's this new memory technique I've developed. I was hoping to try it out.'

I shrug. 'OK.'

We go to his room. 'OK,' he says as I close the door. 'Let's start with French. You know how hard it is to remember if something's masculine or feminine?'

'Do I.'

'OK. Right. When you're learning a word, just visualise the thing wearing either boxer shorts (if it's masculine) or a bra (if it's feminine).'

I laugh. 'You're crazy.'

'So, 'house', in French, is what?'

'*Maison.*'

'Masculine or feminine?'

'Masculine. No, feminine.' I make a face. 'Masculine?'

'OK, imagine a house wearing a bra.'

I can see it. I don't think I'll ever forget it. I laugh.

'What colour's the bra?'

'Blue.'

'See? Told you it works.'

And just like that, I feel like kissing him again.

Saturday morning, Alex wants us to come over. When she gets off the phone, it rings almost immediately. It's Rachel.

'She sounded positive,' she says, hopefully.

'I know. That's what I was thinking.'

Rachel's mum picks me up. And I know the minute I get into the car that Rachel has told her. They're close like that.

When Alex answers the door, she's smiling. I look at Rachel. Definitely positive. We go upstairs. In her room, Alex bursts into a really big smile.

'I told David. We're staying together. And keeping the baby.'

Wow, I think. From being absolutely stuck to full steam ahead.

Rachel hugs her.

Then I'm in there too.

'He's coming home for the scan,' Alex says. 'In, like, two weeks.'

'I knew you could count on him,' Rachel says.

'I was so scared, though, Rache. I practised telling him so many times, in so many ways.'

'But he's David,' I say.

'Yeah. And a baby's for life,' Alex says.

Oh my God. 'Are you getting *married*?'

She shakes her head. 'When I get married, it'll be because I want to, not because I have to. I want the same for David.'

'Did he ask?' I ask.

'Yeah, he asked.'

I think they should. They were made for each other. Why wait? It's inevitable that they'll end up together. 'It's good you're keeping the baby, though,' I say.

She looks at me for a long time. 'Sarah, I didn't really have a choice. That baby isn't just part of me and David, it's part of our mums. It has their genes.' Her voice wobbles.

'Wow.' I never even thought of that.

'What did he say when you told him?' Rachel asks.

'Same thing everyone says, "Are you sure?" He was so shocked. I was so afraid. But then, he just said, "Right. We'll deal with it." And suddenly it wasn't my problem any more, it was ours. I cried I was so relieved.'

'David's the best.'

'Have you told your dad?' Rachel asks.

'The minute I got off Skype.'

'Was he OK?' I ask.

'Not really. He was, like, all distressed, blaming himself for not being around. I think he's terrified.'

'I love your dad,' I say.

'It might even be good for him to have a baby in the house,' Rachel says.

'A bit hasty, Rache,' Alex says.

'Yeah, sorry.'

'Anyone on for going down to the beach?' Alex asks.

It's the first good day of summer. You can actually feel warmth in the air. Which is pretty amazing for Ireland, a country that can take or leave the whole season.

We walk the beach with Homer. And for ages we don't even bother talking. I'm so glad for Alex. So glad she's not alone in this any more. They won't fight over the baby. I know they won't. And David – he'll help with the nappies. Oh my God ... 'Does this mean he's going to move back to Ireland?' I ask.

Alex looks unsure. 'We haven't got that far.'

I feel like apologising.

We're quiet for ages.

'Hey, what's up with Homer?' I ask, eventually. 'I thought

he loved the sea.' He's been walking by our side since we started.

Alex looks at me. 'You're not going to believe this but he won't leave my side. It's like he's protecting me.'

'Ah, bless,' I say.

'And you know what? He knew before I did. I swear to God.'

'Wow. That's amazing.'

Rachel looks deep in thought.

'What are you going to do about school?' she asks.

I want to tell her to leave it. But it's too late. It's out now.

'What *about* school?' Alex asks.

'When are you going to tell them?'

'I'm not.'

'But they'll notice. Eventually.'

'Let them.'

I think of Simon and people like him. 'If anyone gives you hassle, I'll punch their lights out.' I feel so protective of her suddenly.

'Good to know,' she says, and winks at me.

24
PLEASURE

Two weeks later, we're over at Alex's. Getting her ready for David, who's coming the following morning. And I know it's not the most perfect situation in the world, but I still think it's romantic, him coming all this way to be with her. I think of Shane and what could have been if things were different. We're friends again, of course. But it's different. Because you can't really forget. You can't really go back to the way it was. All you can do is try to put it out of your mind. That's what I do now.

Rachel has put this great hair treatment in Alex's hair. While it's doing its work, I'm going to give her a French manicure.

'OK. Hand 'em over.'

Reluctantly, she gives me her hands.

'Oh my God! You've been biting your nails.'

She grimaces. 'I know. I'm sorry. I've just been kind of freaking.' She looks from me to Rache. 'What if he changes his mind? What if he takes one look at me pregnant and goes off me?'

'Alex, you look the same,' I say.

She stands up and pulls down the zip of her jeans. 'See?'

'There's nothing there.'

'I see it. He'll see it.'

'Alex, you do not look pregnant,' Rachel says firmly.

Alex zips up her jeans and yanks down her top. 'Yeah, well I will. I'll be huge.'

'And then you won't again. It's not forever.'

'But a baby is.'

'And David's OK with that,' Rachel says.

But it's like she doesn't hear. 'I'm going to be responsible for this person for the rest of my life. What if I make a mistake? What if I drop it? What if it ends up on drugs?'

I smile. 'Alex, you're going to be the best mum. You know why? Because you *had* the best mum.' (I've given this a lot of thought.) 'You'll know what to do because you've seen her do it. It'll just come to you.' I really believe that.

'You liked her, didn't you, my mum?'

I look at her. 'Alex, I *loved* your mum.' Then I tell her something I've never told anyone. 'I really miss her, you know?' She was so good to me, so warm when my own mum was so distant. 'I know I've no right to miss her. She was your mum.'

'I think it's lovely that you miss her.'

I look her in the eye. 'Alex, you'll be great. I just know it. The main thing is that you stay in school, go to college, keep your options open.'

She smiles. 'You sound like my dad.'

Who, at least, is minted. I see, suddenly, how that's going to help. 'Alex. You can do all that. Just hire a nanny to help you during the day. And a nurse for night feeds. You'll have loads of help. It's not going to be like those girls on *Sixteen and Pregnant*.'

She shivers and I think, *maybe I shouldn't have brought that up*.

'And David loves you,' Rachel says.

'Yeah. He loves me,' Alex says, like she's reminding herself.

Next day is Sunday. We don't hear anything. On Monday, Alex isn't in school. We don't worry. They haven't seen each other in months. And they have a crisis on their hands.

'God, I hope they're OK,' I say to Rache.

'They'll be fine.'

'Yeah.'

'Let me know if she texts you.'

'You too.'

'OK,' I say, but know that if Alex texts anyone, it'll be Rachel.

After school, Shane has news.

'I'm thinking about going home.'

'Wow! You should. Definitely.'

'We went out yesterday for lunch. It was good. Then we went home for a while. They've started work on the house anyway.'

Go them, I think. I smile. 'Then you've no excuse.'

He looks at me for a long time. 'You know, Sarah, if it wasn't for you, I'd still be at that window.'

'No you wouldn't.'

'I'd never have gone outside. Or back on Facebook. Or hooked up with my mates.' He looks at me and smiles. 'You make me want to do the right thing.'

It's the other way around. 'You make *me* do the right thing. Not steal. End it with Simon. See my father again. Study.'

'I'm going back to school,' he says. 'Thanks to you, I'm going to do my Leaving Cert.'

I don't understand. Why waste time (something so precious to him) studying for something he'll never need? 'You're going to do your *Leaving*?'

He becomes suddenly passionate. 'I want to achieve something, Sarah. You were right, my brain still works and it's going to stay working. I'm going to get tired. I'm going to get weak, lose power. And when that happens, I want to be good at something. I'm never going to be an architect. But I can get my Leaving Cert. Sarah, I want to do everything I can do – until the end. I want to live till I die.'

I'm afraid to look at him. In case he sees it. How I feel about him. I seriously, seriously want to kiss him now, just grab his face and snog him to death.

'I don't suppose I could hug you without you getting the wrong idea?' I ask.

'I guess we could try it.' He smiles, teasingly.

It's awkward trying to reach him. He leans forward. I stoop and lean in.

But then we're holding each other and time stops. I close my eyes. Feel his cheek next to mine, feel his arms around me, feel him breathe. I want to stay like this forever. But I pull away before he gets any ideas.

'How was that?' I ask sarcastically.

'That was great.' He smiles.

Then it hits me. If he moves home, goes back to school, I might never see him again.

'What's up?' he asks.

}|{

'What? Nothing.'

'Doesn't look like nothing.'

I shrug. 'We'll miss you at Bingo, I guess.'

'Yeah but *we'll* still hook up, right? Out there.' His face changes, becomes uncertain. 'If you like. Or maybe you wouldn't like . . .' He says it as if he's just realising that I mightn't want to go on seeing him.

'No, no. I'd like. I'd definitely like.'

His face relaxes into a smile. 'Phew. For a minute there, you had me worried.'

And I know, right then, that he is going to break my heart.

On Monday night, Alex calls wanting to meet up in the Jitter Mug after school next day.

'So, it'll be you, me, Rache, David and Mark,' she says.

'Like old times,' I say, smiling. Because it's such a good sign.

'Like old times,' she says, and I know she's smiling.

Yaay, I think when I hang up.

They're there when we arrive. They look happy, relaxed. Normal. Which is a major relief. We go over. David gets up. Gives everyone a hug. Mark gets a back slap with his.

'It's so good to see you guys!' he says, sounding more American than usual.

We sit down.

'How're you all doing?' he asks.

'Great,' Rachel says. 'And you?'

'Great.'

Everyone politely ignores the elephant in the room.

Rachel and I go up to get some smoothies.

'Does Mark know?' I ask quietly.

She nods. 'Once David knew, I asked Alex if it'd be OK for me to tell Mark. I hate keeping stuff from him.'

I know how she feels. I hate keeping this from Shane.

We get to the counter.

'So the surfer dude is back,' Louis says, looking over at the table.

'Yup,' I say lightly, aware of Rachel beside me.

'Cool,' he says, like it's nothing to him.

We collect our drinks and go back to the others.

'Is that your brother up there?' David asks me.

'Yup, that's Louis.' And I get that he likes Louis about as much as Louis likes him.

'So,' Mark says to David. 'How hard is it to get into US universities?'

'You want to come out?' David asks, surprised.

'I'm thinking about it,' he says. 'Like, why stay here in the rain when you could be over there, hanging out in the sun?'

Rachel is staring at him.

'You'd be surprised how much you miss,' David says, looking at Alex. She smiles and I think, *Aw*. 'I can't wait to come back for good,' he adds.

'When are you?' Mark asks. Everyone goes quiet because that's like asking are you moving home when the baby's born?

David looks at Alex when he answers. 'November.' Then he puts an arm around her and pulls her to him. And I think how really lucky she is to have him.

It's Thursday night and there's no news from Alex. She had the scan today. I thought she'd have called. I ring Rache.

}|{

'Have you heard anything?'

'No. I didn't want to call. Just in case.'

'Should we text?' I ask. 'Just so she knows we're thinking of her.'

'Yeah. Good idea.'

When I hang up, I text Alex. 'Hope scan went OK. Say hi to David.' I sign off with the butterfly emote that Rachel, Alex and I always use – only with each other. It's something we've been doing since, like, forever. It always makes us feel like all for one and one for all. And I don't know why but I've a really strong feeling Alex needs us now.

She doesn't text back.

When I'm going to bed at eleven, I call Rachel.

'Any news?'

'No.'

'Maybe she's tired.'

'Yeah, maybe.' But her voice isn't confident.

And neither am I. Something doesn't feel right.

Friday, she's not in school. But she hasn't been in all week. So we tell each other there's probably nothing to worry about. They're making plans. Talking. But I am worried. She should have texted back by now.

Shane asks if I'm OK.

'You seem kind of stressed or something.'

I so want to tell him. But I promised Alex. 'I'm fine.'

'OK, sure.' He knows there's something I'm not telling him. And maybe that's a good thing – for him to think I don't feel close enough to share everything. 'So,' he says brightly, wheeling to one of the cupboards in his room. 'How about giving me some highlights?'

'What?'

'Yeah, I bought a kit in the pharmacy.' He holds up a box.

'Are you serious? You want me to give you highlights?'

'If you don't mind. I don't want to go to a hairdresser.'

I hadn't thought of that. 'Here, give us a look.'

He gives me the box. I check the instructions. Then start taking things out of the box. I always wanted a younger sister to try out stuff like this on. 'Seems easy enough.'

'So you'll do it?'

'Yeah, sure, why not? Should be fun.'

'Great!'

I read the instructions again, check that I have everything. I put the plastic cap thingy on his head. It slips down over his forehead. I have to move it back up. The tips of my fingers brush against his skin. Oh God. Maybe this wasn't such a good idea. I feel myself blush. I keep my eyes on what I'm doing, not daring to look at him. I go around the back to fix the cap there. And to catch my breath. I should have thought this through.

'OK,' I say brightly. 'I just have to pull your hair through these tiny holes with this yoke.' I hold up a gadget with a hook on the end.

He nods, says nothing.

I start to pull tiny clumps of hair through the holes in the cap.

'Just so you know,' I say. 'You look ridiculous.'

'It'll be so worth it in the end, though,' he says in this camp voice.

'Keep your head still.'

I start at the side, work my way back, then round the other side. Then I'm at the front. I feel myself blush again. I feel his breath on my neck. I feel the heat between us. I feel him looking at me. I can't look back.

){{

'So, thanks for coming to my salon,' I say, lightly. 'How did you hear about us?'

I feel him smile. 'You've a great reputation.'

'That's good to know. Now, I'm just going to brush on this ... gunk.'

'Gunk?'

'Bleachy stuff.'

I get the tiny brush they give you and start pasting the gunk on the hair I've pulled through. 'Here goes.' After a few minutes, it's done. 'OK, so now we wait.'

He asks how long I've been in business. I tell him I grew up in the shop. It used to be my mum's. I make up this whole story. And it takes my mind off other things. Then it's time to wash the gunk off.

In the en suite, he tilts his chair back as far as it'll go, towards the sink. I wrap a bath towel around his neck and shoulders, then pour warm water over his head. When the gunk starts to clear, I'm going red again, but not with embarrassment, with panic. It's not supposed to look like this, is it? I keep rinsing, hoping that's all it needs – more water. I grab the towel and rub his hair like crazy, hoping that it'll look OK when dry. He sees my face.

'What?'

'You better look.'

He rights the chair and goes to the mirror. He stares at himself, then starts to laugh. 'Jesus. I look like a hedgehog.'

I feel sick. 'I don't know what happened. I followed the instructions exactly.' He looks like a door mat. Or a sieve. Or someone who's had one of those hair transplants where all the plugs stand out.

'What'll we do? You can't go around like that.'

He shrugs. 'It's just hair.'

'We should dye it all the same colour.'

'OK, sure, whatever,' he says, totally Zen.

I cover his entire head in gunk. Leave it for longer this time. Then rinse it off again.

OMG. His hair is orange with tiny tufts of blonde. I'm not letting him see it.

'I don't think I've left it in long enough. I'm just going to do it again.'

'You sure?'

'Shane, I think you should have gone to a hairdresser.'

'Nah, sure we're grand.'

I've just about enough stuff to go again. This time I let it sit there for ages.

'That must be long enough,' he says finally.

'Yeah,' I say, afraid. Because this is it. The end.

This time, when I rinse the gunk away, his hair is yellow. 'Shane, we're in trouble.'

He goes to the mirror. 'Interesting,' he says.

'I don't have any more stuff left,' I say in full-on panic.

'OK. We'll just shave it off.'

'*What*!?'

'I've got an electric razor thingy in the wardrobe. It'll be grand. Don't worry.'

'I am *not* shaving your hair.'

'I look like a lemon.'

'You'd prefer bald?'

'Definitely.' He gets the razor thingy.

'OK,' he says. 'Let me give you a demo.'

He runs the gadget over his head, leaving a strip of really short hair. Then he hands it to me. 'Now you try.'

He has a bald strip on his yellow head, like a baby lawn-mower just ran over him. I don't have an option here.

}|{

'I can't hurt you, can I?'

'Nope.'

I take a deep breath.

'Hang on, let me take off my shirt.' He yanks his rugby top over his head and I try not to blush. How did I agree to this?

'OK, ready?' I ask. I take another deep breath, then run the razor from the base of his neck to the top of his head. 'Jesus.'

He laughs.

'Keep still or you'll lose an ear.'

The whole thing takes ten minutes. I stand back and look at him. Wow. He's all macho and soldiery. Like the guy in *Avatar*. But better looking. He has a seriously beautiful head. Normally I don't notice actual whole heads, but I guess without the hair . . . He's like a perfect sculpture. His eyes are bigger, his jaw stronger. He is totally and utterly caliente.

'Wow,' I say.

He checks the mirror and smiles. 'You know what I need now?'

I walk up behind him and look at him in the mirror, talking to his reflection. 'I don't want to know.'

'A tattoo.'

I laugh. 'Yeah right.'

'I need a pen.' He looks around and, however he does it, the way his head curves into his neck is like art. I take out my phone and take a photo. I take another. And another. And that is how we are when his mother walks in – Shane, head shaved, chest exposed, and me hovering around taking photos like some sort of groupie.

I stop dead, put my phone in my pocket and step back.

'Good God,' she says. She covers her mouth with her hand.

There is this moment of total silence. Then she laughs.

'Mum, this is Sarah,' Shane says, like he's told her about me.

She takes a long look at me and puts out her hand. 'Finally, I get to meet the girl who convinced my boy to come home. Sarah. It's a pleasure.'

I almost die with relief.

25
FRIENDS

I'm just in the door from Shane's when Rachel calls.

'Where are you?'

'At home.'

'I'm coming over.'

'What's up?'

'I'll tell you when I see you.' She hangs up.

It's about Alex. I can feel it. I spend the next fifteen minutes worrying. When the doorbell goes, I rush to it. She walks in, talking.

'David's at the airport.'

'I thought he wasn't going back till tomorrow.'

'They've split up.'

'What?'

'He just rang Mark. He's a mess.'

'Oh my God. What happened?'

She looks around. 'Louis's not here, is he?'

'Louis? No. Why? He's at the Jitter Mug.'

'Let's go upstairs.' She takes off.

I race after her, wondering what's going on and what Louis has got to do with it.

She shuts the door behind us. Leans against it. And looks at me.

'It's not David's baby.'

'What do you mean it's not his baby? Of course it's his baby.'

'The scan. It showed up that the dates were wrong. The baby's bigger. Alex is more pregnant than they thought.'

'So?'

'David was in the States when she got pregnant.'

'That couldn't be right.'

'It is.'

'But Alex hasn't *been* with anyone else.'

'Apart from Louis,' she says.

I go very still.

'It wasn't long after David left.'

I try to think back. 'But Alex was working in the shop,' I remember aloud. 'How could she have met Louis?'

'I don't know. Does it matter?'

'He asked for her number … But that was later. She was back at school.' I think about them in the Jitter Mug, how they seemed to know each other. How she avoided him after I slagged her about him. How he loves her. It all makes sense. I look at Rachel. 'It's possible. But I can't believe it.'

'What I can't believe is that it's Louis. Of all people!'

'Louis is my brother.' In fairness.

'Louis is also Louis, no offence.'

'Actually, Louis is a pretty caring person.'

'You think he's suddenly going to get all paternal?'

I don't tell her that he loves Alex. Because, with Louis, I don't know what that translates into.

'Anyway, fact is, she's broken David's heart. For good this time.'

'Have you spoken to her?'

'No. And I'm not going to. She's gone too far this time. David was about to give up everything for her. College, the works. And all the time she's been sneaking around behind his back, behind everyone's backs, including ours.'

'What? Was she *two-timing* him?' It's so not Alex.

'No. They'd broken up. But they still loved each other. And she should have told David about Louis when they got back together.'

I think about that. 'Yeah, but that would have broken his heart. I mean, would you do it – to Mark? Seriously? Would you tell him you'd been with someone else?'

'Why are you standing up for her?'

'Because we all have secrets, Rache. We all do things we regret and don't exactly want the world to know about. Alex is our friend. We need to have faith in her. Come on, Rache. At least hear her side.'

'I'm tired of hearing her side. What about David's side?'

'Look, Alex loves David. You know she does. She'd never do anything to hurt him. She thought it was over. She was upset. Not thinking straight. Whatever. The point is, she's lost David. She's pregnant and on her own.'

'Whose fault is that?'

'I can't believe you're being so harsh.'

'I can't believe you're being so naive.'

And just like that, she turns and leaves. She actually walks out on me.

Saturday morning. Alex's dad answers the door. He looks five years older, his face drawn, his mouth a grim line.

'Hi. Eh …' I never know what to call him, his stage name or ordinary name. So I don't call him anything. 'Alex mightn't want to see me right now. But I thought I'd come anyway.'

His face softens and he looks relieved. 'No, no. I'm glad you're here. We don't know what to do with her.' Marsha comes up behind him. She looks as worried as he does. She remembers my name.

Alex's dad shows me up, knocks lightly on the door and opens it. Alex is lying, curled up on the bed, back to the door.

'I'll leave you to it,' he says, and reverses out.

I just stand there for a moment.

She turns around. Her face is red and swollen from crying. 'I've ruined my life,' she says and starts to cry.

I go over, and sit on the bed. 'It just seems that way now.'

She looks at me. 'You don't know what I did.'

'What did you do? You were with Louis when you weren't with David. Big deal.'

She looks at me, eyes wide. 'You should have seen his face, Sarah. He thought they'd made a mistake. He didn't think for one second I'd been with anyone else. I had to tell him. I had to break his heart.' And then she's crying, like she's broken her own. I know then that she's been crying since Thursday. She looks totally drained.

'Come here, lie down.' I lie her down. Stroke her hair. But then she's up again, desperate to tell me everything.

'I should have told him about Louis, the minute we got back together. I couldn't, though. I couldn't hurt him. And now I've hurt him so much more.' Her whole body shudders. 'He came over, Sarah. He was giving everything up. We were making all sorts of plans. Then the scan.' She's crying again. 'I've messed up so badly.'

'Alex, we all mess up.'

'Not like this.'

'Yes like this.'

'It was the day David left. I was just so lonely. And sad.'

'Alex, you don't need to explain.'

'He made me feel better. And I kept going back. I should-
n't have. Oh God, why did I keep going back?'

'Alex stop, you're just upsetting yourself.'

'I didn't tell you. I didn't tell anyone. I was too ashamed.
I thought you'd hate me.'

I close my eyes because I'm going to do it. I'm going to tell
her. 'I got caught shoplifting.'

'What?' She looks confused.

'I got caught shoplifting. After you got back from San
Diego. That's why I've been going to the home. It's my com-
munity service. I didn't tell anyone because I was ashamed.
I thought you'd hate me. So I know what it's like, OK?'

She's just staring at me. I don't know what she's thinking.
But I keep going.

'I went to see a shrink. For a while. To do with the
shoplifting – which was really to do with my parents splitting up ...'

'You thought I'd hate you, didn't you?' Alex says.

'Well, yeah, obviously.'

'Well, I wouldn't have, OK? And I don't.'

I lie flat back on the bed with a bang.

She does the same. But then she turns to me and asks.
'Does Rachel hate me?'

'Of course she doesn't.'

'Then why isn't she here?'

'She's just letting it sink in a bit.'

'She hates me,' she says like it's a fact.

'It'd take more than a mistake for Rachel to hate you.'
And I really believe that. I just have to convince Rache.

We lie there for ages and eventually she falls asleep. I stay
with her, glad that she's finally resting, finally having a
break.

When she wakes, two hours later, I boss her into the shower. When she comes out, I blow dry her hair. Then I order
her downstairs for lunch. Barbara, the most amazing cook
in the entire world, makes us Bruschetta al Pomodoro. And
then leaves us alone. We eat in silence, Alex staring into
space, not really eating at all, just lifting the odd tiny square
of tomato and, eventually, putting it into her mouth. She
looks at me finally.

'What am I going to do without him?' And she's crying
again.

I put my arms around her and just hold her. I don't know
what she's going to do. Because it's not just David she's losing (her Gabbana in life), but the person who was going to
be with her through everything. She's back at the beginning.
Pregnant and on her own.

'You should tell Louis. I know people think he's not a
serious guy, but he's a *good* guy.'

She looks at me in panic. 'No. And don't say anything,
Sarah.'

'I won't. But you should.'

'He wouldn't want to know.'

'He might, though.'

'We weren't in a relationship. It meant nothing to him.'

'Maybe it did.'

'No. It wasn't like that. For either of us. And I don't want

}I{

to go backwards, Sarah. It was a mistake. The biggest mistake of my life.'

'OK. But shouldn't you, at least, give him the chance to do the right thing?'

'What *is* the right thing? I'm sixteen. He's nineteen. We don't love each other. I just want to get through this. I just want to cope. Oh God. How'll I cope?' She starts pulling her hair.

'OK, I don't know *how* you'll cope either, Alex, but you *will* cope. Because people do. You're strong, Ali. And when you know what you want, you're the most determined person I know. If you decide you'll cope you will cope.' She looks mildly reassured. So I keep going. 'You're surrounded by people who love you. Your dad. Marsha. Me. And Rachel.' I'm going to make damn sure she has Rachel too.

She looks at me.

'You're not going to be alone in this. At any stage. And I'm talking until this kid is an adult. OK?'

She smiles a teary smile. 'OK.'

'Now give me a hug.'

And it's only after I finally leave, when I'm walking down the steps of her house, that it hits me. My brother is going to be a father. Which means, I'm going to be an aunt.

26
TIGER

I go straight to Rachel's house. She doesn't exactly look happy to see me. Guess she knows why I'm here.

'Can I come in?'

She says nothing, just opens the door wider. We go up to her room.

'I went to see Alex.'

She shrugs, then looks out the window like it means nothing to her.

'Rachel. This is ridiculous. She's your best friend.'

She ignores me.

'OK, now you're being stupid.'

She turns and glares, but still says nothing.

'Come on. She was lonely. She made a mistake. It could happen to anyone.'

'Yeah, well it wouldn't have happened at all if she'd listened to me and trusted him, waited—'

'Not everyone's as strong as you, Rache.'

'It's not about strong. She always puts herself before David.'

'Not true. It was because she was missing him so much she ended up with Louis.'

She looks at me. 'Sarah, Louis's your brother. Don't you feel just a *little* pissed off that you didn't know?'

'We all hide things, Rache. All it takes is to be ashamed of what you've done.'

'Yeah so what have *you* done?' she asks, like I haven't done anything.

I look at her for a long time. Of all people, she's the one least likely to understand. I take a deep breath. Then tell her. She says nothing, just looks at me. Finally, her face softens and she asks, 'Why didn't you ask me for money?'

'It wasn't about money.' She looks confused. 'It was about controlling my life.'

'*What?*'

'When my parents split up, it was like losing control. Shoplifting gave that back to me.'

'No offence, but you sound like a shrink.'

'I'm quoting one.'

'You went to a *shrink?*'

'To avoid a police record.'

'Jesus, Sarah. Why didn't you tell me? That's what friends are for.'

'Rachel, you're perfect. You never do anything wrong. You never make mistakes. You succeed at *everything* you do. I thought you'd hate me.'

'Well you got *that* wrong. I don't *hate* you.'

'Do you hate Alex?'

There's a silence. Then a quiet, 'It's not the same.'

'Rache, in all fairness, until you've done something that you seriously regret, I don't think you can really judge Alex, you know? She needs us, Rachey. She's so alone, so devastated. So afraid.' I look at her and don't know whether any of this is having an effect. So I add, 'You know, she could have got rid of the baby and never told David. Or anyone. She knew that by keeping it, she could lose him and all of us. She's put that little person before herself. Don't punish her for it.'

We're standing looking at each other. My phone sounds. It's a text from Shane.

'Who's that?'

'Just Shane.'

I read the text. 'Getting tattoo. Wanna come?'

I smile.

'What?' Rachel asks.

'He's getting a tattoo.'

She looks at me. 'You guys are pretty close, right?'

I shrug. 'I don't know. We get on OK, I guess. I think I'll go with him.'

She smiles. 'Do.'

I text back. 'When?'

'Taxi leaving at 3 p.m.'

'I'll b der, psycho.'

I look back at Rachel. 'So, Alex.'

'Alex.' She takes a huge deep breath that could suck a person in. 'Let me think about it, OK?'

I nod. 'OK. Cool.' Because that's a start.

The tattoo place is bright and spacious and smells of antiseptic. A guy is getting tattooed. His shirt is off and he's tilted back in a reclining chair. We wait just inside the door. A girl comes up to us. She's small with short, spiky hair and a

}|{

nose stud. Her arms are covered in colour, her skin a canvas of tropical flowers. Shane gives his name. She runs a finger down the open diary. Her nails are painted black.

'Here you are,' she says in an American accent. 'D'you know the artist you're with?'

'Eh, no.'

She looks over at a guy wearing a beanie, long shorts and a short-sleeved shirt. Tattoos run up his legs, arms and neck. He's twirling around in circles on a swivel chair.

'Tiger's free,' she says, nodding in his direction.

Tiger looks a little doped.

'He did mine,' the girl says, like she can read my mind.

'Oh, right. OK,' I say, embarrassed.

We follow her over. She introduces us to Tiger, who comes alive when he talks tattoos.

'What kind of piece you having – stencil or freestyle?'

'Eh, I'm not sure,' Shane says. 'Four words?'

'Where?'

Shane taps his chest.

'Cool,' Tiger says. 'Does your chair tilt?' He touches the wheelchair.

'Yeah.'

'Easier for you to stay in it then, yeah? What are the words?'

'Alive Till I'm Dead.' Shane looks at me. 'In case I forget.'

I smile, though it breaks my heart.

Tiger sketches out the words in a Gothic design. And suddenly, I know why they call themselves artists. Shane pulls his T-shirt over his head. Oh my God, he is so caliente. Our eyes meet. Quickly, I look away.

The buzzing starts. I watch for a minute, but start to feel

kind of iffy, so I get up and go to the door for air. After a while, I go back. Tiger's still on the first letter. I look at Shane.

'Does it hurt?'

'It's OK,' he says. Which I take as a yes.

I sit with him, just don't look at it. I play a game on my phone. Then we get into this thing of staring at each other. At first, it's funny, like those blinking competitions. Then it's kind of peaceful. Then romantic. Or maybe that's just me. I don't take my eyes away. Neither does he. It's like we're daring each other. And ourselves.

Finally the buzzing stops. I break our gaze to look at the tattoo.

'Wow.' When I look back at Shane, he's still looking at me.

I'm not embarrassed. 'Can I touch it?' I ask, my eyes locked on his.

He nods. Tiger hands me antiseptic wipes. I clean my hands, then trace a finger slowly over each letter. I want so much for things to be different. I look at Shane and wish it. Will it. I get to the last letter, the 'd' of dead. I take my finger away but keep my eyes on his. I want to feel his lips on mine. I want his hands in my hair. And I want him to want me.

He gets his T-shirt on. Pays. And we're out. It's warmer after the air conditioning. Balmy even. Funny how it can do that in Ireland. Surprise you suddenly into summer. The pedestrian street at the very end of Temple Bar is deserted, forgotten. Hardly anyone comes down here anymore. Some of the shops have even closed down. *Shame*, I think.

'Kiss me,' he says. 'Just one fucking kiss, and I swear to God I'll never ask for anything again as long as I live.'

I burst into a smile and before he changes his mind, I bend down, close my eyes and kiss him like I've never kissed anyone, like I've been wanting to for a thousand years. He kisses me back the same way, his hands in my hair just like I imagined. We lose ourselves in each other, forgetting everything. Then he's pulling back.

'Sorry. Sorry, sorry, sorry … we can't …'

I put my hands on the arms of his wheelchair and whoosh myself up, so that I'm kneeling on his seat, one knee on either side of him. I take his face in my hands and I kiss him again, this time with my eyes open. He closes his, like this will be our last and he's going to make the most of it. When we finally pull apart, he looks sad.

'If things were different, Sarah, we'd be together. We'd have been since that time I told you we couldn't be … But things aren't different.'

I'm not accepting that. I'm just not. 'You say you want to live till you die? Well, you're not the only one. You're going to lose power in your arms, your hands. So let's not waste another moment, OK? Let's just be together now for as long as we can be. It's what we both want. So let's just do it.' I take his hands and I put his palms flat against my face. I move them down over my neck, my chest. All the time looking into his eyes. 'I want this. You want this. Ask me out. Go on.'

His voice is hoarse when he says, 'What can someone like me ever give you?'

'You.' I take his face in my hands and look deep into his eyes. 'I'm a big girl, Shane. I know what I'm doing. I know what I want.'

'I'll let you down. It's inevitable.'

'That's what guys do, right?'

He smiles. But then it fades. 'Sarah?'

'Yeah?'

'You have to promise me something.'

'What?' Anything.

'If we do this—'

'We're doing this.'

'I want you to leave, just walk away, the minute, the second, you feel like it. You don't have to explain. I'll know.'

'OK,' I say just to shut him up. I'm not going anywhere. No matter how bad it gets.

'I don't know how fast this is going to progress, but it is going to get bad. I don't want you staying out of guilt. I don't want your charity. Ever.' He looks into my eyes. 'OK?'

'OK.' Then I smile. 'So is that a yes?'

'I need you to promise.'

'I promise,' I say impatiently. 'Now kiss me, *for God's sake*.'

He kisses me. And it's like the best present in the world. He pulls back. And when he looks at me his eyes are so soft.

'Do you know how long I've wanted to do that?' he asks.

I smile. 'How long?'

'Since I first saw you.'

'But you hated me!'

'And wanting to kiss you made me hate you even more.'

'God, you're so mature,' I say, kissing him again.

I go home totally on air. Louis is in the kitchen, biting into a massive sandwich, like he's no worries. I think of Alex, falling apart. I don't care what she says, this is his problem too – or at least it should be. He's nineteen. She's sixteen. She was messed up. He wasn't.

'So what's happening with Miriam?' I ask. Angry.

'What *is it with* you and Miriam?' he asks. Amused.

'Do you love her?'

'Do you care?'

'Do you love her?' I insist.

'It's not that kind of thing.'

'It never is with you.'

He shakes his head, puts down his sandwich, picks up his plate and Coke and starts to leave.

'What are you doing with your life?' I ask, and I know I sound like Mum.

He stops and looks at me. 'Enjoying it.'

'No. You're wasting it. And Miriam's. You only get one life, Louis.'

He squints at me. 'What is *with* you today?'

'If you'd a year to live, what would you do? Seriously? Would you really keep going the way you're going?'

'Sarah. Loosen up, for Christ sake.' He heads for the door.

'OK. Then don't waste Miriam's time,' I call after him.

He turns. 'I don't think *Miriam* would call it a waste of time.' Then he smiles – that lazy, Louis smile and disappears.

After dinner, I'm up in my room, trying to concentrate on French but thinking of Shane instead, when my phone rings. It's Rachel.

'Everything's OK. I went over to Alex today. You were right. She really needs us, Sarah.' And I feel like saying, *welcome back*. 'We should bring her out tomorrow. Somewhere normal. Like the movies.'

'OK.'

'Just to give her a break from all this.'

'What if she doesn't want to go?'

'She won't. That's why we're going to just turn up. And bring her. We'll tell her we've booked the tickets. We'll tell her Mike's waiting downstairs.'

'What if he isn't?'

'He will be. I've spoken to her dad. He's in on this.'

And that is another reason I needed Rachel. She always knows what to do.

Later, Mum calls up to my room.

'I bought doughnuts,' she says. She walks in with a doughnut and a glass of milk.

'Supper!' I say. We never have supper.

She looks at my wall.

'Who's that?'

Instead of my caliente wall are the photos I took of Shane, blown up.

'That's Shane,' I say, proudly. I don't care what she says about his hair, his chest.

'He's … beautiful.' She looks at me, so surprised. 'Your photos are amazing, Sarah. You have real talent.'

'They're just photos.'

'No. Look at the character in his eyes, the curve at the back of his neck. You've captured, my God, so much.'

I look at them closer. OK, so maybe they're good. But that's because they're of Shane.

'There's such intimacy in those shots,' she says. Then she looks at me for the longest time. 'You love him, don't you?'

And that's when it hits me. I do.

I just look at her.

She doesn't say anything. Good or bad. Just opens her arms. I go to her. And she wraps them round me.

27
BORING

Sunday. Because we're bringing Alex to the movies in the afternoon, I call to Shane earlier than usual. He's having physio. So I wait. There's a mass going on in the main room. I sit through it, thinking of him, thinking of Alex, and thinking of exams – which are in two weeks.

At last, he's free. I hurry to his room.

'Hey,' I say feeling my face break into a smile, like a flower opening to the sun.

He looks serious. 'Are you *sure* you want this?'

I go to him, climb up on his chair and kiss him. It is a long lingering kiss designed to leave no doubt. I pull back.

'Are you *sure* you're sure?' he jokes.

'Actually, I don't know. Kiss me again.'

He smiles, takes my face in his hands and presses his mouth to mine. It's a good kiss. It's a great kiss. He pulls back.

'Well?' he asks.

'Hmm. Still not sure.'

He grabs me, crushes his mouth against mine. And then we're seriously snogging. We've been holding back so long, aching for each other, and now we're together, finally together. After I don't know how long, I pull back.

'All right,' I say reluctantly. 'I'm sure.'

Then we're kissing again. I slip my hands under his T-shirt and run them over his chest. I've never been so turned on in my life. He lifts my top over my head. I hold my arms up, like a kid. He looks at me and smiles.

'What?' I ask.

'Better.'

'Better than what?'

'I imagined.'

I smile. 'You imagined?'

'I'm a guy, right?'

He runs a finger along my lips. I bite it. He laughs. There's a knock at the door. I jump up, grab my T-shirt, drag it on inside out, run a hand through my hair. The door opens and it's Christina. She looks at us like she knows something's up. But she says nothing. She tells Shane about an appointment with an occupational therapist, but she sounds distracted. Then she reverses out of the room.

I look at Shane. 'Oh God. She can't stop us, can she?'

'No. It's none of her business.'

'Still, I wish there was a lock on the door.'

'Get back up here.'

Smiling, I climb back up on my perch.

'So how come you're here so early?'

I can't honestly answer that question without telling him about Alex. I've kept it in for so long. We're together now and I don't want to keep anything from him. I know she'd understand. So I tell him.

'Do you think there's any chance they'll get back together?' I ask hopefully.

He grimaces. 'No guy wants to give up everything for another guy's kid.' He shrugs. 'It's kinda the way we are.'

'Shit.'

'What about Louis?' he asks.

'She won't tell him. Even if she did, I'm not sure what he'd do. He doesn't exactly take life seriously.'

He frowns, thinking. And I love that about him, how everyone else's problems are more important than his own.

'That's why we're bringing her to the movies. To force her to get out, get on with life.'

'If there's anyone good at that, it's you.' He kisses me.

I put my nose to his and gaze into his eyes.

'Of course, you know what this means,' he says, fiddling with my hair. 'I'll be going out with an aunt.'

'Marry me and you'd be an uncle.'

'OK,' he says cheerfully.

I look at him.

'I was joking,' he says.

'So was I. But we could.'

'You're completely mad, you know that?'

'And you're a sitting duck.' I start tickling him.

'Get off. Jesus.'

And then we're kissing again.

I expected Alex to put up a fight, say she's not coming. Instead, she allows herself to be herded out the door. And I wonder if that's worse, if it means she has no fight left. Mike drives us to the cinema. Alex doesn't mind what we see. She doesn't want any goodies. And sits blankly looking at the screen. Every so often, she takes out a tissue and blows her nose.

I tell myself it'll take time.

Next day, she is on the DART. She looks weak and pale but she is here. Which means she's not giving up. I stick by her side in case she faints. Rachel's on the other side. And I swear to God, if anyone gets in her way, they're going down.

At school, she keeps disappearing to the loo and coming back with puffy eyes. I'm so worried about her that on her fourth trip, I go after her. She's already locked in a cubicle when I get there. I hear her sniffle. I feel guilty, like some kind of eavesdropper. But I wait. Because I'm determined.

'You OK?' I ask when she comes out.

'Do I look OK?'

She looks even worse than she did when David moved to the States. She goes to the sink.

'Alex? I was thinking. You know the person I went to see … about the shoplifting? She's really good to talk to. When you … need to talk to someone.'

She gives me a look. 'I don't think talking is going to solve my problems. Do you?'

She starts to splash water on her face.

I'm not giving up. I'm not going to let her bully me out of talking about this.

'Look, Alex, I'm the last person to tell anyone to go see someone. You know that.' She looks up from the sink – because she knows it's true. 'But this woman, Mary Gleeson, she's good. She sorted my head out when I didn't think it needed sorting. You know?'

'My head is fine.'

'I thought mine was too. You've so much to cope with, you know? So many decisions to make.'

'I know that. Don't you think I know that?' She's getting stressed now.

'She can help. I know you don't think she can. So I'm going to call her, OK, and ask if she'll see you?'

'I don't want to see her.'

'Can you just let me do this for you?'

'No.'

'OK, well, I'm just going to ask her to call you.'

'Do you ever give up?'

'Not when it comes to my friends.'

She rolls her eyes. And walks out.

But I don't care. She's not stopping me.

When I get to the canteen, she's not there. Neither is Rachel. I go looking for them. But only find Rachel, outside. I know straight away something's wrong.

'What is it?'

'Nothing.'

She's been crying. 'What happened?'

She looks at me. 'We had a fight.'

'You and Alex?'

'No. Me and Mark. It started off being about Alex but then it just blew up into something huge.'

'Why were you fighting about Alex?'

'He was going on about what happened with David, calling Alex a slag and such. I mean, I know he's upset for David. But she's my friend, you know?' Her eyes well up.

'Aw, Rache.'

'I mean, what does he expect?' She breaks down.

I put an arm around her. 'It'll be OK.'

'How did you do it?' she asks me.

'What?'

'Keep coming to school after you and Simon split up.'

'Hang on. This is just a fight, right? You and Mark
haven't actually split up?'

'No, but sometimes I think that maybe we should when
he goes on like that.'

Whoa, slow down. 'Rache, you're both upset about Alex
and David. But you still love each other, don't you?'

'He should know not to do that. She's my friend.'

'And I'm not standing up for him or anything, but maybe
he's so angry for David he's not thinking before he's speaking, yeah?' She shrugs. 'Maybe you just shouldn't talk about
David and Alex for a while – if you're just going to upset
each other.'

'Yeah, but we should be able to talk about anything,
shouldn't we?'

'I don't know. Isn't that expecting a lot? I mean, there are
things you wouldn't bring up with your parents because
you'd know it would upset them, right?' She looks at me
blankly. And I think, *does she really tell her parents everything?* 'Do they know you drink?'

'I don't drink much compared to most people.'

'Rachel. Do you tell them you drink?'

'Well … it's not like I bring it up.'

'There you go.'

She thinks about that for a moment. 'So, I should just
avoid talking about it?'

'Until it dies down anyway.'

'What about the rest of it?' she asks.

'What?'

'The fight.'

'What else were you fighting about?'

'God. Everything. How he doesn't take anything seriously.

}}{{

How he thinks I'm too serious. *He called me boring*!' she says
with the same horror as if he'd called her a crack whore.

I laugh.

'What's so funny?' she asks crossly.

I shrug. 'I just think he wants more fun, Rache.'

'Like, what, I'm a comedian?'

I'm laughing again. 'Sorry.'

'So that's a yes, obviously.' She is seriously angry with me.

'Do you love him?' I ask, knowing the answer.

'I guess,' she says, despondently.

'Why?'

'I don't know. He's cute. And fun. And witty. And I
don't know, he's just Mark.'

'And you don't really want to change him, do you?'

She thinks about that for a long time, then she smiles.
'No.'

Going home on the DART, it's just me and Alex. Rachel and
Mark have gone off somewhere to make up.

'Want me to go with you to Dalkey?' I ask.

She looks at me like she's coming out of a trance. 'What?'
I ask again.

'Eh, no. Thanks. I'm fine.'

'Maybe Mike should pick you up from school for a while,
even for a week or two.'

'No! I don't want to change anything. I don't want anyone to know.'

'OK.'

As we approach the stop for the home, I put my bag on
my lap ready to get up.

'How's Shane?' she asks, surprising me.

I want to tell her. But I know what she'll think – that I'm making the world's biggest mistake. So I just smile. 'He's good. Moving home soon.'

I expect her to say something bland, like 'great.' But she surprises me with, 'You'll miss him.'

'We're going to stay in touch,' I say, lightly, afraid she's sussed me. But she's gone again, miles away, back to her own, worried world.

When I get off the DART, I take out my phone. And call Mary Gleeson.

That night, Rachel calls.

'Oh my God, we just had the best time.'

'You and Mark?'

'Yeah. We just hung out and had a laugh.'

I smile. 'So it's not over, then?'

'No. It's not over.' I can hear the smile in her voice.

'Good. Cause you make a great couple.'

'I need to loosen up. I don't know why I get so uptight.'

'You're a high achiever, Rache. But, hey, look at what you've achieved.'

'I could have lost him, though. It was going that way.'

'Nah. He's too mad about you to let that happen. He's good for you, Rache. You don't need to worry about the other stuff. You're bright. You'll so get there. You know?'

'What are you up to?' she asks.

'Would you believe, studying?'

And we laugh.

28
CHINESE

The exams drop on me like something falling from the sky. I sit, waiting for our first paper (Maths, oh joy) to hit my desk. I look around. Everyone's so relaxed. Which isn't a total shocker. Transition Year exams don't matter to anyone. Except me. My heart is beating even faster than it usually does at exam time. Which is impressive.

And here it comes, the paper.

I lift it up. Turn it over, expecting the worst. I look at the first question. And think, *Oh my God. I can do this!* I come to the next question. And I don't get that this-is-Chinese feeling. I know what they want. I close my eyes and give Shane an imaginary high-five. It. Is. Amazing. I get all the questions finished. And for the first time, probably ever, I come out of an exam hall smiling.

'What did you get for number four?' I ask Rachel and Alex.

They stare at me. Because normally the last thing I want to do is discuss the paper. If anyone starts, I usually disappear.

As soon as I get to my locker, I call Shane. I tell him everything that came up and how I answered them. I'm on the phone so long, the others go ahead to lunch. Shane seems even happier than I am. I'd give anything to be with him right now.

In the afternoon, I actually *enjoy* an exam. Which is a bit freaky.

At dinner, I tell Mum, in total surprise, that I think I did well.

'Well, you've been doing a lot of study.'

'Yeah but it never feels like study with Shane.'

'You know,' Mum says, 'sometimes I wonder if getting caught shoplifting wasn't the best thing that's happened you.'

I stare at her. But then I start to think. If it wasn't for the community service, I'd never have met Shane.

'And maybe,' Mum says, 'the best thing that ever happened me was your father meeting someone else.'

Wow.

Shane moves home. And invites me over after school. His mum, Deirdre, answers the door. Before I know it, she's hugging me.

'Thank you,' she whispers in my ear. When she pulls back, her eyes are glistening. I love her instantly.

Shane appears behind her. 'Yo, homey. Welcome to my crib.'

I smile. 'Hey.'

I don't kiss him. His mum's there. I just follow them into this huge open-plan space containing kitchen, sitting and dining areas. It's bright and modern with enormous cream tiles, under-floor heating and cool leather furniture. It has amazing views out over Dublin Bay.

'Would you like a drink?' Deirdre asks.

'Sure, I'll get them in my room,' Shane says.

His room is on the same floor. The door slides open using remote control. It's amazing. Huge, for starters. Instead of windows there's a wall of glass which slides open to a balcony with views of the sea, right out over to Howth. But I'm a gadget person and his bed looks seriously interesting.

'Can I try it out?'

He hands me a zapper. I go through all its functions. Moving the head up and down, rotating the bed from side to side, starting a ripple movement on this special mattress.

'Look up,' he says.

And there are my stars. Aw.

'Your crystal's over there.'

'*Your* crystal.'

'OK. My crystal.' He smiles.

His favourite buildings are over his bed. On the wall opposite is a giant TV. He's got an X-box 360 and a Wii.

'Do you have the cow race game?' I ask enthusiastically.

He smiles. And nods.

'I am moving in.'

He gets me a Coke from a cool, miniature fridge.

'Oh my God, there's Quagmire.'

He smiles. 'You meet at last.'

Quagmire lies motionless under a red lamp.

'Does he do anything?'

'He gets interesting when he eats.'

I shiver. 'I'll take your word for it.'

'The couch pulls into a bed,' he says. 'For anyone who wants to stay over.'

}|{

'Is that an invitation?' I flirt. Then I climb up on his chair and kiss him. 'Have you told your parents that we're together?'

'Course I have.'

'What did they say?'

He looks at me, suddenly serious. 'They were worried. For you.'

'Yeah well I hope you told them not to be.'

'Sarah, *I'm* worried for you. Have you been on Google Images lately?'

'Oh my God, Shane. You know I've looked it up. You know I know. Everything.'

He doesn't back down. 'I meant what I said about leaving. Any time.'

I put my face right up to his. 'I know you did. But I won't be going anywhere.' I kiss him. 'Any time.'

'You know,' he says. And he's smiling now. 'You're my mum's hero.'

I smile. 'Yeah, well, you're mine.'

I feel bad that I haven't told anyone about us. It's like I'm not proud of him. Which I so am.

He raises his Coke. 'To home.'

'To home.'

'And you.'

I smile. 'And me.'

We kiss.

'OK, you've exams tomorrow. Let's study.'

I groan. But take out my books. Because he is always, always thinking of me.

Next day is another good-exam day. Wahoo! On our way out of school, I tell Alex and Rachel about Shane.

'I kinda guessed,' Alex says.

'You think I'm mad, don't you?'

'No, I don't. I think you're brave.'

'He must be really special,' Rachel says.

'He is. He really is.'

'When are we going to meet him?' Alex asks.

'Oh my God, I'd love that. I don't know. I'll check with Shane.'

'Call him,' Rachel says.

'What, now?'

'Yeah, why not?'

I shrug. Smile. 'OK.'

I make the call.

'Thought you'd never ask,' he says.

We arrange it for Saturday afternoon. As soon as I put down the phone, though, I start to worry.

'Don't be nice to him,' I say. 'Just be normal.'

They nod.

'Like, give him the usual grief and stuff.'

'OK.'

'Slag him, like.'

Rachel smiles. 'It's OK. We get it.'

I nod. 'Good.'

'Don't worry. It'll be great,' she says.

'Where'll we meet?' Alex asks.

'The Jitter Mug has wheelchair access,' I say, but then remember. 'But that might be, like, awkward for you ... with Louis there.'

Alex looks at me. 'No. I've decided from now on, I'm going to be as ballsy as you.'

I don't know why that makes me teary but it does.

'You were right about Mary Gleeson,' she says.

'Who?' Rachel asks. And I think it must be a record. For me to know something she doesn't.

'Sarah's shrink.'

'Did you actually go see her?'

'Not yet. We just spoke on the phone. But you were right. She makes you feel that you can do stuff, that you have choices. I'm going to see her tomorrow.' She smiles across at me. 'Thanks, Sarah.'

I smile back. I feel closer to her than I ever have.

Friday night, I'm on a high. The exams are over and not one was a disaster. I'm going upstairs, when Louis comes out of his room. He gives me this strange look.

'What?' I ask.

'Nothing,' he says. And walks into the bathroom.

I shrug and head up to my room. I go on Facebook, chat to Shane and forget all about Louis.

29
GOOD LUCK

First thing Saturday my phone rings. I sit up in bed. It's Alex.

'Hey,' I say, surprised. 'What's up?'

'I told Louis.'

Oh my God. That explains last night. 'What did he say?'

'It's OK. I told him I didn't expect anything.'

'What did he say?' I ask, impatiently.

Another pause. 'Good luck, more or less.'

'Good *luck*? That's *it*? Oh my God. I'll kill him.'

'Sarah. I don't want anything from Louis, I told him that. I was just letting him know, so I've nothing to hide. Mary Gleeson made me see it – a lifetime secret would be too much.'

'So you're still going to keep the baby.'

'It still has my mum's genes.'

'I can't believe he said "good luck". I mean what kind of guy says "good luck"?'

'Sarah I'm glad he did. We're not in a relationship. This would just tie us together.'

}|{

'So he gets away scot free?'

'I just want to get on with this. I don't want hassle. I don't need his help.'

'He has responsibilities. He's my brother. *I* feel responsible—'

'Well don't. Because you're not.'

'I feel it.'

'Sarah, you've been the best friend about this. Do *not* feel guilty.'

'He's my brother. You'd never have even met if it wasn't for me.'

'OK now, stop. This way is best. I've told him. He knows. And I'm not tied to him. I'm free. Free to bring this baby up the way I want to.'

'Still—'

'Sarah, stop. I mean it.'

'OK.' Then I think about today. 'What about this afternoon? The coffee shop.'

'What about it? Louis made his choice. And that's fine with me. I'm not letting it get in the way of my life. I'll have coffee where I want to have coffee.'

I march straight down to him. Burst in his door.

He's still in bed. Of course.

'"Good luck"? What kind of guy says "good luck"? Oh my God, you're such a wimp.'

He sits up. Has the decency to look guilty. 'Right, OK. I'm a wimp.' He reaches for a T-shirt and drags it on.

'Alex is my friend. How could you do it?'

'It wasn't some evil plan.'

'She's sixteen.'

}|{

'Jesus. Can you keep your voice down?' He's out of the bed now, dragging on his jeans.

'So, you still enjoying life?'

He runs his fingers through his hair, walks to the window, looks out, turns around. 'She doesn't want anything from me. She made that clear.'

'Did you *offer* anything?'

He looks down at his feet.

'You're going to be a dad, Louis. You're going to have a son. Or daughter. Our dad walked out on us. You going to do the same?'

'I'm going out with someone.'

'Oh my God. Suddenly you're going out with someone? Would that be Miriam by any chance?'

He turns from me, stretches out his arms on the window sill and leans forward. Finally, he turns back.

'Alex made her choice. It was the surfer dude.'

'What?'

'She didn't want me. She wanted him.'

I don't get it. 'You asked her to choose?'

'No.'

'Then what are you talking about?'

'Nothing.'

'By the way, the "surfer dude" was standing by Alex till it turned out it was your baby.'

'Good for him,' he says, like he hates him.

'Aren't you even sorry?'

'Of course I'm sorry.'

'Then do something.'

'She doesn't want me to, OK?'

'How convenient.'

'It's not convenient. It's a bloody fact.'

'So how'll you feel when your kid looks you in the eye some day and doesn't know what you are to them?'

'Relieved. Probably.'

'Asshole,' I say, and leave.

When Shane and I get to the Jitter Mug, Alex and Rachel are already there. I wave. They wave back. Shane waves too, messing. We laugh. I introduce everyone. Shane asks if he can get them anything.

'No, we're fine thanks,' Rachel says.

He looks at me. 'What are you having?'

'Sure, I'll go up with you.'

'No. Stay. You're grand.'

'OK, thanks,' I say, because I know he wants to do this.

I tell him what I want, then sit down, hoping he'll manage.

'He's lovely,' Alex whispers.

'Kind of adorable,' Rachel says.

I smile. Because he is both those things. And they see it.

'Don't look now,' Rachel says, 'but guess who's just walked in.'

We look – of course. It's Simon. And Amy. Luckily, they're too into each other to see us. I turn around to see how Shane's doing. And smile. He's on his way. I get up and pull a chair out of the way to make space for him.

'My God,' Shane says to me. 'There's a guy at the counter looks just like you.'

We all look at each other. I laugh.

'That's amazing. No one ever thinks we look alike. That's Louis, my brother. Oh God, sorry. I should have introduced you.'

)I{

He looks back at Louis. 'I can't believe no one sees it.' He turns to Rachel and Alex. 'You don't see it?'

Then, like they've known each other all their lives, they're talking. I guess that's when I realise how nervous I've been about this whole thing.

We're there an hour when a shadow falls over us. I look up.

'I *thought* I recognised you!'

It's Simon. And he's talking to Shane, who he has never met in his life.

Shane smiles. 'Simon,' he says.

That's when I get it. Facebook.

Simon turns to me. 'You left me for *this*.' He looks at Shane as if he's dirt.

I stand up. 'Piss off, Simon.'

He smiles. 'Or else?'

I panic. Or else what? 'I'll tell them about your little secret.'

'What secret?'

There is no secret. 'How small you are.'

He laughs like I'm hilarious.

So I look down at his crotch. 'There isn't even a bulge, Simon.'

Everyone automatically looks. Including Amy, who's standing beside him, sidekick to bully.

Simon looks at Shane, then at me, with his eyebrows raised. 'So you've a bulge now, Sarah? Is that what you're saying?'

I stand tall. 'What I'm saying is that Shane is more of a man than you'll ever be.' And I'm so sorry to be standing here discussing Shane like he's invisible. How did we get to this?

'You know, I always thought you were sad,' Simon says. 'But this is seriously sad.'

'Not as sad as you,' is all I can think of to say. I'm shaking. With rage. With humiliation for Shane.

'Back off, asshole,' Shane says, his voice clear, strong, confident.

Simon laughs. 'What are you going to do, wheel on me?'

'Is everything OK here?' It's Louis, arriving over, full of authority. I've never seen him like this.

'Yeah, fine,' I say. 'Simon was just leaving.' I stare at him to make sure he does.

Simon shakes his head, as if he's seen everything. 'Big brother saves the day,' he says sarcastically.

Louis walks right up to Simon. He's about five inches taller, with a lot more muscle.

'I'm sorry,' Simon says to Louis, 'but do you own the place? Or do you just act like you do?'

Louis smiles. 'You're barred, buddy. I don't want to see you in here again.'

'Best news I've had all day. I hate this dump.' He turns and walks, Amy hurrying to keep up.

Why don't cruel diseases ever hit people who deserve them? I think, sitting back down. Everyone in the coffee shop is staring. Louis and Alex are looking at each other. His eyes seem sorry. Then he seems to wake up.

'Everyone OK?' he asks.

'Yeah, thanks,' I say. My face is red and I want to punch my fist through something. Preferably Simon's face.

'I'll get you some more drinks.' Louis looks to see what we're having and is gone.

I look at Shane. His jaw is tight, his face dark. He looks like he could kill.

}|{

I try to make a joke of it. 'That just proves what a loser I was before I met you – going out with a-holes like him.'

'Let's go,' he says.

'Are you sure?'

'Tell Louis thanks for the drinks,' he says to the others.

They nod. 'OK, yeah, sure,' Alex says.

'Good to meet you, Shane,' Rachel says.

He forces a smile. 'You too.'

'See you,' I say to them, trying not to cry. I wanted so badly for this to go well. Now it's ruined.

Alex smiles a chin-up smile.

Rachel puts a hand up in a kind of wave.

I go after Shane, who's already outside.

'How dare he talk to you like that!' he says, so angry.

'I can handle myself.'

But it's like he hasn't heard. 'All I had to do was stand up. And he'd have backed off. Just stand up. I couldn't even do that.'

I look at him straight. 'Trust me, if that was an option, he'd never have come over. Simon is the world's biggest wimp.'

'Let's get out of here.'

His mood is low all the way back to his place.

In his room, he says, 'I can't protect you. I can't stand up for you.'

'I don't need you to.'

'*I* need me to.'

I'll kill Simon. I swear to God, I'll kill him.

He looks down at the wheelchair and slams his fist against it.

It is ages before either of us speaks. We just sit there. I

regret everything. Ever going out with Simon. Trying to stand up to him and only making it worse. Not leaving when I saw him come in.

'This defines me,' Shane says, looking down at his body. He sounds beaten.

'Not to me.'

He looks at me like he doesn't believe me. 'What was the first thing you thought when you saw me?'

I think back. 'I wondered why you were turned away from everyone.'

'OK, the second thing.'

'I thought your beard was terrible.'

He smiles despite everything. 'OK. After that.'

'I wondered what age you were.'

'Are you normal?' he jokes.

'Probably not.'

'OK. If you'd seen me *on the street* for the first time, what would you have thought – there's a guy in a wheelchair?'

'I don't know. Maybe.'

'There you go. It does define me,' he says gloomily.

'To strangers, maybe.'

'Mostly everyone is a stranger.'

'Since when do strangers matter? They don't know you. You'll never see them again. Fuck them.'

He looks at me for a long time. Then he quietly says, 'You're great. You know that?'

'Course I do.' But the funny thing is, before Shane, I did care what people thought, what everyone thought. I've changed. And it's because of him.

'Don't suppose I could have one of those hugs?' he says.

'No.' I walk away from him. Over to his music system. I turn on some dance music. Then I lock the door.

'What are you doing?'

'Shh.'

I stand before him, holding his eyes with mine. I start to move to the music, move my hips, dance for him. Slowly, I unbutton my shirt. I whip it off and throw it at him. The corner of his mouth twitches into a smile. I unzip my skirt. Let it fall to my ankles. I step out of it with one leg and fling it at him with the other. He laughs. In my bra and thong I dance towards him. I take his face in my hands and kiss him. Then I dance away again, teasing him. I close my eyes and start to really get into the music. Finally, I go to him. I hooch myself up so that I straddle him.

'Free lap dances for moody men,' I say in a fake accent, maybe Russian.

He smiles.

'I said *moody* men.'

He frowns. Then laughs. And I know I've won.

Now that I've offered, I've no idea how to lap dance. But I use my imagination. I rotate my hips, forward, back. I move my body close, then away. I raise my arms over my head, moving to the music. I'm enjoying it, turning him on, the power of that. He reaches for me.

'Ah, ah. No touching. Is not professional. I am professional.' I keep the accent up.

He laughs.

'No touching till I finish.'

'Then hurry up.'

'Shhh,' I say. 'No talking. No touching.'

In the end, I touch him. I take his hands and put them on me. 'OK. Touching.'

He pulls me to him. And our mouths meet with an aggression that hasn't been there before. I push him back and rip his top over his head. I kiss his tattoo. He opens my bra, throws it aside and curses. His touch is light and rhythmical, like he knows how to be with a woman. I feel things I've never felt before. I rock back and forth, wanting more. I reach down, open his belt, his trousers. Then suddenly I'm stopping. I'm looking up at him in shock. And we're laughing because everything's working down there. He shrugs.

'So we do more than lap dance,' I say in that voice I'm beginning to like.

I jump up, get naked. Then I stop, remembering the one thing that could screw up my life – the one thing that has screwed up Alex's.

'Do you have something?'

'Bottom drawer by the bed. Hidden.'

I hurry over. 'Bingo,' I say when I find one.

He laughs. 'Bingo,' he says, like he's remembering how it all started.

Then I'm back.

He looks at me. 'You sure?' he asks.

I answer him with my body.

Alex was right. It *is* different with someone you love. But not just that, it's different with someone who cares about you. And who knows what he is doing. Shane is amazing. He makes me feel things I've never felt before. Pleasure I never thought possible. Until my neck falls back and my whole body floods with waves. I hear him curse. I open my eyes to see the guy I love explode. It's the best feeling in the world. He opens his eyes. We laugh in shock at what's just happened between us, then cling to each other. Then, out of nowhere, tears spring to my eyes because I can't help thinking, what will I do without him? I stay clinging to him, so that he doesn't see my tears.

)|(

'You OK?' he asks.

'No,' I say, without moving. 'I'm much better than OK.'

And by the time I pull back, I am, again.

I hate having to leave him. And go home. I lie on my bed, trying to relive every moment, when there's a knock on my door.

'Hey,' Louis says, coming in. 'How're you doing? What was all that about today?'

I'd almost forgotten the Jitter Mug. I turn on my side and raise myself onto an elbow. 'Just my ex-boyfriend being an asshole to my current boyfriend.'

'You're going out with the guy in the wheelchair?'

I sit up. 'His name is Shane.'

There's a long pause. 'No offence, but aren't you complicating your life a bit?'

'Some of us aren't afraid of complication, Louis.' Hint, hint.

'Have you really thought this through, though? What if you want to end it? You're going to feel pretty shitty walking out on a guy in a wheelchair.'

'Unlike you, Louis, I'm not always planning my next exit.'

It's like he doesn't hear me. 'What happened him? Car accident?'

'Shane has motor neurone disease – if you must know.'

'Come again?'

For the first time in my life, I stun my brother into silence with a medical fact.

Finally, he speaks. 'Do you love him?' he asks carefully.

'Yes, I love him.'

'And you're on for this?'

'Yes, I'm on for this.'

'Then you're a braver person than I am.'
'You could be brave. You have a chance.'
He gets up. Stretches (like we've been discussing the weather). And leaves.

30
REINDEER

Sunday, I call Alex.

'Did you get a print-off of the ultrasound?'

'Yeah, why?'

'Can I borrow it?'

There's a pause. 'Why?'

'I'm going to be an aunt. I want to photocopy it.'

'Oh my God, I never thought of that. Wow.'

'We'll be *kind of* related? Well, not actually related, but you know, connected.'

'That's amazing!'

'And you know Rachel could be godmother and we'd all have, like, a job.'

'You always cheer me up,' she says but sounds kind of sad.

'So can I've the ultrasound picture?'

'Sure.'

'Will I call over for it?' I want to make sure she's OK anyway.

'Yeah sure.'

*

She takes it out of a small brown envelope and hands it to me without looking at it. It's black and white and grainy.

'Oh *my God*. It's so cute. Look at its tiny little hands.' I hold it out to her.

She takes it, looks at it, then puts the back of her hand to her mouth. She starts to shake, silently crying.

'Oh God. I'm sorry,' I say. 'This was a mistake.'

She shakes her head. 'No. It's just … First time I looked at this, David was beside me. We were together, making plans, telling each other how cute the baby was. It was the loveliest moment. Then …' She looks up at me. 'I still can't believe it. One split second and everything changed. I've lost him forever. I miss him so much.' She looks at me, her eyes filled suddenly with fear. 'I don't know if I can do it on my own.'

'Course you can.'

'Oh yeah, what about school? How'll I go to school with a baby? What about college?'

'Alex, come on. Think about it.' (I have.) 'Your dad's minted. He can hire nannies, nurses, whatever you need to help with the baby. You can still have a life. And look at this little person. So beautiful. So magical.'

'So delicate. So vulnerable.'

'We were all vulnerable. Look at us now.'

'Yeah, but what do I know about babies? What kind of mum can I be? I'm *sixteen*.'

'You'll be seventeen. And all you have to do is love it.'

She looks at me, eyes wide. 'What if I can't? What if I hate it?'

'You won't. It's impossible to hate a baby. Nature makes them cute for a reason.'

'I *could* hate it. For ruining my life.'

'It won't ruin your life.'

'It already has. I've lost David. And no guy will ever go near me for the rest of my life because no guy wants to be an instant dad and I don't even know why I'm *thinking* of that because I don't want anyone else, only David.'

Oh my God, I think. *It's a total mess. And I haven't a clue what I'm talking about.*

'*Do* you hate it?' I ask. Afraid of the answer.

She looks at me for a long time, her eyes wide and frightened. And just when I expect her to say yes, she shakes her head.

'I can't.' She shrugs. 'It's not its fault, is it? It's mine.'

Which leads me to another terrifying thought: 'You don't hate yourself, do you?'

'No, but I really tried.' She smiles suddenly, and it's like the sun coming out.

'Can I plait your hair?' I say.

'Why?' she asks, surprised.

'I don't know. I just feel like it.' And we've talked enough and worried enough and sometimes it's just nice for someone to play with your hair.

She smiles. 'OK, go on then, knock yourself out.'

'Have you a comb?'

She gets one, then sits down. I start by combing her hair through. Soon I'm plaiting. For a long time, there's just this pleasant silence.

Then, out of nowhere, she says, 'You'll be there for me, right? No matter what, right?'

And because it's Alex, the person who never needs anyone, it's extra sad. I let go of her plait and come round to face her. 'No matter what. One hundred per cent.'

She closes her eyes and nods. 'Good.'

I bang the ultrasound picture down in front of Louis.

'Meet your baby.'

He closes his eyes, tips his head back and groans. I pick up the picture and put it in his hand. I lift his hand up to his face. He opens his eyes and looks at it. For ages, he says nothing. Then, 'How old?'

'Thirteen weeks when it was taken. More now. Obviously.'

He doesn't take his eyes off it. 'Boy or girl?'

'I don't know.'

For ages, he just stares at the picture. Then he looks at me. 'It's not as easy as you think. I like her, OK?'

'Isn't that a good thing?'

'Not if she doesn't like me. Which she doesn't.'

'Can't you just forget that?'

He laughs like that would be totally impossible. 'Would you get involved with someone who doesn't want you involved, someone you like but can't have?'

'You more than like her, don't you?'

He puts down the picture. Sighs deeply. 'Yeah, OK, I more than like her, which is why I can't play happy families.' I feel like hugging him. 'You have to give up on this, Sarah, OK? Alex doesn't want me involved. Let's leave it at that. And make it easier for everyone.' He pushes the scan across his desk. 'And you needn't tell her I like her.'

I wouldn't do that to him. Or her. 'It's OK. I won't.'

Minutes later, I hear him pounding on his drums. He hasn't played his drums in years.

)|(

*

When I call to Shane after school the next day, Deirdre isn't her usual friendly self. Oh my God. Could she have heard us?

'Is your mum OK?' I ask when we get to his room.

'Just a bit pissed with me.'

'*Why?*'

'I cancelled my physio.'

'Why?' He needs his physio.

'The physiotherapist couldn't do his usual time and you were going to be here.'

'Shane. I don't mind waiting. Seriously.'

'I know, but I get tired after physio. I don't want to be tired for you.'

'OK. Here's what you do. Have the physio. Sleep for an hour. I'll hang out with your mum.' I've no idea *what* we'll talk about but I'm sure we'll come up with something.

'You don't want to hang out with my mum.'

'Shane. If you don't do your physio, I'll leave. I mean it.'

He holds up his hands. 'OK, OK. I'll do my physio.'

'And you have to sleep after.'

'You better wake me after half an hour.'

'An hour. And, yes, I'll wake you.'

'Promise?'

'Jesus. I promise.'

'OK.'

We go out to tell his mum.

'Thank you, Sarah,' she says. 'At least he listens to you.'

We call the physio and all have coffee together until he comes, then Shane heads to his room with him.

'I was just going to sort through old photos,' Deirdre says. 'Would you like to help?'

}|{

'Sure.'

She disappears for a while and returns with an armful of shoe boxes.

'Would you believe I never put them in albums?' She tips the boxes over and hundreds of old photos fall out all over the table. 'Dive in,' she says. 'Just help me put them in some sort of order. If you can.'

The first photo I pick up is of an angel. He's about three with big blue eyes and blond hair. He's wearing reindeer antlers and a little red nose.

'Aw, bless,' I say, and hand it to her.

She looks miles away, her face soft and dreamy. And I think, *of all people, this is hardest for her*. She's loved him for nineteen years. She knows him better than anyone. Loves him more than anyone. Even me. I pick up a photo of Shane in rugby gear. His kit and knees are covered in mud. She looks at it.

'He was eleven. This was taken just before he heard he'd been put on the C team. He was devastated. I told him it was a good thing because it would teach him how to deal with disappointment. He looked at me like I was mad. But he picked himself up, turned up early to every training session, every game. Gave it his all.' I smile. That'd be Shane. 'He loved rugby,' she says, and her eyes fill.

And even though I don't know her, I know what she's feeling. I reach for her hand and squeeze it. She looks at me and smiles.

'What would we do without you?'

The physiotherapist leaves. We stay, sorting photos, a whole record of Shane's life. After an hour, I go in to wake him.

But how can I when he looks so peaceful, away in some other world where he might be running, playing rugby or diving into the sea? I take off my shoes and slip in beside him. Slowly, so he doesn't wake, I snuggle up to him. I inhale the smell that is uniquely his. I kiss his neck softly. Then I slip my arms around him.

He stirs.

'Hello,' he says.

I smile. 'Hello.'

'This is nice.'

'I could stay here all day.'

'Let's,' he says.

'OK!'

'I was joking.'

'I wasn't.'

I start running a finger along his back, then remember a game we played as kids, outlining a letter on someone's back and having them guess what it was. I trace a letter.

'T,' he says.

'Yep.' I do another.

'U.'

'Yep.' Another.

'Q.'

'This is too easy. I'm going to do words.'

'OK.' He settles himself like he's going to concentrate. Like he's having fun.

I trace the letter 'I'.

'I thought we were doing words.'

'I is a word, you retard.'

He laughs.

I don't set out to write it. But I do end up writing it. I

trace the letters L. U. V.

'Love?'

Then I trace the letter U.

It takes a second, but then he turns his head. 'You love me?'

'I love you.'

He smiles. 'Come over here.'

I climb over him. Then lie facing him.

'That's the nicest thing anyone's ever spelled on my back.' He smiles, leans forward and kisses me. 'I love you,' he says.

'You do?' I didn't expect anything back, just wanted him to have that, my love. I kiss him. So happy.

'I'd have told you sooner but I didn't want to trap you with it.'

'How can you trap something you already have?'

'God, I love you.' He moves my hair from my face. 'In fact, I more than love you, I wuv you.'

I smile. 'I wuv you too.'

'Want to know when I knew?' he asks.

'Absolutely.'

'The lap dance.'

'That *late*? Really?'

He shrugs. 'I always thought you'd leave, so I didn't let myself. But then the lap dance. It was just so you. So wonderfully you. I couldn't stop it anymore. I didn't want to. And when I fell, I fell big time. It was like being hit over the head.'

I feel my heart swell.

'Want to know when I fell for you?' And it's only now I realise the exact moment. 'The day you were waiting outside for me with your woolly cap on.'

He smiles. 'How could that be love? You didn't even know me then.'

'I knew you.'
'It was the hat?' he says, baffled.
'It was the hat.'
Then he smiles and says, 'That's so you.'
And then we reach for each other.

31
FAMILY GUY

The last week of school flies. It doesn't even feel like school
– we do nothing. Friday night, we party. Saturday, I get a
new client, a little Scottie, called Scottie. He's so cute, with
an old man's face and long white tufts of hair falling down
over his eyes.

'When are you going to get a proper dog?' Louis asks,
walking into the kitchen carrying a load of books.

'What's a proper dog?'

'A Boxer. An Alsatian. Not these fluff balls. I feel like
drop-kicking them.'

'You don't even play rugby.'

Scottie runs to him and starts licking his bare feet.

'Jesus,' he says. He climbs up on a chair.

I laugh. 'He's not a mouse.'

'You sure? Here, throw me my runners, will you?'

I get the runners and throw them to him, one at a time.
'What are you doing up so early anyway?'

He drags the runners on. 'Thought I'd cram a bit.'

'*You*, study?'

'It's been known to happen,' he says, climbing down. I give him a look. 'OK, it hasn't. But given that I'll probably have to repeat—'

'Oh God. Will you?'

'It's OK. I'll pass next time. The trick is studying.'

'Jesus, Louis.'

He gestures to the books. 'You're looking at a new man, here.'

He does look different. Maybe it's just the books. I've never actually seen him study. Not that he's opened anything yet. He's looking at Scottie.

'Think you might have a problem there,' he says.

Scottie's dragging his bum along the floor.

'What's he *doing*?' I ask.

'Scratching his ass.'

'What? Why?'

'He's got worms.'

'Oh my God. How do you know?'

'*Family Guy.*'

'*Family Guy?*'

'There's this episode where Brian has worms.'

My whole face wrinkles up. I look at Scottie like he's evil. 'What'll we do?'

Louis looks like he's trying to remember. 'Stewey gave Brian pills. Google it. You probably get worm pills from the vet or something.'

'Great! Just what I need.' Hassle.

'Jesus, he licked my feet,' Louis says.

I had him all over me. Ee-ew. I let Scottie out into the garden, run upstairs, have a shower, change my clothes and go on Google. I text Scottie's owner. He texts straight back

)I(

(from Sweden) and apologises. He says he'll 'sort me out' when he gets back. He *better*. I rush to the vet in Dun Laoghaire, get the treatment, go to the chemist and get worm tablets for us. Then I go back and try to get the dog to eat his tablet.

He won't. So I put it in his food. He eats the food and leaves the tablet, which is now soggy, half dissolved and covered in dog food. I pick it out of the empty bowl (ee-ew) and look around. I get some kitchen paper, put the tablet on it, go to the sink and scrub my hands. Then get a piece of steak from the fridge. With the sharpest knife I can find, I cut a secret hole. I slip the tablet in. Then put the piece of meat in his bowl.

He eyes me suspiciously but then gulps it down anyway. I almost sink to the ground in relief. I have to clean everywhere because – wait for the worst bit – worms lay eggs. The dog's bed is machine washable (thank you, God). I wash his bowls, the kitchen, the hall, the sink. Then I shower again, just in case. I knock on Louis' door. He opens it in his Jitter Mug gear.

'You have to take this.' I hand him his tablet and a glass of water.

He doesn't ask questions, just knocks it back.

'Don't tell Mum, OK? Or she'll never let me have another dog.'

'Sarah, you have to get her to swallow a tablet.'

I wonder if I can hide it in her food.

I've just walked out the front door with Scottie to bring him for a walk when Rachel appears at the gate.

'Hey, just in time for a walk!' I joke. She likes walking about as much as I do. Though it's different with dogs. She's piling through the gate like she hasn't heard.

}|{

'You know that girl I don't like? The one on David's Facebook page? Jenny something?'

'Yeah?'

'Well, they're together.'

'Who's together?'

'Her and David. Mark just rang.'

'I don't believe it.'

'Believe it.'

'It's just so not like David though.'

'Are you walking that guy?' she asks, looking down at Scottie.

'Eh, yeah.'

'OK, let's go.'

We start walking. I have to trot to keep up with her.

'That cow,' she says. 'I knew she was just waiting for her moment.'

'What'll we tell Alex?'

She looks at me. '*Should* we tell her? I don't think she's ready for that just now.'

'You're right.' But then I think. 'Is she ever going to be ready?'

Rachel stops walking, turns and looks at me. 'Would *you* like to know – if it was you?'

I think about that. 'I guess.' I look at her. 'Would you?'

She nods.

'Then we should tell her.'

'I don't know if I can.'

'Me neither.'

'OK, let's just think about this for a minute,' she says. She starts walking again, slower this time.

After a while, I think of something. Something important. 'What if she finds out on Facebook?'

'Oh God.'

'We'll have to tell her.'

She looks like she's in pain. 'When?'

'The sooner the better. You know Facebook. She could find out any minute.'

'Will we go after this?' she asks, like she's talking about the dentist.

'I'm supposed to be going to Shane's. He wants me to meet his friend, Peter.'

She looks relieved. 'OK. Tomorrow.'

'Or we could do it today. I'm sure Shane wouldn't mind.'

'No. Tomorrow,' she says. 'Let's leave it till tomorrow.'

Deirdre answers the door. She looks tired. But smiles.

'Hi, Sarah. Go on in, he's out on the balcony with Peter.'

I go into his room and see them sitting outside. I go out. Shane turns. His face brightens. I smile and kiss him hello.

'This is Peter,' he says.

I turn. His friend is looking at me curiously like he's trying to understand what I'm doing with Shane. It makes me feel like I'm some kind of novelty, like those women who date prisoners on death row. I want to tell him to shag off. The only reason I don't is because Shane has been dying for us to meet. So I smile. For him.

Peter stands and puts out a hand. Surprised, I shake it. He looks me in the eye, the way honest people do.

'Here, you sit down,' he says, nodding to his chair and heading inside for another. *Maybe he's not so bad*, I think. *But then maybe he's just one of those charmers.*

'So, how're you doing?' Shane asks me.

I tell him about David.

)|(

He shrugs. 'The guy's human.'

I stare at him. 'Really?'

'Sarah. You're chewing your finger off there.'

I take it from my mouth. 'I have to tell Alex.'

'No, you don't.'

'Someone has to.'

'Eh, no.'

Peter's coming back so I clam up. I look at Shane, thinking how different guys are from girls.

'So,' Shane says to us both, but looking at me. 'Thought we might all go to that table quiz thingy.'

'Seriously?' I've been trying to talk him into this fundraiser for research into motor neurone disease. He said it'd be full of people in wheelchairs.

He shrugs. 'Might be a bit of a laugh.'

'That's great,' I say. Because this means he hasn't totally given up on the idea that they'll find a cure in time. 'Cool.'

'So, just the three of us?' Peter asks.

Which worries me a bit. 'We're not going to take this too seriously, though, right?' I look at Shane. 'You know I'm not great on general knowledge.'

'What are you talking about?' he says. 'You know more celebrity news than anyone.'

'Like *that's* going to help.'

'Have you ever *been* to a table quiz?' he asks.

'No.'

'Well, then, you won't know. You've got to have a celebrity expert. After that, we're covered. Pete's a walking encyclopaedia.'

'You make me sound like a geek.' Peter looks at me. 'He's ten times smarter than I am.'

Then I think of something. 'I could ask Rachel and Alex. Rachel's a genius. And Alex is amazing on music and movies. And she's a bit of a genius too.'

'Any of them single?' Peter asks.

I think about that. And feel for Alex all over again. 'Not really.'

'How can you "not really" be single? You are or you aren't, aren't you?' He smiles.

'It's complicated.'

'Ah,' he says, like case closed.

It hits me then what Alex said about guys – no one will want her with her 'complication'. She's only sixteen. She should be having fun.

'You should invite them,' Shane says to me. 'It'll be fun.'

'OK,' I say, thinking that maybe it would be good for her to get out, have fun, forget about everything, just for one night.

Next morning at nine, I get up to let the dog out. It's not the total crack of dawn but for Louis it is. But there he is, at the kitchen table, studying before he goes to the Jitter Mug. Maybe I underestimated him. I thought this would last a week, tops. I let Scottie out, then sit at the table and reach for the Coco Pops. They're nearly empty. Which reminds me. I haven't seen Miriam in two weeks.

'Where's Miriam?' I ask.

He looks up from a gigantic book. 'Huh?'

'Miriam. She hasn't been around.'

He shrugs. 'Oh, right. That's over,' he says casually. Then goes to back to his book.

'Seriously? Why?'

He looks up like I'm bothering him. 'Sarah, aren't you tired? It's, like, nine in the morning.'

'I'm never tired when there's crucial news breaking. So who ended it?'

He sighs. 'Me, if you must know.'

'Why?'

He looks at me like he knows there's only one way to shut me up and that's tell me. He's right. 'It was going nowhere.'

'Wasn't that the point?'

'I got tired, OK?'

'Of what?'

'Of there not being a point.' He gets up. Leaves his books open on the table and disappears. I look after him, and think, *weird*.

Alex has started to wear her T-shirts baggy. But she's still wearing skinny jeans underneath. And you really wouldn't know.

'You look amazing,' I tell her, because her hair is so glossy and her skin so clear.

'You mean for someone who's pregnant?'

'No. I just mean you look really pretty today.'

'You haven't seen me naked.'

'Alex, Jesus. Too much information.'

She smiles. 'So we going out?'

'Yeah, sure, great,' Rachel says. We weren't sure she'd want to.

'Where to?' I ask.

'I thought we'd get some sushi in Dundrum.'

Rachel and I look at each other.

'Raw fish?' Rachel asks. 'Is that OK?'

She groans while we google it on her iPhone.

Some sites say it's OK. Some say it's only OK if it's been frozen first. Some sites say better not.

'We better not then,' Rachel says.

'Might as well stay here,' Alex says, moodily.

Hormones, I think.

Rachel looks out the window. 'I'm not staying in today.'

She's right. It's gorgeous out there. And anyone who knows anything about Ireland knows that hazy blue skies are not a regular feature.

'Let's go to the beach,' I say.

'If you think I'm getting into a pair of togs, you can forget it,' Alex says.

'We could just paddle.'

'You've a Frisbee, haven't you?' Rachel asks Alex.

She looks miles away suddenly. 'Yeah, I've a Frisbee.' She sounds sad.

'You don't want to go,' I say.

'No. We'll go.'

'Are you sure?'

'Yeah. It's the best place for beached whales, isn't it, the beach?'

Rachel and I look at each other.

'It's all right, I'm joking.'

We've played Frisbee. Had a picnic (packed by Barbara and delicious). We've had a sandcastle competition (Rachel won). Now we're back on the rug, drinking Coke. And I can't do it. I can't tell her. I look at Rache. I know what she's thinking: Do we really want to ruin such a perfect day?

We lie on the rug. It's lovely, feeling the sun on my skin, listening to the waves breaking and the sound of people on the beach. I'm beginning to think we shouldn't say anything. Just leave it be. Hope for the best.

}|{

Alex sits up, facing the sea, and wraps her arms around her legs. 'Do you think there's any chance that me and David will ever get back together?'

I don't move.

'Rache?' she asks.

I hear Rachel clear her throat and sit up. I seriously want to stay put. But I can't leave Rache do this on her own. So I sit up too.

'I think maybe not,' Rachel says, carefully.

'Really?' Alex asks. She sounds so disappointed, I want to cry.

Rachel looks at me. I widen my eyes in warning. Don't say it. Don't do it to her. Just don't. Not now.

'What?' Alex asks, catching me.

'He's seeing someone,' Rachel says quickly, like she's pulling a plaster. 'That girl, Jenny.'

Alex's hand goes to her heart, like she's been stabbed there. 'How do you know?'

'Mark. I'm sorry.'

She faces forward and stares at the horizon. For ages.

'I can see them together,' she says, so quietly it's like she's talking to herself. 'I can actually picture them.' She's gone so white I'm afraid she's going to faint. Then, all of a sudden, she starts to get up. She's stumbling.

I think, *Not a good idea.*

'Where are you going?' Rachel asks, starting to get up too.

Alex is walking, no, running away from us now. We look at each other. Then we hurry after her.

She stops and turns. '*What?*'

'I don't know,' I say, awkwardly, not knowing what to do. 'Want company?'

}|{

'No.'

So we stand there like retards as she marches off along the beach.

'Shane was right,' I say. 'We shouldn't have said anything.'

'When did he say that?'

'Yesterday.'

'Then why didn't you listen?'

'Like this is *my* fault?'

She stops suddenly. 'Sorry.'

'It's OK.'

She looks along the beach. 'Is she running again?'

I shield my eyes, squinting into the sun. 'I think so.'

'We should go after her. Just slowly.'

We follow, at a distance. I feel ridiculous.

Finally Alex stops and turns around and starts to walk back. When she sees us, she says, 'Are you following me?'

'Just making sure you're OK.'

'I'm OK. I could just kill someone. So watch out.'

I smile. Because I know she's OK.

We link arms and walk together back to the rug.

'She didn't wait long, did she?' she says. 'And he didn't exactly fight her off. Grr.' She actually makes a kind of growling noise.

I laugh. Then I'm disgusted with myself. 'I'm sorry.'

'You know what? I'm sick of being sad. I'm sick of missing him. I'm sick of being lonely. That's it! I've had enough. If he can forget me that quickly, I can forget him.'

She starts marching again, back to our things. She drops to her knees and starts stuffing things into bags. And I think, for the first time, maybe we've a fighter here.

Two weeks later, the quiz is on, in a hotel in town. I arrive first, with Shane and Peter. There's a really great buzz in the room. Groups of people are standing around chatting, people of all ages. There are maybe seven or eight people in wheelchairs, mostly men in their forties, some with more advanced disease than Shane. Suddenly, I get it. Why Shane didn't want to come. He didn't want to be reminded of the future. I feel so stupid. So sorry. But when I look at him, it's like he hasn't seen them. It's like he's decided he's out for a laugh. And he's sure as hell going to have one.

We get a table and a number. Rachel texts to say that she and Alex are in the lobby. I go out to meet them. Alex looks seriously beautiful, hair falling in waves, and wearing this really pretty black dress, like she's out for the night and nothing else matters. Go, Alex. Rachel looks like she always does. Perfect.

We go inside. Shane introduces everyone. I see Peter looking at Alex. And later when the others are chatting, he turns to me and whispers, 'How complicated?'

I smile. Because he's reminded me of something I've forgotten in all of this – Alex. Some guy, some day, will come along and won't care about complications. Suddenly, I know, it's going to be a great night.

Peter asks Alex and Rachel what they're drinking and disappears to the bar. We try to pick out a name for our table. In the end, Alex comes up with one. 'Clueless'. One of our favourite movies.

The quiz kicks off. A lot of the time, I'm quiet. But I do know who the yellow Teletubby is. I know what actress Ryan Phillippe was married to. And I can identify a baby picture of Barack Obama. Apart from that, I live down to our team name. The others are amazing, though. Kind of unbelievable really. It doesn't stop us messing. For Tiger Woods' first name, Peter suggests 'Down'. For the most common blood type, Shane says 'Red'. What makes me really happy, though, is seeing Alex laugh, forgetting everything and just having fun.

Later, I kiss Shane goodnight. He looks at me with the biggest smile.

'I knew you two would get on,' he says, referring to Peter, like that was the most important thing about tonight.

'You know what?' And I can say this now. 'I didn't think I was going to like him.'

'Why not?' He sounds surprised.

'Oh, I don't know, the way he looked at me when we first met, like I was some sort of novelty for going out with you, or something.'

'Pete's not like that. He was probably just wondering who this girl was that I keep going on about. You do know I never shut up about you?'

I smile and kiss him. 'That's the way it should be, Owens.'

But he is serious. 'You are the best thing that's ever happened to me, you know that?'

'Same,' I say, choked with emotion. And I just wish, wish, wish he could be here forever.

32
BIOLOGY

Weeks pass. It's my happiest summer ever. I see Shane every day. We chat for hours. Make out. Snuggle. Practise safe sex. Play on his consoles. Go to the movies. Shop. Laugh. Live. We go out in groups, sometimes the five of us, sometimes only me, Shane and Peter. I turn down an offer of going to the south of France with Mum to be with Shane. Because when it comes to choosing between Shane and the one place I've always wanted to go, there is no contest.

I get my exam results and can actually celebrate. On my report card, the principal congratulates me. This is a first. I hope it won't be a last. It feels like I have changed, turned a corner. I don't want to go back.

It's weird. I knew Alex was pregnant but, for some crazy reason, I never thought she'd *look* pregnant. Maybe because she's only sixteen. But as the summer goes by, she starts to show. I know, then, that I have to tell my mum – before she works it out for herself. I also know she'll freak. I mean really freak. As a social worker, she's seen so many girls 'ruin their lives' by getting pregnant – she's warned me against it often enough. She has no clue that any of us are having sex. Even if I manage to convince her I'm not (which I will have to do to stay alive), what if she thinks Alex is a bad influence and makes me leave Strandbrook after all? And what if we start hating each other again?

I'm still talking myself into telling her when the whole thing blows up in my face. But not just *my* face. When Mum walks into the sitting room, she's so fixated on me she doesn't notice Louis studying quietly in the corner.

'Sarah,' she says. 'Do you have something to tell me? About Alex Newman.'

I feel Louis suddenly paying attention.

I sit up. 'Eh, yeah, I was going to tell you about that.'

'When? When were you going to tell me?' Shit, shit, shit. 'I just got off the phone with Rachel's mother. Who rang about something completely different, by the way. She assumed I knew about Alex. Because Rachel had told her.' She pauses. 'Like I would have expected *you* to tell *me*.'

'I was going to—'

'Alex Newman is *pregnant*,' she states, like she's announcing the end of the world.

'*So?*' Louis says.

Mum turns and notices him for the first time. 'Louis, I'm talking to your sister.' As in, leave.

He stands up but doesn't go, just folds his arms. It's like he wants to stand up for Alex or something.

'How long have you known?' she asks me, like he's not there.

I shrug.

'Did you know she was sexually active?'

'Mum!'

}I{

'Well, did you?'

'No.' Bizarrely it's not a lie.

'I hope *you're* not.'

'Oh my God, Mum.'

'I don't want you hanging out with her.'

I feel like telling her that the father is standing right behind her. Which makes her the granny. I look at her for a very long time.

'It's not contagious.'

Her expression changes as if she realises how Old Mum she's sounding.

'Alex messed up,' I say. 'She's going to pay for that for the rest of her life. I'm not going to ditch her now that she's in trouble. She's on her own. She needs me.'

Louis, looking seriously guilty, turns and goes.

Mum takes a deep breath and lets it out slowly. 'All right. But please, Sarah, be careful, for God's sake.'

'I think Shane would take that as a compliment,' I say to annoy her.

I go up to my room to recover. At least she knows, I tell myself. At least I don't have to hide it any more. There is relief in that.

One lazy afternoon, me and Rache are hanging out with Alex up in her room.

'Dad thinks I should take a year out of school,' Alex says.

I stare at her. My immediate reaction is nooooo.

'What do *you* think?' Rachel asks Alex, cautiously.

She looks at us seriously. I hold my breath.

'Do you really think I'd leave you guys to go on without me?' She breaks into a smile.

)|(

'Phew,' I say. It would have been awful without her. And
what if she never came back? Blew her chances, her future?

'I'm not letting this baby change my life.'

'Go you,' I say. And we hug her.

As the weeks pass, Alex starts to look really pregnant.
People start to look. Stare. Comment. I stare back like I'm
some kind of psycho that could explode at any moment.

Towards the end of the summer Alex has her first ante-
natal class. She wants me and Rache there, which is great.
Thing is, even though there's Google, none of us really
knows what to expect.

In the hospital, we're directed up three floors and down
endless corridors to a grim, grey room with big windows.
It's filled with plastic chairs, the ones with the holes at the
back and metal legs. A window is open and you can hear the
traffic outside. We sit at the back and watch the room fill. I
thought we'd be the only teenagers. I was wrong. There are
loads. Most are older: eighteen, nineteen. They're wearing
tracksuits, trainers and tight T-shirts that gape over the
belly. Marsha, who has been designing the prettiest tops for
Alex, would be disgusted. There are older women of course,
some *ancient* women. A few men have come along to offer
moral support. Alex is the only one who has brought
friends.

In the end, there are about twenty or thirty of us.

A woman walks in, wearing a blue uniform and sensible
shoes. Her hair is short and brown and she looks as sensible
as those shoes. She stands in front of the blackboard – I
swear to God, there's a blackboard. Her welcome is busi-
ness-like, then she orders us to move our chairs into a U

shape. I think of school. And wonder if you ever really escape.

She starts to talk about labour. It can take hours and hours, she says. She has a doll. And a dummy pelvis. She shoves the doll, head first, through the pelvis. She says the bones separate to allow the baby through. I don't look at Alex. Just hope she's OK.

'Mummies, make sure you breathe,' she says. 'And Daddies, you can sit and rub Mummy's tummy.'

What if there's no Daddy? I think. Hasn't she looked around the room and seen the number of teenagers? Hasn't she factored that in? She talks about the pain. And how you can take gas. Which can make you feel sick, but is still probably a good idea.

'Now, Daddies, Mummy's tummy might be in pain now, so she mightn't like you rubbing it any more. So maybe ask her where she'd like you to be.'

'Hong Kong,' Alex whispers. 'I swear to God, if she mentions Daddies one more time I'll hit her over the head with that freaking doll.'

She talks about the first signs of labour. Rachel leans forward, all ears.

'So you might get a show,' she says. 'That's a plug of mucus being released.'

Released from where? I think. Then I get it. *Ee-ew.*

'Try to have a good look at it.'

Jesus.

'See if there's much blood in it. You don't want there to be clots. Because that wouldn't be a good sign. If you're able, capture some of it in a bowl and bring it in ...'

Capture it? Like it's going to run away?

}|{

'If she thinks I'm going to go looking for a bowl and bring it in . . .,' Alex whispers, her face screwed up.

'This is disgusting,' I whisper.

'Shh,' Rachel says crossly.

I start to giggle.

The midwife looks at me like I'm some giddy kid in Sex Ed class. I feel like saying, this is a million times worse than Sex Ed class. In fact, if they gave this class instead of Sex Ed class, no one would ever have sex. And we wouldn't be here. Fact. Finally, once she's made sure that we all know the true horror that lies ahead of Alex, she lets us go.

'That's the last one of those I'm going to,' I hear a man say.

'I'm with you on that,' Alex says.

Luckily, I brought chocolate.

September approaches like the Grim Reaper. Going back to school will mean being apart from Shane for entire days. How will I bear it? I tell myself that Alex needs me. The baby's due in November. And though it's not absolutely, totally, in your face obvious when she wears the clothes Marsha designs, she really can't hide it any more – especially in her uniform, which makes everyone look like a whale anyway. If school's going to be hard for me, it's going to be a hundred times harder for Alex. She is going to be the big news. And I'm so ready to floor the first person who makes a smart comment. Alex's dad has told the principal. Who has probably told all the teachers. To everyone else, though, it will be a surprise. Because what can the school do, make, like, an official announcement – Alex Newman is pregnant everyone, be nice? I don't think so.

First day back. On the DART, we're quiet. Alex looks so pale.

'You OK?' Rachel asks her.

She looks down at her bump, then up. Her face becomes determined. 'Yeah, I'm OK. This is not going to mess up my life. I'm going to work harder. I'm going to keep my grades up. Go to college.'

I haven't heard her so determined about anything since her mum died. And I think how cool it would be if the baby gave her all this ambition, instead of ruining everything, like she thinks it will.

'Go you,' I say.

'If anyone says anything – you know, today,' Rachel says. 'Just ignore them. I mean don't let it get to you. Half of them are retards, you know that.'

Alex nods, but she looks worried.

'I swear to God,' I say. 'If anyone says anything, I'll floor them.'

Alex smiles.

'I mean it.'

'We should have a plan,' Rachel says. 'Like, just act like it's life as usual, like we're above anything anyone might say. Yeah?'

'OK,' Alex says.

I'm still not going to take any shit.

We walk side by side, up the corridor, heads high, inde-structible. It starts almost immediately, the double-takes, the staring, the huddling, the whispering. And I'm sure the gloating too. As a rock star's daughter, Alex has never been an ordinary person. Now she's fallen from her pedestal, and that makes some people happy. I sense all this while I look dead ahead, and keep on going.

We get to our lockers and have to split up, not much, but enough to break the armour of togetherness. I'm waiting for it, the first catty remark. I'm waiting and I'm ready to spring. I don't think my ears have ever been more alert.

It doesn't take long.

'Looks like Alex had a busy summer.'

I turn. It's Amy Gilmore, standing, arms folded, flanked by Orla Tempany and Robin O'Neill. She looks so smug. I say nothing. Just walk slowly up to her, look her in the eye, and slap her, hard, across her long, puppet face. The sound echoes in the high-ceilinged room. I smile, surprised by how good it feels.

'Ouch,' someone says.

'Exactly.' I look around to see if anyone else wants some, knowing that from now on, I'll be The Weirdo. Hanging out with The Slag. There was a time that that would have freaked me out. Now I don't care. I catch Simon staring at me. And it's like the weirdest thing. I've just whacked his girlfriend and, for the first time ever, he's looking at me with something that resembles respect. I slam my locker shut and go up to Alex.

'You ready?'

'Ready, Mike Tyson.' And it's great to see her smile.

We go to our first class.

It's TipToes. Who spent all of last year talking about fuzzy things like friendship. Today, it's all talk of Leaving Cert timetables and good study habits. It's enough to make you get up and go. I think of Shane and wonder what he's doing. Playing on his X-box, maybe. Though he hasn't been doing so much of that lately. I check my watch. Physio. God, I miss him so much. I close my eyes and imagine his touch on my skin, imagine his mouth on mine ...

'Sarah Healy, am I boring you up here?'

Actually, yes, I'm so tempted to say. But I control myself

and tell her what she wants to hear. 'No, Miss.'

'Good, well, when you're *sure* you're ready maybe we could open our books and get to work.' I stare at her. She sounds like Roz in *Monsters Inc.*, like she has a pair of half-assed vocal chords that let too much air through. Now that would be an interesting dissection.

After class, we stand up to go. TipToes sees Alex's belly for the first time and the corners of her mouth turn down in disgust – as if it stands for everything that's wrong in the world. Alex might as well have handed her a piece of poo. I glare at her. But she doesn't see me. So I go up to Alex, and glare from there. This time she does see me. She drops her eyes immediately and starts shoving her book into her tatty, leather briefcase. She hurries out. I close my eyes and will her to trip. She doesn't.

'Don't mind her,' I say to Alex.

'Cow,' she says under her breath.

'More like a heifer,' I say. 'She's *never* had sex.'

'Maybe that's her problem,' Rachel says, joining us.

We walk out.

And it's like we've contacted some rare, highly contagious disease. There's all this empty space around us, like the atmosphere around the world. It's like no one else has ever messed up.

Class follows class and it just gets worse. People look at her like she's trailer trash. Girls are the worst. Well, girls and female teachers – the ones you'd think might be sympathetic. I don't know how Alex doesn't just walk out.

At first break, we queue in the canteen.

'I wonder who the father is?' says a whispered voice behind us.

'David McFadden, of course. Daw.'

I swivel around. Jennifer Byrne and Rebecca Hyde, the token fat nerds in our class. They clam up immediately. One of them blushes. And you'd think because they're geeks, they'd have a heart.

'You know, Jennifer,' I say, 'the thing about pregnancy is that it ends. You're stuck with those cankles.' I turn back.

Rachel and Alex are laughing.

We take our trays to an empty table.

'First day's the worst,' Rachel says encouragingly.

'It better be,' Alex says. She looks down at her tray like she's wondering why she bothered getting anything.

'Hey,' Rachel says brightly. 'Amy Gilmore's face after the slap . . . '

Alex turns to me. 'You realise you're my hero, Sarah.'

'Hey, you just gave me an excuse. I've been wanting to slap that ho for a very long time.'

'You can't keep slapping people, though,' Alex says.

'No. I should probably punch a few, maybe pull some hair. Vary it a bit, keep them on their toes.'

We laugh.

It's like the whole canteen turns and stares. Like we've lost it.

'I love you guys,' Alex says, but her eyes well up.

A tray lands down on the table.

We all look up. It's Mark.

'Hey,' he says, like it's totally natural for him to sit here.

Rachel's face lights up like she's falling in love all over again.

He sits down. Then he looks at me.

'Good *slap*,' he says, the same way the guy in *Legally Blonde* says, 'good *snap*'.

We're laughing again.

}I{

After school, I'm dying to see Shane, but Rachel wants to go to the Jitter Mug. To make a statement. To let everyone know it's business as usual. We are not intimidated. I text Shane to say I'll be a bit late. It's a while before he texts back, which isn't like him.

'Take ur time,' he says, and a smiley face.

We haven't been to the Jitter Mug since the Simon incident. Now we walk in, heads high. Anyone who knows us is looking. And whispering. And sniggering. We walk up to the counter. We queue. Finally, we get to the top.

Louis takes one look at Alex and goes white.

'Hey,' he says, without taking his eyes off Alex.

She goes kind of red.

I tell him what we want, to move it on. He seems to jolt back to reality.

We get our drinks, find a table and sit.

'Poor Louis,' Alex says.

'What do you mean *poor* Louis?' Rachel says, crossly.

'He looked like he was going to have a nervous breakdown.' I wonder if she really thinks it's funny or if she's just saying it to break the ice.

I look up at the counter and wish he'd get over how he feels, just put it aside. And be there for her. In some small way. I sigh.

'What?' Rachel asks.

'Nothing.' If I told them he loved her, they wouldn't believe me. And he would personally kill me.

Luckily, Mike drops me to Shane's so I'm not ridiculously late. I feel kind of wrecked from the early start this morning. Shane looks wrecked. He always tires as the day goes on. Today, though, he looks extra tired. I kiss him hello.

'You OK?'

'Yeah, yeah, grand. I might get into bed though. Colm will be in in a minute if that's OK?' Colm is his nurse.

I smile. 'Sure.' I tell myself not to worry. Shane can be extra tired without it having to mean anything. Everything's fine. His disease is not getting worse.

While we wait for Colm, I tell him about my violent streak. He laughs.

'Wish I'd been there to see it.'

'Surprised you didn't hear it from here.'

He laughs again. 'Remind me never to get on the wrong side of you.'

'Never get on the wrong side of me.'

There's a knock on the door.

I go out while Colm helps Shane into bed. Staying would just make him feel helpless. And Shane is so independent.

As soon as Colm comes out, I go back in. I climb up on the bed beside Shane.

'What are you doing out there?' he asks.

I smile, and slip under the quilt. We snuggle up together and chat. We do not plan to fall asleep.

I'm woken by my phone.

'Where are you?' It's Mum.

I check my watch. It's seven-thirty. 'Oh God, sorry. I'm with Shane. I'm on my way.'

'I'll collect you. Dinner's ready.'

'You sure?'

'Yeah, I'll be there in a minute.'

'OK, thanks. I'll start walking.'

Shane's still asleep. I kiss him goodbye and write him a note saying I'll talk to him later on Facebook.

'How's Shane?' Mum asks when I get in the car.

'Tired.'

And I wonder if it's the way I said it, because she turns to me, her face serious, and asks, 'Is that a bad sign?'

'Just this time of day. Mum, do I really *have* to go to school?' I ask, though I know the answer.

She smiles. 'Yes, you really have to go to school.'

We drive in silence.

'I've some news,' she says after a while.

I look at her. She seems happy.

'I've got a new job.'

'Really?' I didn't know she was looking for one.

'One I always wanted. And talked myself out of.'

'What is it?'

'A promotion, office-based.'

'I thought you liked working in the community.'

'A certain person thought it more worthy.' I know who she means and am glad she said it like that because it doesn't sound like she's blaming him. 'But, actually, I can do more at this level, have more impact. And I'll get paid more and work fewer hours.'

'Wow. That's great!'

'I know. We can spend more time together.'

And I think how amazing that would have been a few months ago. 'Except that I'll be at Shane's most afternoons.' Meaning all.

She looks at me cautiously. 'You sure you're not spending too much time over there?'

'No.' I'm not spending half-enough.

'You sure?'

'Yeah, Mum, I'm sure.'

'It's going to be hard.'

'Yeah, Mum, I know.'

}|{

'All right.' She takes a deep breath. Then looks at me. 'OK, well, I'm here, all right? Anytime. You know that, don't you?'

I nod.

'And from next week, I'll be home by five.'

'Thanks, Mum.' I look at her. She's not changing job for me, is she? She wanted that job. Definitely. She wouldn't do something so big for me.

After dinner, I go on Facebook. Oh God. Everyone's talking about Alex. Not only on Facebook but on Twitter. Like it's this great scandal. They know she can read what they're writing. They know anyone can.

There's a knock on my door. I click out of Facebook. Look up. It's Louis.

'It's everywhere,' he says.

'Yeah,' I say, miserably.

'How's she doing?'

I tell him about school.

'Jesus.'

Another knock at the door. We both look at it.

Mum walks in. 'Is Alex OK?'

Even Mum's noticed? 'You should see the way people look at her, Mum.'

She folds her arms. 'It's not going to be easy.'

'Ever,' I say.

She looks at me. 'I was wrong before, Sarah. I'm glad you're standing by her. She needs her friends right now.'

The door closes. Louis is gone.

Mum looks after him. 'It's good you two are spending more time together. Have you been on to your dad lately?'

'I'll give him a ring.' I've been so busy with Shane, with

Alex. I start to feel guilty. But then, he hasn't exactly been calling me.

Next day at school, Alex gets word that the principal wants to see her.

'What for? My dad spoke to him. Even though I didn't want him to. This is none of their business,' she says, but looks worried.

'You're right. It's not,' Rachel says.

We walk Alex to the office, grumbling about how unfair this is. We wait with her until she's called in. Then we go back to class, still grumbling but really worrying about what's happening behind that door.

When class is over, we hurry to our lockers. She's there, waiting. We go straight up to her.

'What did he say?' I ask.

'He was OK. Actually, he was pretty sweet. He wanted me to go see the school counsellor. I told him I was already see-ing someone. He said that if anyone gives me a hard time to go straight to him.'

'Does that include teachers?' I ask.

'Yeah.'

'Did you tell him about Tip Toes and some of the others?'

'No. It might just make them worse.'

Right, I think, *if things get bad I'll tell him.*

'Did I miss anything in Biology?' she asks.

I was so busy worrying about her I didn't take anything in. I look at Rachel.

'I'll give you my notes if you like,' Rachel says.

'Great. Because I'm *not* going to fall behind.' There's that determined voice again.

'Could I've a look at them too?' I ask. Because maybe I'm

feeling a little more determined too. Don't want to slip back to the way I was.

'Let's go to the library at lunch. At least we'll get some peace.'

After school, we don't hang around. Obviously. We're almost at the school gates when I see Louis, leaning against the pillar. He straightens up and walks to us. Automatically, I think something's wrong.

'What are you doing here?'

'Waiting for you … Well … all of you.' He looks at Alex.

Suddenly, it's like we get it. Alex blushes. Then we all start walking in silence. Louis falls behind with Alex.

'Here, can I carry that?'

'It's OK, thanks.'

'OK.'

Rachel and I walk a little ahead to give them privacy. But people start to stare, so, nervous of another scandal, we fall back again. I'm glad Louis is doing whatever he's doing. I just wish he wasn't doing it in full view of the entire school. At least she didn't let him carry her bag.

On the DART we sit together.

'Aren't you working today?' Alex asks him, awkwardly. It's so weird. I still can't imagine them together. They're just so unalike.

'Not today,' he says. And I wonder if he took it off especially for this.

'Cool,' she says.

'I'm cutting back on my hours a bit. To study.' He sounds so serious. For Louis.

I was going to get the DART to Shane's but I get off with

}|{

Louis so – for all those watching – it looks like he came to school to collect me. We walk away from the DART in silence.

'You think that went OK?' he asks.

'Depends what you were trying to do.'

'I don't know. Show some support. What with everyone giving her a hard time and that.'

'Support's great. But they'll give her an even harder time if they see her hanging around with someone other than David.'

He hits his forehead. 'I can't believe I didn't think of that.' It's the first time in my life I've experienced my brother lost.

'It'll be fine,' I say. 'I'll just let on, tomorrow, there was some big family thing or something.'

'It was a mistake. She didn't want me there, did she?'

'She was probably just thinking about the gossip. She has to go in there tomorrow.'

'Jesus.'

'You'll find a way to be there for her. I know you will.'

He doesn't look so sure.

When we get home, the car's outside.

'Could you run me over to Shane's?'

He makes a face.

'Please.'

'I'm going to have to teach you to drive.'

'Oh my God. Yes. Definitely.'

He smiles. 'I'll go get the keys.'

Shane's already in bed. He says it's easier, rather than have Colm interrupt us later. I jump up on the bed beside him.

'Want to play the cow game?'

'Nah, I got a movie.'

'OK, cool, but could we have just one game first? We haven't played in ages.'

He makes a face.

'Come on.'

'OK, just one.'

I get out the controllers, hand him his. I set everything up, then we're off. I go mad, like I always do, screaming when I do something stupid (most of the time) and shouting at the screen. I'm not the kind of person who can keep an eye on her opponent while she's racing herself so when I win it's a total shocker. He did terribly. I look at him.

'You let me win.'

'No, I didn't. I swear.'

'We have to do it again. And this time don't let me win.'

'Sarah, can we just watch the movie?' He sounds tired. 'I don't feel like the Wii.'

'What's the movie?'

'*Precious.*'

'You're not serious?'

'No, I'm not.' He smiles. 'I know how much you love *Precious*. It's *Red*. Peter says it's great.'

'Oh, yeah. Alex was going on about that.'

We snuggle up together on the bed to watch it. And we're not disappointed.

'You remind me of Helen Mirren,' he says when it's over.

'What? Helen Mirren is like sixty or something.'

'Yeah and she's still spunky. I bet you'll be like that when you're sixty.'

And it must hit us both at the same time, that he won't be with me, because we stop and stare at each other, then I wrap my arms around him and hold him tight.

}I{

At the weekend, I meet Dad in the same restaurant as last time.

'Sorry I haven't been in touch,' he says. He looks at me like he's dying to tell me something. 'I've been writing a book.' He says it like an announcement. Like he's really pleased.

'That's great,' I say, but I'm cautious. 'What kind of book?'

'Well, psychology.'

'Not based on real life?'

'Not really. Mostly it's advice ... With a few case histories.'

'No shoplifting,' I say, to be sure.

'No shoplifting.'

'Good.' Then I think of something. 'Are you *allowed* to talk about your patients? Like didn't you take the Hippocratic oath or something?'

'That's for doctors.'

'Yeah, I know, but people's privacy—'

'Will be protected. And I have their permission.'

He's tetchy. Like I couldn't just be happy with his success, so I say, 'I'm sure it'll be great.'

'Yeah.' But he doesn't sound so sure any more. 'So how are you? Back at school?'

He always knows how to cheer a person up. 'It *is* September.'

'Good, good. Any news?' he asks.

I wonder what he'd say if I told him my friend was pregnant and my boyfriend had a terminal illness. 'Not much.'

'How's Louis?'

Going to be a dad, I think. But say, 'Grand.'

'I really must give him a call.'

'You know, if you're busy, you could see us both together.'

}|{

I can't keep the bitterness from my voice. What's wrong with me? He's my dad. The only one I have. I want to get on with him. I just can't help feeling he hasn't room for us any more. Or he'd have called.

'I'm not busy,' he says. 'OK, well I have been. I got a bit carried away. With the book. But I'm here for you both, any time, you know that.'

I look at him and try to pretend that his words don't sound hollow.

33
Go

Shane's not using his right hand. It sits on his lap while he reaches across with his left to work the controls on the wheelchair. I look at him, questioningly, telling myself it's nothing. He's just extra tired. Again. But he looks straight at me, his eyes telling me that it *does* mean something. I stop breathing.

'I've known for a while,' he says, and he looks so sad. 'I've been hiding it. Even from myself. I didn't want to know.'

Oh God. I think of the texts, so slow in coming back. I think of how tired he's been. I think of the Wii. I guess I knew too. Just didn't want to admit it.

'I want you to go,' he says. 'Before it gets any worse.'

I hold his eyes with mine. 'You don't know me very well if you think I'm going anywhere.'

'Sarah. It's creeping up. So fast. Faster than I thought.'

What does this mean? How much time does he have? Do *we* have? I'm so afraid. But can't let him see. If I let him see, it will be over.

'It's OK,' I say. But it isn't. What about everything he wants to do? What about us?

'Sarah, please. I want you to go.'

'No, you don't. You're just trying to protect me. But I don't want to be protected. I love you. And I want to be with you till … I can't be any more.' My voice cracks because the thought of that breaks my heart. I get up suddenly.

'Back in a sec,' I say, brightly. And run.

I race up the hall, then bend over and burst into tears. It's so not fair. What did he ever do to anyone? Why couldn't he have more time? I think of the Leaving Cert, the one thing he wanted to achieve.

His mum comes out of the kitchen. Oh God.

'I'm sorry,' I say. But I can't stop crying.

'Come here.' She's smiling.

She puts her arms around me and holds me. Then we're both crying.

Then she laughs.

'Look at the pair of us.'

I try to smile but then I think of him hiding it from me. Hiding it from himself. And I'm crying again. Worse than ever.

'Come on. What we need is a cup of tea.' She puts an arm round me and walks me to the kitchen.

I don't even like tea. But I can't go back to Shane. Not yet.

Finally, I do go back. I kneel up on his chair. Look into his eyes. I take his right hand in mine. I kiss it, then put it to my face.

'This is how I want to live,' I say. 'With you. That's it.'

'Sarah. You know how I'll go.'

'I've known that a long time and I'm still here.'

'I'm going to be ugly. Useless.'

Suddenly, I'm angry. 'You know, Shane, strangers aren't the only ones who think that this defines you. *You* do.'

His eyes widen in surprise.

'You just don't get it, do you? You changed my life. You saw the good in me when no one else did. Before I met you, I was a mess. Going out with a guy I didn't even like. Shoplifting stuff I didn't need. Envying friends I loved. I was so unhappy and I didn't even know it. I hid nothing from you and you still accepted me. You saved my life, Shane, and I love you. This disease is a pain in the ass. But you're still you. You're such a strong person. You're wise and caliente. And caring. And funny. You make me so happy. Every day. Do you really think I'm going to walk away from that?'

He looks at me so sadly. 'I'm going to leave you behind.'

I take a deep breath. 'And I'm OK with that.'

'I'm not.'

'Well, you don't have a choice. Because I'm not going anywhere. In fact, I'm sleeping over. I've cleared it with your mum.'

At last, he smiles. 'What about *your* mum?'

'She doesn't have a choice. I'll ring her in a minute.'

His eyes are moist when he says, 'You realise you're the most amazing person I've ever met.'

'Course I do.' I smile and kiss him.

'I love you,' he says.

'You should,' I joke.

'Want to know why?'

'Course I do.' My favourite kind of conversation. Someone telling me how brilliant I am.

'I love you because you're you.'

'That's it?'

He laughs. 'You see?'

'No.'

He laughs again. 'Want me to spell it out?'

'Absolutely.'

He smiles and kisses my nose. 'You pile into everything; you say what you're thinking no matter what it is. You love dogs and *Desperate Housewives* and the cow race on Wii and Perez Hilton. You make me laugh like no one else. You care – about everyone. You're beautiful and smart—'

'*Smart*?'

'Yeah, smart. Maybe that's the best thing about you ...'

'What, that I'm smart? I'm not smart, Shane.'

'Let me finish.'

'Sorry.'

'You don't get how great you are.'

'Go on.'

He laughs.

'You're a sex kitten.'

I growl.

'You frown when you're concentrating.'

'And that's *good*?'

'You're frowning.' He kisses between my eyebrows. And we snuggle up.

'You know,' I say, after a while, 'when I met you first I was afraid of you.'

'What? The dangerous guy in the wheelchair?'

'Trust me. You were scary.'

'Scary's good, though. I'm still scary, right?'

'You're the scariest, most gorgeous guy I know.'

And I wonder, when my mum turns up with my pyjamas,

my toothbrush, a change of underwear, even my squidgy pillow, has she changed into the mum I've always wanted. She even hugs me before she leaves. She looks like she's going to say something but seems to change her mind. Then, as she's about to get in the car, she turns.

'I love you,' she says.

'I love you too.' And I'm smiling. Because I realise I mean it.

Wow.

We lie facing each other, planning all the things we're going to do. It's like suddenly there's a bigger hurry. He's bringing me to a restaurant for my birthday next week. At Halloween, we'll have a party with fireworks. We'll go to the first rugby international of the season. We'll even go to Paris.

'Marry me,' I say.

He laughs.

Which is when I realise: 'I'm serious.'

He looks at me like I've lost it.

I haven't. 'Remember when you asked me what I'd do if I'd a year to live and I said I'd fall in love and get married? Well, I've fallen in love. Now I want to get married.'

'But you don't have a year to live.'

'How do you know? Are you God? I might have less than a year.'

'Except that you don't. I do.'

'OK then, I want to live till you die.'

He smiles sadly. 'And I want you to be able to walk away.'

'I already told you. I won't be walking anywhere.'

'Let's think about it,' he says.

'Fob off.'

'I'm not fobbing you off. I just want you to think about it. What if I live to be as old as Stephen Hawking? You'd be stuck with me.'

'Do you know how happy I'd be if you lived that long?' I start to get teary.

He hugs me.

My cheek against his chest, I make a wish.

'Let's think about it,' he whispers.

We start to get sleepy.

'You better set up the pull-out bed,' he says.

'Why?'

There's a pause. 'Colm comes in every two hours to turn me. I could pull myself over – until the hand.' He looks down at it.

I'm so stunned by how much this has taken from him that I forget to speak.

'And I'm not a great sleeper,' he adds. 'I'd keep you awake.'

'OK,' I say. Feeling tears come again, I kiss him on the cheek and get up.

'All the stuff you need is in the first cupboard.'

'OK.'

I make up the bed and while I'm in the bathroom, Colm comes to help him into his.

I lie in the semi-dark, feeling miles away from him.

'You OK over there?' he asks.

I get out of the bed and start to shove it so that it is beside his, with enough room for Colm to do his thing.

I jump in and turn to face him. 'That's better,' I say.

He smiles. 'Much.'

I don't get much sleep. Colm is in and out. And Shane must be getting nightmares because every so often he groans. Once, I hear them whispering.

'How's the breathing?' Colm asks.

His breathing? There's nothing wrong with his breathing.

'I think I need to go up higher,' Shane replies.

Colm adjusts the head of the bed and the pillows.

'How's that?'

'Good, thanks.'

I lie with my eyes open, stressing. *His breathing now*?

As soon as Colm leaves, I say, 'Why didn't you tell me about the breathing?'

He jumps. 'Jesus, you gave me a fright.'

'You're fine during the day.'

'I know. This is just a night thing. I didn't want to worry you.'

'I'm more worried when you don't tell me stuff and I find out myself.'

'Sorry.'

'It's OK. Are you all right up there?'

'Now that I'm facing you.'

'I love you,' I say. But I'm thinking, *What will I do without you*?

He hears me sniffle. 'Are you OK?'

I nod.

'That's why I want you to go.'

'I'm *not* going.'

'I wish you would.'

'Oh God, can't you just be a little bit selfish for a change and just goddamn marry me?'

He smiles. 'Wuv you.'

It's the first thing I say to him in the morning.

'Marry me.'

It's the first thing I say whenever we meet up.

'Marry me.'

He always laughs.

There are variations. Like when he asks what I want for my birthday.

'An engagement ring.'

Or when he mentions Paris.

'Oh you mean the honeymoon?'

'Can you even get married at sixteen?' he asks.

'With parental consent you can.' I've looked it up (of course).

'Ah,' he says.

34
LEGO

I'm seventeen. Yaay!

At breakfast, Mum gives me vouchers for driving lessons.

'Oh my God!' I scream and throw my arms around her.

'Nothing like a bit of independence,' she says, smiling.

I don't see Louis, but on the table he's left an envelope. Normally, he's not one for gifts, so I rip it open. It's a card featuring Peter from *Family Guy*. Inside, he has scribbled a note that says, 'I O U, 10 driving lessons.'

Wahoo. The more I get, the sooner I pass.

At school, Rachel and Alex have my locker decorated with sweets and jokes. It's kind of a thing we do in our school. And I love it.

At first break, Simon comes up to me and wishes me happy birthday. I'm so stunned, he's walked away before I can respond.

After school, we go to the Jitter Mug. Just Rachel and Alex and me.

Together, they hand me a present.

'I love the paper' – silver with a blue ribbon around it. I look up and smile. 'Thanks guys.'

I don't want to open it straight away. I want to guess. The box is light. About the size of a giant box of chocolates. But it's not heavy. So it couldn't be chocolates. (They'd never buy me chocolates anyway.) I shake it. No sound. So. It's light and rectangular and soundless ... I haven't a clue.

'Open it,' Alex says, smiling.

'No, no, I want to guess.'

'OK, go on then.'

'I don't know. A box of silent cereal?'

They laugh.

'No.'

'Open it. Come on. You're killing me.'

'Give me a hint.'

'No,' Alex says.

'It's blue,' Rachel says.

'Blue?' Oh my God. It couldn't be. They couldn't have. And I don't guess, in case it's not it. Because it'd be too much.

'OK, I'm going to open it.'

I rip off the paper. Inside is a box of ... '*Lego*?'

But it didn't make a noise. I'm totally confused.

'Open it,' Rachel says.

I do. Inside the box of Lego is the most beautiful evening dress I've been saving for, for months. I look up. 'You guys.'

'The Lego box was my idea,' Rachel says, proudly.

'Good one.' I get up and I hug them. Suddenly, I've something to wear tonight. For my dinner with Shane. 'You're just unbelievable.'

'Yeah, we know,' says Alex.

I smile across at her. It's so amazing to hear her just be normal, not worried, not scared. Just herself. I think that maybe everything's going to be OK.

*

Mum calls up to say the taxi is outside. I'm not ready. I could throw my eyelash curler, mascara and lip gloss in my bag and go. But it'll just take two minutes and I want to look perfect. I want everything to be perfect tonight.

'My God,' my mum says when I come downstairs. 'My little girl has grown up.' She hugs me extra tight. 'Have fun.'

'Gotta go.'

I hurry out. Greg, our regular taxi driver, hops out and opens the door for me. I thank him, climb in the back, kiss Shane and sit on the chair facing him. In his jacket and tie, he looks like James Bond – the only caliente Bond, Daniel Craig. His hair has grown again and he's it gelled in a kind of a higgledy piggledy way that makes me feel like ruffling it even more. I could eat him up. I really could.

'You're beautiful,' he says, kind of hoarse. 'Isn't she beautiful?' he says to Greg.

'Beautiful,' Greg says. Like he has a choice.

'Thanks,' I say, kind of embarrassed. 'Let's go.'

The restaurant is the one in Monkstown that Dad took me to.

'I love this place!' I say.

He looks at me. 'I know.'

He picked it for that reason. Without telling me. I smile. He's the best. He just is.

Inside, the restaurant seems different to how I remember it, cosier, warmer and buzzier, so pretty by night, with candles on the tables and everyone dressed up. I'm out to dinner with the guy I love. It feels right, for seventeen.

'Thank you,' I whisper to him.

They show us to a table by a roaring fire.

'Wow. Cool table,' I say when the waiter's gone. 'I can't believe we got it.'

)l(

'I picked it out last week.'

'You came in specially?'

'Course I did.'

Oh my God. I love this guy.

The waiter comes back and Shane orders champagne. Just the thought of it makes me giddy.

'Celebrating?' the waiter asks with a smile.

'It's my birthday,' I say. And, just in time, stop myself saying I'm seventeen.

We have monkfish and the tastiest chips I've ever eaten. We chat and laugh and tease each other like always. Over dessert (yummy ice cream), he says, 'I got you something.'

'This meal,' I say, because I seriously hope he hasn't got anything else. This will cost a fortune.

He puts his hand in his pocket and pulls out a small gift-wrapped box. I recognise the wrapping from the shop Alex did her work experience in. So classy. The way it's tied, the paper, the string …

'Oh my God, I love their stuff.' I look up at him. 'You shouldn't have.'

'You haven't opened it yet,' he says with a smile.

Whatever it is, I know it's going to be perfect. Slowly, I open the wrapping, wanting to make the moment last. I take out a small velvet box, look up at him, smile, then open it.

'Oh my God. It's gorgeous. I love it.'

'It's not much. But it's all I could afford.'

'What are you talking about? It's beautiful.'

I put it on my finger and it sparkles. I look down at it with all my fingers straight out. Funny. I've put it on *that* finger. And it does look like …

'Do you still want to get married?' he asks.

Everything stops. Even my heart. I never thought he'd do it. Every time I asked, I never thought ... My hands go to my face. 'Really?' He's planned all this. Gone to all this trouble. Picked out the table. The most beautiful ring. Dressed up. God. I well up.

'Is that a yes?' he smiles.

For once in my life I can't speak.

He goes all serious. 'Are you OK?'

I put my hand to my mouth. Nod.

'You're crying.'

'I'm just so happy. They're happy tears.'

'Are you sure?' He still looks concerned. 'Maybe—'

'You are *not* taking it back now,' I say crossly, covering my hand with the other one.

He bursts out laughing. When he stops he looks relieved. 'I'd get down on my knees if I could.' Instead, he reaches across the table for my hand. 'Sarah Healy, will you marry me?'

I smile. 'Yes, Shane Owens, I will absolutely marry you.' This, more than any other, is by far, the one and only, best moment of my life. 'Wow. God.' I can't believe it.

He kisses my hand. I get up, go over to him and kiss him properly.

'I love you so much,' I say.

'I love you so much.'

'I love you more.'

'No, I love you more.'

'Wanna fight over it?' I ask.

'OK, but I'll win.'

'All right then, just give me a kiss.'

He laughs and does.

)|(

When I sit back down, the waiter arrives with more champagne. He looks almost as excited as we are. 'That was so romantic,' he says, so enthusiastically I wonder if he's gay.

When he's gone, I look at Shane for a long time.

I smile. 'So. What made you change your mind?'

'I didn't. I always wanted this. Just wanted you to make sure you did. And call me old-fashioned, but I wanted to surprise you. I wanted it to be romantic. For you. And I guess I wanted to ask.' He shrugs.

'Wow.'

'At least, if it's a disaster, you won't be stuck with me forever.' His smile is wobbly.

'If that's a joke, it's *not* funny.' But I don't care because . . . 'We. Are. Getting. *Married*!'

'As long as your parents agree.'

I look lovingly at my ring. I hold out my hand to him. 'They'll agree.' Even if it has to be at gunpoint.

He takes my hand in his and kisses it. He looks right into my eyes. 'You're definitely sure about this?'

'I've never been surer about anything in my life.'

I walk in the front door, on air. I sail into the kitchen, humming. I'm engaged!

'Someone had a good time,' Mum says, coming with an empty mug from the TV room.

I hold my hand out. I thought about breaking the news slowly but I want her to see how happy I am, how happy he makes me.

She's gone white. 'Is that—?' she stops like she's afraid to say it. 'It is.'

She looks from it to me. In shock. 'I can't believe he asked you to do this.'

'He didn't. I did.'

'Sarah, you're seventeen.'

'With your consent—'

'No, no. Hang on. Sarah, you have to think this through, the practicalities … Where would you live – for *starters*?'

'With Shane, I suppose. Together anyway.'

'Has he asked his parents?'

'I don't know. I presume—'

'Don't presume *anything* about marriage.'

'Mum, it'll be OK.' I shouldn't have told her. Not yet. She's ruining everything. Tonight, I just want to be engaged to the guy I love and not worry about all this *stuff*.

'Sarah, marriage is not something you go into lightly—'

'I know that.' But she's not stopping me just because it didn't work out for her. 'I'll be eighteen next year and I won't need consent.'

'I think that's a better idea. Wait till next year.'

'No. I love him and I want to be with him now. We don't know how long we have together. We mightn't even have a year.' It kills me to say it.

She looks at me.

'Please, Mum. It's what I want more than anything in the world. Shane is my life. I love him. I want to be with him.'

'Sarah, do you know about this disease, what it will do to him? How hard it will be?'

'Of course I do, I'm not stupid. Seriously, Mum. Have *some* faith in me.'

'Who's going to nurse him? You?'

'He already has a nurse.'

'Let's sit down.'

'I don't want to sit down.'

'Sarah, I understand. This is so hard. And you're emotional.

Understandably. But you've always been such a romantic. Marriage doesn't mean happy ever after.'

'Don't you think I know that?' I've watched one fall apart right in front of me. I try to calm down. 'Mum. He's going to die. Can't we just have this?'

'I need to sit down.'

For a long time, she just sits at the kitchen table, like she's arguing it out in her head. Finally, she looks up. And my heart stops.

'I want to meet him,' she says.

'OK.'

'I want to see for myself that he loves you.' She'll see that. 'I want to know that he's thinking of you.' That too. 'And that, somehow, he'll take care of you.'

'I can take care of myself.'

'Good. That's good. But this is going to be a bumpy ride, Sarah. Someone has to be making sure you're OK.'

'His parents are lovely, Mum.'

'Yes but they're not *your* parents. And you can't expect them to be.'

'I know.'

'Their priority is Shane. Just like my priority is you. And that's why I can't just give in, like snapping my fingers. I want you to be happy, Sarah.'

'Then just say yes.'

'I want to meet Shane. And I want to meet his parents.'

Oh God, I think, wondering what she's going to ask them, wondering what she's going to say. But it's my only way forward, so I say, 'OK.'

35
IT'S YOU!

On the DART in the morning, Rachel spots it.

'Is that a new ring?'

I lift my hand up. 'That?' I ask as if it's nothing. 'Yep, it's new.'

'It's on your engagement finger, Sarah,' Alex says.

'Oh, yeah,' I say, as if I hadn't noticed.

'So it's *not* an engagement ring?' Rachel says, cautiously.

'Oh, no, it is,' I say brightly.

'Oh my God!' they say together.

'Last night?' Rachel asks.

'Yep.'

'Did you know?'

'No clue.'

'Wow.'

'My God.'

Then Rachel goes all serious. 'Can you even *get* married at seventeen?'

'With your parents' permission.'

'Do you think they'll give it?' she asks, doubtfully.

'I asked Mum.'

'And?'

'She wants to meet Shane. And his parents.'

'Yikes.'

'I know.'

'And your dad?'

'I kind of started with Mum.'

'Sarah,' Rachel says. 'Are you sure about this?' She looks all concerned. 'I mean marriage is for *life*.'

I look at her. 'Life can be kinda short sometimes.'

She swallows. 'I'm sorry.'

I shrug. 'It's OK.'

'No. It's not. It's terrible,' Alex says. She looks like she's going to cry. 'Why does there always have to be, like, a catch, you know? Why can't it be simple?'

'Alex, it's OK. Seriously,' I say.

She shakes her head. 'No. It's so unfair. It's so *sad*.'

'No. Honestly. It's great. I never thought he'd ask. I really didn't.'

'I know, but life – it's such a *bitch*.'

I smile.

'And *what* are you smiling about?' she snaps.

'I don't know. You're just so hormonal or something.'

'What?' She's outraged. 'That's like saying, "Are you having your period?"'

I laugh. I can't help it. 'It's your hormones, Alex. Definitely.'

Rachel puts an arm around her. 'I guess it's not sad if Sarah's happy, right?'

Alex looks at me. '*Are* you?'

I smile. 'Incredibly.'

'Well then,' Rachel says, as if that's that.

And I love them both. I really do.

*

)|(

In school, one of the nerds spots the ring and tells the other nerd. Next thing I know, they're in my face with questions. So I just tell them, straight out, 'Yeah, I'm engaged.' That's when it hits me – being engaged is one thing I have. Whatever else happens, no one can take that from me. Wahoo.

The nerds practically wet themselves, they're so excited to be first with the scandal. It flies around the class like a physical thing, an orange being passed from chin to chin. The orange reaches Simon. He looks at me for a long time.

I look back. *I don't care what you do. I don't care what you say. Bring it.*

He takes Amy aside. And I'm waiting for them to add wheelchair to the story, some spice to turn me into a bigger freak than I already am. But, actually, it's starting to look like they're having some sort of argument. I wonder what they could be fighting about. Which one of them will break the news? How to? When? In the end, Amy walks away, looking seriously pissed off.

All day, I wait for Round Two of the scandal to break. It never does. The word 'wheelchair' is never mentioned. And when we're finally leaving for the day, and I see Simon ahead of me, I think, maybe he's not the world's biggest jerk after all. Or maybe he's just making me sweat.

Shane calls to say that Deirdre would like to 'talk' to me when I get there.

'Just me?'

'Is that OK?'

'No.'

'Really?'

'No. I'm joking. It's fine.' It's not, though, really. It's terrifying.

'You sure?' he asks.

'My mum's talking to you, remember?'

'Yeah. When's that happening?'

'Don't know. I gave Mum your number last night.'

'Cool,' he says.

Even though we both know – it's so not cool.

Later, I walk up to the house, terrified. Even though I like Deirdre. She answers the door. I can't see Shane anywhere. Crap. She brings me into the kitchen and offers me a drink.

We sit at the table, her with a tea, me a Coke. And if I was Shane, I'd be listening at the door.

'So, big news,' she says.

'Yeah.'

Then no one says anything for ages.

'You've been very good to Shane,' she says.

'No I haven't,' I say, because I don't want her to think that that's what this is about – me being good to Shane.

She smiles. 'Let me rephrase. You've been very good *for* him.'

'*He's* been very good for *me*.' I sound defensive. I can't help it. I just wish people would leave the freaking disease out of it.

She smiles again. 'You're a sweet girl.'

'No. I'm an ordinary girl. I just love him.'

She looks at me for a long time. 'Shane is very sick.'

Oh. My. God. Do people think I'm blind? Deaf? Dumb? Living in a vacuum? Retarded? 'I know he's sick,' I say, as calmly as I can. Which probably isn't as calmly as it should be.

'He's losing power. All the time.' Her voice wobbles. And

I remember how hard this is for her.

'Deirdre,' I say. 'I know all about motor neurone disease. Every little thing. I've read about the research. I've read about disease progression.' Might as well use all those words I now know. 'I've seen photos. I've seen people whose disease is more advanced. I know,' I finish up.

She nods, slowly. 'I just want to be sure you know exactly what you'd be taking on. It's my duty to you, Sarah, as Shane's mum.'

'And I get that. But it's not the disease I'm marrying. It's Shane.'

'It comes with him.'

'I know that.'

'You're a very determined young lady.'

'When it comes to Shane I am.'

'But are you strong?'

'I don't know.'

She thinks for a while. 'Your parents. What have they said?'

'My mum wants to talk to you.'

She nods. 'Good, because I want to talk to her.' She smiles then. I don't know why – to calm me down? 'And your dad?'

I clear my throat. 'He doesn't know yet.'

She looks surprised.

'They're separated. I'm calling him tonight.' I've just decided.

She nods slowly and is quiet for a while.

'Sarah,' she says then, like she's made a decision. 'Fred and I have no say in this. Shane is over eighteen. He can do what he likes. I just want you to know that if he wasn't eighteen and we had a say, it would be 'yes'. If your parents give their consent, we'd be delighted to have you as part of our family.'

Then it hits me. What exactly they'd be taking on.

'Thank you,' I whisper, kind of bowled over.

'And I don't care what you say,' she says, firmly. 'You *are* a very special person. And I'll be telling that to your mother. In case she doesn't already know.' She winks.

And I blush because I'm not special. I just want to be with the person I love.

I don't actually ring Dad that night. I chicken out until two nights later. Mum has gone to meet Shane's parents and I have to take my mind off that.

'Sarah!' Dad sounds happy I've rung.

'I was hoping we could meet up.'

'Sure. Will we go back to the restaurant we were in last time? You seemed to like it.'

The happiest moment of my life was there. It seems like a good sign. 'Yeah, that'd be great, thanks.' I wonder if I should warn him that I've some news. No. He'll just try to get it out of me. So I just hang up. Immediately, I start to write out a list of reasons he should say yes.

I'm still at it an hour later when Mum comes up to my room. I try to work out from her face how it went with Deirdre. But I can't. She sits on the bed.

'So,' she says. 'I've been to see Deirdre.'

I know. I know, I think. *Just tell me what she said.*

'She's a lovely woman.'

Oh my God.

'And Shane. Shane's a very impressive young man.'

Please, God, don't let her next sentence start with 'but'.

‘He's also a very convincing young man.' She smiles.

‘Oh my God. Does that mean yes?'

She raises her eyebrows, smiles and nods.

‘Really? Are you serious?' I jump up from my desk and run to hug her.

She pulls back and looks suddenly serious. ‘Sarah, there's still your father.'

He's always been the easiest. ‘I'm meeting him Saturday.'

It takes forever to get to Saturday, but it finally arrives. We walk into the restaurant. The waiter takes one look at me and says, ‘It's you!' like I'm some kind of celebrity.

Oh God.

Dad looks at me for an explanation.

I shrug. I will the waiter to say nothing. Say nothing. But he does say something. It's like he can't hold it in.

‘This young lady got engaged in our restaurant only the other night.'

I stand very still. Dad looks from him to me, then down at my finger. He turns the colour of salt. ‘What's going on?'

The waiter clears his throat. ‘Let me show you to your table.'

Oh my God. It's the same table Shane and I were at. I look at the waiter to see if this is some kind of joke. But he's not looking at me any more. His shoes have his full attention now.

We sit down. The waiter hands us the menus, avoiding our eyes. He tells us the specials, stumbling over the words. All the time Dad's just staring at me. When the waiter finally leaves, I speak before Dad does.

‘That's what I wanted to tell you.' I smile. ‘I'm getting

married ... I just need your consent.' Best way to put it, I think, under the circumstances.

'If it wasn't for that stupid bloody waiter,' he says, 'I'd think this was some kind of joke. What's going on, Sarah?'

I shrug. 'I'm getting married.'

'Of course you're not. You're sixteen.'

'Seventeen. I had a birthday. You forgot.'

He looks confused. Like how could I have had a birthday without him knowing? He shakes his head. 'You still need to be eighteen.'

'Unless you get parental consent.'

His eyes narrow. 'Who *is* this guy? And *why* do you have to get married?' Then his eyes widen. 'Are you in trouble?'

'No, Dad. I'm not "in trouble".'

'Then *why*?' As if there could be no other logical reason.

'Because we're in love. And don't have much time.' I tell him everything, beefing up the tragedy element.

It totally backfires. 'You're not ready for this,' he says, firmly. 'This is far too traumatic for someone so young.'

'How do you know? You don't know me.'

'I've lived with you all my life.'

'Not quite.'

'Almost.'

'Mum said yes,' I say, using it against him, making him the bad parent, the old-fashioned one.

'I don't believe that. She wouldn't.'

'She obviously has more faith in me than you do. She said yes, Dad.'

'Well, I'm saying no.'

I lose it. 'You left. You can't boss me around now, just so it looks like you care.'

'I *do* care. Which is why I'm not allowing it.'

}I{

'Why is it always about what *you* want? You don't care about anybody but yourself.'

'Sarah, for someone who wants to get married, you're sounding very juvenile right now.'

I want to throw my glass of water in his face and ask him how juvenile that is. But I want this so badly. 'Please, Dad. I don't ask you for anything. This is all I want. Just this one thing.'

'No, Sarah,' he says, like Peter at the Gates of Heaven. 'I can't let you do this to yourself. I won't.'

'Yeah, well don't think that makes you a good father. Because you're not.' I get up and walk. Hating him all over again.

'How did you get on?' Mum asks when I walk into the kitchen. Then she sees my face. 'Oh.'

I burst out crying. 'He doesn't know anything about me, about Shane. And he didn't try to find out. He just thinks he's God.' I slump into a chair.

'It's OK,' she says. She rubs my back.

'It's all I want,' I say, tears streaming down my face.

She's silent for the longest time. Then she says, 'I'll talk to him.'

I look up at her in shock. She hasn't spoken to him since the shoplifting incident and that was only because she had to.

'You'd do that. For me?'

She takes my face between both her hands. 'You're my little girl. I'd do anything for you.' She kisses my forehead.

'But—'

'Sarah, you've grown up so much in the past few months. *So much*. In fairness to your father, he hasn't seen enough of you to realise that. I have, and I know how much you need to do this. I know that if you don't, you'll regret it for the rest of your life. It's going to be hard, no question. But you can come home anytime. No one will blame you. Shane will understand. We've spoken about that.'

'Mum, I won't leave him. No matter how hard it gets.'

'OK. But you need to know that you can – for down the road.'

No one thinks I'm strong enough for this. But I am. I'll show them.

'So, do you want me to talk to your dad?'

'Mum, that would be amazing. But talking to Dad …' I make a face.

She smiles. 'Come on. I have to stand up to him some time. Here's my chance.'

36
WOMAN

I try to be like Shane and not think about the bad stuff (my dad), just think about what I've got. I'm engaged. And I've ten driving lessons to use up. So when Louis offers me my first lesson, I take it.

We walk out to the car.

'So when do I get to meet this guy?' Louis asks.

'You already have.'

'I mean properly.'

'You're not, like, the man of the house or anything, Louis. You don't get to vet my … fiancé.' Ooh, I like the sound of that.

'I'm not vetting anyone. If he's going to be part of our family, I'd like to get to know him.'

'Oh, right.' OK. That's different. And maybe kind of sweet. 'Thanks.'

He looks at me. 'Sarah, if it wasn't for you, I'd never have had the guts to go back and talk to Alex again.'

'What did I do?'

'You inspired me.'

I laugh. 'I *inspired* you?'

'The way you piled in there with Shane, no worries. Wheelchair, so what?'

'I love him,' I say simply.

'I love *her*.'

I smile. 'Told ya. How's that going?' I ask, instead of getting in.

He shrugs. 'At least, I can be with her without going crazy for her, which is an improvement. It's like I'm there to protect her now or something.'

'Really?'

He grimaces. 'OK, it's kind of old fashioned.'

'No. It's how I feel too. Like I'd kill anyone who got in her way. You know?'

'So I'm *not* mad.'

I smile. 'Unless, of course, we're both mad.'

'A distinct possibility.'

I smile again. 'So Alex is OK with you being around?'

He shrugs. 'As friends, I guess. Why? Has she said anything to you?'

I shake my head. 'Alex is kind of private like that.'

He smiles. 'I know. She's great, isn't she?'

'Yeah.'

We get into the car, but I don't want to get going just yet. 'What are you going to do when the baby comes?' I ask, seeing as we'll probably never have a chat like this again.

'I don't know. Whatever Alex needs, I guess.'

'You going to tell Mum?'

'I'm not going to tell anyone unless Alex wants people to know.'

I wonder how that must feel – the girl you love not wanting

to admit you're the father of her baby. 'Doesn't it bother you that she doesn't want to tell people?'

'Sarah. A few weeks ago, *I* didn't want to know. Come on, we better get going. Mum will want the car back.'

I'm sitting in the driver's seat of my mum's car, suddenly terrified. I've been so excited about these lessons. But now all I can think is what if I manx the car?

'So how much do you know?' Louis asks, matter of factly.

'About driving?'

'Yeah, you know, from watching.'

'I don't watch. Usually, I look out the window.'

'OK.'

He points everything out. Accelerator. Brake. Clutch. Gears. He tells me what to do. I ask him to repeat the first bit again. I follow his instructions exactly: turn the key, press the clutch, go into gear, ease off on the clutch while pressing on the accelerator. The car revs up. Then stalls.

'What did I do wrong?'

He taps the hand brake.

'Crud.' I forgot to let it off.

I try again, remembering the hand brake. The car cuts out. I feel like a retard.

'What did I do *now*?'

'You let off the clutch a bit fast. Just *ease* it off. Try again.'

I start again. And stall again. 'Jesus. What's wrong with me?'

'Just try again. You'll get it.' He's so patient, it's abnormal.

'Were you this bad?' I ask.

He lights a cigarette, opens a window. 'Probably.'

'Jesus, Louis, why are you *always* so laid back?'

'What, you want me to start yelling?'

'It might help.' The whole Zen approach is getting on my nerves.

'Jesus H. Christ. Start the fucking car,' he shouts.

And we burst out laughing.

Next day, at school, Round Two finally starts. I realise this when Orla Tempany decides to check the truth of the story with me.

'Are you seriously engaged to a disabled guy?'

I smile. It's almost a relief. People are so predictable.

'So you're not?'

'No, I am. I just think it's funny that this is your latest big deal.'

'Oh my God, she is.' Orla turns and hurries away to spread the, now confirmed, news.

'You'd think I was going to marry an actual wheelchair,' I say to Alex, rolling my eyes.

'They're assholes.'

I remember how I used to live on gossip. Was I really like that? I mean, they're happier that I'm engaged to a guy in a wheelchair rather than just engaged.

After school, Simon comes up to me at my locker.

'Are you OK?' he asks.

'Yeah, why wouldn't I be?' I ask coldly.

'It wasn't me.'

'You know what Simon? I don't care. It doesn't matter. None of it does.'

'Well, I think it's pretty fucking cruel.'

'Actually, it's the truth. I am engaged to a guy in a wheelchair.' I shrug and turn to go.

'I'm sorry,' he says. 'I tried to stop her.'

'Who?'

'Amy.'

'Yeah well, maybe Amy wouldn't have thought it was such a big deal if you hadn't made it such a big deal in the coffee shop.' Then I do go. Leaving him standing there. With his stupid sorry.

Later, I get a call from Rachel.

'It's all over Facebook. Simon ended it with Amy.'

'I should probably care, right?'

'It was over the wheelchair thing. She started the rumour.'

'It's not a rumour.'

'I know. Still, maybe he's not a complete a-hole after all.'

'You know what, Rache, if he was a frog that turned into a prince, I still wouldn't care.'

That night, Mum calls me down to the kitchen.

'I spoke with your dad.'

Oh God. I think my heart has stopped. '*And*?'

'He said OK.'

'He said *OK*? *Are you serious*?' I put my hands to my face and scream. I run to her and fling my arms around her. 'How did you do it?'

She shrugs. 'I just explained.'

'And he went for it?'

'OK, I had to use a little guilt.' She smiles.

Then I'm hugging her again. 'Thank you *so* much. You're a genius … Oh my God. I have to call Shane.' *We're getting married. We can be together at last.* I start towards the door.

'Wait,' she says.

}|{

I stop and turn.

'You have to come see me,' she says. Suddenly, I see it. Mum finally stood up to Dad and got her way. Only it's not her way. It's mine. This isn't what she wants – for me to leave home at seventeen.

'Of course I will.'

'At least once a week.'

'More.'

'Maybe every Sunday for lunch. Both of you. And one night during the week?'

I smile. 'That'd be nice.' I really want to ring Shane now, though.

'Sarah, you have to promise me something.' I look at her. 'Hold on to your independence. Stay yourself.'

I almost cry for her. 'I promise, Mum. I swear.'

She smiles. 'I'm going to miss you so much.'

'Mum, you'll see me all the time.'

'At least I'll have you for a few months yet.'

Months? 'I thought it'd be sooner than that.'

'It takes a bit of organisation, Sarah. You have to wait in line for a priest, a church …'

'Really?'

'And there'll be paperwork. Especially given your age.'

'Damn.'

'It might be no harm, Sarah. It'll give everyone time to get used to the idea.'

She means Shane and me. 'We *are* used to it. We just want to be together.'

'You spend most of your time together as it is.'

'Except for school.' Which I resent. I really do.

'Which you'll have to keep up.'

}|{

'I know.'

'So there's no rush, Sarah.'

'Actually, there kind of is.' But now, at least, we can be together properly. We can fall asleep together, wake up together, use every bit of time we have to be together.

'Mum, can you do me a favour?'

'Shoot.'

'Can you drive me over? I don't want to tell him over the phone.'

She smiles. 'Sure. I'll just go get the keys.'

'You look suspiciously happy,' he says, when he sees me.

I put my hands on my hips and wiggle them. 'You're looking at your future wife.'

He smiles. 'Seriously?'

'Seriously.' I run to him, vault myself up and fling my arms around him. The chair almost topples over.

He laughs.

I pull back and look at him. 'I'm going to be a wife!' I say unnecessarily.

'A missus.'

'A kept woman.'

'A frau.'

'What's the word in French?' I ask.

'There is none.'

'Then what do they say?'

'Woman.'

I laugh. '"Come here, woman."'

'I like the sound of that. Fetch my slippers, woman. Put the cat out, woman.'

'Shut up.' I laugh. 'Let's get your laptop.'

}|{

'Why?'

'To plan our big day.'

He smiles. 'You don't waste time, do you?'

'Are you kidding? If we could get married right this minute, we would be getting married right this minute.'

'Here, give me a kiss.'

'Give me your laptop.'

It's Louis who picks me up.

'I'm getting married before you,' I tease.

'Good,' he says. But he's smiling. 'Congratulations, squirt.' He ruffles my hair and makes me feel like a kid again.

Fifteen minutes later, I'm rushing into the kitchen to see if Mum has my birth certificate. She's on the phone, her back to the door.

'I'll be lost without her,' she's saying. I think of Dad leaving. Now me. And I know Louis will be gone as soon as he can. God. She's going to be all alone. 'Are you joking?' she says. 'Louis's never home.' I reverse out. The house will be so quiet now. Just when she changed job to finish early. Slowly, and kind of bewildered, I walk upstairs.

I want to tell Alex and Rache in person. I manage to hold off till the morning, then ride the whole way on the DART without saying a thing.

'What are you smiling about?' Alex asks suspiciously.

'Nothing.'

But as soon as we're out of the DART station, I stop walking. And smile.

'Who wants to be a bridesmaid?'

'Oh my God,' they say together. They burst into smiles together. And hug me together.

Then Alex loses her smile. 'You have to wait till I have the baby. I'm not waddling around in an amazing dress looking like a whale. OK?'

The baby's due in two months. The paperwork's going to take that long anyway. 'OK, sure.'

'What kind of wedding are you going to have?' Rachel asks, sounding excited.

'What do you think? The works. Church wedding. Like, *loads* of flowers. Doves, definitely.'

'Doves?'

'Yeah, doves.'

Alex laughs.

'Would doves and balloons be too much?' I ask.

'The balloons might frighten the doves,' Rachel suggests.

Alex smiles. 'And the doves might burst the balloons.'

'So just doves then,' I confirm.

After school, we get off the DART early to check out a shop that sells wedding dresses. We walk in. A bell rings overhead. Two assistants chatting to each other at the counter,glance at us, then at each other. I remember we're still in uniform. One of them approaches, like she's coming to get rid of us. Maybe she thinks we're just messing. *Not a bad idea*, I think, *spending an afternoon trying on wedding dresses. Wish I'd thought of it before.*

'Can I help you?' she asks, like that's the last thing she wants to do. But then she sees Alex's bump and her whole attitude changes. She smiles at her.

'When's the big day?' she asks.

'You're talking to the wrong person,' Alex says. Kind of rudely, which is why I love her.

'Oh, sorry.' She actually blushes. 'So, who is the bride?' she asks carefully.

'That would be me,' I say. 'And these are my bridesmaids.' Suddenly, it hits me. We're really doing this. I feel like whooping and doing a little dance.

'Of course,' she says, not exactly grovelling but not far off. I remember the recession. Things must be bad. 'What price range were you thinking?' she asks.

'What price ranges do you have?'

'They start at five hundred, for the sale items,' she looks over at a rack of sad looking dresses, 'and go up to eight thousand,' she turns to the Vera Wang range.

I'm screwed. But don't let on. Don't want to give her the satisfaction.

'Great!' Alex says. 'We'll see all of them,' she says with the confidence of someone who is minted. 'And the bridesmaids' dresses too.'

'Follow me,' the assistant says. She starts to walk down the shop.

Alex whispers to me. 'Don't look at the labels. Just pretend you're Cinderella.'

I smile. And think, *Why not enjoy the afternoon anyway*?

The assistant starts to actually assist, pulling out dresses and talking about 'features'.

Alex dismisses her with an 'It's OK, thanks. We'll take it from here.'

The dresses are amazing. We end up heading for the fitting rooms with about fifteen, draped over each of our arms. Wow, they're heavy.

'Just a moment,' the older assistant says. 'I'll accompany you.'

'What, into the fitting rooms?' I say.

'Not quite that far.'

Just outside the fitting rooms, there's an area with gigantic mirrors and a rack to hang the dresses. That's where everyone waits while I go in, with one dress at a time.

I step into the first dress. It's so soft, so silky but so cold. I shiver. I stand up straight and look in the mirror. It's beautiful. But it's not me. I know that straight away. I go out anyway because it took so long to put on.

'Wow,' Rachel and Alex say, together.

The assistant zips me up, in silence, without me even asking. She doesn't 'ooh' or 'ah' and I think that maybe I can trust her to, at least, be honest.

She doesn't take the next dress in line, but roots through them. Then she takes out the sixth or seventh from the front and looks at it for a moment. Then she hands it to me.

'Try this.' It's a sexy sheath of silk, low neck, no sleeves. Very simple.

'You think?' I ask, unsure. It seems kind of plain to me.

But this time, when I look in the mirror, I almost don't recognise myself. I look so grown up. So sophisticated. This is my Cinderella moment. All I can do is stare. When I (finally) come out, there's this gasp, followed by silence. The assistant smiles like she's satisfied, like *this* is why she does her job. She zips me up and I allow myself a swirl in front of the mirror. How did she know?

Alex starts taking photos on her phone. Front. Side. Back.

'I'd prefer if you didn't,' the assistant says.

'Why not? They're just photos,' Alex says.

'She's so beautiful,' Rachel says.

'All right, go on then. Though strictly it's not allowed.'

'I'll just take one last shot,' Alex says. She takes it, then says, 'OK. Done.'

'So,' the assistant says to me. 'Would you like to see any more?'

I shake my head.

She lifts the price tag. 'Five thousand euro.'

I nearly collapse. 'Oh. OK. Good.' (Good?) 'I'll have to come back, though. With my mum.'

'Of course,' she says. And I can't tell if she believes me or not.

She unzips me and I return to the changing room, so careful not to damage the dress. If I damage it or mark it, they might make me pay for it.

Outside the shop, I remember the bridesmaids' dresses. 'Oh my God, we forgot you guys.'

'Good,' Alex says. 'You think I'm trying anything on looking like this?' She looks down at her bump. 'I need chocolate.'

'Let's go to Starbucks,' Rachel says.

'Best idea I've heard all day,' I say. Still thinking about the price tag.

'No,' Alex says. 'You're about to *hear* the best idea you've heard all day.'

I smile. 'Does that even make sense?'

'It's going to,' she says. 'Marsha!'

'What?'

'Marsha'll do it. Marsha'll make the dress.'

}|{

'Oh my God. *Would* she?' I ask.

'Why d'you think I went mad with the camera in there? So I can show her what you'd like. Of course she'll do it. If I ask her nicely. She's been so sweet since I got pregnant.'

'She was always sweet,' Rachel says.

'I know but she's insanely sweet now. Making baby clothes. Loads and loads of the cutest baby clothes. She'd almost make you look forward to it.'

We look at her.

'Almost.'

Next day, we go see Marsha. She's all excited that I'm getting married. She wants to see pictures of Shane. I hand her my phone. She loses her smile. Then produces a fresh one. Manufactured. She looks at me like she's looking at a different person. A particularly good person.

'Right. Let's see those shots you took of the dress,' she says to Alex.

Alex fiddles with her iPhone and passes it to Marsha.

'Oh, wow,' she says. She looks up at me. 'You're beautiful.'

I smile. Embarrassed. In that dress I just may be.

'It's a stunning dress. Good photography, Alex, very professional.'

'Why, thank you.'

'Right,' Marsha says. 'First thing we do is measure you up.'

'I'm an eight,' I say.

She tsks. 'No one's *just* an eight.' She whips a measuring tape from her back pocket and moves like a bullet, taking the measurements as automatically as someone brushing

}|{

their teeth. She pulls a pencil from behind her ear and starts to scribble notes. Then she starts to sketch the dress. 'It looks very simple,' she says as she draws. 'It isn't. The important thing is to get it to fall right.'

I nod seriously.

'I'm pretty sure where I can get the fabric. How long have we got on this?'

'Actually,' I say with a grimace, 'we've probably got a few months. It's, like, impossible to get a church.' Which I think must be some sort of cosmic revenge for all the thousands of masses I've skipped.

'I'll work ahead anyway,' Marsha says.

And I hate to bring up money but I have to know if I can make this. If I don't ask, I'll be stressing the whole time. 'How much do I owe you?' I ask, quietly.

She looks at me like I've just called her a hooker. 'I'm not *charging*. You're a friend.'

I stare at her. 'Oh my God. That's so sweet.' My hand goes to my heart. 'But I have to pay you something. For your time. For the fabric.'

'No,' Marsha says. 'This one's on me. I want to give you a present anyway. Now I won't have to think.'

I don't remind her that I hardly know her because I know she'd be insulted. So I just hug her.

'Thank you so much. You're the best,' I say, and there are tears in my eyes.

37
OXYGEN

Weeks pass. The weather gets colder, the days get shorter and Alex's bump gets bigger. One day, in the middle of October, when I switch on my phone after school, there's a message from Shane.

'Call me. Nothing to worry about. Just not at home.'

It's too noisy to call back so I grab my stuff, lock my locker and tell the guys I'll meet them outside. On my way out, I start thinking: *Does anybody say 'there's nothing to worry about' unless there is?* Worried, I call him.

'Hey,' he says. He doesn't sound right.

'Where are you?'

'In Raphael's.'

'*Hospital?*'

'Eh, yeah. It's OK. I've just a little pneumonia.'

'A *little* pneumonia?' It's the biggest killer of people with motor neurone disease.

His laugh turns into a cough.

'Can you've visitors?'

'That's why I was calling.'

'Can I come now?'

'I was hoping you'd say that.'

'I'm on my way.'

'Any chance of some Jelly Tots?'

'Definitely,' I say, relieved. He mustn't be too bad if he wants Jelly Tots.

A nurse directs me to Shane's room. He's sharing with two other men.

'He's at the end,' she says. She smiles and hurries away to answer a call bell.

I look in but can't see him because the curtain around his bed is pulled forward slightly. I smile at the man in the first bed as I start to walk in. He looks about eighty. He raises his hand to say hello. It's attached to a drip. I hope it's nothing serious. The next man looks younger – by about ten years. Sound asleep, he's lying on his back with his mouth wide open, snoring so loudly you can probably hear him in the next room.

When I get to Shane's bed, it's Deirdre I see first. She's scraping butter onto toast for Shane. She sees me and smiles brightly like this is all cool, like she's making a picnic and we're off to the beach. Then I see Shane.

Oh my God. 'Is that *oxygen*?'

'It's OK,' he says. 'I just need a little extra till the antibiotics kick in. Did you bring the Jelly Tots?'

I pull them from my pocket and open the pack fully, so he can get them out easily.

'You're a life saver,' he says. He takes a few at a time, like a junkie getting a fix.

Deirdre pushes the tray of tea and toast up to him. Then she turns to me.

}|{

'How are you, Sarah?'

'Good, thanks,' I say, as jolly as she is. But I don't feel jolly. I'm worried as hell.

'I might just nip out for coffee,' she says.

'You should go home,' Shane says. 'You've been here all day.'

'Are you sure? Just for an hour or two. I've a few things to do.'

'Mum, go. I'll see you tomorrow.'

'You sure?'

'I'm a big boy now,' he says, kind of narked, like she makes him feel useless or something.

'I'll see you tomorrow then.' She sounds hurt. She loves him so much; she just wants to help. But I see his side too. It must be awful having to rely on his parents for everything.

Deirdre leaves. I go up to him and sit on the side of the bed.

'How're you doing?'

He nods. 'OK.'

'You don't look OK, Shane. This happened kind of quickly. You were fine yesterday.' Actually, now that I think of it, he *was* pretty tired.

He shrugs. 'I'd a bad night.'

'Shane, this doesn't mean that your chest muscles have weakened, does it?' I'm so afraid of the answer.

'No. They said I'm in pretty good shape.'

'Honestly?'

'I wouldn't lie to you about this.'

I close my eyes in relief.

'With some serious physio and intravenous antibiotics I should be out of here in a week.'

I let out a huge breath and help myself to a Jelly Tot. I lie up on the bed beside him and we watch a movie from the eighties called *Splash*, about a mermaid who falls in love with a guy. I'm loving it, but Shane's exhausted and the nurses keep hassling me about visiting time being over. I get up, put on my coat. I don't ever remember October being this cold. I heave my bag onto my shoulder.

'How're you getting home?' Shane asks.

'DART.'

'Why don't you get a taxi?'

Being minted, he has no clue about money. 'I'm fine.'

'I know, but it's late and you're on your own.'

'Ooooh, look at you, getting all husbandy already.'

He smiles. 'I'm serious though. Get a taxi. I've money.'

'It's OK, seriously. I'll be fine.' I bend to kiss him.

He turns his face so that the kiss lands on his cheek. 'We don't want you to end up in here beside me.'

'There's an idea!' I kiss him on the mouth. 'Love you,' I say, then I walk backwards out of the room, blowing kisses, wondering if they would let me stay if we were married.

The DART is practically empty. There are only two other people in the carriage. A guy in his, I don't know, thirties, in a long dark coat, sitting nearby. And a little old woman, farther up. I look out the window but because it's dark, I only see my reflection. After a while, I notice the reflection of the guy. He's looking at me. So I look away from the window. And just stare straight ahead. I still feel his eyes on me so I take out my phone and send Shane a text. I glance at the window. It's not my imagination. He's still looking. This is starting to creep me out. I think of getting up and going to sit next to the woman. But that'd be kind of dramatic –

given that he's probably just bored and doesn't realise he's staring. Finally, we pull up at my stop. I get up and walk to the door, hoping he doesn't follow and telling myself I'm being paranoid for thinking he might. The doors open and he's still sitting down. *Phew*, I think. But I only fully relax when the doors close behind me and the DART pulls away – and he's still on it. Maybe Shane was right about the DART. Maybe I should be more careful. Still, I can't afford a taxi. And there's no way I'm leaving any earlier than nine.

Three days later, in Biology, I notice Alex gripping her tummy under the table. She's breathing deeply. Looking pale. Oh my God. It couldn't be. She's not due till November.

'Are you OK?' I whisper.

She nods. 'Just cramps.'

Cramps! 'We need to get to the hospital.' I try to stay calm.

'No. It's OK, they're just false contractions.'

'*False* contractions?'

'Sarah Healy,' the teacher barks.

I look up in shock. 'I was just asking—'

'I don't care if you were asking for OXYGEN!' Her piggy face has gone even more piggy pink. Her full-on unibrow is frowning. Hasn't she heard of a tweezers? I wait for her to turn back to the board. I look at Alex.

'I'm fine,' she whispers.

'You sure?' I whisper back.

'Just my body getting ready.'

'SARAH!' Miss Piggy has just whipped around with impressive non-piggy speed.

'Sorry,' I say.

For what's left of the class, I pretend to listen. But how can I concentrate on some boring experiment when who knows what could be happening beside me. I mean that's real biology. In action. I sneak a peak at Alex to make sure she hasn't gone into silent, secret labour ... if there's such a thing.

As soon as the class is over and we get out onto the corridor, I turn to her. 'Have they stopped?'

She shakes her head. 'All I can say is, if these are false contractions, I can't wait for the real ones.'

I stare at her. 'Alex. Maybe they're the real thing. Maybe we should—'

'No. They're not regular. And they're too far apart.'

'But what if they *get* regular and close?'

'*Then* we worry.'

Oh my God. 'OK, give us plenty of notice.'

'Sarah, babies take hours and *hours* to be born,' Rachel says, sensibly.

'Thanks, Rache. Comforting thought,' Alex says.

Rachel looks at her. 'You'll be grand. As long as you go for the epidural.'

'Can we stop talking about this?' Alex has gone even more pale. She looks like she's going to faint.

'Are you OK?'

She looks at me, eyes wide. 'No. I'm not ready. I'm not ready for this. I'll never be ready.'

Oh, crud. I don't know what to say. All I know is, if it was me, *I* wouldn't be ready either. And someone telling me I was would *not* help. I find a chair and order her to sit.

Rachel squats down beside her. 'No one's ever ready for

this,' she says, sounding so wise. So Zen. And, not for the first time, I'm glad she's here.

After twenty minutes the 'cramps' subside and Alex is OK again. We're given out to for missing class.

I climb up onto the bed with Shane and snuggle. I tell him about school. About Miss Piggy and her oxygen remark. 'She's such a pig,' I say, unnecessarily.

'God, I miss school,' he says.

I stare at him. Then get it. I'm actually lucky to be able to go. I guess.

'Would you mind getting off the bed?'

I look up. There's a nurse standing at the end of the bed. How did she do that? Just appear so quickly.

'Hygiene,' she says.

I get up. Why is the world so full of people with rules? I sit on the chair beside the bed and feel miles away from him.

'Give it a minute,' he says, 'then pull the curtain and come back up.'

God, I love him. I wait three minutes, exactly, then pull the curtain and climb back up. I put my face up to his, nose to nose.

'Hello,' I say.

He smiles. 'Hello.'

We laugh.

'I was thinking of fortune cookies for the wedding.'

He smiles again. 'You really want this, don't you?'

I've a sudden moment of panic. 'Don't *you*?'

'More than anything.'

'Then hurry up and get better.'

'I'm trying.' He looks at me. 'It's four days. I thought I'd be off the oxygen by now.'

Oh my God. He should be, shouldn't he? 'Why aren't you?'

'I don't know.'

'Have you asked the doctor?'

'No. But I will in the morning.'

'Good.'

A tray of food arrives. He ignores it.

He needs to eat. So I get up and do what Deirdre normally does. Then I move the tray up to him. He smiles thanks. But only picks at the food. I have this feeling that if I wasn't here, he wouldn't bother.

'Here, you have the dessert,' he says.

'Nah, I'm grand.'

'Go on, I'm stuffed. It'll just be dumped.'

I am actually starving. And it *is* ice cream. 'You sure?'

He hands it to me. Then lies back, looking exhausted. I get up and move the tray away. His eyelids look heavy, like he's fighting to keep them open.

'Sleep,' I say.

He looks relieved. 'Would you mind? Just for a few minutes.'

'Yeah, sure.'

'Wake me up in ten, OK?'

'OK,' I say, just so he'll sleep. I'm not waking him.

'You should get some homework done.'

'You sound like my mum.'

He smiles. 'You don't want to fall behind.'

'I won't.'

'Life goes on, right?' Meaning he wants my life to go on smoothly after he's gone.

'I hate when you talk like that.'

'I don't care. It's important.'

'Sleep,' I say, instead of shut up. I love him so much.

His eyes close. Like they're relieved.

After ten minutes admiring him, I get kind of bored. I think of all the freaking, useless homework I have to do. Why was it ever invented? I mean, what idiot came up with that idea? Some sort of sadist, obviously.

Finally, and only because I don't want to be up all night, I take out my stupid homework.

Shane keeps on sleeping. Someone takes his tray away. A nurse comes to inject drugs into the thingy in his arm. Still he sleeps. Two other nurses come to turn him over. They wake him but by the time they're finished settling him, he's asleep again, just facing the opposite direction. The hum of the hospital continues around us.

At seven, Peter arrives. I shove my books into my bag.

'You don't have to put them away.'

'Trust me. I was looking for an excuse.'

'What were you doing?'

'Ecosystems.'

'Ah,' he says, like that explains it.

He looks at Shane. 'How's he doing?' he whispers.

'Still waiting for the antibiotics to kick in.'

He leaves a few packs of Jelly Tots on the bedside locker. 'His fix,' he says.

'He's already had a pack. You don't want to send him over the edge,' I joke.

He smiles, then pulls up a chair beside me. 'How long's he been asleep?'

'About an hour and a half.'

'You think he's gone for the night?'

'Don't know. Maybe. You should have come in earlier.'

'That's your time with him.'

'I can share,' I smile.

'It's OK. He called me after school and we'd a chat so it's grand.'

'Then why did you come in?'

He shrugs. 'Thought you might need a lift home.'

'Who thought? You or Shane?'

'He wants you to be safe.'

I didn't even *tell* Shane about my silent freak on the DART.

'Look, you don't need to—' I start.

'I want to.' He lowers his voice. 'It's something I can do for him. You know?' He looks at the person who's always thinking of everyone else. My throat burns and I well up.

'It's not fair, is it?' I whisper. 'I mean, why did it have to happen someone so great?'

And when he looks at me, I see that mine aren't the only teary eyes in the place. 'Come on, let's go.'

I go to the head of the bed and cup Shane's cheek in my hand, then I bend down and kiss him. 'I love you so much,' I whisper, then I force myself to leave.

38
Pyjama Woman

Next day, Shane's bed is empty. I stand in the doorway looking at it. Wondering where he's gone. *Worrying* where he's gone.

'He's been moved, love,' the man in the first bed says. 'Into a private room.'

'Oh, right,' I say.

'Ask one of the nurses.'

'OK, thanks.'

But I don't need to ask anyone because, back on the corridor, I see Shane's parents. They're talking to a doctor. Actually, the doctor's talking. They're listening, his father frowning, his mother looking worried. I walk closer. I glance into the room behind them. Shane's lying on his side, eyes closed, wearing one of those oxygen masks that cover your face. He's on a drip. He's covered by only a sheet. A fan is blowing air around the room. Suddenly, it's me who's cold. I start walking, like I'm in a trance. His parents finish with the doctor. Turning, they see me.

'Sarah!' Deirdre says.

'What's wrong?'

It's his father who speaks. 'They think he has an infection on top of his infection.'

'Is that serious?' It looks serious.

'They're doing tests and changing his antibiotics,' he says. He's so formal – like he's still on TV.

I look at Deirdre. She smiles but only with her mouth. 'Would you like to see him? We'll wait out here.'

'Would you mind?'

'We've been with him all day. Oh, you have to wash your hands.'

I look at her.

'Just a precaution.'

For who? I wonder, but don't ask.

I wash my hands, then go to the head of the bed and sit, waiting for him to wake. Willing him to. He looks so much weaker. His chest rises and falls so obviously when he breathes, like it's taking huge effort. I want to touch him, tell him it'll be OK but I don't want to wake him.

And then, like he's psychic, he opens his eyes. And smiles.

I take his hand. It's so hot. I smile to hide my fear. I'm about to ask how he is, when I decide that's obvious. And I don't want him to waste energy talking.

'How're the wedding preparations coming on?' he asks.

I burst into a smile. Because that's what we should be doing, planning for when he gets out, not even thinking about the infection.

'Great! If it wasn't for the priest and the church, we could actually do it now.'

He takes off the mask. 'Then let's do it. Let's get married here. We don't need a church. There's a priest here. I was talking to the chaplain yesterday,' he says.

'The chaplain?' Last time I heard that word, Alex's mum was dying. 'Why?'

'He just called around.'

'Why, though? You're not holy.'

He smiles. 'They call to everyone. I was talking to him about you – like I do to everyone – pathetic, right? The wedding came up.'

I'm worried about him having the mask off. 'Shouldn't you put that on?'

'I will in a minute. So what do you think?'

I want to get married more than anything. But I want it to be the best wedding ever – especially for him. 'I'd prefer to wait till you're better,' I say. 'Till you're out.' Maybe with something to fight for, he'll get out sooner.

He gives me this look.

'What?' I ask.

'Nothing. They're changing my antibiotics.'

'I know. That's good, right?'

He puts the mask back on. And nods. He rests his head back and closes his eyes, like that one conversation has taken all his energy.

I glance out to the corridor to see if Shane's parents want to come back in. His father has his arms around his mum and she is crying into his chest. And I have that cold feeling again. Like there's something they're not telling me.

I stay with Shane for hours. Mostly, he sleeps. His parents wander in and out. Sometimes they sit for a while. Finally, his dad has to go. Deirdre does all these little things for Shane that never occurred to me to do. Which makes me feel useless. When the night nurses come on, she goes out to talk to them.

Peter arrives. He looks totally shocked. 'What happened?'

I shrug. 'An infection on top of his pneumonia. They think.'

'Shit,' he whispers, looking at Shane. 'How long's he been asleep?'

'Ages. He's sleeping pretty much all the time at the moment.'

When Deirdre comes back, Peter gets up.

'I'm going to bring Sarah home,' he says to her. 'If Shane wakes will you tell him I called?'

She smiles, like she's realising she's forgotten the other people who're worried about him. 'Of course.' She hugs me goodbye.

In Peter's car, rain pelts against the windscreen and coloured leaves smash against the glass. He turns up the heating.

'What did the doctors say?' he asks.

'I don't know. They were speaking to Shane's parents. I only got what they were telling me. Which wasn't everything.'

He looks at me. Then, out of nowhere, my stomach rumbles really loudly. We laugh in embarrassment.

'You hungry?' he asks.

I shrug. 'A bit.'

'There's a space!' he says, swerving into it like some kind of Formula One driver. 'Come on, let's grab a McDonald's.'

Now that he's parked, I can't exactly say no.

There's a free table by the window. He tells me to take it and asks what I want. Then he heads to the counter. Which is busy tonight. I sit looking out at the rain. A car pulls up outside, mounting the path before coming to a stop in the wheelchair space. The car door opens and a fat, blonde chick gets out. Using both legs. I sit up. Check. There's no one else in the car. No one disabled in the car at all. I feel pressure building in my head.

She's in pyjama bottoms and a vest top. Her arms are heavily tattooed. Her face is tough, her eyes hard. She's not the kind of person you mess with. Don't care.

When she walks in the door, I stand up.

'It's a miracle!' I call out. She turns and looks. 'Oh my God,' I say. 'She can *walk*.'

And she does walk. Over to me, her chin jutting out like she's dying for a fight.

'You got a problem?' she asks, in a strong Dublin accent.

'You just took that wheelchair space out there.'

'*So?*' Her whole head juts forward now.

'So someone in an *actual wheelchair* might need it.'

'You think I fucking care?' she sneers.

'I think you'd *fucking care* if something happened *your* fucking legs.'

A kid at the next table bursts out laughing. His mother glares at him to stop.

'Go fuck yourself, you skinny bitch,' Pyjama Woman says, and then, like I'm too skinny to bother with, she marches to the counter.

No way. No *way* am I letting her away with it. I hurry out into the rain. I look up and down the street. Where are all the cops when you need them? It's Dun Laoghaire. There's a station around the corner. *Right*, I think, and start to run. This is important. This is critical. I round the corner, so angry I could hit someone. Then, hallelujah, strolling towards the town, head tipped down against the rain, a cop.

I run up to him, tell him what happened, realising as I do it's probably not an actual crime. He looks at me. Then he starts to walk. Fast. I have to trot to keep up.

Pyjama Woman is actually sitting in the car, munching on her burger, when we get there. *Unbelievable.*

The guard taps on the window.

She lowers it. 'Yeah?' she says, her mouth full. And I think, she's not afraid of anything.

He asks for her driver's licence.

She doesn't have it.

'Step out of the car,' he says.

On the side of the street, in the rain, he takes out a notepad. He takes the registration number, then asks for her name and address. As she stands there giving out her details, her T-shirt starts to go all see-through. It's not a pretty sight.

She glares at me.

I smile.

And then something I don't expect. He breathalyses her. Yes!

I think of Peter and glance inside. The whole of McDonald's is looking out now, including Peter, who is standing with the food in his hand and his mouth open. I watch as Pyjama Woman gets back into her tiny car, her fat jowls blaring red, like some kind of tropical bird, her T-shirt clinging to her lady lumps. With the guard watching, she belts up. And just before she drives away, she glares at me. I give a little wave.

I can't believe that, even now, with Shane so sick, I still have to go to school. Everything seems so irrelevant. The teachers seem like people who've never gone out in the world and had adventure, taken risks. All the kids seem like ... kids. It doesn't feel right to be here any more. But not just for me ... Alex looks like she's going to have the baby at any moment. She spends so much time going to the loo and is constantly chewing heartburn tablets. It's like we've outgrown school.

As soon as the bell goes, I head to the hospital. I go straight to the Nurses' Station and ask to speak to Shane's doctor. After my clash with Pyjama Woman, I'm not afraid of anyone. Doctor or no doctor. White coat or no white coat. I deserve to know what's going on. Even if I am seventeen.

I have to wait fifteen minutes before the doctor is ready to speak to me. She's young, blonde and pretty with her hair tied back into a ponytail.

'I'm enquiring about Shane Owens,' I say, trying to sound grown up. 'He has an infection on top of his infection, I know that. I just want to know what that means exactly.'

'And you're ...?'

'His fiancée,' I say firmly, confidently.

She looks surprised. Like she's trying to work out if I'm for real.

'He just seems to have got so much worse,' I say.

She nods. 'Have you spoken to Shane's parents?'

'Of course. But there's something they're not telling me. I mean, how bad is it? I need to know.'

She takes a deep breath. 'You're right, Shane has acquired an infection on top of his initial pneumonia. It's taking quite a toll on him. He's fighting. But it's a big fight.'

'What do you mean?'

'His cultures have grown gram negative bacteria.'

'I don't know what that means.' How am I supposed to?

'It means that we don't have as many options as we'd like to when it comes to antibiotics.'

I stare at her. 'So you're saying what?'

She puts a hand on my arm. Which freaks me out. I know from Alex: when doctors touch you, it's serious. 'I'm saying, we're doing our best. We're working with what we have. And hoping for the best.'

'But he *is* going to get out of here, right?'

'We're doing our best.'

'Oh my God.' My hand goes to my mouth. My legs buckle.

She grabs a chair and I drop into it. She asks a passing nurse for a glass of water.

'Breathe deeply,' she says.

I don't want to breathe at all.

39
SMOKE

I'm standing outside the hospital. Smoking. I hurried out to get air. And that's what I was doing when this guy in pyjamas came out for a smoke and offered me one. I thought, *These things kill you, right?* So I'm standing here, swallowing back smoke, trying not to cough, to just hold it in for as long as I can before blowing it out to breathe again. I'm not going back inside. I can't face Deirdre. I can't face Shane. I can't face the truth. All I can do is stand here with a knot in my stomach and smoke in my lungs.

'Are you *OK*?'

I turn. It takes a second to focus on the person who's just walked up to me. Peter.

I squint at him. 'Why're you here so early?' Has he heard too?

'It's seven.'

'It couldn't be.'

He picks my second cigarette out of my fingers and flicks it away. 'Come inside, you're freezing.' A bit late, I remember my coat. He takes my arm and guides me back into the hospital. He stops at a line of chairs that are facing out.

'Sit,' he says.

It seems like the easiest thing. He sits beside me.

'What happened?' he asks after a while.

By the time I finish telling him, I'm crying. He puts an arm around me.

'It's OK,' he says. 'He'll be OK.'

'They don't think they have the antibiotics to fight it.'

'But they're trying new ones.'

I nod.

'So they might get lucky.' There's a long pause. 'They never said anything about a superbug?'

'No.'

'Well, that's good.'

I look at him again. 'Does it matter what they call it, if they can't fight it?'

He sighs. 'Does Shane know?'

'I don't know.'

'Does he know you know?'

'No.'

'Have you been in to him at all?'

I shake my head. 'I can't.' I think about Shane waking and wondering where I am and feel so bad.

'Come on,' he says, grabbing my hand and dragging me up. 'We're going up.'

He seems so strong and I think, maybe I can do this if he's with me. Because I do want to do it.

Going up in the lift, I realise, 'I stink of smoke.'

He puts a hand in his pocket, pulls out some gum and hands me a stick. The lift doors open. We step out in silence. I'm suddenly terrified.

'What'll I say?'
'It'll come to you.'

Shane's asleep. Deirdre's staring out the window. She senses
us standing in the doorway and turns. She quickly wipes a
tear and forces a smile. And suddenly I know what to say.
Because I don't want her to have to hide it any more.

'Deirdre, I know,' I say quietly. 'I spoke to the doctor.'

'Oh, Sarah.' She comes to me. 'I'm so sorry,' she whispers.
'Shane didn't want you to worry. He wants to fight it. He
thinks he can beat it. He really does.' She looks at him with
so much love.

'Then don't tell him I know.'

Her eyes well up. Next thing I know, we're hugging each
other. Then abruptly she says she's going for a walk. She
gets her bag and wraps her cardigan around her, then, head
down, looking almost old, she leaves.

I sit with Shane, my face close to his. I take his hand in
mine and kiss it.

He opens his eyes. Then smiles. 'Hey.'

I smile. And try not to cry. 'Hey.'

And then, without even knowing I'm going to say it, I'm
saying it, 'I want to marry you. Here, in the hospital.
Whenever you're ready.'

His face lights up. 'You sure?'

'I'll talk to the chaplain,' I say. 'I'll arrange it.'

He nods. 'Cool.'

I smile and kiss him. Then I remember. 'Peter's here.'

Peter leans across me so Shane can see him. 'Hey, mate.'

Shane smiles. 'Wanna be my best man?'

'Is the Pope Catholic?'

)I(

*

Two days later, Alex and Rachel are at my house, getting dressed into bright red bridesmaids' dresses that Marsha had been secretly busy with. They've helped with my make-up and hair. And fussed over me till I told them we'd be late. Alex looks at herself in the mirror and closes her eyes.

'Sorry for not waiting – till the baby,' I say.

'Sarah, this is your day. Do you really think I care that I look like a beached whale?'

'Yes.'

She laughs. 'OK, maybe a little. But at least I won't out-shine the bride.'

Bride? Oh my God. 'I really am getting married.'

'You really are getting married.'

Mum calls upstairs. 'How're we doing?'

'Nearly ready,' I call down. We've only, like, half a million things to do.

Louis has cleaned the car and attached tin cans to the back. He opens the front door for me like a chauffeur. He actually looks like one in his dark grey suit. The Mother of the Bride climbs in the back in a seriously cool suit, all fitted and clingy. The bridesmaids (gorgeous, of course) squish in beside her. Everyone's chatting. It feels like we're going to a party.

When we pull up outside the hospital, I start to get nervous. I'm really doing this. I'm really getting married. We hurry inside out of the cold. People stare. And it does seem as if we've got off at the wrong stop.

The three of us do our usual, I-don't-care walk. We're pretty good at it now. We all go up in the lift, mixed in with people in dressing gowns, one even carrying a catheter.

When the doors roll open, there is my father, standing at the entrance to the ward. I stop. Because I didn't expect that. I feel kind of weepy. I walk slowly over.

'Hey, pumpkin,' he says, something he hasn't called me since I was little.

'Hey, Dad.'

He opens his arms and suddenly I'm glad he's here, even though he didn't really want this. He didn't want it because of me. And he's allowing it for the same reason. His hug gives me strength.

'Ready?' he asks.

I nod.

'Then let's go.'

I look up the corridor and can't believe it. It's lined all the way up with white ribbons and roses. Like the aisle of a church. I turn around.

And there they are, my two best friends. 'Did *you* do this?'

They smile. And then we're all hugging each other.

'I love you guys,' I say, and feel suddenly teary.

Over Rachel's shoulder, I see my mum. She's looking past me at – it can only be Dad. There is no hate in her face now. Her eyes are soft. They seem to say, 'Can you believe it? Our little girl is getting married.'

I pull back from Rache and turn around. He's looking back at her, and smiling.

'OK, let's not keep the groom waiting,' Louis says, behind me.

And then we're walking, in three pairs, me and Dad, Rachel and Alex, Mum and Louis, up our makeshift aisle. At the door to every room, patients have gathered. It is seriously embarrassing. At the Nurses' Station, the nurses stand like some sort of guard of honour. One of them, eyes red, is blowing her nose. I feel like telling her to smile.

Dad opens the door to Shane's room.

Wow. There are lilies everywhere. The pink ones, that smell of celebration. Shane's parents are there, smiling at me. Marsha, too. And Peter, in a suit that matches Louis'. And there he is, sitting out on his chair, in a grey suit, white shirt and silver cravat. His hair is spiked. And he looks gorgeous. The oxygen is gone, the drip too. And I know it's only for this. His eyes hold mine. Suddenly, there's no one else in the room, just the two of us. I go to him and kiss him.

'You're beautiful,' he whispers. 'Like an angel. My angel.'

I'm sure it's not the most romantic wedding in the world. But it's *my* wedding. To the guy I love. Who is still the guy I love, no matter what. The vows don't take long because Shane doesn't have huge energy. And needs to get that oxygen back on. I kneel up on the wheelchair, careful not to lean on him. We look into each other's eyes as we are 'joined together as man and wife'. We kiss when we are told we 'may'. Then we cling to each other like we never want to let go. And speaking for me, I don't.

Clapping erupts, reminding me that we're not alone. I look around and notice how much love is in this room. It's in the music – compiled by Alex. It's in the wedding cake – made by my mum who worked through the night to do it. It's in the photos – taken by Louis. It's in the speeches – made by Peter, my dad and Shane's dad. It's funny to have our lives dissected, to have our parents remember bits that we'd forgotten. It's weird to hear my dad describe the person that is really me. I didn't think he knew. And I didn't think he was proud.

}|{

Shane's speech is the shortest. It's also my favourite.

'Today, I am the luckiest guy alive. Thank you all for being here, for sharing the happiest moment of my life.'

He kisses me again.

When I turn around, both our mums are crying. Even my dad is crying. And I'm wondering if it's for more than it seems. But then I jump up and shake the first bottle of pink champagne. I pop it open and let it spill everywhere because you live once, right?

When everyone's gone, Shane's exhausted. I wait in the corridor while the nurses make him comfortable and set him back up on his oxygen and drip. I'll spend my wedding night on a camp bed beside his. But at least I'll be with him. At last. When the nurses leave, I slip into the bed beside him and snuggle up. I put my arm around him and my mouth to his ear.

'We did it,' I say.

'I love you, Mrs Owens.'

'I love you, Mr Owens.' I kiss his neck. 'Are you happy?'

He nods. 'Happiest day of my life.'

'Me too.'

40
CENTIMETRES

My honeymoon is a week off school. And it *is* like being in another world. Everything starts so early. Doctors' rounds. Bed baths. Drug trolley rounds. Nursing staff changing over. Some nice. Some not. We travel the world on the internet. We safari in South Africa. Surf in Australia. Sunbathe in Bali. Mum brings in exotic food, each day to match where we are. But Shane's not hungry, and all the time he's getting weaker.

I spend a lot of time hassling doctors. Try another antibiotic. Try five, why don't you? I learn about blood gases. Blood cultures. Results. What's good. What isn't.

After a week, he sends me back to school.

'Life goes on,' he says, making me want to scream.

It's weird, though. I didn't want to come back. But school is kind of a relief. Everything's so normal. So familiar. So manageable. It's so good to see Rachel and Alex, to be hugged by them, to go to the canteen like a normal teenager.

'Oh my God, you're *married*!' one of the nerds says.

'Yeah and the sex is great,' I say, just to confuse her. Sex and wheelchairs? That should keep her busy.

}I{

*

I alternate between hospital and school. Mum helps out, picking me up from school, dropping me home to shower and change and eat 'some decent food', then driving me to the hospital. Someone calls to leave their dog with me. I have to turn them down. There is no way I can mind a dog right now. Though I would so love to.

One Saturday, Mum tells me she's taking me out for the day.

'But—'

'You've no choice in this, Sarah. It's booked. We're going. Pack togs.'

It turns out to be the nicest day. Just the two of us, in this really Zen-style spa. First we go for a swim. Then a jacuzzi. Then we each have a back massage. Oh my God, the smell of the oils is, like, so amazing. I think I might have been a bit tense.

I wake with a hand on my shoulder and someone calling my name. Oh my God, I fell asleep. Worse, I've been drooling. Luckily, I'm face down with my head in a hole, so she can't see. Still, I'm mortified. I don't move.

'I'll just leave you a moment to put on your robe. Take your time.'

Afterwards, we sit in this lovely room looking out onto a tropical garden. I can't believe how quiet it is here. Especially compared to the hospital and school. No wonder I fell asleep.

'Thanks, Mum. That was amazing.'

She smiles. 'It was good, wasn't it?' she says, like we've just done something decadent.

I feel more able for the hospital now. More able for the camp bed. At the entrance to the hospital, she hands me a little make-up bag. I zip it open and there are all the things I love, all the things that make a day a better day. Lip gloss. Sparkly eye shadow. Fake eyelashes. False nails. I look at her. These are the kind of things she'd never have given me before. These are the kind of things she'd have frowned on.

'The fake eyelashes look fun,' she says, enthusiastically.

I look at them. They look like black feathers with green spots on them.

'That they do. That they do,' I say in a funny voice.

'Here. Give me a hug.'

I reach over to her and we hug.

'I'm so proud of you.'

And when she talks to me like that, I'm still kind of surprised.

It's now November. Shane just keeps going, getting no better, no worse. Just more and more tired. And I'm so afraid. He sleeps most of the time now. And the packets of Jelly Tots pile up. I hate leaving him to go to school, but he insists I do. And the only reason I listen is that I don't want him to have to fight me. He needs all his energy to fight this.

Nothing that we're learning seems relevant. None of it means anything. Then again, I'm not sure it ever did. It's Friday and I'm in the canteen with Rachel, eating a proper lunch (Mum's idea). Alex has gone to the loo again. Just as well this is her last day at school before her 'maternity leave'. It's two weeks now before the baby's due and, honestly, she spends more time in the bathroom than the classroom.

'Something's wrong,' Rachel says.

I look up from my lunch. Alex is walking towards us. She looks like she's seen a ghost.

'I've had a show,' she whispers in horror.

Oh my God. 'Does that mean you're in labour?'

'I don't know. I can't remember. Don't you have to be in pain?' She looks at Rachel.

'Yeah, I think so,' Rachel says.

Phew!

'Did you capture it?' Rachel asks Alex.

I laugh. Then realise she's serious. 'Sorry.'

'Yeah, I have it here in my pocket,' Alex says sarcastically.

'Was there blood?' Rachel asks, ignoring us both.

'No. No, I don't think so.' Alex looks worried again.

'We should get to the hospital,' Rachel says. Her voice is so calm it's freaky – like someone telling you not to panic when that's exactly what you should be doing. 'Let's go to the office. We have to ring your dad.'

Automatically we get up, leave our trays, and start walking, heads high, cool.

Out on the corridor, Alex starts to panic. 'This isn't it, is it, Rache?'

'Think so.'

'But it can't be. It's too early. Like, for the baby.' She looks so worried.

And even though I'm freaking, here, I do spot a good sign: Alex is worried for the baby.

'It's only two weeks early,' Rachel says. 'Babies are born premature all the time.'

'Mike, slow down,' Alex's dad says. 'You'll get us all killed.'

'Sorry,' he says, and slows.

They're up front. We're in the back with Alex. At the RDS, the traffic gets heavy and grinds to a halt.

'Go in the bus lane,' Alex's dad says. He looks like he's having the baby. Mike doesn't look too great either. Which makes me worse. I remind myself that Alex isn't in labour. We're just being careful.

Beside me, she grips her stomach and groans. I stare at her.

'False contraction?' I ask hopefully.

Her face contorts in pain. 'Doesn't feel false,' she says, through gritted teeth.

Oh God.

'Mike, speed up, for Christ sake,' Alex's dad says. He turns around in his seat. 'Are you OK, sweetheart? Hang on, we're nearly there.'

At the hospital, they get Alex a wheelchair. Every time she gets a contraction, she grips the arms and leans forward. God. Her whole face is screwed up.

'Can we have an epidural?' I ask the nurse.

She looks at me and smiles. Like I'm some sort of cute kid or something.

'I'm serious,' I say.

'We'll have to examine Alex first. Don't worry, we know what we're doing.'

Alex gets another contraction. Her knuckles go white. She grits her teeth. When it's over she says. 'Sarah's right. I need an epidural. Now.'

'Let's get you to the ward and have a look.' I don't want to think what she'll be looking at. 'Then we'll know better where we're at.'

Alex is brought to an empty ward. The nurse helps her into bed, then asks us to leave while she examines Alex. She pulls

}|{

the curtains around the bed. We disappear down the corridor, looking at each other in silence.

After a few minutes, the nurse comes out to us.

'She's two centimetres dilated,' she says.

I look at Rache.

'Not very advanced,' she whispers.

'Labour has started but we'll be here for a while,' the nurse continues.

'So do we go back in to her?' I ask, keen to be with Alex.

She looks at us. 'Maybe just two of you.'

'I'll wait outside,' Mike says.

'Do you mind if I just see what Alex wants?' her dad asks the nurse.

'Of course.' She smiles.

We go in to Alex. She's hooked up to some kind of machine.

'What's that?' I ask.

'A monitor to make sure the baby's OK.'

'Cool.'

Her dad asks her who she wants with her. She chooses me and Rachel. 'No offence, Dad. But they're, like, *girls?*'

'It's OK. I understand.' Actually, he looks kind of relieved. 'I'll just be outside in the waiting room. Call if you need me.'

'OK. Thanks.' She smiles. Then she gets a contraction.

'What about the epidural?' I ask when it's over.

'They said it's too early. It'll just slow the thing down.'

'Jesus,' I say. 'Do you want me to rub your shoulder?'

'Touch me and you die.'

I back away. From the one ante-natal class we went to, I try to remember what to do ... Daddy could be stroking

Mummy's tummy now ... *If he is suicidal*, I think. But speaking of Daddy ... what about Louis? I look at Alex. Would she want him here? Would her father? Or would they kill him on sight? He should know, though, shouldn't he? He's been, like, around and stuff. Oh God. I'm not sure if I should bring him up right now, though. Alex just told the nurse to go fuck herself. And she's a pretty nice nurse.

While Alex gets contraction after contraction, I get more and more convinced that Louis should be here. Or at least he should know. I look at her, gripped by another contraction. If I ask her, she'll say no. But if I don't ask and he shows up, she might actually be glad. It'd show he cares. And that she's not on her own. Which, of course, she's not – we're here. But still. When her latest contraction eases, I tell her I have to go to the loo.

'Need anything?' I ask.

'Epidural,' she says through gritted teeth as another contraction hits. God they're coming very quickly now. Maybe they need to examine her again.

I go outside to the waiting area. Her dad looks at me as if to ask, 'any news?' Suddenly I think, *he's this shit-hot rock star. If anyone can get Alex an epidural, he can*. I tell him she really needs it now.

'Leave it with me,' he says, getting up like he's glad there's something he can do.

I hurry outside to call Louis. When I turn on my phone, though, I see a load of missed calls from Deirdre. I start to call her but before I can, the phone rings. Oh God, it's her.

'Hello?' I say, heart pounding.

'Sarah. Thank God I got you.'

Oh God. 'Is everything OK?' My voice sounds very small.

'It's Shane. He's asking for you.'

'Is he OK?'

There's a long pause. 'I don't think so, Sarah,' she says, and her voice breaks. 'You need to come.'

I just hang up. I run back into Alex.

'Are you *OK*?' Rachel asks me.

'There's something wrong with Shane. I gotta go. I'm so sorry Alex.'

'Don't be silly. Go. I'll be fine.'

I hug her. Then I run.

I burst into the waiting area. Alex's dad stands immediately. I put my hands up.

'It's OK. Everything's fine with Alex. I just have to go.'

He looks at me, all concerned. 'Is everything OK?'

'No.' I tell him about Shane, talking so fast my words merge.

'Mike will drive you,' he says.

'There's no need—' I start.

But Mike stands up. 'Let's go,' he says.

'Thank you,' I say to both of them. I look back to where I've just come from. Then I look back at Alex's dad. 'She'll be OK,' I say. And it's funny how much I need to hear those words.

'The anaesthetist is on her way with the epidural. In a few minutes, she won't feel a thing. Don't worry. She will be fine.'

I feel like hugging him. Then I remember. He's a rock star. So I just go.

We rush through traffic, in silence. I think about Alex. I close my eyes and pray that she'll be OK. Then I remember Louis. I take out my phone.

'Sis!' he says cheerfully.

'Alex is having the baby.'

Silence.

'She's in hospital.'

'Oh, Jesus. Is she in pain?'

Seriously, what a question? 'She's having an epidural.'

There's a long silence. 'I should go in,' he says, but sounds unsure.

I say nothing. It's up to him.

'Who's with her?'

'Rachel and a nurse.'

'What about her father?'

'In the waiting room.'

'Fuck. And you?'

'On my way to Shane. Something's happened. He's asking for me.'

Another pause. 'Do you want me to go with you?'

'No. His parents will be there. But tell Mum so she knows where I am, OK?'

'Sure.'

'Are you going to Alex?' I ask.

'Did she ask for me?'

'No. But that doesn't mean she wouldn't like you to be there. Or at least know you're there, you know, outside, in the waiting area.' We pull up in front of the hospital. 'Louis, I've to go.'

'OK, OK, good luck,' he says. 'Call me if you need me.'

I hang up, thank Mike and hurry into the hospital.

41
STAY

At the entrance to the ward, I stop. Two weeks ago, I stood here with Dad, looking up a corridor of flowers. Now the flowers are gone and I feel like I'm in a nightmare. I take a deep breath and hurry. I'm almost at Shane's room when the door opens and a nurse comes out. It's Emma, who is young and fun and never gives out about me lying on (or in) the bed. When she sees me now, she looks so sad, like she's actually going to cry. Fear grips me. She hugs me. Which is terrifying. I pull back.

'He's going to be OK, isn't he?' I ask desperately. *Please say yes. Please say yes.*

She presses her lips together and her eyes fill.

'He's waiting for you,' she says, and pushes the door open. Oh God. Oh God. Oh God.

The room is in shadow. Everything still. His parents are by his side, Deirdre holding his hand, his dad's arm around her. Shane is lying flat, on his side.

'He's not supposed to be lying down!' I say. 'It's bad for his lungs. And where's his oxygen?' I look around for it.

They turn together. Oh God, their faces. Oh, Jesus. Oh
God. Oh, no.

Deirdre gets up. She comes to me and hugs me. Her body
shudders and she starts to cry. I pull back. Not wanting this.
But she takes my hand and brings me to the top of the bed.
To Shane. Who said he could fight this.

'He can still hear,' she says.

I stare at her. This isn't happening. It can't be happening.

'Sit with him, Sarah,' she says. 'He's been waiting for
you.'

What do they all mean, waiting? Waiting for what? But I
know what. I sink into the seat. I take his hand. Oh God, it's
so cold. I cover it with the blanket. It hurts so much to see
him like this – so weak, so *exhausted*. His eyes struggle
open. He smiles so weakly like it's taking all his energy.

'Hey,' he whispers. But it's his eyes that speak. They say,
'Here we are. Can you believe it? Already?'

I try to smile. But tears are clouding my eyes.

'I wanted one last hug.'

I cover my mouth. It's just so final. I try not to cry (he
won't want me to). But my whole body shakes with a massive sob and I can't stop myself.

'I'm sorry,' I say. Why can't I be brave? Why can't I be
brave like Deirdre?

'God, I love you,' he says. He closes his eyes, exhausted.

I put my cheek to his and I tell him I love him. I put my
arms around him so gently. This couldn't be it. Our final
hug.

He whispers something. I move back to see his face.

'I'll never stop loving you, Sarah.'

Oh God. I can't let him go. I just can't. 'Shane. It's OK.

It's just a bug. A stupid bug. We can fight it. You know we can.' I squeeze his hand. 'Please, Shane. I love you so much. Do this for me. Fight it. Please.'

Behind me, his mum breaks down.

He closes his eyes.

'Shane?'

He doesn't answer.

I turn around in panic. Another nurse, an older one, comes up to the bed. Has she been there all this time or did she just arrive? She takes Shane's pulse. All three of us look at her. Hoping. Praying this isn't it.

'He's sleeping,' she says.

I breathe again.

All through the night, Shane's breathing becomes weaker and shallower and slower. Every breath brings me one step closer to admitting that he has lost the fight, that he really is slipping away. I am losing him. I look at Deirdre. I can see her heart breaking in her face. I slip my hand from Shane's. I take hers and put it in his. This is her boy. Her child. No one's pain is greater than hers. Even mine which is so huge. She looks at me and smiles. So sadly. She takes my left hand and puts it in his left. She holds my right in her left. She holds his right in her right. We form a circle. And all I can think is, his dad is left out. But when I look behind, he's actually fallen asleep. I sit, arms aching from holding hands for so long, listening to every breath, knowing now, admitting, that we're just waiting for the end.

And then, after hours, Shane's breathing stops. His mum gasps. We both turn together, to look for the nurse. She checks the pulse in Shane's wrist, then his neck. Then she

}{{

checks her watch. Automatically, I check mine. Four a.m. She shakes her head.

'I'm sorry.'

His dad, awake again, reaches for Deirdre. Giving me a moment alone with Shane. I bend over him and whisper in his ear.

'I love you so much. I'll never stop. I swear.' I squeeze his hand so tightly. I kiss his cheek and can't believe that soon I'll never be able to do that again. I don't want to let him go. I don't want to leave. I want to stay here forever. I want to die too. Go wherever he's gone.

No one shoos us out. The nurses let us sit with him. They let us cry. For hours. And when we finally walk out of that room, *oh God*, the sun's coming up. Pink and golden. How can the sun rise today? How can life go on, just like that?

Out on the corridor, Deirdre holds my hands and smiles. Her face is swollen and red.

'I'm sorry you never got to live with us. I'd have liked that.'

And I'm crying again, thinking of what could have been. She hugs me then. She smells of him. Oh God. Finally, she lets me go. She smiles. 'This isn't goodbye. I'll be calling you, OK?'

I nod. She grips my arms, looks into my eyes.

'He wanted you to be happy. To go live your life. You know that, don't you? You've given enough now, all right? Go live your life.'

Which sets me off again. I'm not just going to head off into the sunset. *He* was my sunset. And he's gone. I wipe my nose with the back of my hand. And, so she thinks I'm OK, I smile.

'Thanks,' I say.

They walk down the corridor, holding each other, looking

like they've lost their entire world. I know what that feels like.

I stand, stunned and so alone, wanting to sneak back in to him but knowing the nurses are in there now. And it's too late. I take out my phone to call my mum. But one of the night nurses – a woman I've never met before – tells me that Mum is in the Day Room. She's been here all night.

The nurse puts an arm around me and walks with me to the room. And even though I hate strangers touching me, I don't fight it. What's the point? Through the glass windows, I see Mum, sitting on one of those hard armchairs, in the semi-dark. And I'm crying again. Automatically. Before the nurse even opens the door, Mum's up. And coming to me. She thanks the nurse, who leaves us alone. Mum takes me in her arms and holds me. My whole body shakes against hers. She holds me tighter. She says nothing to make it better. Which is good. Because nothing can. She stays holding me for a very long time. In the end, she pulls back, brushes the hair back from my face and wipes a tear.

'Let's go home.'

Something in my head tells me I can't. I remember Alex. I look at Mum. 'Alex is in hospital. She went in yesterday to have the baby.'

She looks at me, then checks her watch. 'She might still be in labour.'

'No. She couldn't …'

She raises her eyebrows and nods.

I turn on my phone to see if there are any messages. Nothing. From anyone. I think of her still in labour. 'Oh my God. I hope she's OK.'

'Do you want to go in?'

I nod. I can't go home anyway. It wouldn't feel right. To

just carry on like everything's normal. Nothing's normal. And it feels like nothing will ever be again.

We leave the hospital as the nurses change shifts, as the cleaning people buff the floors. And another day begins.

Outside, daylight stings my eyes. My head aches. And my nose feels like I've been inhaling raw chlorine. I follow Mum to the car.

It's Saturday morning and there's no traffic. But Mum stops at every orange light (they all seem to be). When I drive, it won't be like this. Then I think, how can I drive? Without him? My heart feels like it's exploding into a million pieces. Tiny bits going everywhere. *Where are you?* I think. I feel like there's a hole in my heart.

At the hospital reception, Mum asks for Alex Newman.

The guy behind the desk looks at us carefully.

'Are you relatives?'

I worry that something has happened.

'No,' Mum says.

At the same time I say, 'Yes.'

They're both looking at me.

'What kind of relative?' he asks me.

'Aunt,' I say but don't expand.

Mum stares at me, clearly thinking I'm lying.

'I'm sorry,' the guy says. 'You'll have to come back during visiting hours.'

No. No way. I have to see her now. It's like, suddenly nothing else matters.

'*Louis?*' Mum says.

I turn. Louis is walking into reception from the wards. He stops when he sees us.

}|{

'What are you doing here?' Mum asks.

He hesitates. Then straightens up like he's decided something.

'I've just become a dad.'

'*What?*'

'Baby girl. Eight pounds, three ounces. She's beautiful.'

'Oh my God,' I say. 'Is she OK? Is Alex OK?'

Mum looks like she's going to pass out. 'You and Alex Newman?'

Louis doesn't even hear her. He's looking at me like he's in awe. 'She was amazing. She didn't want me there till it was over, but when I went in, straight after, there she was, sitting up in bed eating toast after eighteen hours of pushing.'

'*Eighteen* hours?'

'Baby was born at four.'

'Four, *this* morning?'

'Yeah.'

'Four, exactly?'

'Yeah, why?'

I stare at him. Not believing. 'Shane died at four.'

He loses his smile. His whole face falls. 'I'm so sorry, Sarah.' He comes to me and hugs me.

'He was asleep,' I say. 'He just slipped away.' I say it for him but it makes me feel better to think of him asleep, in the middle of a dream. He could have been walking, swimming, hand gliding. Laughing. Suddenly, that seems so important.

'You want to see Alex?' he asks.

I nod. 'But *he* won't let us.'

Louis turns to the guy on reception. 'I'm the baby's father. I need to go back for a minute. With my sister.'

}|{

Without waiting for an answer, he puts his arm around me and starts walking.

'Fifteen minutes,' the guy calls. He checks his watch to make a point.

'I'll wait in the car,' Mum calls. She frowns at Louis. 'I'll talk to you later.'

He just smiles.

Going up in the lift, I turn to Louis. 'So everything's OK? Alex is OK? The baby's OK?'

He nods, smiling. 'She looks like me.'

And when he says that, I know for sure that everything's fine.

'Her name's Maggie.'

I look at him, hopefully. Alex would never have called the baby after her mum if she didn't love it.

'She is the most beautiful thing I've ever seen.' His voice is filled with emotion.

And I smile. Because months ago, he'd have been heading for the hills.

42
MAGGIE

Alex is lying on her back with two pillows. She looks pale and tired but unbelievably peaceful – considering. Like the weather after a storm. She smiles when she sees me.

'Hey,' she says, and sounds so Zen.

'Congratulations.' I smile. 'It's cool you called her after your mum.'

'Kind of made sense.'

'Sorry I couldn't be here.'

'Is Shane OK?' she asks, cautiously.

I bite my lips together. Shake my head. And try, so hard, not to cry. She looks at Louis, who shakes his head.

'Oh my God, Sarah.' She flings back the covers and starts to get up.

'Stop!' Louis calls, rushing over. 'You've had an epidural. You have to lie flat for another hour.'

'Crud,' she says, angrily. Then, 'Sarah come here.' She sounds so bossy, I almost laugh.

'You sound like a mum already,' I say.

'Get up here,' she says, patting the bed beside her.

I climb up. I remember Shane and feel suddenly hollow, like a wind is blowing right through me. I shiver.

'Lie down,' she says.

Suddenly, tiredness overwhelms me and I do what I'm told. Alex turns on her side, to face me. She strokes my hair. Like an expert, like a mum.

I look at her. 'I can't believe it, Alex. It happened so fast. In the end.' And I'm crying. 'I'm sorry. I shouldn't have come. You've enough—'

'Shut up. This is exactly where you should be. OK?'

'You warned me. You said it would hurt.'

'Yeah, but I bet you wouldn't change a thing.'

I look at her. 'No.' And I'm sobbing again. 'I loved him so much.' I close my eyes and see his face. I hear him telling me, 'Life goes on.' It's like an order. I sit up.

'Where's this baby of yours?'

She smiles. And I think, *Wow, she's smiling at the thought of her baby. Something's right in the world.*

'Louis. Will you get Maggie?' She talks to him like they're a couple, like they're a real mum and dad. And even though I know they're not together, I pretend. Because I can have that, can't I? Just for today.

Louis stoops so gently over the little cot and scoops up the tiny bundle so easily, like this is what he was born to do. The world is a very strange place. He carries the baby to Alex. And I take a second, just one second, to look at Alex's face before I look at Maggie's. It goes all soft and even though this is the saddest day of my life, I feel happy. *Something good*, I think. *Something good.* And then I look down at the most beautiful face in the world.

'Oh, Alex, she's beautiful.' She has the tiniest pixy face

with a little pointy chin and those cupid lips that babies have. She is like a little elf child and I love her instantly.

'Want to see her hair?' Alex pulls off the tiny white cap.

Out pops a huge tuft of dark hair, the kind that Asian babies have.

'Oh my God!' I say, and laugh.

'Want to hold her?' Alex asks.

'No, thanks. I don't want to wake her.' Or hurt her or do anything stupid.

'Hold her,' she bosses.

And I laugh again, wondering if it's like a switch, if the minute you give birth, you get all this authority. Then I feel guilty. I shouldn't be laughing. Not today.

'Hold her,' she says firmly, passing the baby to me.

I take her into my arms like she's a bomb that could go off at the slightest movement. I take her. And hold her. And then, the weirdest thing, I look down at her sleeping face and feel this huge wave of calm settle over me. I stop worrying, stop grieving, just watch her. And then, like magic, her eyes pop open. They are blue and hazy and probably can't see very much. But they're looking up at me and suddenly I feel all this love coming to me, like a wave of energy. I look up, so surprised, to see if anyone else feels it.

'Hello, Auntie Sarah,' Alex says in a baby voice.

I look at her and laugh. And I know. It's what Shane wants. For me to laugh. And live. And breathe. And enjoy *every* moment.

I'm getting married to Shane. We're on a beach. He's standing, waiting for me to walk up the aisle (a sandy path, between rows of golden chairs). He is in his rugby gear with big mucky patches on his knees. The golden chairs are empty. But a penguin looks on from the side. When I reach Shane, he smiles, then he picks me up, throws me over his shoulder, slaps my bum and carries me off. I'm laughing. But then I'm thinking, this must be a dream because now we're cavemen. There's a knocking sound. A man on the beach is hammering at an upturned boat.

'Sarah?'

I open my eyes. It's dark. And Mum is in the room. The knocking was her at the door.

'Hey,' she says gently, and sits on the side of the bed. 'How're you doing?'

'What time is it?'

'Half nine. You've slept twelve hours solid.'

'Half nine at night?' I ask, trying to adjust.

She nods. 'Peter's downstairs. He says he has something for you.'

It's taking a while to work that out.

'Why don't you come down and see what it is?'

'I'm OK,' I say.

'It's something from Shane,' she says.

I'm up and down the stairs in seconds.

Peter looks wrecked.

'Hey,' he says.

'I'll leave you to it,' Mum says. 'Nice to meet you, Peter.' She disappears into the kitchen.

'How're you doing?' he asks.

I shrug. 'You?'

'OK,' he says, sounding so not OK.

'He was asleep. In the end,' I say. 'He just slipped away.' I think I'm going to be saying that a lot – out loud and to myself.

He nods. 'His mum said.'

'Did she ring you?'

'Yeah.'

'That was nice of her.' Given that all I've been able to do is sleep.

He holds out a memory stick. 'Shane asked me to give you this.'

'What is it?'

'Something he wanted to tell you, I think.'

Suddenly, I want to be upstairs at my computer, with Shane.

And Peter must get that because he says, 'Well, I better get going. Take care, yeah?'

I nod. 'Thanks, Peter.'

We hug. I walk him to the door. Then I'm racing upstairs. Opening the computer and inserting the memory stick. None of it is happening fast enough. And then he is suddenly there, looking right at me. Alive again. Oh God. He's in the hospital. Sitting up in the bed, no oxygen on, freshly shaved. When was this? It must have been at the beginning because he looks so strong.

'Hey.' And I love the way he says it, like the word is full of love. 'Things aren't looking too good right now. So this is just in case.' He clears his throat. He pauses, looking straight at the camera. I reach out and touch his face. And then he's speaking.

'I've worked it out,' he says. 'Love. It's like energy. It doesn't die. It just changes from one kind to another. I'll never stop loving you, Sarah. I don't know how, but you're still going to feel my love after I've gone. You won't be alone. I honestly believe that. And I want you to believe it too.' He sounds so sure. 'Sarah, you're the best thing that's ever happened to me. I've lived more in the last six months than I did in my entire life because of you. If I hadn't got sick, we'd never have met. And I wouldn't swap that for anything. I want you to look after Pete, OK? He might look like he's got it all together, but he's a pussy. He's going to need some help. And there's my mum. She loves you, Sarah. Call on her sometime – maybe when Dad's at work and she's alone? Just call and have a chat. OK?'

'OK,' I say. And remember. He's dead.

'There's something else I want you to do. I want you to be happy. OK? Live like we did, like there's a deadline. Make the most of every single day. Love that baby when it comes. You'll make a great aunt. The most fun aunt ever.' He smiles. 'OK. Better go.'

'No. Don't.'

'Physio's coming to beat the shit out of me. I'll just close my eyes and pretend I'm on the rugby pitch.' He smiles. His last words to me are 'I love you.'

The screen goes blank.

I snatch at the mouse. And click back to the start. Then I watch it over. And over. And over.

Two days later, in the church, Louis and Mum sit on either side of me. It feels like they're propping me up. I hear the church fill, behind me. I don't turn around. Then Dad is there, at the end of the pew. We stand to let him pass, first Mum, then me, then Louis. He squeezes my hand on his way by. Then he sits the other side of Louis. Since the wedding, it doesn't seem so odd now for the four of us to be together.

The priest is the one from the hospital.

}|{

'I didn't know Shane for very long,' he says, 'but I knew he was special straight away. Shane had motor neurone disease. But he never let that stop him. Shane always put others first. His top priority in hospital was to make sure that things were in place for those he loved after he left. He made sure I'd be here today, someone that he knew, 'not some stranger', as he put it himself. Shane had great faith. Not in the traditional sense. He strongly believed that his love for those he loved in this life would not die with him but would surround them after he was gone. I have no doubt that it will. I feel honoured to have known Shane Owens for the small period of time that I did.'

After the service, I walk out of the church, into the sun. Louis passes me some blackout shades and, gratefully, I hide behind them. Up ahead, Shane's parents, looking broken, are swamped by people. I back away from the fuss. I try to hide. But someone is standing in front of me. Blocking out the sun.

'What do you want?' I ask, my voice ice, when I see who it is.

'I came to say sorry. For that day in the coffee shop. I was an a-hole.' I stare at him. Today is not about him. It's about Shane. 'I liked you, you see. Didn't know how much till it was too late. I guess I was upset. Anyway, sorry.' He turns and walks away, leaving me standing there, stunned. But it doesn't matter. Nothing about Simon does.

'What did that creep want?'

I turn around. It's Alex and Rachel. And Maggie.

I burst into a smile. 'You came!'

'You think we'd miss this?' Alex says, then her face changes. 'Jesus, you'd think I was talking about a *party* the way I said that.' She looks sick. It's then I notice they've both been crying.

'It's so good you're here. Is Maggie OK? I mean, it's not too cold or anything, is it?' I look towards the church. 'We could bring her inside.'

'They said she'd be fine if I wrapped her up.'

I look at her, all cosy in her one-piece coat and her little striped cap.

'She's so cute.'

'Want to hold her?'

'Do you mind?'

I put out my arms for her.

'Oh my God,' Alex says. 'Every time you hold her, she opens her eyes.'

I smile and carry her higher so she can see my face. And the feeling floods back, the feeling of calm, of warmth, of love. I think of what Shane said about love not dying. I think of the timing, one leaving, one coming. And I wonder …

'Hello, you little angel. I'm Auntie Sarah. Yeah, that's right. Saa-rah. Very important word.' I look up at Alex. 'Never too young to start.' She laughs. 'We're going to have so, much, *fun*, you and me.'

'It's time to go,' a voice says. It's Mum. I didn't see her coming. 'They're waiting.'

I look over and the hearse is loaded up and ready to go. I look down at Maggie. And smile. I bend down and kiss her forehead. 'I will see *you* later.' I pass her back to Alex.

'I won't bring her to the graveyard, if that's OK,' Alex says.

'God, no, that's fine. I wouldn't want you to.'

'I hate those places,' Alex continues. 'Windswept and cold.' She looks at me. 'He's not going to be there, Sarah. He'll be somewhere else. Remember that, OK?'

I nod. 'OK.'

Alex was right. The graveyard is windswept, cold and bleak. After the prayers are said and the body (God) lowered, I turn to walk away, to forget that I was ever here.

Then someone is beside me.

'Hey,' Peter says.

I look at him and smile. Because he's the one person who understands, the one person who knows. 'Hey.'

We walk in silence, our feet in step. Outside the gates, we stop. He turns to me.

'He asked me to look after you, you know,' he says.

'He asked *me* to look after *you*. Said you were a pussy.'

He laughs. 'Bastard.'

And then I'm crying. I've managed to hold off all day. Now it hits me.

He's gone. And I'll never see him again. Peter puts his arms around me.

'It'll be OK,' he says, his voice right by my ear. 'I know. I'm psychic.'

I pull back. 'He'd it all planned, hadn't he? For us to look out for each other.' I remember when we met first, how much Shane wanted us to get on. He'd planned it even way back then.

Peter smiles. Then nods.

We walk together out the gates of the graveyard.

'There's Mark Delaney,' he says, casually. 'What's he

doing here? He didn't know Shane. Did he?'

'No. He's a friend of mine – from school. Actually, he's Rachel's boyfriend.'

'*That's* the Mark she's always talking about? That's so weird.'

'Why? Do you know him?'

'Wait a sec. That means you must be Sarah.'

'What are you talking about?'

'You're the Sarah I was supposed to meet at the Amusements in Bray that time.'

I stare at him. 'Oh my God. You're *Peter*? The guy who didn't show up.'

'Couldn't show up. My aunt died.'

'Mark said it was a family thing.' Which, I realise, it was. 'Sorry. I just thought you stood me up. Family thing is just a standard, like, excuse.'

'It's OK. I forgive you … Weird, though.' He seems lost in thought. 'Wonder what would have happened if I'd been able to make it?' He looks at me.

'I'd probably have hated you,' I joke. But I think back and realise it would have been the other way round. Because I wasn't very likeable then. I've changed so much. Because of Shane. I look at Peter, suddenly filled with determination.

'I'm going to get the best Leaving Cert I can get.'

He looks confused.

'I'm going to visit the Guggenheim, the Sydney Opera House, the library in Ringsend.'

He smiles, then, like he finally gets what I'm on about. 'Me too.'

'I'm going to be the best aunt I can be.'

'I might give that one a rain check.'
'But, most importantly, I'm going to live till I die.'
For him.